# Multiple
# Listings

# Multiple Listings

*A Novel*

---

## TRACY McMILLAN

Gallery Books

New York   London   Toronto   Sydney   New Delhi

Gallery Books
An Imprint of Simon & Schuster, Inc.
1230 Avenue of the Americas
New York, NY 10020

First Gallery Books hardcover edition March 2016

GALLERY BOOKS and colophon are registered trademarks of Simon & Schuster, Inc.

For information about special discounts for bulk purchases, please contact Simon & Schuster Special Sales at 1-866-506-1949 or business@simonandschuster.com.

The Simon & Schuster Speakers Bureau can bring authors to your live event. For more information or to book an event, contact the Simon & Schuster Speakers Bureau at 1-866-248-3049 or visit our website at www.simonspeakers.com.

Cover design by Lucy Kim

Cover image © Thomas Northcut/Getty Images

Manufactured in the United States of America

10  9  8  7  6  5  4  3  2  1

Library of Congress Cataloging-in-Publication Data is on file.

ISBN 978-1-4767-8552-3
ISBN 978-1-4767-8554-7 (ebook)

*For Joseph*

# Multiple Listings

# PROLOGUE

―――――

## Down Payment

# NICKI

My doorbell just went off. It's the worst possible moment—I'm in the middle of putting the food on the table for a family dinner, which never happens. Between my very busy day job, the restaurant my boyfriend and I are in the process of opening, and my teenage son, we almost never eat a meal together, so the fact that I managed to pull this off is a big deal. Of course the Jehovah's Witnesses would decide to show up now.

"Jake! Can you get that? It's Jesus at the door!" I wait, but I can't hear any footsteps. "Cody? Can you get it? Hello?"

I turn back to the kitchen and grab the large orange ceramic platter of meat. I'm not really a cook-cook, but with a stick of butter, salt, pepper, and onions, I can totally make something nice happen to a pork loin. And if I put it on some great Fiesta ware, I almost look like I know what I'm doing. As long as you don't mind the fifteen million calories.

"*Somebody! Anybody?*" I call out.

I guess it's nobody. Nobody but me. This platter is heavy and I really don't want to have to go to the door with it. But the doorbell is ringing so incessantly it looks like I might have to.

"Hang on!"

Just as I give one of those *does-it*-always-*have-to-be-me* sighs and walk over to the front door, I hear Cody's footsteps.

"I'm coming, Mom," he says.

"Never mind," I say. I'll admit I can work a tiny martyr streak when I want to. "I got it."

I walk to the door, my gold clogs pounding the original creaky wood floor. Cody always says how I drive him crazy with my clomping, but I have a thing against walking around with bare feet in the house—I can't stand the grime—so, oh well. If he didn't want to listen to my feet, he could have gotten the door himself.

I'm almost there when I catch a glimpse through the beveled-glass window . . .

I promptly drop the platter to the floor.

*Oh my God.*

I can hear the platter smash into fifty pieces and I can see there's a huge brown stain spreading all over the white rug, but I can't even pay attention to it because—

*How is this possible?*

My father is standing on my front porch. I have not seen him in seventeen years.

# PART ONE

———

## Multiple Listings

Nine days earlier

# 1
—

# NICKI

I'm waiting for a sign. A large black crow, maybe, or a coincidence of some kind. Just something to tell me: this is it, this is the place. The place I'm supposed to live. The place I'm supposed to be. I've got questions, too—about the thing I'm supposed to do, the person I'm supposed to love, and what's going on with my kid—that I'd love signs for as well, but I know that's a lot to ask for. Too much, probably. So I'll just settle for some kind of heads-up on The Place. Would a burning bush be too much to ask for? I could really use one of those right about now.

How many houses have we looked at so far anyway, thirty? Forty? Fifty? I lost count sometime after deciding we should shift our search from Northeast Portland back to Southeast Portland. Which was a couple of weeks after shifting our search *to* Northeast Portland *from* Southeast Portland, and that's not counting the two lofts we looked at in the Pearl District, or the two weeks we spent nosing around the West Hills (as if).

We saw some great houses, but none of them said anything like This Is The Place. We've seen a lot of This Is Somebody's Place, But Not Mine, a few examples of This Would Be The Place, If You Were into Granite, and of course, enough This Is Absolutely Positively for Sure Not The Place to last a lifetime. Everyone says the same thing: *You'll know it when you see it*. But at this point, I'm wondering if it'll ever happen, and if it did, how would I know?

Which is why I really need a sign.

Jake doesn't believe in signs. At all. Jake is my twenty-six-year-old boyfriend. (That's eleven years' difference, for those of you who are counting, and we've been together for two years.) Jake is just sure about stuff—about houses, about the restaurant, about life. He doesn't think in terms of places and signs. He thinks in terms of his mind and what it's telling him. His mind *is* the place. He knows in an instant what he wants. Like me, for example. On our third date he told me I was *it* for him. That he could see himself with me forever. At first I was a little bit suspicious, but he won me over. Scratch that. At first I was thrilled—like the homecoming king had just asked me to go steady. *Then* I got suspicious and he had to win me over. I can tell you the exact moment of my conversion, too. About a month after we started dating, I had to go to San Francisco overnight for work. The next morning, I woke up to room service knocking on my door. Jake had ordered me a full breakfast over the phone, paid for it, and had it delivered to my room with a note that said: *From Jake, with love.*

We've been together ever since.

Weirdly, I know in an instant what Jake wants, too. Like the house at 2325 SE Burnett. The moment we pull up in front of the Open House sign, I know that he's going to want this one. Really want it. I can tell just from the house numbers. Big, sleek ones in matching brushed-satin-nickel-stainless-steel-whatever. The kind that scream Cool People Live Here, like a dog whistle specially tuned to a pitch that only guys with tattoos and piercings can hear. In other words, guys like Jake.

"I love it!" See, we just rolled up and Jake's already sold. It's the orange door, obviously. "Don't you?"

"It's nice," I say tentatively. I don't want him to get any big ideas so soon. We just got here. "The foundation work is great, I'll say that." I will always pay respect to a good foundation.

If I had to give Jake a one-line bio, the kind you'd ironically put on a Twitter profile, it'd say something like: *I do life like a black-diamond run.* Jake's the kind of guy who skis fast and hard down the most challenging, most dangerous mountains—literally and figuratively—and gets off on it. Jake is bold. It's what I love about him, and, of course, what sometimes drives me nuts. But I deal with it because he's not intimidated by me, and that's a relief. The more successful I've become, the more I've realized that there's something about a woman who can take care of herself that can make a guy feel insecure. Men like to be needed; it makes them feel safe. Too often they want a woman who is "less" than they are—at least in their minds. My guess is it's because little girls can't hurt you the way big ladies can. Very few men have the strength to be with a woman who wants them but doesn't *need* them.

Jake is one of those men. He manages The Echo—named "Best Restaurant to See and Be Seen In" by *Portland Weekly*—and he makes it look easy. Jake has a U.S. senator's ability to make people do what he wants, and a pimp's ability to make them feel special while they do it. (Or is it the other way around?) He's not only the most ambitious guy I've ever met, he's one of the smartest—all wrapped in a physical package (face, body, clothing) so attractive he could be (and actually has been) cast in a cell phone commercial. Jake's dream is to open his own restaurant—and I'm going to help him do it. We're going to do it together. I've always fantasized about the idea of working with the person I'm partnered with, and now it's going to happen.

"You can't possibly not like it, Nicki. What's not to like about it?"

*Can't possibly?* Ugh. It worries me that he can just *fall* for a house like this so quickly. He just met it! Can't he see how cliché that orange door is? Or how that brushed nickel is trying too hard? The house is like a girl who posts too many selfies on Facebook. What Cody would call *thirsty*. But I'm not in the mood for a confrontation, so I keep silent, for the moment.

"If this place is half as good inside as it is out here," Jake says, "I approve."

I already know what's inside. Carrara marble, white subway tile, dark wood floors, undermounted kitchen sink: pick any three out of four. After all, assessing houses is my business. Literally. My real estate appraisal firm somehow (if I'm honest, it seems like an accident) managed to become one of the busiest in Portland. I not only handle all the refinancing appraisals for Oregon's biggest mortgage company—which amounts to taking a spin through the house, making sure it isn't going to fall over anytime soon, and that'll be six hundred dollars, please, thank you very much—I have a ton of residential clients as well. Not bad for someone who can't solve for two variables.

"Wow." Jake stops just inside the doorway to take it all in. "I love it."

Even I have to admit this place does not disappoint. A huge open space with vaulted ceilings and walls of glass overlooking an amazing garden. "I feel like we tripped and fell into a Crate and Barrel catalog," I say.

"I'll take it," Jake says. Then, "I could really see us here, Nicki."

He smiles at me, his dark brown eyes all excited, and that makes my heart spin like a pinwheel. This is when I love him the most, when we're out exploring the world together, even if "the world" is just every open house, every Sunday, in Southeast Portland. I've never had a better running buddy. Somehow, the two of us walking into a house is like opening the door to a whole potential life, a life that can be ours for 20 percent down plus closing costs. Do we want a Craftsman life, a midcentury life, a modern life, a two-story life, or a condo life? It almost doesn't matter. For these three hours—Sundays between 1 and 4 p.m.—I have no doubts about my life, or anyone in it. I'm going to buy a great house, move in with Jake, and be happy. And I mean officially move in, not like the makeshift situation we have now where he crashes at my house all the time, but still keeps an apartment on Twenty-Third and Northwest Hoyt.

But that's just for three hours on Sunday. The rest of the time, I'm looking for a sign.

"Welcome! I'm Sue!" A bubbly, fortyish agent appears out of nowhere and thrusts a setup sheet into my hands. "Three bedrooms, two full baths, a total redo, and as you can see, it's delicious."

"Yum," Jake says, possibly mocking Sue, but also possibly not—Jake has a way of mirroring people when he wants to be liked. Like if you have a French accent, then sometimes so does he.

"Been looking for long?" Sue asks casually. I'm sure it's taken her years to perfect this question. A less-experienced buyer would hardly suspect she's trying to turn them into a client.

"A little while," I say. I'm not committing to anything at this point, not even a conversation. Which isn't stopping Sue.

"Is it just the two of you?" She glances at my belly, like she might find some more information down there. *Um, no.*

"I have a sixteen-year-old son," I offer. I just decided Sue is okay, and we can be friends. Probably because I sort of liked how audacious Sue was about the "pregnancy" that doesn't exist and never will.

Jake looks at me. He's asked me to tell people *we* have a sixteen-year-old son, but I always forget. I've been saying *my kid, Cody,* for sixteen years, and it's hard to break the habit. I think it's sweet that Jake wants to present us as a family—it feels like he's committing to me—to us—for good. "Well, *we* do."

"You have a teenager?" Sue is gushing at me. "You're kidding. You don't look old enough to have a *teenager!*" She says *teenager* like it's herpes.

"Thanks, that's really sweet," I say. I do totally mean it.

"What, were you twelve when you had him?" Sue's genuinely curious. People always are. I'm mostly happy to indulge them. I think maybe I'm trying single-handedly to dispel the struggling single mother stereotype one person at a time.

"I was young, but not that young." I'm thirty-seven, but I come across like someone Jake's age. It's the combination of my supersized green eyes—I feel weird saying it, but they're really big and pretty, the only things

I have to thank Beth, my mother (but just barely my mother), for—and my olive skin that still hasn't started to wrinkle.

"The thing is," I say to Sue, "at sixteen, Cody's a full-on *guy*. It's like living with another adult."

"Well then, you are going to *love* this layout. It has double masters!" Sue pronounces this in the same tone you would use to say *I'm going to Disneyland!* "Buckle up, because you are going to be wowed."

"I want to be wowed," Jake echoes.

"Okay, fine," I say, fake-begrudgingly. "Go ahead, wow me."

I really, really don't want to like this house.

————

"It's pretty much perfect," I say, plunging my feet into the plastic dish tub full of lukewarm water. I'm talking about 2325 SE Burnett. I fiddle with the buttons on the chair massager and scooch around until the mechanism is working the middle of my shoulder blades. That's where all the tension from a lifetime of A-studentness holes up like a crazed conspiracy theorist in a Montana cabin. "It's really . . . it's . . . just . . . perfect." Though I wouldn't admit this to Jake, I really did love the house.

"You say that every week about *something*. And every week, you forget about it, and move on." Peaches shoves her massage controller into my hands. "Make this thing chop me."

Peaches and I have a standing mani-pedi date every Sunday at 4 p.m.—right after the open houses. We're like sisters—we met in fourth grade and bonded immediately over being forced to slog through the same lame childhood: crazy single moms, a pile of stepdads, every year a new apartment and a new school. But through it all we stayed best friends.

The interesting thing—and no doubt a big part of our attraction to each other—is that the same lame childhood spun us in completely opposite directions. I became an overachieving compulsive saver with an eight hundred credit score who is addicted to having my shit together, while Peaches turned out to be a waitress with a special love for motorcycles and pit bulls who has never had a relationship last longer than it takes a jar of salsa to go bad in the fridge. Kids are almost certainly never going to happen for Peaches, and trust me, that is a good thing.

"There, abuse yourself." I hand the controller back to Peaches, who rolls her eyes back into her head as she settles into the visibly buzzing chair. She's one of those women who likes it rough.

Peaches might drive me crazy, but I've never found another person who understands, really and truly, what it was like to grow up rain soaked and benignly neglected in the Northwest, in the eighties—back when it was still about guns, logging, and sheep, not coffee and craft beer—by moms who probably meant well but totally misinterpreted feminism to mean you could just do whatever you want whenever you wanted and your kids would be fine because they can't be happy if you're not happy and besides kids are "really resilient" so don't even worry about it.

They probably should've worried about it.

Oh, and we argue like sisters, too.

"Face it, you're the George Clooney of house hunting. You're going to just keep casually dating houses for the rest of your life—because you're never going to meet the gorgeous, skinny, Audrey Hepburn–like, international lawyer of—" Peaches cuts herself off, holding up a bottle of nail polish in a shade of yellowish acid green. She has no attention span to speak of. "What do you think about this one?"

I fake-retch a little. "I think I don't get why you want to look like someone barfed on your nails." I seriously do not understand why Peaches, who at thirty-six has the looks, hair, and body of a Miss Texas—or a porn star, take your pick—wants to wear ugly colors on purpose.

"You need to relax, as usual," Peaches says. "This color is edgy. It goes with my tattoos. And my nipple ring."

"Eww. Why do you have to talk about your nipple ring all the time?" I give a pretty pale blue bottle of Essie nail polish to Hua, the only woman in all of Portland—including myself—allowed to touch my cuticles. I change the subject back to the house. "Anyway, Jake really wants to make an offer on it. And it's the only home we've found that would work for all three of us."

I can hear myself selling the idea to Peaches. It's like I can't help it. Long ago, I gave Peaches a papal-like authority to approve or reject decisions in my life and, surprise, surprise, Peaches has never given the authority back. "It has two master bedrooms!"

Somehow that doesn't sound as great as it did when Sue said it.

In any case, Peaches isn't buying it. "I hate how real estate people always call houses *homes*. It's like how lawyers always say they're *attorneys*—so fake. I really wish you would stop."

"Whatever, Peaches. Okay, the *house*—"

"And can we just get something straight? *Jake* is not going to be making an offer on anything." She gives me a full serving of side-eye. "*You* are. And the fact that he even *says* that worries me." Peaches speaks in italics a lot.

"I didn't say he said, 'I want to make an offer.'" I'm always defending Jake. Peaches doesn't see how sweet he is to me, how he brings me little gifts (a scarf here, a ring there), makes me a perfect cappuccino every time he sleeps over, *and* scratches my back every single night exactly the way I like it—one long stroke from top to bottom, right to left, like mowing a lawn. She doesn't see any of that and I don't mention it, because it would cheapen the whole thing. I don't have to prove Jake's love to Peaches, of all people. "He didn't say that."

"Fine then. What did he say?"

"He said *we* should make an offer."

"Well, what he *should* have said is, 'You, *Nicki Daniels*, should make an offer, with the money *you* have worked your ass off to earn, starting with the paper route you had in sixth grade, and continuing until this very day when you are *still* working your ass off, *and* taking care of your kid, *and* dealing with my entitled ass.' When I say entitled, I mean Jake, not me."

She pulls one foot out of the water and offers up her toes for a helping of puke green/yellow. "Speaking of which, does he still want your money for a restaurant?"

Of course she would bring that up. About a month ago, I mentioned in passing that I was thinking of investing in Jake's restaurant, and I've regretted it ever since. Peaches makes it sound like Jake is some sort of male gold digger who is only with me for my money. I don't even have that much money. At best, a guy could dig for bronze. To me she just sounds old-fashioned. This is the twenty-first century, people. So I have the money, big whoop, why feel bad about it? I can't deal with the idea that it's okay to be a woman who makes money as long as you're partnered with a man who makes more.

"It's not like that," I say. Conversations with Peaches can sometimes start to feel like dropping a piece of paper on a windy day where your only hope is to stomp on it the moment it lands. Otherwise you're going to chase it all over tarnation.

"Oh really, then what's it like?"

"I'm not the only investor. The contractor guy, Miguel, is putting in all the labor and materials—which is worth way more than my share. Jake is putting in the sweat equity. And I'm underwriting the lease. We're all three equal partners."

"So you've already committed to this?" Now Peaches is accusing me. "You didn't tell me that."

"I didn't have to!" I can hear myself going on the defensive, which I hate. But Peaches is partly right. Until now, I've been making it seem like the restaurant thing is more of a maybe than a yes. Probably because I knew she would have such a big, fat opinion about it. Peaches has big, fat opinions about a lot of things in my life.

And I let her get away with it, probably because she's not just the closest thing I have to a family—she's *all* I have for a family. With no brothers or sisters, a mom who is God knows where (seriously, she could be dead for all I know, but I don't know because I'm really great at practicing Don't Look, Don't Find), and a dad in prison I haven't spoken to in years, I am alone in the world. Except for Cody—and if I ever decide to marry him, Jake—I am essentially an orphan. For a very long time, Peaches was The Most Important Person in my life, and just as Bill Clinton is still called Mr. President, it's not a title Peaches is going to relinquish anytime soon. Like, ever.

Which is why Peaches hates all my boyfriends. Whenever a new guy comes along, Peaches drops down to third in my Netflix queue of people. She could handle becoming number two when Cody was born. But for her, being number three is just not acceptable. Peaches believes no man is as trustworthy as she is, and in some ways she's right. Love has a tendency to make even good people turn shady. Or maybe I just like guys who have a little bit of shady in them.

"I don't know, Nick." Peaches has that skeptical tone in her voice. "Maybe you should slow your roll with Jake. It's fine to boink him, but you don't need to give him a job, too."

"Peaches, I'm sorry, but I'm not taking relationship advice from you."

"Why not?"

"Because you wouldn't know the difference between a good boyfriend and Charlie Sheen."

"Charlie Sheen is hot."

"Exactly." I practically snort, I'm so right. "Anyway, I don't think you get it. Jake loves me. He wants to marry me—"

"Ohhhhhh! So that's it! He said the magic words! *I want to marry you.* Okay, now I get it. This explains everyth—"

"Peaches, please."

"You're going to tell him the house is yours, though. Right? *We're* not buying it, you are, and *your* name is going to be on the deed. The *only* name."

"Peaches."

"If he's cool, he'll have no problem with that. If he's not cool with it, he's a taker, Nicki."

"Peaches! He's not a taker."

Hua looks up from my cuticles. "Peaches right. No one ever says, '*I'm a taker.*'" It would be just like Hua to interject once in her broken English, but totally make it count.

"*Yes!*" Peaches gives Hua a high five. "Hua, you kill me, woman. Thanks for the assist."

"Maybe you're right," I say. I've learned this is the best way to get Peaches to stop talking about something. She's like the drunk driver of BFFs—she has a way of jumping the curb and plowing right through any sobriety checkpoint you try to set up.

"Just ask him if he's okay with his name not being on the deed. I dare you," she says.

I can't even look at Peaches, I'm so mad. I just stare at my *OK!* magazine and pretend to be absorbed in the latest Jennifer Aniston pregnancy rumor. There's a long silence.

"Okay, now can we *please* talk about something else?" Peaches says impatiently. She's pretending like *she's* the one who can't take it anymore. Nice move. Classic Peaches.

"I wish we would," I say, still staring at the extreme close-up of Jennifer's womb area. It's got a red box on it to indicate where the baby would be. If there were one.

"No, *I* wish we would."

"No, *I* wish we would, first."

It's hard not to laugh. Peaches and I have a way of keeping a fight going *and* laughing about it *and* playing it like a scene in a movie—all at the same time.

"Fine."

"No, *I'm* fine!"

"Fine. Be fine, then. I'm not stopping you."

"I will."

"Go ahead," Peaches says, letting her head bob just a little. "I'm waiting for you."

"I'm doing it," I say. "Right now. This is me being fine." I exaggeratedly do my best impression of "fine"—supercalm face, Mona Lisa smile, eyes forward, head just slightly tilted to the left. "You like it?"

"I love it." Peaches laughs and holds up her hand for a high five. "You're effing hilarious."

I slap her hand. "No, you are."

And as both of us dissolve into giggles, Hua tries not to ruin my cuticles.

# 2

# RONNIE

After church, I always clean. Every Sunday I pick up each of my thirty-two possessions and carefully wipe off every speck of dust. Every last morsel. Done right, this kills a good two hours.

Which is great, because Sundays are long. I don't have to go to my job, and normally that would be a good thing, but not here. Because the kitchen where I work is probably the most happening spot in the whole place: giant vats of boiling water for the mashed potatoes, huge ovens filled with industrial-sized trays of "meat" loaf, and massive sheets of gooey paste that pass for apple cobbler. The kitchen also has the one thing that's always in short supply on Sundays: regular people to talk to. Employees, who just work here, not live here. They come and go as they please.

I love to talk to regular people. I like to hear about their lives: their kids, their cars, their struggles, their TV shows. I want to know them and feel them and live vicariously through them. It makes me feel alive. It wasn't always like this. One time, doing reps in the gym, I realized that all of the relationships I had before I got here were either with people who a) I was using or b) were using me. To the 1998 Ronnie Daniels, human beings worked in one of two directions—you could put something in, or you could take something out. These days, I see myself more as someone sitting next to the mailbox observing everyone who comes up and saying hi and good-bye and trying to make their day a little brighter.

It's a lot better this way.

My books take the longest to clean. They are my prized possessions and I do them one at a time, all fourteen of them. I have spiritual stuff like *The Holy Bible* (King James Version), *The Tibetan Book of Living and Dying,* and the *Tao Te Ching;* some general interest, like the copy of *Tuesdays with Morrie* someone gave me, and a thick and unreadable hardcover about investing in stocks—which I've always planned to do someday. But the majority of my books are about psychology. Over the years, I've read it all: child development, evolutionary psychology, marriage and family therapy, self-help. My favorite book is this one on attachment theory—because how people bond to their moms is *the way they do life*. Seriously. You think you have free will, you're making choices about how to be, whom to love, and how to love them. Not really. It was all set by your first birthday. You didn't choose shit. Your mom came to you when you cried, or she didn't, and she read the signals you were sending, or she didn't, and the rest is an episode of *Divorce Court.*

When I'm done with the books, I give a once-over to my two legal pads and my pen—I have one of those blue Paper Mates, not the Bic Cristals I really like. Even after all this time, I can still remember how much easier the ball rolls on those Bics, and I like the darker color of the ink, too. I got an eye for stuff like that. I'm stylish. Even in here. I used to shy away from saying so, but now I'm old enough to just be real. That's how it is and why lie? Sure, maybe I'm not as cut as I used to be, but for fifty-seven, I'm still good-looking in an Alec Baldwin sort of way. I got a full head of hair, piercing eyes, and a voice made for phones (or pillow talk).

I definitely still have it, or I would if there were anyone to give it to.

I'm just about to start on my two photographs—they're my prized possessions, so I always save them for last—when I hear the sharp clatter of jingling metal against metal stop right outside my door.

"Hey. *Ronnie.*"

It's Dacker, one of the younger guards. There's a sharp, *listen-up*–type of urgency in his voice.

"Dacker?" I can see Dacker's right eye through the square window. "What's goin' on?"

This is unusual. It's fifteen thirty on a Sunday and nothing else is supposed to happen around here until dinner. I hear a key slide into the lock—my lock—and the next thing I know the heavy metal door is swinging wide open. I can see Dacker, all of him, not just the part of his face visible through the cell door. He's a good-lookin' kid, Dacker. Maybe all of twenty-nine.

"Warden wants to see you."

"On a Sunday?" This could be alarming. You never really want to see the warden in the flesh, much less on a weekend. Last time that happened, that snitch Eyelash went and lied his way out of trouble by throwing four innocent guys under the bus. All four ended up in The Hole for a month. I was one of them. "What's he want to see me for?"

"Don't ask me, man. I just do what they tell me." Dacker says this like he and I are basically in the same boat. I guess in most of the major ways, we are. We spend all our time behind bars, don't we?

"And they told you to come here and get me and take me down to see Warden Moline?"

Dacker shakes his head. "Naw, man. It's the other one. The assistant warden."

"Reeves."

"Yeah, man. That's him."

"The red-faced guy. Who can't dress."

"The very same." Dacker cracks an almost imperceptible smile as he swipes a pair of handcuffs off his right hip in one clean, practiced motion. He's not supposed to enjoy spending time with the inmates—*fraternize* is the official word for it—but sometimes he can't help it. Some of us, like me, are cool people. Probably makes his job less depressing. In fact, if Dacker wasn't so nice, he'd probably be working the Monday-through-Friday nine-to-five by now. But he still has some humanity, and around here that means the JV squad—nights, weekends, holidays. "Turn around."

"Oh, you wanna boogie?" I do a little dance move as I turn around. Seventeen years in this place hasn't taken the boogie out of me. I'm proud of that. Besides, I know these guards so well—the way they move, how they handle me—I could go on *Dancing with the Stars* with any one of them and win the mirror ball trophy. (Dudes in the joint love that show. It's as much skin as they're going to see this side of the barbed wire.) "Does anyone say the word *boogie* anymore?"

"No one ever did," Dacker deadpans.

He gives me a little nudge and we start moving toward the door of the cell block.

"How's your girlfriend, Dacker? She still giving it to you good?"

"She is," Dacker says evenly.

I'm the go-to guy around here for advice on relationships. Sort of like a jailhouse lawyer, except a jailhouse therapist. I know women so well, and I've done so much reading, dudes just started coming to me and talking to me about their problems, especially with the ladies, and pretty soon I was up to my ears in cigarettes and candy bars that I was taking in trade. Along with the spiritual stuff—meditation, Buddhism, and this Egyptian theology you've probably never heard of—I got turned into sort of a guru in here.

This time, though, Dacker's all business. "Let's see what the warden wants, huh?"

I wince at the reminder of where we're going. "Yeah. Let's see what old Assistant Warden Bob Reeves wants with me on this fine Sunday afternoon."

As we walk, I'm reminded of the hook on an old disco song and I break into an a cappella version—*"Cause boogie nights are always the best in town . . ."*

And inside one of the cells, someone claps, because I can really sing.

———

Reeves lurches in wearing his weekend clothes: a pair of oversized jeans and a size XXXL T-shirt from a local fun run he obviously didn't do. At his weight—he must top 250, at least—Reeves couldn't do a five foot, much less a 5K. He perches on the edge of his desk, his massive left buttock holding him down, while his right one hangs free.

I shift in my chair, poised for anything. Encounters with a warden are tense. My first tour of duty in the joint, I used to spend hours playing chess, and it's a lot like that. You never know what's going on in the other guy's mind. This could very easily end with a trip to solitary, or a punch in the face.

"Now, now, you can relax," Reeves says. He's looking straight at me, which in prison means he's waiting for a response. "Take a load off."

*Pawn to d5.*

I'm flipping through my mental Experiences in Prison file, looking for a match. Nothing's coming up. I have no idea what's going on here. I decide to play it safe by keeping it very neutral.

"Thanks," I say. "Don't mind if I do."

*Okay, pawn to d6.* Just match him, nothing more.

Reeves clasps his hands together, winding up for his next move. It's disturbing to see how much he enjoys this. There's a thing in the psychology world called *sublimation,* where, for instance, people who want to inflict pain become dentists. Wardens are people who in another era would have become overseers on plantations, but since slavery is outlawed, they become wardens instead. It's a real ugly profession. Anyway, I watch as Reeves arranges his face into "thoughtful," then says offhand, "I'm going on vacation tomorrow for two weeks and I'm in here trying to clear off my desk before I leave. Heading to Bend; I got a place out there."

*Boom!*

*Cxd4, bitches!*

Reeves just upended the board. A warden referring to his *personal life*? Telling me something about himself and his world outside the armed guards and the electronic gates? That just does not happen.

"And since I'm going to be gone for two weeks," he continues, "I realized I needed to let you know what's happening so you could make some plans."

*Plans?*

"Uh, Warden. Excuse me," I say. I just realized candid is the way to go here. "Can I ask you a straight question?"

"Sure, Ron. Go ahead."

"What is happening here?"

"You're getting out of here, Ron. That's what's happening." Reeves grins so wide it almost erases the contempt that permanently roosts on the left side of his upper lip.

*You're getting out of here. That's what's happening.*

My large intestine almost drops through my lap and out the bottom of the chair. Those are the most life-changing words to crash into my psyche since the jury foreman stood up seventeen years ago and said, *We find the defendant guilty . . .* Reeves keeps chattering, as if he doesn't understand that my ears have gone deaf.

"The way it happened was, I found out Friday that you became eligible for that new early release program back on September 29," he says. "I was feeling generous, because that's the kinda guy I am, so I decided to do you a solid and take care of it before I left on vacation."

*You're getting out of here. That's what's happening.*

Suddenly, I'm time traveling back to that federal courtroom in 1998. To the moment I heard the word *guilty*. It was as if I died on the spot. And dying was just like people said it would be: there was a long tunnel with a white light at the end and in a flash, I saw my whole life—random scenes of it anyway—peppering my eyes like machine-gun fire.

*The alley behind my childhood home in Seattle.*

*The first time I scooped the money off the table, hustling pool.*

*A dinner I'd had with Beth at a revolving restaurant in a San Francisco hotel.*

*The time I fired a gun at a man, missed, and vowed never to do it again. I didn't.*

*The face, during orgasm, of the last woman I had sex with.*

Then I died. I was taken away by the bailiff, put in a cell, and kept there until this very moment, when Reeves called me into this office and brought me back to life.

"You're supposed to be happy, Ronnie. Thank me. Say something." Reeves is talking, and I shake the memories out of my head, returning to the present. All those years of meditation can't keep me present for what's happening now. "Ronnie?"

"What? Oh. Thank you."

Reeves chuckles at me and keeps moving. "Since the early release program is new, who in hell knows what's going to happen? Most likely you'll be in the halfway house for thirty to sixty days. Then you get released to home detention for another thirty to sixty days. You got someone lined up you can do your home detention with?"

"Sure," I lie. I would say yes to anything Reeves asked me right now. "I got a daughter."

"If you don't line something up, you'll have to come back here. But I trust you'll—"

"No, no! She'll be thrilled."

*Eventually. I hope. She'll be thrilled, right?*

"Good." Reeves locates a folder with a short stack of documents inside and signs as he speaks. At one level, the prison system is an exercise in filling out forms. Dozens of them. For everything. "Okay, here's the order remanding you to the halfway house in Portland. It's a crappy place, and you'll have an ankle bracelet on, but at least you can look out your window and see a real titty walk by every once in a while." He looks at me and winks again. "So it's not all bad."

I flash back again to the last lady I had sex with, wondering if I still have her phone number.

"I'm sure they're gonna miss you in the kitchen. You're pretty much an A student down there. Wish everybody in this place did time like you."

"You're right about that, I am good at doing time," I say. "You know what they say. The way you do time is the way you do life."

"Is that what they say?" Reeves isn't even listening. He's putting his stapler right where he wants it and his pens back into the pen holder. "Um, um, um."

This is what people don't understand about prison. It's a life. It's not the life anyone in here dreamed of, but it's a life. If you can adapt, and I'm a world-class adapter, you will be okay. You'll figure something out. Me, I made learning my thing. I've learned more in prison through correspondence courses and self-study courses and certification programs than most of the guys I grew up with who went to college. I got an education in here. People think prison is all bending over in the shower and gang rape. But it's really just another version of the same thing human beings do everywhere they are: living.

There are guys in the joint who have cell phones, and blenders, and drug problems, and cooktops. If it's out there, it's in here. I've followed the rules because my third time around, I figured out that your integrity is the only thing they can't take away from you, so I was going to do the hell out of my integrity. It took time, but I finally understood that the ultimate responsibility for my being here was mine. Sure, I could blame the guy who turned state's evidence on me, but he couldn't have turned on me if I hadn't already done something wrong. Since then, I've been the model prisoner. I've gotten fourteen different commendations while doing my time, all signed by the warden. Just trying to dismantle all that old karma by meeting each new moment as the person I aspired to be. Instead of the person who committed all those crimes.

"Always the philosopher, aren'tcha, Daniels." Reeves looks at me serious. "You think you can get a job with that? Let's hope so."

He signs the last page with a flick of the wrist worthy of a concert pianist, or a hip-hop deejay. "There you go, Mr. Ronald Daniels. All set. A free man. Almost."

"Hard to believe this is really happening," I say, thunderstruck. "I can't believe it."

"You should see the look on your face." Reeves looks at me and laughs— at me, not with me. This is the Reeves I know. A bully who's found a job that's a perfect fit. "You guys all react the same way. Like little kids.

"I've been doing this a long time, Ronnie. And you know what I think?" Reeves lowers his voice, like he's about to give up a state secret. "I think you're terrified." There's something threatening about the way he leans toward me, resting on his forearms. "I think you're just now realizing you weren't in here because society had to get *you* away from us. You're in here because *you* had to get away from *society*." Reeves looks at me dead in the eye. "Because it scares you."

My face is burning red and my forehead is breaking out in a sweat. I hate Reeves for knowing this, and for saying it. Even more, I hate that it's true. He probably says this to all the guys. It's his way of grabbing power one last time before setting us free. Asshole.

Reeves stands up and shouts, "Dacker!" Dacker comes in and throws the cuffs back on me. Reeves goes back to sounding all hearty, like he's giving a graduation speech. "Time to move on to some new challenges, Ronnie. You still got some time left on the shot clock. Make it count."

*You're getting out of here. That's what's happening.*

"Some days, I really do love my job," Reeves says to nobody.

*I'm getting out of here.*

*I can't believe it's happening.*

# 3

## NICKI

I was afraid something like this was going to happen, and now it has. I'm sitting outside the principal's office at Cody's school staring at a poster with a bow and arrow on it that says Take Aim At Your Future! while Cody simultaneously picks at his cuticles and surfs the Web on his phone, his blond hair falling in his face. I'm not sure why I'm here yet, only that I was up to my statement necklace in Excel spreadsheets when I got a call from the vice principal telling me to come down to the high school immediately. I grabbed my stupidly huge purse, my seventy-five-dollar calfskin-fringe key chain—the one I just had to have—and raced down here as fast as I could.

"Can you please not look superworried about me?" he says in his customary monotone. "It makes me feel weird."

"I'll try not to, honey," I say evenly.

Oh boy. How does he manage to sound so provocative and bored at the same time? I'm actually getting pretty good at not reacting to the teenagey tone—because, as one of my older mom friends says, you always gotta ask yourself, "Do I want to die on that hill?" And the answer is almost always no. But then it does seem like Cody is always upping the ante, coming back with some version of, *Well, how about this hill? Or this one? Or this one?* Then I have to decide I don't want to die on those hills, either.

The truth about me and my son is that he is, in some essential way, a mystery to me. He always has been. I hear people talk about how innocent and amazing and wonderful and magical childhood is. Their kids say cute things about the moon and choo-choo trains and peanut butter. They love puppet shows and building block towers and licking the spoon. My kid wasn't like that. I never knew what he was thinking. And often, I still don't.

From the very beginning, Cody's been this perplexing combination of totally easy and totally hard. I realized he wasn't like other babies in the first week. Every time I tried to set him down in the bouncy chair, he would immediately start crying. If I picked him up, he would immediately stop. For two weeks, I attempted to train him to sit in that chair, but he wouldn't do it. Finally, I gave up and strapped him into the BabyBjörn and wore him around all the time—just to get some peace. Once I did that, he was easy as pie.

Eventually, I discovered that Cody was just easily bored. Even in infancy! I had no idea an infant could be bored. While another baby might stare at his mobile or look out the window at the leaves on the trees, Cody wanted full-on engagement all the time. When he was a toddler, I used to park in front of construction sites so he could watch the drills and the backhoes. I'd get out my paperwork—this is when I was still doing my mortgage job—and jam through half a day's work while he looked out the window. He had the concentration and attention span of a grown-up—he could sit there so quiet, so well behaved, for two hours!—as long as he was fully immersed in something he loved. If not, though—watch out. It was nonstop complaining, fidgeting, and whining.

I'll admit I overrelied on the video games, the computer, and the TV. As a single mom, I had to. When he was little and I would get home from work, the only way I could get dinner on the table was to plop him in front of *Teletubbies* or *Rugrats*. I didn't feel the least bit guilty, either! I looked at my mom friends trying to do it by the book—no screens, no sugar, no MSG—with pity and, sometimes, judgment. Most of them were a lot older than me, with husbands, and all the ambition they used to put into their jobs they were now putting into their children. I swear they were doing more harm to their kids with their perfectionism than I was doing with the Happy Meals. At least I didn't yell (very often). If I had to choose between being in constant conflict with my child and another hour of Game Boy, there was going to be no contest. Bring on the Game Boy.

Things changed when Cody was eleven and my appraisal business took off. Within a few months I was making more money than I ever imagined—not like fuck-you money, but nice upper-middle-class money—and could work my own hours. So if Cody had a school performance, or a doctor's appointment, or the flu, suddenly being a good mom didn't always have to go on the back burner to making ends meet. We didn't have to deal with crappy apartments anymore, either, with their broken dishwashers and laundry room at the end of the hallway. When we went to Target, we could load up on large sizes of everything and backup toothpaste. When we lost something, we could easily replace it. And the car never broke down because we always had a new one. Life got a lot easier.

After a year or two of this, I discovered most of the problems associated with being a single mom have nothing to do with not having a man and everything to do with not having a man's earning power. Give a single mom a cardiologist's money and all of a sudden she looks a lot less sad/pathetic and a lot more like someone who has figured out that traditional marriage is a bummer if you like freedom. Also, by then I had not only learned the ropes of motherhood, I'd figured out who I was the mother *of*. Okay, so my kid is a baffling combination of well-socialized and introvert, of easy and hard, of sweet and distant? Fine. I'm happy to be that guy's mom. From there on out, I put all my energy into accepting Cody on his own terms. Not an easy task with anyone, maybe least of all your kid.

And I thought I was doing great. Until now.

I reach over toward his hand. To my surprise he lets me rest my hand on his for a full three seconds before shifting his weight in such a way that the connection is broken.

"Whatever it is, honey," I say, "we'll get through it."

He looks at me for a half second, and I can see in his eyes that he's sorry. "Thanks, Mom."

The thing is, Cody really *is* a good kid. I know everyone says that about their offspring, but in this case it's true. He's polite to teachers and other kids' parents. (Is any teen polite to their own?) He doesn't have crazy anger issues or smoke more than the normal amount of weed. His problem is this: he's apathetic. If he had a motto, it would be *non mihi curae est*—Latin for "I don't give a fuck."

About anything.

Wait, I take that back. He cares a lot about one thing: Magic: The Gathering. Not the kind of magic where you saw a lady in half or pull a rabbit from a hat. This Magic (or MTG, for short) is a card game that you play at comic-book stores. As I understand it—and I don't really understand it—Magic is sort of like Dungeons & Dragons meets poker meets chess. You make a deck out of all these little cards that cast spells and have drawings on them and cost a lot of money and end up all over the bedroom floor—then you go to a comic-book store where you battle your deck against the decks of other guys who will someday do great on the math part of the SAT. There's a lot of strategy involved, and the whole shebang is way too complicated for most regular people to understand. Also, there are tournaments in every city in America, and even a world championship that Cody plans to win someday. Oh, and some people call it Cardboard Crack.

That's it. The only thing Cody seems to care about. Not school, clothes, sports, or girls. Okay, maybe girls—but so far they don't care about him back. And yes, he has friends, but mostly of the backpack-and-comic-book-store persuasion.

It wasn't always like this. He used to care about video games and stuffed animals and *iCarly* and drama club. But the passageway from child to man has been really narrow for him, and he's having a hard time moving through it. Something I chalk up to him not having a dad.

I think back on my own sophomore year. I did some shoplifting, dabbled in drinking, smoked the occasional cigarette. But my house was so chaotic, so disorganized, I actually wanted to follow the rules. My big giant middle finger to my mother was to get Bs, have a nice but average boyfriend, and come home before midnight—all of which Beth found terribly amusing. (It's probably an act of rebellion that in adulthood, I often refer to her by her first name.) She laughed out loud when I announced I was trying out for the school play—*What would you want to hang out with those nerds for, anyway? And wear some stupid costume? Losers.*—then took a long, last pull on her Menthol 100 and stubbed it out in the grimy ashtray she got at the Grand Canyon. I didn't care what she thought of me, though. I mean, how upset can you get when a woman who wears curlers to the grocery store calls you a loser? Not very.

Not that following the rules worked, necessarily. I've done everything right that my mom did wrong, and I'm still sitting outside the principal's office. I'm not trying to feel sorry for myself, but is that fair? We had some tough times when Cody was little, but once I figured out how to make money, I gave him everything you could give a kid—not spoiling him or anything, but he got the new video game on the day it came out, and he's always had clean hair and nice shoes on. We eat organic! We own a house! He's totally vaccinated! I really thought if I was just the most together mom ever, I mean really, truly crushed the whole motherhood *deal*, I could make up for the fact that his dad bailed before he was born.

I really did.

I was only twenty years old and five quarters away from college graduation when I met Gio. I was so sure of myself then! My rotten childhood was over, and I was free for the first time in my life—or I thought I was. Within ten minutes of locking eyes, Gio convinced me to leave Peaches and the other girls in the nightclub and walk around the block with him. I definitely felt like I shouldn't say yes, but the second I looked at him—I mean really looked at him—there was absolutely zero chance I was going to say no.

His eyes were the craziest amber/yellow/blue. My first thought was: *danger;* my second thought was: *this is the most beautiful boy I've ever seen,* ever; and my third thought was: *danger.* I took the walk.

One block turned into another and another and another until we watched the sun rise while running across the Hawthorne Bridge, holding hands. Along the way we talked about things I never even knew I had words for: feelings, sensations, hopes, fears. Gio had seen and done so many things. He'd been to war! He'd seen a man's leg get blown off! He'd been to Japan! He was like a character out of a fairy tale. Not the prince on a white horse, the other kind of prince, the wounded kind. Like the boy in my favorite Hans Christian Andersen story, who along with his ten brothers gets turned into a swan, and whose sister, in order to reverse the spell, has to knit them all sweaters from yarn made of stinging nettles. In the story, the sister isn't able to finish all eleven sweaters in time, which leaves the youngest brother with a beautiful swan wing in place of his left arm.

Gio was sort of like that. A creature who belonged to this world and another world at the same time. I knew he would eventually fly away, and one night he did. It was almost as if he went out for a pack of cigarettes and never came back, but in this case, the pack of cigarettes was a willowy Reed student named Rachel who ate avocados and adhered to Third Wave Feminism. But I'd kept a part of him. I had Cody, my beautiful boy.

The lady from the office pokes her head out into the hallway.

"Ms. Daniels? Cody?" she says. "You can go in now."

Maybe Cody is part swan, too.

———

"Mrs. Daniels, let me cut right to the chase." So this is Principal Borman. He's about forty-two, probably a little OCD, married. He doesn't seem mean, just cold—more reptile than coyote. He seems like a teacher who moved into administrating for the power and the increase in pay. "Cody's being suspended. For truancy."

I gasp, then cover my mouth, because I sort of promised not to overreact, and gasping probably falls into the category of "superworried." I look over at Cody, but he's got his head down, so I can't see his eyes.

The principal continues. "He skipped his first two hours again today, and missed a test in Life Sciences. Which makes"—he consults his computer screen—"twenty-six absences this term. At the moment, he's in danger of failing all six of his classes."

I turn to Cody. "Is this true?"

"Not Choir," he says. "I'm not failing Choir."

Principal Borman looks again at his screen. "You're right. I take that back. You're getting a C-minus in Choir."

I'm in shock. Cody looks like he goes to school every morning, and he looks like he's been at school every evening. He carries a backpack that looks full and he looks like he's doing homework. To find out he's just blowing off classes left and right, well, I'm having a hard time wrapping my head around it. Basically it means he's been lying his ass off. Not only did I not know he was capable of that, he's always been especially scrupulously honest. I mean, this is the same child who in third grade insisted we go back to the store when he realized he'd accidentally left carrying a small kaleidoscope without paying for it. So, yeah, this comes as a complete and utter shock.

"I'm *sorry*." He doesn't sound sorry. He sounds indignant.

"What have you been doing while you're not in school?" This sounds like the wrong question the moment it leaves my mouth. But it's not.

"With all due respect, Mrs. Daniels, what difference does that make?"

"It's Ms. Daniels."

"Ms. Daniels."

"With all due respect, Principal." I'm being sort of cheeky to use his language, but I do it anyway. "What I'm trying to figure out is, is he skipping *against* school? Or *for* something else? If he's going to be punished, we should at least punish him for the right thing."

Principal Borman doesn't say anything in a *that-makes-sense* kind of way. I look to Cody. I wait for an answer. "Cody?"

Cody cracks his knuckles and shrugs. He has as many variations on a shrug as Eskimos have words for snow. There's one-sided, two-sided, with an eye roll, a head wag, both, or neither. For someone who says so few words, he definitely manages to communicate a lot of information.

"Cody!" I'm not mean, but I mean it.

"I don't know," he says finally. Now I feel bad, like I crossed the line.

Principal Borman steps in. "Cody," he says, "your mom asked you a question. Give her an answer."

Cody fidgets. "What was the question?" He's not exactly being defiant, he really doesn't remember. It's like he's missing one marker on the memory gene.

"Why have you been skipping school?" Principal Borman says again. I'm starting to get why he's the principal. He's really authoritative, without raising his voice at all. And Cody, by some miracle, is doing what he says. "What have you been doing with that time?"

"Fine," he concedes to Principal Borman, then turns to challenge me. "Mom, why do you even care about that?"

"Because I care about that." It's interesting to me that he thinks I should explain myself before he explains himself. Is that what things have come to? When I was growing up, this was called sassing, and you could get a bar of soap in your mouth for it. There are moments I wonder about all the so-called good parenting I've done, and this is one of them. "Answer me."

Cody glances at the principal, then back at me. "Usually I go to the comic-book store and play Magic. But other times I just ride the bus. Or go home and hang out in my room."

Cody's getting fired up now. "Because school is stupid. I just sit here and watch, like, boring PowerPoint presentations, while the teachers drone on and on about boring shit. I haven't learned anything since ninth grade."

I look at Principal Borman. Cody might be wrong, but he's not irrational. His explanation makes perfect sense, even if it's sixteen-year-old-guy sense.

But Principal Borman only cares about the rules. Because he's a ruler. He's not worried about crossing the line. He's worried about drawing it. "Well, Cody. Truancy is wrong. And you're being suspended."

"Whatever."

*Non mihi curae est.*

"You'll be back in school on Monday. Obviously, you're going to take a fail for the test. It's up to Mr. O'Brien whether he'll let you make it up or not. Same with your other teachers. If they don't let you catch up on your work, you may have to do it in summer school. Several of your classes, Life Sciences included, are required for gradu—"

"Great." Cody glares at him and shoots me a pleading look. "Can we go now?"

"Sure." Principal Borman stands up. "I'd say we're done here."

Cody practically knocks his chair over he gets up so fast. He's out of the room in a flash.

"Thank you, Principal," I say confidently. "I don't think it will happen again."

"Ms. Daniels, can I be frank with you?"

I pitch my shoulders back a little. I wasn't expecting anything beyond a polite good-bye. "Sure. Of course."

"You seem like a nice person. I can see that you care a lot about your son."

"I do."

"I can see that." He takes a breath, like this is important, or hard for him to say. "Skipping school may not seem like that big a deal. But your boy is asking for something. Rules. Structure." Another breath, deeper this time. "Cody's not gone yet, Ms. Daniels. But if something doesn't change, he will be."

He doesn't even make nice at the end with a little smile. He just holds out his hand to shake mine. My lip is trembling, and I grab my bag and blindly fish around in it, furiously scraping the contents from one side of the bottom to the other, trying to find my key chain. Stupid fringe.

As I step out of the office, I see Cody at the far end of the long hallway. My kid is in trouble. Not huge trouble, but trouble just the same.

Maybe no one can make up for it when your dad bails.

———

We ride home in silence. Until I had Cody, I thought silence was emptiness, a lack of communication, but it's not. Silence is as full of information as talking is. Cody entered the world knowing this, and he's been teaching it to me for sixteen years. Sixteen very quiet years. It's a big part of his essential mystery.

When he was little I used to try to encourage him to talk, with lots of questions and conversation. Somewhere around year nine, I gave up, and that's when I realized how much communicating he was actually doing. Like right now. He's hurt and angry and ashamed and indignant and defiant and proud of himself, all at once. He also knows another mother would be yelling at him on this car ride, and not that he would ever say this, but he's grateful I'm not. I read in a parenting book once that when a kid becomes a teenager, they fire you as a boss, and if you've done a good job, they rehire you as a consultant. This is one of those situations. The classes have been skipped, the boy is suspended, what's done is done, and stupid rhetorical questions like *what were you thinking?* aren't going to undo it. He skipped school for a reason—he wanted to let us all know we can't control him—and he accomplished his objective. We all know we can't control him. Especially me.

I pull into the driveway and Cody's got his car door open even before I throw the gearshift in park. He heads for his room without looking at me, which stings, but I know this is part of the show—he's performing Person Who Isn't Under Anyone's Control—and he's all the way committed to the role. Knowing this doesn't make it any less painful.

"Cody." I say it softly, because I want to make sure he knows I'm not forcing him to talk, but it might be a good idea if he would. "Please, let's sit down for a minute and talk about this."

Instead, Cody slams the door to his room, his door scraping against the frame with a sharp sound. I know everything about Cody's emotional state based on the pitch and decibel level of that door hitting that frame. I now respond to it like Pavlov's dog.

I'll be honest. At times like this, I wish there was someone to help me. I wish there was someone to call, someone to come over, someone to sit with me so I don't feel so alone. It's not even that I'm wishing Cody had a dad—to be honest, I kind of like doing everything my way—but how great would it be if someone walked through that door right now who could say the right thing, give me some hope, tell me everything's going to be all right? Someone who could hold half of my fear, like carrying the other end of an especially heavy sofa on moving day? Someone whose investment in that kid equaled mine?

How great would that be?

*It would be so great.*

But it's not going to happen.

I heard a Christian minister on early-morning television say once that men don't follow institutions or ideas—they follow leaders. All this time, I thought I was doing Cody a favor by not getting married, but now I'm not so sure. I thought it would undermine his security if, for instance, he asked if we could go to the county fair and I had to say *Let me check with Bob first*— instead of just making all the decisions on my own. I thought Cody would be traumatized if suddenly he had to deal with some guy named Bob whose authority derived solely from the fact that he was having sex with me.

Maybe it's time I admit that Cody has needed a man in his life all along. Not to be his father—that ship has sailed—but to be someone in his life who isn't so worried about crossing the line that he fails to draw one at all. Because that's what men do, don't they? Like Principal Borman, they draw the line.

I can't give Cody his dad back. But I could give him a man in his life. That structure thing? *That* I can do. Until now I've been happy just to have Jake as a boyfriend—a side dish, even—who never has to be fully integrated into my life. I haven't needed a man for the traditional reasons: money, or status, or to give me a baby. I have all of that. But what I do need a man for is Cody. My son, who has lived for sixteen years without a father figure—and who desperately needs one. I've done everything for him but the one thing I cannot do myself: create the kind of structure and stability that comes with a traditional family.

I've always thought Jake was too young for that, but maybe this is the sign I've been waiting for. Maybe Jake is the guy. Now that we're taking everything to the next level, maybe his age doesn't matter so much anymore. He loves me, he wants to commit and run a business together. What more could I ask for? It's all right here. I'm flooded with hope that we can do it—the house, the relationship, the restaurant, the family, all of it. Is this what it feels like to know it when you see it?

I pull out my phone to call Jake. He answers on the first ring.

"Baby? I think I'm going to make an offer on that house."

# 4

# RONNIE

By the time I board the bus to Portland, there are only two seats left: the one next to the toilet, and a window seat next to a young mom whose kid has green stuff oozing out of his/her right nostril. I pick the one next to the mom, even though it's clear from her body language that she wants the space all to herself and her kid despite not having a ticket for him. Or is it a her? I feel bad, but I stand at her row anyway and finally she looks up at me like *Who, me?* Which forces me to be the bad guy.

"Excuse me," I say, "that seat open?" I nod in the direction of the seat. I can't even really make eye contact because this is basically the first real live woman I've spoken to in seventeen years and it's overwhelming.

Reluctantly, the girl swings her knees into the aisle, giving me room to pass. I stand there a second, unsure which way to face as I slide into the seat—should I put my ass or my package in this young woman's face? When you imagine your first forty-two minutes of freedom, this is not what you think about.

I finally decide on ass and move so quick I almost fall into the window seat, startling the toddler, who begins to wail. The oozing green stuff moves up and down, getting closer to cresting her/his top lip with every shudder.

"Sorry about that, young lady," I say, nodding politely to the mom. I've always had nice manners. I believe presentation is a form of respect. Even if all I had to wear was the standard-issue uniform at FCI Sheridan, there were going to be sharp creases in my khakis and high shine on my shoes. "Sorry about that to you, too, little one."

I flip on the sparkle switch. The kid literally stops whimpering on the spot and just stares at me, because my eyes are *that* blue.

As the bus pulls out of the station and heads toward Interstate 5, I look around trying to get a feel for what's different. White paper coffee cups, for starters. Those mothers are everywhere. Water bottles. People drink water from bottles now? Who knew? Piercings. I see three people with metal in their faces just on this bus—that wouldn't have happened in 1998. Electronic stuff is everywhere—even the destination sign on the bus is all lit up. A lot of women are wearing tights as pants. Now that's a trend I can get behind. And last but definitely not least, every man, woman, and child on this bus seems to have some sort of gadget in their hands that they're clinging to for dear life.

The baby starts to fuss again and the mom glances at me apologetically.

"Sorry," the mom says. "It's nap time."

"I remember those days," I say. The girl will relax if she knows I'm a parent, too. "Your life is ruled by the schedule, right? What's her name? Or is she a he?"

"Kelsey." The girl wipes the big booger from Kelsey's nose, the way a person starts cleaning when someone drops by. "I'm Chloe."

"Ronnie." I hold my hand out like a flipper, because there's not enough space between our bodies for a full handshake.

"I'm not going for the K thing, like the Kardashians—my name starts with a C. I just like the name Kelsey." I can tell Chloe has explained this a lot of times.

"Gotcha," I say. "The Kardashians are krazy, huh? With a *K*?"

This gets a smile out of her.

As far as pop culture goes, I'm probably way more current than the average fifty-seven-year-old. Prison is filled with young men, coming in and out, and they keep you up to date on all the latest music and lingo and girls who are famous for their booty.

"How many kids you got, Ronnie?"

"One. A girl, her name is Nicki." Last time I saw her she was right about Chloe's age. Now she's gotta be thirty-six or thirty-seven. Is that even possible? I wonder what she looks like now, if her hair is still long and curly, and whether she's plump or thin. To say I've missed her all these years—that doesn't even come close. It's been more like a death. Or a kidnapping, because you never stop holding out hope that you might actually see the person again.

I'm never going back to prison.

Yes, I know I said that in 1988, and I said it in 1993. But it really is different this time. Because this time I learned my lesson. This time I educated myself. I read the books! I took the courses! I did the work—inner and outer. I know *why* I became a criminal and made the life choices I did. I built a new character.

I forgave myself.

"Only one?" Chloe sounds a little disappointed.

"Well, you know what they say." I grin playfully. "God only gives you what you can handle."

This time, I'm going to stay out. I'm going to avoid trouble, keep my nose clean, do the right thing. Because I've got a daughter I've missed, a grandson I've never met, and there is a lot of making up to do.

There's only one problem: Nicki hasn't spoken to me since before I went to prison this last time, and she doesn't know I'm getting out.

But I can get around that. I have to.

———

I line up the small plastic container in front of my fly and wait. This is going to be my life now: pissing into cups and handing them to Melissa Devolis, a thirtysomething plain Jane who probably studied social work because she wanted to save the world. That's how all these caseworkers are. They think they're going to do something for the less fortunate. "Something" ends up being a job as a reentry caseworker at the Oregon Residential Reentry Facility, which turns out to be essentially a babysitter for grown men who have no skills for the real world.

I exit the bathroom, still screwing the lid onto the warm cup, and hand it to her.

"I'll take care of this"—she means the pee—"and meet you in my office in five"—she means minutes. "You go ahead and take a seat in there."

Two minutes later, she slides her largish ass into the cheap office chair, the weary springs protesting her every movement and her extra twenty pounds. She's obviously tired of this job, and probably her life. There's something sad about the way she does her hair, a half-assed ponytail with grown-out bangs that she bobby pins off her face. It's a hairstyle that says *I've given up.* She pulls out a folder with my name on it and opens it. Surprise! It's jam-packed with forms that have to be filled out and signed.

"Let me start by saying very few guys in this place ever successfully make it back into the world." Melissa's real down-to-business. She takes her job seriously. "And I doubt you will, either."

"Why would you want to start like that?" I give her some serious eye contact, with twinkling. My whole spiritual practice is built around the idea of being present and knowing that you create your life with your intentions. And here this woman is predicting that I'm going to fail. I'm not mad at her, but I would like her to question that, just for a second. The best way to do that is to turn on the sparkle. "You've never met anyone like me before."

Melissa looks up from my file and holds my gaze. She takes a full breath and lets it out in a long sigh.

"Mr. Daniels, you can't possibly think you are the first man to get out of jail one day, then sit down in that chair and try to charm me the next." She pauses. "Can you?"

"*Hah!*" I clap my hands and laugh out loud. "You did not just say that! You're great."

She didn't expect this response. I can see that she's slightly suppressing a smile.

"Melissa Devolis, you are straightforward. I like that in a woman," I say. It's true, I really do like that in a woman. I call her out. "I can see you're trying not to smile. Don't front. We're going to be spending a lot of time together, so we might as well be friends."

Melissa takes another full breath. She brushes a piece of hair away from her face and in the process shows me her wrist.

*Bingo.*

She likes me. She doesn't know it yet, but she does. I know because those two gestures—hand to the face and showing the wrist—are both things female human beings do when they're sexually attracted. When you know evolutionary biology, the world starts to get a lot less confusing.

"Let's get down to business, Mr. Daniels." Her smile disappears. She hasn't lost her temper, but she's not exactly keeping perfect track of it, either. "Okay?"

*Let's get down to business, Mr. Daniels.*

Her abrupt shift in tone immediately causes my heart to rev and my mouth to go dry. I have to unstick my lips from my teeth. My whole body is on alert. Which means I haven't changed that much. Female anger still scares me. I take two breaths from as deep in my belly as I can get my breath to go.

This is what I mean by I know myself now. The second Melissa uses that clipped tone with me, I'm no longer sitting in a chair at the Oregon Residential Reentry Facility. I'm back in my childhood home, my overworked, overburdened mother shutting me up with just a glance across the room.

In the past, I would have reacted. I would have come back at Melissa with some anger of my own. I would have made trouble for myself by getting mouthy. And that would be how, not two hours after getting released from prison, I would have taken the first step toward committing my next crime and going back. But now I'm different. Now I have choices.

Now I can spend a few minutes thinking about how my life of crime mirrored my childhood. How growing up, I was always in trouble—the crazy one, with the ten hundred questions and the ability to charm—and my mother only really noticed me when I told a bad joke or sang too loud or laughed too much or talked too fast while she was trying to watch her favorite shows—she loved her cop shows. I guess I learned early on that if I couldn't get attention for being a good boy, I'd get it for being a bad one. Maybe my mother was so hard on me because I was the spitting image— in looks and behavior—of her own dad, whom she worshipped, but who drank and womanized and, according to my mom, made the whole family's life miserable. I met Grandpa Ross one time, at his funeral. You could tell he was a scoundrel even when you saw him lying in that coffin. He had a full head of slicked-back hair and a thick mustache, and despite being dead, he was still handsome. I was twelve years old, and I never forgot the image of my mother going up to him and kissing his dead forehead. Then she said, *Fuck you*, and walked away. Is it any wonder I could never please this woman?

As the fifth of seven kids—officially by two fathers, but in truth, prob-ably three—I enjoyed the benefits of being mostly ignored. For one thing, I didn't have responsibilities like my older sisters. I never had to babysit, mow the lawn, cook, or do dishes. Instead, I basically "starred" in the life of our block—a sort of smoking, shoplifting, pyromaniacal Huckleberry Finn, who was known all the way at the other end of the street as the best-looking, boldest, craftiest little shit in the neighborhood.

Yeah, I was proud of that. I'd go where no one else dared go, say what no one else dared say, and steal what no one else dared steal. I had cojones. By the time I was in fifth grade, I'd already perfected my first con: a fake charity where me and a couple of my little sidekicks would head over to the area north of Gilbert Avenue and go door-to-door asking for money for "needy children." Two hours later, we'd be feasting on Charleston Chews and maybe passing around a new yo-yo. What? I was needy, wasn't I?

By high school I was pulling down a retail manager's salary selling marijuana and Quaaludes. In my senior year I got myself an apartment a block from campus, making sure to dress well, keep my hair cut, and maintain a decent grade point average (I'm not bragging; I mean above a C minus) because, like I said, presentation is key. I knew: a) the teachers assumed the "good"-looking kids were good and the "bad"-looking kids were bad, and b) being a drug dealer in high school is like being the biggest store in a very busy shopping mall—it's all location, location, location, and then let the game come to you.

I went "pro" in my early twenties, almost by accident. In addition to my small-time drug and pimping hustle (two girls I was screwing were also screwing the occasional john I set them up with), I had a sideline going at the biggest pool hall in Seattle. I used to regularly take guys for two, three, four hundred dollars a shot. Half my success there was my understanding of psychology. Where a normal hustler is just looking for drunk and stupid, I picked my marks based on how they were acting. Were they insecure about their place in the group and had to prove something to their buddies? Were they wishful thinkers who had fantasies of being Paul Newman in *The Hustler*? Were they unable to back down from a challenge to their ego? I'd exploit vulnerabilities you didn't even know you were showing.

Eventually, I caught the eye of a guy named Diamonds (I never did know his real name) who had gotten into the cocaine business in the eighties, just as it was going mainstream. He owned the whole Seattle market, at least at the wholesale level, and wanted to branch out to Portland, but needed help. He picked me. I didn't know dookie about Portland, but I had balls and the name of someone to get in touch with. I drove my first pound down there in a maroon 1979 Cutlass Supreme, and that was it. I'd found my calling. I got the break of a lifetime when Diamonds got busted nine months later. It was too soon for me to be implicated in his business, but long enough that I knew a few players in his distribution network. I took over his business, relocated to Portland, and suddenly, now I was The Man.

But for all my swagger, I always had that soft spot where I never got Mama's love. And it drove me. I didn't know that at the time, but it's clear as day now. I was going to make women love me. All of them. The ones doing the Jane Fonda workout. The ones waiting tables. The ones who were married. The ones who were hos. If I had to seduce, finagle, lie, beg, or coerce—I would make them love me. Unfortunately, no matter how nice my car, no matter how much cocaine I moved, no matter how many hundreds I had in my pocket, or how many women I could get into my bed—no matter *what*—there was one place I could feel like Little Ronnie again in a hot second. And that place was in a woman's eyes. All a female had to do was *whisper* anger, frustration, judgment, or, worst of all, disregard, with her eyes and I'd feel smaller than a cockroach.

Sort of like how Melissa's got me feeling right now. She might think I'm attractive, but she still has the power to send me back to prison, and that's a fact. She's the one who decides if and when I leave this halfway house. She's the one I need to keep happy.

Which makes me wonder about her superpower.

Every woman has a superpower—the thing *she* thinks makes her special. Not what a man would notice about her, necessarily. Men are all about the goodies—a stacked chest, a round ass, long legs. But most girls have something they love about *themselves*: their smarts, their cooking, that space between their teeth. If you can figure out a girl's superpower and tap into it, if you can reach her there, you got her. She'll smile at you and talk to you and maybe even give her body to you. And if she gives her body to you, her heart is just a matter of time.

Knowing a woman's superpower is my superpower.

"Mr. Daniels?" she says. "Mr. Daniels?"

"Yeah?" I snap back into the room. "You really got to call me Ronnie," I say. "Since we're going to be spending so much time together."

"Can you stay with me here, Ronnie?" She smiles just a little bit. "We're almost done."

"Actually, I can't. Hold on a second," I say. I make a *hang-on* gesture and bow my head a little and concentrate because an insight is coming—this is the whole reason I meditate, by the way, because it has turned my mind into a fifty-five-thousand-watt radio station that picks up signals from the past, present, and sometimes future.

"Mr. Daniels. Ronnie," she says. But then she stops talking and watches me with curiosity. She's probably never seen one of her clients meditate before. "*What* are you doing?"

"I'm getting an insight," I say. "From you."

This is what I'm getting. Every woman who has ever given in to me, and probably every woman I've ever been attracted to, had a father who failed her. That Daddy failure—that spot where he left her—cuts a door out of a woman's mind, and that's where the bad boy, the flirter, the cheater, the drinker, the workaholic, enters. Where *I* enter. There's no force, no masked men, no home invasion—there's just a door that a guy like me walks right up to (he might even knock) and the woman opens it. And then he's inside.

This is why women go after bad boys. A regular guy—a guy with a good job, nice parents, and the ability to commit—could never walk through that door. He doesn't even know where that door *is*. Only a "bad" man can do that. What a woman wants is a guy who has the potential to abandon her exactly like Daddy did, but then doesn't. *Right!* She desperately hopes that somehow she will take the "bad" man and turn him good. She'll take him in and fix him up. She wants him to turn good on her shift. For *her*.

I'm getting all of this from Melissa. This is what Melissa wants. This is why she's in her thirties and single. Because so far, all the bad boys just keep acting like Daddy.

Melissa's superpower is that she needs to be needed.

Well, I need her. A lot.

"Melissa?" I say softly. "You know what?"

She looks up at me. I hold her gaze and watch her pupils dilate. She really is attractive when her face is relaxed. "Yeah?"

"I need your help," I say.

———

"She really looks like you," Melissa says, staring at the computer screen. "*Really* looks like you. She's beautiful."

"Oh, so that means you think I'm good-lookin', then?" I'm ribbing Melissa. Partly because I like her, and partly because I'm nervous. I asked if she would look Nicki up on Facebook, and now it's taking forever for her to turn the computer screen toward my chair. So I can see my baby. "Can I see?"

Melissa struggles with the cords that are preventing her from being able to turn the monitor. "Here, come over here." She tugs my chair toward hers. "You can't see all of them because of her privacy settings. But these are the ones that are public."

I have to get up and move the chair, and as I stand—

*God.*

*There she is.*

Nicki. On that Facebook thing.

Nicki.

She *is* beautiful.

She looks like a woman now. Not older really, but grown, like she has responsibilities and she carries them out. Her eyes are still so big. Yellowy-orangey-green—depending on the light. I can see Beth in her, too. Something in her expression. Intelligent, but with a sweetness that Beth never had.

*Don't think about everything you missed.*

"That's her?" Oh my God. My daughter. "I can't believe it. I really can't believe it." Obviously, I know it's her, but I'm trying to process it. "That's her."

"Didn't she send you pictures? Or come to visit?" Melissa points toward the right-arrow key on the computer. "There are lots more here, looks like. Just keep clicking that."

"Not in a while," I say.

I can't tell this woman I haven't spoken to my daughter in seventeen years. Melissa is a prison official. Even if she was capable of understanding—and she isn't—I could never risk the truth. Because if she knew that I don't have anywhere to live after this, well . . . Let's just say I can't let that happen.

I click through photos of Nicki's life. At her birthday party. With Cody. He's about thirteen or fourteen in the picture—it's a graduation of some kind, junior high maybe?—one foot in puberty, the other in childhood. There's Nicki and Cody in Paris. *Paris? My little girl went to Paris? And took her son?* There they are at the Grand Canyon and in Venice. There are photos of a man who must be her boyfriend. I guess he looks all right.

"So, what do you think?" Melissa asks. "She must be so excited to see you!"

*She's not.*

I have to be very careful. I don't want to slip and fall into one of the excruciating places—*I've missed my daughter's life! My grandson has my eyebrows*—that I've avoided for so long. Because I don't want to die of grief or lose my mind. I just want another chance. So I say, "I think she's beautiful."

"She is beautiful. And your grandson is so handsome," she says.

*She doesn't even know I'm out.*

The reason she stopped speaking to me is my own fault. I thought surely I would get off on the charges, so I didn't tell her I got arrested. I almost told her right after I got popped, but before I could spit out the news, *she* told *me* she was pregnant. Pregnant! And once she said that, I couldn't very well talk about going before the grand jury, could I? I couldn't explain that one of my distribution guys had turned state's evidence, and now there was a very good chance that I would be going away for a long, long time.

So I didn't say anything. I put it off another day and another day and another day, and next thing I knew the jury foreman was reading the verdict.

*Guilty—guilty as charged.*

Melissa can't possibly understand what it's like to call your daughter from prison to tell her that you're going to be there for the next 239 months. I don't blame Nicki for hanging up on me. I don't blame her for blocking my calls from that day on. I was guilty of so much more than conspiracy to distribute cocaine. I was guilty of depriving a twenty-one-year-old girl of her father, just when she needed him most. I was guilty of abandoning my grandson, before he was even born. When you betray people like that, you have to know you might never get them back.

But I believe—I *have* to believe—that Nicki will let me into her life again. She'll do it because I'm her father and she needs me, and her boy needs me. And I need them. Not just for somewhere to serve my home detention, either, though I wouldn't blame someone for thinking that. I have a genuine desire to be in her life again, to make up for all the ways I've disappointed her, to be the man I never had the ability to be. Until now. Whether she knows it or not, she still needs her dad. Because no girl should have to go through life without the love and care and support of her father if he's still breathing. I'd go to the ends of the earth for that little girl and her son. As long as I'm still alive, I'm not going to give up trying to be part of her life. She'll love me again. I know she will.

I just have to explain things to her, that's all.

# PART TWO

———————

In Escrow

# 5

# NICKI

The sellers accept my first offer on the Southeast Burnett house without even countering and, of course, now I think I overpaid. I'm filled with anxiety and it doesn't feel like the regular old buyer's remorse I had last time—that was more of a low hum and this is more of the sound of high-tension wires—not that it matters, because either way, I'm in escrow. Which means that sometime in the next thirty-six hours I have to—oh, sorry, *get* to—write a check with six figures before the decimal point and pretend like it doesn't scare the shit out of me. And sometime after that—thirty or forty-five days and five thousand phone calls and inspections later—they're going to hand me an eighteen-inch-tall stack of papers and I'm going to sit in a room with terrible fluorescent lighting and sign them all.

I told Cody about the new house and he shrugged. "Why are we moving? I like it here," he said. Not exactly the reaction I was hoping for. I told him how Jake and I have decided to make it official—instead of just keeping half his clothes here and sleeping over all the time, we'll be moving in together permanently. Without trying to sell it too hard, I said how I'm especially excited to have the kind of family structure we've never had before. That prompted Cody to ask if we're getting married, naturally, a question I dodged by saying I think that'll happen eventually, but for now we're as good as married, we just don't have a contract with the state about it. He gave a *fine, then* shrug, which was less enthusiasm than I might have liked, but at least it wasn't protest.

I'm contemplating all this as I walk up to the restaurant. It is hard not to love this place. It's on one of those perfect little corners in Southeast Portland where everything you could ever imagine wanting—a swell vintage clothing store, a bookstore, an art gallery, a boutique—is just waiting for you. Never mind the fact that there's not one thing in any of these stores anyone actually needs. It's all about desire. A whole intersection devoted to things that are so damn irresistible, so *wantable*, that people with more money than they need can't help it—they are moved to open their wallets.

The day Jake brought me here to show me this place he said, "The only thing missing is a restaurant," and he was right. Then he launched into a detailed rundown of the economics. "Rent is twenty-three hundred a month. I figure we can fit fourteen two-tops and ten four-tops. That would allow us to do one hundred forty-five covers a night. Plus breakfast and lunch." He scooped me into a hug and held me tight. "Babe, this is the project we've been waiting for. All you have to do is say yes."

All I had to do was say yes. That's it.

I've never been one of those girls obsessed with Cartier boxes or Tiffany ads or getting a big, fat diamond ring. I've never craved a proposal where the guy drops to one knee and asks me to marry him. But somehow, hearing Jake say those words—*All you have to do is say yes*—moved me. It spoke to something deep in me that has always wanted to be in one of those relationships where you live and love and work together so well that *Portland* magazine wants to do a feature story on you. Maybe it's because I'm such a workaholic, but working together—*that* has always seemed like the ultimate partnership to me. Because then you're both equally invested in the thing that matters most besides children—your work. Your kids will leave you eventually, but your work never will. And of all the guys I've been with in my life, Jake is the first one I could really start a business with. He has the personality, the know-how, and the will to succeed. I completely trust that he will make this place a success. Completely.

So I said yes.

We showed our business plan to the owner of the building and put in a bid, and when we got it over five other bidders, it seemed meant to be. Now I'm Nicki Daniels, restaurant owner. Or, co-owner. An added bonus is that the restaurant is only six blocks from the new house, which means not only that we're going to be putting down deeper roots in our community, but Cody can be a big part of it, too.

I can see Jake through the plate-glass window. He looks like a prize-fighter—wiry, pumped, thrilled. He's going over the plans with our contractor and third partner, Miguel, moving through the space, making big arm gestures and motioning where things will be added, and where they'll be taken away. This is Jake in his element: doing something daring, executing a vision, making shit happen. It gives me chills.

I really do love him.

It seems like only yesterday I was delivering papers off Sandy Boulevard, wondering if I'd ever (I mean *ever*) even have a real pair of Nikes. I had to wear the fake, cheap ones they sold at Payless. They were plastic and made my feet stink and all I wanted was for my feet to smell okay at a slumber party. Now look at me—upstanding lady, owner of two businesses, mother, girlfriend, and home owner. Crazy.

"Hey, babe," Jake says, kissing me. He's all business. "Can I talk to you?"

"Sure." I throw a quick nod to Miguel as Jake leads me by the hand through the kitchen, out the back door, and into the parking lot out back. "Where are we going?"

We're lucky to have Miguel. He's not only a really talented general contractor—he's very well known in Portland for his great taste in materials and design—he's stable, methodical, and family oriented. Miguel is in his midthirties, on the stout side, with square hands and a striking pair of pale brown eyes. *It's that face that gets him all those jobs*, I think. At one

point, I thought Peaches might totally hit it off with him, but I always
stop just short of introducing them because that wouldn't be a fair thing
to do to Miguel, not to mention his two kids. For a one-third interest in
the business, Miguel is putting up all the money for materials and labor
to transform this eighteen-hundred-square-foot space from a crappy café
that serves food out of cans into the kind of place Portland is known for:
stylish, with high-quality local ingredients, but low key enough to take a
toddler to.

Easier said than done.

Once outside, Jake stops in front of his car door and puts one hand on
each of my arms. He looks me in the eye silently, then leans in and gives
me one of those kisses he knows how to do. Soft, but *there*. Really there.
"Baby, I love you."

I open my eyes wide, delighted. I like what this project is doing for our
relationship.

"I want you to know how much I love you," he says, kissing me again.
He's blinking a lot, like it's making him nervous to say this, and that's
making me nervous. "I'd do anything for you."

"I love you, too, baby." I give him a big hug, like, *snap out of it, you're
being too serious*, and he shoots back a sexy smile, like, *I know I'm a lot to
handle sometimes, but I love you*. He opens the rear door of his vintage Toyota 4Runner—and takes out one of those big paper bags from Anthropologie, the kind with the rope handles.

He hands it to me. I'm not prepared for how heavy it is, and my arms
drop a good six inches. "Whoa. What's in here?"

Jake smiles his devilish smile. "Look inside."

I open the bag and paw through a couple of layers of pink polka-dotted
tissue paper. That's when I see it/them. *Holy crap*. The bag is stacked with
bricks of twenty-dollar bills.

"It's twenty thousand dollars." Jake breaks into a wide grin. He's proud
of himself.

And I'm terrified.

"Are you crazy?" I drop my voice to a whisper. I'm sure I'm making one of those facial expressions that he really can't deal with, too. "We could get robbed!"

Jake's smile leaves the building. "What? This is what you asked for. Double what you asked for."

"Okay, but I didn't ask for it *in a paper bag*!" All I can think about is how twenty thousand dollars would turn even good people into armed robbers.

I can see the left side of Jake's face beginning to twitch. I know that means he's getting angry. "Nicki, you told me you wanted me to put up money. I went out and called in a bunch of favors, I went out on a *limb* for this, and got you twice what you wanted. Because I love you and I want you to trust me. And now here you are making me feel like shit."

After my conversation with Peaches that day, I realized she was right and asked Jake if he could put up ten thousand dollars. Just to have some skin in the game, as they say. At the time he'd looked worried, but he didn't protest at all, and to be honest, I sort of forgot about it. I really just wanted to know that he *would* if I asked him to.

"I trust you! I do! I just think it's dangerous to carry all this money around!" He's overreacting and I don't really know why. It seems pretty straightforward to me. "Why wouldn't you just get a cashier's check?"

"I thought it would be cool to see the actual money. I thought it would be romantic. I was wrong. Again. Nothing I do is enough for you, is it?" Jake gets into the car. "This is bullshit."

"Jake, don't! I'm sorry. I wasn't trying to make that big a deal out of it."

"Yeah, well. Too late." He starts the car and throws it into gear. "You're welcome."

He takes off.

I stand there. I know what just happened: Jake flew into one of his moods, where he gets all hostile, then, in a split second, spins off into the wind. Because that's what he does. He's impulsive and at times has difficulty handling his feelings. He'll be back in an hour or two, probably with a bouquet of leaves or something, so I'm not especially worried.

But what I am wondering is this: what am I supposed to do with all this cash?

———

"Are you effing kidding me?" Peaches is sitting in the front seat of my car, staring into the Anthropologie bag, looking at the bricks of bills. "I can't decide whether to steal it or make it rain." She picks up one of the stacks and starts dealing twenties off of it the way rappers do in music videos. "Damn. Maybe Jake isn't so bad after all."

"Please stop that. I swear, even Cody wouldn't do that."

"Yeah, maybe. Because he'd be afraid you would ground him," Peaches says. "But he'd want to."

"Probably," I say. I grab the twenties off the floor and furiously restack them. "Let's go inside."

I called Peaches to the bank because I felt like somehow if she's with me, I can't get robbed. Peaches is useful like that. One time in our early twenties, I happened to get two free plane tickets to New York City (long story), and on the first night, while walking down Thirteenth Street, a guy ran up behind me and yanked the little purse dangling from my hand. It happened so fast and was so unexpected I was sort of like, *Oh well, whatever, isn't that what they said New York City was like?* But Peaches immediately went tearing after him. She starts yelling, *Stop, you asshole! That's not yours!* She even hollered at people passing by, *Stop him!* And in half a block she'd made such a commotion, and was gaining on him so fast, he tripped and fell and she stepped on him with her pointy heels and grabbed the purse back while a crowd cheered her on.

"Peaches," I say calmly when the bell dings. Our teller is ready for us. "C'mon. It's our turn."

I hoist the bag onto the narrow little counter in front of the teller window. "I'd like to make a deposit, please." I hate trying to talk to someone on the other side of security glass. I always think they can't hear me. Then I have to shout and everyone can hear my business.

"Go ahead, slide it under the window," the teller says. She motions to the little dish.

"*No, we have cash*," Peaches says, way too loud.

"Peaches!" Of course she has to tell the whole bank we have a bag full of cash. "Be quiet!"

I read once that the first ten years of a marriage are a power struggle between the couple—each person vying to get the other one to do things *their* way—and after that people sort of just accept the other person for who they are. That's pretty much where Peaches and I are now—I accept her. She's an exhibitionist, she likes having—no *making*—people look at her. Even though she sometimes embarrasses me, I get it: that's Peaches. She's going to talk too loud at the bank, try to engage strangers in conversations about random stuff, and possibly (probably, even) give her phone number to some dude without a muffler on his Harley. I'm also taking into account that she's especially giddy at the moment, probably because she's in the presence of so much money.

I open the bag and show the teller the stacks of bills. The girl's eyes widen. She motions to the door at the end of the row of windows. "Meet me at the door over there."

Other people in line are now looking at us—exactly what I didn't want. Our heels click as we walk across the terrazzo floor—*nothing like a great sixties floor*, I think—and when we reach the door, a heavy lock clicks, and then—

*I'm eight years old, waiting for my dad to appear at the end of the long, long room. This is my second or third time visiting prison, and everything about this place fascinates me. The guard stands next to a door that slides open with a loud mechanical sound. Rrrrr-clatch! A guy walks out, but it's not my dad—his uniform is kind of messy and he's not smiling. My dad always has shiny shoes and creases in his pants. Behind him is another guy, also not my dad—he's not handsome at all. Another guy, then another guy, then the door shuts and . . . nothing. My dad isn't there.*

*I sit back down on the row of chairs, Mommy lights another cigarette—how long is this going to take? Then the door lurches open again,* rrrrrr-clatch! *And then—there he is.*

*My dad.*

*His eyes are so blue! I always forget how much they sparkle, and before I can even finish that thought he scoops me up and I'm sailing over his head and he's saying my name and my middle name—Nicole Marie! Nicole Marie! My little girl, you're getting so big!—and all the crazy butterflies I had in my stomach a minute ago are gone now and I'm just flying through the air in my dad's arms—*

"Can you swipe your card, please?" The manager is waiting for me.

Peaches pinches my arm. "Lady, wake up."

I got lost there for a second. I forgot that I'm holding a bag with twenty thousand dollars in it.

"Oh, sorry," I say. I hand the manager the money and she tells us to have a seat while she counts it.

I follow Peaches to the waiting area, basically a square with two sofas and two chairs. It's been two hours since Jake took off and he should be texting any minute now to say he's sorry he lost it and he really didn't mean anything by it. That's what he always does.

"Now that you've got the money, I have to say I'm kind of excited about your restaurant," Peaches says. Just like her to hate on something until it happens, then declare it awesome. "I'm actually thinking I should ask you for a job."

"Of course you are," I say. Because of course she is.

———

I go over to Jake's house later that afternoon, unannounced. I rarely do that. We spend so much time together that when we're apart—even if it's after a fight—I like to give him his space, but I feel terrible about how the thing with the money went. I know he was just trying to do something cute, and I didn't handle it right. One of my big flaws is that I'm sort of a perfectionist. I think there's a certain way to do things, and when it doesn't happen, I blurt out how I think it should have been, and people's feelings end up getting hurt. It's not that I'm stuck on people doing things my way—it's more a matter of efficiency. To me, bringing twenty thousand dollars in cash in a paper bag just isn't efficient. Too many things can go wrong with that plan—losing the bag, having it rip, having it stolen—and if something did, you'd kick yourself because you'd look back and see how big the downside was for so little upside. I mean, there's no gesture cute enough to warrant risking twenty grand. It just doesn't make sense.

But making sense doesn't necessarily matter when it comes to the heart. Jake just wanted me to know that he was 100 percent in on the restaurant deal. That he was holding up his end of the bargain and not trying to take advantage of me. That he loves me and wanted to do what I asked of him. I should have been able to see that. Which is exactly what I say when he opens the door.

"I'm sorry," I say. "I wasn't thinking."

It has taken me a long time to learn how to say I'm sorry. I always used to say something euphemistic like, "I apologize," because it somehow sounded more powerful, less like I was begging the other person to forgive me. Even now, I often want to say *I'm sorry*, then immediately explain why I did the thing I did. Probably because I grew up with Beth, who could give you the silent treatment for a whole day if you did something wrong. The solution was never to admit any wrongdoing, or, if you did, then follow it up with a whole lot of verbal dancing around that would hopefully distract her from your original transgression.

But lately I'm figuring out that if I want to have a long-term relationship, I need to be a little softer, a little less argumentative. Jake is not Beth—I shouldn't react to him as if he is.

"Will you forgive me?" I say.

"It's okay," he says. He pulls me into a hug, then shuts the door behind me. For a long moment, we stand there, my cheek on his shoulder. "I love you, Nicki. More than anything. I wish you believed in me," he says. "I just want to make you happy."

This is where I want to say something like *No one can make another person happy*, but I decide against it, because that's just me trying to be right again. I search my brain for the correct response. What would I say if I believed in him?

In the beginning, I absolutely believed in him. We met in 2012 at The Echo. I was there with two of my mom friends, Sara and Robin, for an early dinner to celebrate Robin's birthday. It was a Thursday night, I remember because we were laughing at how lame we'd become that going out on a Thursday was now considered living dangerously. I was thirty-four, Cody had just turned thirteen. We were all complaining about having teenagers when a round of apple martinis arrived at the table out of nowhere. We looked around at the nearly empty restaurant—our reservation was for 5:30 p.m., that's how bad our Mom Situation was—trying to figure out who could have sent them. Seconds later, Jake breezed over and, looking straight at me, said, *You ladies are too gorgeous to have teenagers. Here's a little something to take the edge off.* It never occurred to me that this young, beautiful guy would find me attractive, but he asked for my number that night, called me the next day, asked me out on a date for the coming Sunday night—where he took me to Beast, at the time the most happening restaurant in Portland, where he introduced me to the chef, Naomi, who proceeded to send out course after course of mind-blowing food.

Our first six months together were a whirlwind of activity. Jake is the kind of guy who pores through the listings in the *Bridge City Weekly* every Friday night, and surprises you with tickets to a George Clinton concert, or signs up for a truffle-hunting excursion, or a group hike halfway up Mount

Hood in the middle of summer just to see the stars. I'd never met someone with so much energy, curiosity, confidence, and sex appeal. I knew I would never be bored with this guy and I fell completely, hopefully, in love.

The thing about Jake was there was nothing standing in our way. He wanted to be with me, and there was no fear of commitment to keep us apart. He was present and accounted for from the very beginning. He went out on a limb and declared his love for me and it felt good. It felt safe.

But the closer I get to taking that final leap into the relationship, the more my old fears come to the surface. I'm sure this is normal, right? But if I keep doing what I've always done—pushing people away—I'm going to keep getting what I've always gotten.

"You do make me happy," I say. I look up at him, completely unguarded. "You really do."

There's something about surrendering to him, to the relationship, that's like turning on a blowtorch. He kisses me ferociously and pulls me to the sofa and in seconds we are making love right then and there, amid the old beer cans and the mail stacked up on the table. It's crazy amazing.

Like it always is.

When it's over, we lie there, breathing heavy, bodies tangled, not saying a word. This is the only time in my life—after orgasm—that I'm perfectly still, perfectly quiet, perfectly at peace. As I watch the sun set through the leaded glass window, I think to myself *thank you*.

All I had to do was say yes.

———

A few days later I surprise Jake with a picnic lunch at the restaurant. He's been working around the clock—nights at his regular job managing The Echo, and days at the new place, which still doesn't have a name, by the way—and I thought I'd do something nice and bring him a Vietnamese *banh mi* sandwich made of sliced pork and cilantro on a gum-destroyingly amazing French baguette. It's one of our favorite things to eat together, when he's willing to eat gluten.

I walk into the main dining room, where the linoleum has been ripped up and now sits in a pile the size of a small shack. You can see what this place is going to be. The ceilings soar to twenty-two feet with exposed ductwork and track lights. The old tin that lined the walls has been cleaned up and it's gleaming. The way the light is coming in, it's really special. I've got to bring Cody down here. Between my job and the insane amount of paperwork I've had to pull together for the loan on the new house, I've been too busy to rip him away from his bedroom long enough to come with me. Not surprisingly, Cody's fine to let the whole restaurant happen without him. He considers it my project, and therefore, boring. I'd like to think he might see it and be inspired to consider what he'd like to do with his future. I mean, beyond his current plan, which is "to be rich and play Magic."

I scan the room looking for Jake and immediately trip on a pipe sticking up out of the floor—I should definitely not be wearing three-inch platform espadrille sandals in this place, but that's just my level of commitment to fashion.

"Jake?" I look up at the two mask-wearing guys, but they shrug. "Jake?"

Miguel comes in from the kitchen area, wiping his hands down on his jeans. He manages to look stylish in a T-shirt and work boots. He gives me one of those "hugs" where our right shoulders briefly touch, so none of the dirt gets on me. "Sorry," he says.

"It's okay." I'm assuming he means the dirt. "Jake around?"

Miguel looks up. "Uh . . ." He obviously feels like he needs to explain, which is weird, but whatever. "He took off a little while ago. Said he'd be back after lunch."

It already is after lunch. That's what I get for trying to surprise him. I shrug. "Okay."

"Don't worry about the plumbing thing, by the way. I think we got it."

"What plumbing thing?"

Miguel's head turns sharply. Then just as quickly he turns back. Like he's suddenly worried Jake's going to come walking through the door. "The thing in the kitchen."

Obviously there's something Jake didn't tell me, and Miguel isn't going to rat him out. Which is fine. I don't want to have to worry about every little thing down here. I'm actually glad Jake is taking care of things without bringing me into it. I need the space on my hard drive for other things.

"Jake's on it. I don't think it's going to be something we're going to have to worry about."

He doesn't sound all that sure.

"That sounds like maybe I should worry," I say with a laugh.

Miguel laughs with me, but he's looking at me a little weird. I can tell he doesn't want to step into the middle of anything between me and Jake. "It's probably nothing," he says finally.

"It looks amazing in here, by the way," I say, changing the subject. "Or like it's going to be amazing. Do you mind if I wait a little while? I need to make some calls."

I have three more appraisals to do this afternoon. Good news, since I spoke to the lender this morning and my new mortgage is going to be double the old one. I can handle it, though. I can. I swear.

"Sure. Go ahead," he says.

I perch at the edge of the counter and whip out my laptop. Twenty minutes of emails later, Miguel comes back over.

"Jake called," he says. "He's not going to be back for a little while. Said not to wait."

"Oh, okay," I say, wondering why he didn't call me himself. I don't want to make Miguel any more uncomfortable than he obviously already is, so I just fake being fine with it. "I'll get out of your way."

"Take your time," he says. "Stay as long as you like."

"Thanks, Miguel."

People told me I shouldn't go into business with my boyfriend, and I know why they said that, in theory. But right now, watching Miguel go back to tearing up linoleum, I'm starting to get it.

This could be harder than I thought.

# 6

# RONNIE

I'm coming back from another long, meaningless day of job hunting when I run into Melissa, on her way to her car. Ever since that first day, she's been dressing nicer, wearing perfume, putting a little bit of effort into her hair. She's been so helpful, too. She's done everything but write my résumé for me—she taught me how to get an email account, apply for jobs on the Internet, and use a printer. Sometimes she's even seemed downright flirty when it's been just the two of us in the computer room.

Or maybe I'm making that up.

"How'd the job search go today?" She stops and really looks at me, her caseload bag swinging forward from the abrupt change in momentum. She twirls a lock of her hair.

*I'm not making it up.*

"Not great," I say.

"What happened?"

If I tell her what really happened she'll feel sorry for me. How I walked into Acme Hardware to ask for an application and the kid working the cash register—probably eighteen or nineteen, definitely into heavy metal—couldn't stop dillydallying with his phone. How I stood there, chest tight, pits stained, until he glanced up, gave me a once-over, and went back to whatever game he was playing on his phone. "You mean for a job?" he asked without looking up, thumbs flying. *Yeah, I mean for a job. What do you think, asshole?*

"Are you okay?" Melissa's eyes move up, down, back, forth—examining every inch of my face, or whatever she can see of it in the fading light.

"Yeah, I'm fine," I say. I'm not convincing, though. Because this is where it all falls apart for me every time. This is the level of the going-straight game that I can never get past—the part where you have to get a job and become a productive member of society. If I could do that, I would never have become a criminal in the first place. Not that there was a point before I turned into a criminal. There wasn't. I was always a criminal. Antisocial behavior happens because you weren't socialized properly from the get-go. I wasn't a socialized kindergartener. I wasn't a socialized seventh-grader. And I wasn't a socialized adult. There was virtually no chance I was going to drive a bus for a living, or deliver the mail. The people who do that are the same people who raise their hands to erase the chalkboards and join the debate team or the football squad. I was out there shoplifting and hustling for Charleston Chews. I was never normal. Not one fucking day.

But I was good inside. Always. I just didn't get enough love and I didn't know anything and that made me ripe to try to get love in all the wrong ways, from getting money, to using women. We lived in an area on the edge of the hood in South Seattle, and there was all kinds of negative stuff happening there. I had lots of company. Sooner or later you catch a case. Then once you're in the system, you do a bid or two in the pen, and from there on out, it's basically over. You can never go back to the world that regular people live in, the one with choices and options.

Crazy me, I thought all the changes I made in prison this time around would help me once I got outside. I thought I'd be able to make a place for myself out here. I thought knowledge would be power. But outside is outside. It's cold out here.

"Ohhhh, you're not okay," Melissa says in a voice you would use to comfort a hurt child. This is the social worker part of her, the part that rescues wounded birds and nurses them back to health. "Ronnie, I'm sorry. I really am. I know it's hard."

"Thank you," I say. It feels good to have someone care about how hard it is. Usually people say that you did the crime, and so the "doing time" part, however hard it is, you have it coming. They don't want to feel for you or hear you complain. You made your bed, you gotta lie in it. "You don't have to say that, but it feels good that you did."

We stand there a moment, watching the trees in silhouette. It's a beautiful night.

"Wait, I know!" Melissa says excitedly, and skips down the steps. She clicks her key chain. *Chirp-chirp!* She opens the passenger door, all excited. "Get in."

I cast a side-glance toward the car door. It is absolutely forbidden for inmates and staff to "consort" with each other. If we got caught, I could be sent back to prison immediately. Melissa could lose her job. I look all around us, checking to see if the coast is clear.

"It's fine," Melissa says. She waves off any suggestion of danger. She's surprisingly cavalier. What do I know? Maybe they're lax here at the Oregon Residential Reentry Facility. "No one cares."

I get in.

As I click the seat belt shut, knees up around my chin, my heart is beating a million miles a second. *I'm sitting in the front seat of Melissa Devolis's car.* I keep stepping on something down by my feet and whatever it is crunches loudly, but I'm not sure what it is, since I'm so squished into the seat everything below my knees is out of view.

"It's just old water bottles," Melissa says. "Feel free to move your seat back."

I've been wanting to ask why everyone drinks water out of bottles now, but this isn't the right moment. Instead I say, "Is there a lever?"

I feel around, find nothing, then realize I'm looking in the 1997 place. In 2015, you move your seat back with a button, not a lever. And it's motorized, not mechanical. And it's on the side, not underneath. Which about sums up the world: everything's moved and now I have to figure out where they put it.

"Found it."

I smile sheepishly. Melissa smiles back.

"We're going to get ice cream, by the way, because ice cream can fix anything," Melissa says. "Do you like ice cream?"

"Sure." I'm wondering if this is a trick question.

"You don't sound very enthusiastic," she says.

"No, I like it a lot. Really. I like it a bunch." I can't believe I just said the words *a bunch*. I'm nervous. Melissa is making me nervous. This whole situation is making me nervous. Sick to my stomach.

"Because it sounded like you only like it a little bit."

"Okay, then, how's this: *I love ice cream!*" I sing it out loud, like I'm Teddy Pendergrass or someone. As if I'm making love to the sentence *I love ice cream.*

Melissa laughs at what can only be called the top of her lungs.

"You are so effing funny, Ronnie!"

"I've heard that before."

"Were you always like this?"

"Yes, I was. As a matter of fact, I still am."

"You don't seem like the other prisoners," she says. "You're different. You're not hardened."

"I did a lot of work in there," I say. "I made it my job to get myself right."

My stomach is starting to flip. I don't feel so good. "Hold on." I turn down the music. I'm distracted, and feeling a little sick. "Can you pull over for a second?"

"Are you going to throw up?" Melissa looks worried.

I shake my head. I don't know how to tell her I'm worried this ice-cream cone is going to cost me my freedom.

"I shouldn't be in your car," I say. "And you shouldn't have me in your car. If you want ice cream, you can surely find someone to go with you who won't get you fired. And if I want to take a ride in some woman's car, it probably shouldn't be yours."

Okay, so I did have to vomit. Words.

"I'm sorry." Melissa drops her head. Her eyes are welling up. "You're mad at me."

"Not at all. I just thought . . ." Shit, I didn't mean to make her cry. After making a woman mad, making a woman cry is the second most frightening thing I'm capable of. "I'm just trying to be responsible."

"And I'm trying *not* to be!" There's a real edge to her voice, almost a desperation. "That's all I ever do! The *right* thing. I just feel like—" She stops herself. "I thought it would be okay to break the rules. Just once. Is that such a big deal?"

Melissa digs an old fast-food napkin out of the center console and uses it to wipe her eyes and blow her nose. It's a pretty loud *honk!* for such a mousy person.

I reach over and put my hand on her arm. I'm only trying to comfort her, but the moment I touch her I get that electrical jolt. My stomach flips again and I get a ping. Down there. Right in the root chakra. *Damn.* I pull back my hand almost the moment it touches her.

Melissa looks at me like I've seen a million women look at me.

"Don't," she says. She takes my hand. Puts it back on her arm. "I want it there."

*Shit.*

I search her eyes, looking for some little bit of hesitation, some little bit of doubt. Some sign that I shouldn't do what I'm about to do. What Melissa wants me to do.

"Please?" she says.

So I do it. I just lean over and kiss her. Her lips are so soft, my whole body is immediately flooded with sex and I'm drunk with being inside another person's mouth for the first time since Bill Clinton was president.

You'd think I would want to devour her whole body on the spot, but it's the opposite. I want to go slow and savor it, because it feels so deep and thick and tastes so good I think I might die of pleasure. And I want that. I want to die of pleasure. After a long, long minute, Melissa pulls back and looks at me. She silently starts the car, checks her mirror, rips a U-turn right in the middle of the boulevard, and begins driving away from the halfway house. I don't even have to ask where we're going.

We are going to her house, where we are going to have the best sex I've ever had.

————

An hour later, we're back in the car, crawling along surface streets, making our way back to the halfway house. We're not saying much, maybe because we know what we just did can't be undone—and also because we know we're going to do it again.

There's no way we're not going to do that again.

Melissa is taking a left on Southeast Hawthorne when I suddenly realize where we are.

"Wait. Can you take a right at the next corner?" I point toward a big tree up ahead. Even though it's dark, I can see the fall colors from the light of the streetlamp, and it takes my breath away. There are no fall colors in prison. There are no colors, period. "I just want to check something out."

"Sure," she says. "Up here?"

We turn down Southeast Thirty-Seventh. This is it. This is her street. I didn't imagine it would be this cute, lined with little bungalows. I scan the doors for addresses. I know Nicki's by heart, of course. I've written it on a dozen birthday cards and letters over the past seventeen years. She may not have wanted to talk to me, but that didn't mean I was just going to go away. I remembered every Halloween, every Thanksgiving, every Easter with a Hallmark card. I never wanted her to think I forgot about her.

I'm filled with something—hope? Joy? Pride? Dread? Fear? Relief? All of those. But mostly I can't wait. Because this is my chance.

"A friend of mine lives right here," I say. I point at Nicki's house. "You mind if we stop for a quick second? The lights are on and it would be fun to say a surprise hi."

"It's not really in the rules," Melissa says. She's got sort of a bashful smile on her face, still in the oxytocin and dopamine haze. "But why not, I guess."

"It'll just take a second, I swear." I get out of the car. My heart is like a fist squeezing over and over in my chest, but since I know Melissa's watching, I have to make like everything's fine, everything's normal, I'm just here to say hi to an old buddy. It's too late to turn around, there's no way to explain my way out of it, and besides, I don't want to turn around. For all these years I have wanted to see my daughter, to talk to her, and she wouldn't let me.

Well, now she can't stop me.

I know I'm taking a chance, just showing up like this. But I also know the power of surprise—it disarms a person. It's been easy for Nicki to ignore me over the phone. She could be logical, a left-brained, rational person who doesn't want to see me for this reason, that reason, and the other reason—reasons she's been rehearsing over and over until she got to the point where she believes that she doesn't even need *her own father* in her life.

But she's wrong. She does need me.

All she has to do is see me.

# 7

# NICKI

The moment I see him it's as if someone pushed the whole house off a very tall building and I'm falling and it's the panic part, before I realize death is inevitable and just relax and let my life flash before my eyes.

*My dad is standing there.*

Ronnie pushes the doorbell again, he probably shouldn't do that, it's just scaring me more, this whole thing is really intense and—

"*Go away!*" I can hear myself yelling at him, but it doesn't sound like it's coming from me. Now I know why people say that in a crisis time stops and you leave your body. Because it's true. "*Go. Away.*"

"Baby! It's your dad! It's me, open up," he says. "Please open up." He tries the door, but it's locked.

I am frozen in place.

"I'm out! I'm just here to say hello." He's attempting to sound light and happy like he's dropping by for coffee. "I'm sorry, I didn't mean to scare you, I thought it would be fine—"

"*Jake! Jaaaaaaake!* Come here quick!" I flip on my heels and lunge toward the back of the house, in the process slipping on a piece of pork loin. My ankle twists and I almost go down, before catching myself in a large comic gesture. As I get back on my feet, I pass Cody, who has heard my yelling and has come out of his room to investigate.

"*Mom!*"

Cody's already to the door and looking through the window and I can see that he knows who it is. My dad. I don't know how he knows—I guess I've shown him pictures—but the recognition is moving across his face like one of those skywriting planes pulling a banner: *you know this guy, you know this guy, who is this, who is this, it's your mom's dad, it's your mom's dad, it's your mom's dad, Ronnie, Ronnie, Ronnie, Ronnie . . .*

"Cody! *It's me.*" Ronnie can see that Cody recognizes him, so he starts knocking harder, shouting loud enough to be heard through the door, while still managing to come across as nonthreatening. To everyone except me. "It's your grandpa."

"*Tell him to go away,*" I shout. I'm heading toward the kitchen now, turning around every other step, to see if the danger is still there. Whatever's happening in me is primal. I can see that Ronnie's not going to hurt me, but something in me is so scared I can't do anything but run. My reaction is frightening Cody—it's obvious by the look on his face.

"Nicki, *please!*" Ronnie is knocking on the glass now, trying to get Cody to open the door. "Cody, can you open the door? It really is okay, son."

"Mom, I think it's okay," Cody says. "Really." He opens the door. "Let's just talk to him."

*No way.* I scurry the rest of the way to the kitchen, hiding just to the side of the door frame. Listening.

Jake comes in from the garage. "What's going on?"

"Make him leave," I say.

"Who?" Jake's craning to look past me into the living room. "Is that your dad?!"

"Thank you, son, for letting me in," Ronnie says to Cody. He holds out his hand. "I'm your grandpa, Ronnie."

"Hi." Cody shakes Ronnie's hand. He likes him already. I don't want my son to like my dad already. I want my dad to have to earn it. "I'm Cody."

"Nice to meet you, son. I know your mom's upset, but it's okay. She's just taken by surprise." Ronnie hollers in my direction, not threatening, but to make sure I hear. "*Nicki, come on out here, sweetie.*"

He waits a few seconds, but I refuse to answer him. He keeps talking, sort of like a hostage negotiator. "Nicki Beans! I'm sorry, baby. I didn't mean to scare you. Come on out."

Cody laughs at my nickname.

*Nicki Beans.* My dad's name triggers some small sliver of my mind that I'm not in real danger. My dad's never been a violent person—he's never hurt anyone. I want him to go away not because he's a bad man, but because somewhere along the way I decided he's a Leaver not a Stayer, and I can't stand to be left by him one more time. If he's going to leave, I'm going to be the one to make him go. Sooner. Like, now.

"Go away, man," Jake says. "Seriously. Leave us your number and she'll get in touch with you when she's ready. I don't know what you were thinking. Surprising her like this."

"He's *selfish*," I say, making sure he's hearing me. There is something really satisfying about shouting at Ronnie. About telling him what I really think. I have a flash of wanting him to stay just so I can read him the riot act for a while. "That's how he is. He only thinks of himself."

"What was I supposed to do?" Ronnie says excitedly. He's psyched I've decided to speak to him at all. "You wouldn't take my call! You just stopped picking up the phone! I don't even know why."

"Because I didn't want to hear from you, that's why," I say. Heartless. "Now go away."

"I got it, I'll go," he says. I can tell from the sound of his voice that he's going to leave now. Thank God. "I just thought you should know I'm out."

Jake comes back toward me, holds his arms open. "You okay?" He wants to hug me, but now that I know Ronnie's leaving, I feel energized enough to go out there and watch him go. I walk back toward the front door, careful to avoid the pork loin strewn everywhere.

"I don't hate you or anything, I just want you to leave," I say. That's as close as I'm going to come to an apology. "You shouldn't have shown up like this."

"I'm sorry, Nicki. I didn't know what else to do," he says. "I really am sorry."

I forgot how blue his eyes are.

He's not a bad person.

How weird that I was just thinking of him today in the bank. I don't really even believe in psychic stuff, but who knows? It does seem awfully coincidental.

"I'm glad you're out," I say. "Good for you. Really. I'm happy for you."

"Tell you what," he says. He's being like a child who can't bear to leave Chuck E. Cheese's and is trying to buy another minute. "Let me give you my phone number. Just in case. I don't know, maybe we could have coffee or something sometime. Call me if you ever need anything at all. Anything. Do you have a pen and paper?"

"No," I say. "Just go."

"I'll take it in my phone," Cody says. He jumps in there a little too eager. It's as if he likes my dad—but how can that be? He doesn't even know him. Cody pulls his phone out of his pocket. "Go ahead."

Ronnie gives Cody the number, and the moment he's finished, I take Ronnie's shoulder and literally push him out the door.

"Good-*bye*," I say. Then, even though I know it's unnecessarily dramatic, I slam the door in his face.

———

In the bedroom later, I'm silent. I can't cry, I can't talk. I can only binge watch episodes of *House Hunters International*. I know that eventually, I'm going to run out—of episodes, I mean, not run out of this room; actually,

I might never leave this room—and I can't even think of what will happen then. As an anesthetic, nothing works like *HHI*. It's the gold standard of numbing out—pure television Novocain. Or what's that stuff that Michael Jackson used? Propofol. It's pure that.

The only time I even come close to thinking about my dad is when I'm blazing through the commercials—five quick pops of the forward button on the remote—and the advertisements roll by. If you ask me, prison was a good place for him. He'd always seemed fine with it. Really. On all my childhood prison visits and phone calls he'd always seemed upbeat and settled. He had friends, a job, a communal TV, dental care, food, clothes, and books. He didn't talk about the bad parts except the food, so I could only assume there weren't any. Or there weren't any bad parts that were so bad he made sure never to return.

I think back to the last time we spoke. When he called me from prison that very first night, without giving me the chance to have so much as one last visit with him on the outside, I wasn't worried about him. I was worried about *me*. I was furious, but not at him. I was furious *for* me. Pregnant and alone, I needed a father—and now I wasn't going to have one. I already didn't have a mother. Which was bad enough.

Not only that, from the moment he called me, I knew this is the direction the energy was going to travel from now on:

ME → HIM

Being in a relationship with a prisoner is very one-sided. You can't call a prisoner if you had a bad day at work, or need a friend. They call *you*, when *they* feel like it. They can't help you move, fix your screen door, come over and hang out. This is what people—the prisoner, especially—don't understand.

Where was Ronnie when Beth was parading her stupid boyfriends through the house and went to Puerto Rico on vacation, leaving me to walk through the high school graduation ceremony with no one in the audience? He was in prison, that's where. How embarrassing was it to wander around aimlessly pretending my parents were there? I would have skipped the whole thing, but I was goddamn not going to miss the all-night senior class party.

And what about the night Cody was born? Where was Ronnie then?

In prison.

How about when we lived in that house where the roof caved in and we couldn't afford to fix it? Where was Ronnie then?

In prison.

The day I got my first period?

The Daddy-Daughter dance?

In prison, in prison, in prison.

Without a dad, I was forced to depend on my mother, and she was a terrible person to have to depend on—the word *terrible* having its origins in the Proto-Indo-European verb "to shiver." I bet the first time she scared the hell out of me, I was still lying in a bassinet at the hospital.

So now he wants to stand at my front door seventeen years later feeling bad I stopped talking to him? Is he serious, he can't figure out why?

What was he thinking—that he would just knock on my front door and I would open it and say hi, oh shit, long time no see?

I was fine without him.

———

Around ten o'clock Jake's phone vibrates with a text. He's been sitting beside me for the last hour, his arm behind my back, helping me watch TV. I'm sure his arm must be hurting at this point. But his body next to me is the only thing comforting me right now, and it feels so good I don't give a fuck about his arm.

Whatever's on his phone, though, it's making his whole body shift.

"Uh, Nick?" He says it tentatively. "Nicki?"

*Shhhh.* I put a finger to my lips. "Honey."

"I need to talk to you."

"I can't talk," I say. "I'm watching this."

I'm still in a trance. I've been forced to move on to domestic *House Hunters*, which is basically a whole lot of tray ceilings, granite countertops, and statement two-story foyers, but I'm fine with it. That's how desperate I am for relief.

"Nick," he says, easing his arm out from under my body. "I have to run out for a minute."

"What?" I jerk forward, springing back to life like a toddler you think is asleep until you try to sneak out of the room. "You can't go! Where are you going?"

"I have to. It'll be quick."

"Jake, no! I can't be alone!"

"I'll send Cody in here," he says. As if Cody can sit still next to me with his arm behind my back without needing years of therapy afterward.

"I can't let Cody see me like this. I need you!" My voice is whiny and trembly like a little girl's. I'm actually panicking at the thought that he's going to walk out the door—even if he's going to be back soon. "I need you, Jake."

"What about Peaches?"

It's Thursday. Peaches is getting laid right now. Duh. Besides, Peaches would make this all about my dad—what he said, what he did, what he looked like, if he was still hot—and I'm concerned about me right now.

"Jake, I need *you!*" My blood pressure is going up. My throat is scratchy and my mouth is very dry. In the beginning of our relationship, he never would have left if I'd asked him to stay. "What is so important that you have to leave the house right now? It's nine thirty at night."

"It's just an errand. It'll take twenty minutes. I'll be right back."

"You can't leave me, Jake. Please don't leave me. Please—" I say. I sound pathetic, but I don't care. He can't leave now. Not now.

Jake gets up. "I'll be *right* back." He grabs his jacket and his keys. "Please! I'll be back in a half hour."

"You said twenty minutes!"

"At the most. A half hour at the most. I wouldn't go unless it was really important."

Jake's looping his other arm into his navy blue hunter's jacket, the one I got mail order from J. Crew. I was worried it wouldn't fit because it was final sale, but when it arrived it was so perfect he didn't take it off for a month. That jacket became proof of how well I knew him, how much I loved him—better than anyone ever had. I knew it was because I was a mother, where most of the other girls he'd gone out with were just that, girls. They worried about their careers and their thighs and had wine nights with their besties and never really cared about anyone but themselves. Not me. I could love him like a woman.

"What could possibly be so important?"

"It's about the restaurant," he says. "I have to meet with one of my investors."

"Now? Can't it wait until the morning?"

"No, it can't," he says. "I'm sorry."

"Jake, please!" I know I sound lame, but then why wouldn't I? My dad just showed up at my door after seventeen years and now my boyfriend has some urgent errand he has to run. At ten o'clock at night. Do I not have the right to ask him to stay with me? "Are you making me beg?"

"Not unless you want to," he says. When I get really emotional, Jake becomes like a contestant on week one of *The Biggest Loser*—no stamina whatsoever—who can only run a block before Jillian Michaels has to step in and start barking orders.

Cody wanders by. "What's going on?"

"Nothing," we say in unison.

Cody goes into the bathroom. I hiss at Jake. "You really suck sometimes."

"No. You're just really controlling."

"Yeah, well, that's how you're getting the restaurant you want, isn't it? You like how controlling I am when it means I can cough up thousands of dollars for your dream."

That was low. I know it the minute I say it, but I'm human. The way I see it, he's leaving me in my time of need. And I came through for him in his. Why shouldn't I mention it? Okay, maybe I should've used a nicer tone of voice, but the truth is the truth.

"Jake, wait." I feel bad. "I'm sorry."

"Too late, Nicki."

I hear Jake say good-bye to Cody on his way out, which makes me feel like he's definitely the better person between the two of us. But still, in the bottom of my stomach there's a thick glob of indignation and victimhood. How can he leave me like this? Right when I need him the most?

I turn over and pull the blanket up over my head.

He'll be back.

# 8

## RONNIE

Melissa calls me into her office and shuts the door. She looks serious. There's a large paper shopping bag on her desk, which I'm guessing are the rest of my things. It shouldn't surprise me that this is happening. Freud said (I think it was Freud) that people have two urges: the life urge and the death urge—and for me, the death urge is prison.

*She's sending me back.*

"I want to talk about last night," she says. There's a tension in her body that tells me something's definitely going on. Is she trying not to cry? Did someone find out and she lost her job? Or did she—oh, hell no—did she *confess* to someone?

"Are you sending me back to Sheridan?" I search every inch of her face for information. I'm trying to sound calm, but my voice is a little off-key.

"That was your daughter, wasn't it?"

"Please, Melissa. *Please.*" I say it a lot louder than I mean to. "Just tell me if you're sending me back."

If she is going to send me back, I need to know now. I need time to prepare my mind and body for The Hole, which is where I will almost certainly go once I am officially transferred back to Sheridan. When you're in The Hole, you have to live in an unheated, windowless concrete cell not much bigger than a large bathroom stall, where the lights are kept on twenty-four hours a day. To call it "living" is generous. It's more like existing, and barely that. It's twenty-three hours a day—all day on holidays and weekends—with one hour for "recreation" in a ten-by-ten-foot fenced-in piece of dirt that looks just like a dog run. But the physical part isn't even the worst of it. It's what happens to your mind. Your emotions. The loneliness, the emptiness, the desperation. It's like an insane asylum. You can't see anyone, but you can hear the screams. My first bid, I did three tours of duty in The Hole—I was young and wild and I couldn't say no to trouble. At one point, I was dealing drugs in the joint, allowing myself to get caught up in the bullshit. This time, I only did one. I kept my nose clean, stayed away from the drama, was loyal to other guys, helped them when they needed it. That's why Reeves called me a model prisoner. Seventeen years and only one trip to The Hole and it wasn't even my fault? Unheard of. But breaking parole would doom me to thirty or sixty days at least, possibly one hundred and twenty or more.

That is, assuming I get transferred back to Sheridan. They could decide to punish me even more by sending me far away from Oregon, far away from Nicki and Cody. I can't even think about that.

Melissa doesn't even flinch. "I think we should talk about it, Ronnie."

My Adam's apple is throbbing. I can't even swallow. Much less talk.

"When I came in this morning, I checked your paperwork," she says. As she flips through my file, it's hard to believe this is the same face I watched come last night while Earth, Wind & Fire played. "You said here you're going to do your home detention with your daughter. But then I saw that look on her face at the front door. She didn't know you got out, did she?"

The familiar shame of being caught in a lie rushes through me. But I'm also relieved. Because if this is her second question, she's not planning to send me back. If she wanted to do that, she'd have said it already.

"You're right," I say. The best defense is no defense—it's the truth. Always. "I thought I'd have it figured out by now."

"What are you going to do, Ronnie." She doesn't even put a question mark on the end of it. She's got me. I'm trapped.

"If you're going to send me back to Sheridan, just do it," I say. "Don't humiliate me."

"I'm not trying to humiliate you," Melissa says. Her voice is quiet. "I'm trying to help you." She hands me the bag. "Here. Open it."

I set the bag down at my feet and pull out the first thing in it: a brand-new cell phone. Still in the plastic packaging. "Are you kidding?"

Melissa takes it from me and begins cutting off the top of the package. "It's prepaid," she says. "It means you pay by the month. I covered the first month. When you get a job, you take it from there."

I reach in again. There are some clothes. Then a wallet, which I open. There are a bunch of twenties in there, maybe three hundred dollars' worth.

"Where did this come from?" I ask.

"My bank account."

I shove the bag and everything back toward Melissa. "I can't take money from a woman."

Melissa flashes me a broad smile. "Ronnie, that's bullshit. You've taken plenty of money from plenty of women."

I have to laugh. "There you go, calling me out again."

"Yeah, well. Somebody needs to." She studies me a moment. Screws up her courage. Leans in and lowers her voice. "Ronnie, I have an idea. I want you to hear me out." She holds my gaze. "Come stay with me."

*Stay with Melissa?* Craziest thing I've ever heard.

But it could also work.

My mind immediately starts calculating pros and cons. It would definitely solve my biggest current problem—that without somewhere to go, I'll be forced to go back to Sheridan. Huge pro. Then I mentally map the location of her apartment—could I get in and out of there without being seen by the wrong people? Yes. Next I have to size up Melissa's psychology. She's doing this to meet a need—that's why everyone does everything. Probably she's lonely. But is she emotionally stable enough to keep the secret?

In ten seconds I've made a decision.

*Yes.*

But first I have to test her.

"I can't do that," I say. She can't think I'm just going to jump on this opportunity. She won't trust me. And if this plan is going to work, Melissa has to trust me. Completely. "I'll figure something out. Something will happen."

"Something *has* happened, Ronnie," Melissa says. She leans in to me even closer. "I fucked you. *And* I learned your secret." I wish I had a picture of her face right now. It would be Exhibit A in my theory that criminal justice system employees and criminals are no different—except one group has committed crimes and the other hasn't. "You can't undo that, Ronnie."

Young guys in the pen always used to talk about Basic Bitches and Bad Bitches—it's one of those rap things—and right now I'm trying to figure out how this timid woman went from Basic to Bad so fast. I knew I was great in bed, but damn. I turned this woman out in a night.

I tap my fingers on the desk, trying to look more worried than I am. "What if someone finds out? You could lose your job."

"That won't happen," she says. Damn she's confident. "The system here has more holes than Swiss cheese."

Once I see her arrogance come into play, I know I gotta keep her building that up. Make her sell her*self* on this plan. Make her trust her*self* so much that she doesn't question it. At all. The way to do that is to keep giving her objections that will force her to drill down into her own belief that this plan can work. Because I'm not so sure.

"You're not doing this for me," I say. "I don't need you like that."

"You're right. I'm not. I'm doing it for me."

"Are you sure?" I say. "Because you'd be risking a lot."

"I'm sitting here rotting away, Ronnie," she says. She's getting fired up. "Whatever happened last night—that's the most alive I've felt in years. Maybe ever." She pauses, thinking it over. "I can't go back to the way I used to be."

"Don't think you're in love with me. You're not."

"I know that," she says. "Believe me, I'm a realist."

I'm doubtful about this. Her brain is wired to make her think she's in love; that's how the brain's chemistry works, at least for women. Men are different. I know the moment I meet a woman whether or not I could ever fall in love with her. Though Melissa is interesting, and the more I get to know her, the more I like her, she will never inspire me to fall in love. She just won't. It's not her fault. She's probably not enough like my mother. If I had one piece of advice to give women everywhere, I'd tell them: *Don't ever fall in love with a man who's not already in love with you.*

Someday I want to write a book just breaking it down. I'd call it: *Baby, I Got Your Money: A Hustler's Guide to Love and Relationships.* Ha! I'd sell a million copies of that shit.

I'm thinking about my name on top of the best-seller list when I realize Melissa's waiting for an answer.

"So will you?" I notice she's looking sweeter than usual. "Will you come live with me?"

———

An hour later I'm opening the door to Melissa's apartment. The condominium complex is big and sprawling: six buildings, each with its own parking lot. There's no way anyone will know who I am in this place, much less which one of these boxes I'm living in. It's exactly the kind of apartment I would never choose to live in—because I need my shit to be *special.* In my career, that was my downfall. I needed to dress sharp, get noticed. That'll get you laid, but it'll also get the Feds on your ass. I learned that on my first arrest. Turns out the FBI had me under surveillance for six months before they had enough evidence to make a case against me. I had no idea, because at that point, I was twenty-four years old, I'd only been in the game three years, and I was still immortal. When they finally arrested me—at six thirty in the morning; Nicki was only four and slept through the whole thing—I had to sit through a six-hour interrogation. The very first question the agent asked is where I worked. I told him I had a warehouse job out there on Northeast Halsey. It's true, I visited there often, because it was a drop spot for my distribution activities. He laughed and said there's no way I was dressing the way I was, driving the car I was, living in the house I was living in, on a day job. He said he'd been watching me for months now, and he knew every move I made, how much tail I was getting, and how fly I thought I was. He wanted to know, was it worth it now that it was going to cost me the next four years of my life in a prison cell? The truth is, at that moment in my life, I probably thought it was. Goes to show you. Anyway, the point being that I know guys in the game a lot longer than I was who never got caught. They dressed ugly.

You make your trade-offs in life.

The moment I walk in the front door, last night comes flooding back to me: that sofa, the bad carpeting, the smell of cheap air freshener. After all those years of living with men only, you forget how sweet women like things to smell.

I set my bag down and wonder what to do next. The first thing I notice is that I feel disappointed. Lonely. I've been surrounded by people every minute of every day for almost two decades! And now I'm finally in a room by myself with a lock on the *inside* of the door. This should feel like the first real freedom I've had in seventeen years. But it doesn't. True freedom would be having the ability to do whatever you want. And what I want is to be with my family.

*I wonder how Nicki's doing today. I wonder how Cody is.*

Funny, because if you asked me three months ago if living rent free in a nice place with a woman who's going to let me have sex with her every day would be enough for me, I'd say hell yes.

It isn't.

One thing I could do is head down to my old stomping ground, the Hi-Lite, just to see who's still around. I know Mal's down there. And maybe

I could hook up with Beamer and Two-Shots. Just *talking* to any of them could get me arrested, but I'm not trying to get involved in some business deal. I only want to catch up, see my old friends, maybe not feel so isolated. I've been out of Sheridan for eighteen days now and believe it or not, I'm bored. I was busier in prison! At least there I had a job.

I wander into the tiny kitchen. The spotless stove confirms what I would have guessed: Melissa doesn't take care of herself—oh, I bet she can cook, she just doesn't, because she doesn't think she's worth it. She's probably waiting for some man to love her before she'll make love to herself with a good meal. I open the fridge and, yep, it's empty. An expired container of yogurt, a couple of to-go boxes and a half-empty jar of pickles. Sad.

That's when I decide that for my first official act of freedom, I'm going to do what any self-respecting kitchen man would do. Go shopping.

———

I grab a shopping cart and push it down the aisle. I walked almost a mile to get here and it was worth it. I've heard of Whole Foods (don't people call it "Whole Paycheck"?), but nothing could've prepared me for this. First off, these customers! When did supermarkets become sexy? Every woman here looks like a homecoming queen. Second of all: *where did all this food come from?* The last time I went food shopping, $8.99 organic red muscato grapes out of season hadn't been invented yet. Neither had pizza stations, sushi stations, or massive steam tables serving everything from Mexican to Indian by the pound. I thought the three hundred dollars Melissa gave me was a lot of money, but I could blow all that before I get to meats.

I'm about to snag a yellow cherry (yellow!) and sample it, when I notice a security guard tracking me. Damn, that didn't take long. People in the world of law enforcement—even rent-a-cops—automatically know when you're an ex-con. They notice the cagey look in our eyes, the tense way we move, the shallow breathing that begins the moment you get locked up and ends, well, never. You carry it with you the rest of your life.

"Afternoon!" I say to him. "Nice day out there."

"It's okay to have a sample," he says. "But you can't just stand there."

"Sure thing," I say. I pop the cherry into my mouth and *oh Lord*. That is heaven right there. I grab one of the small brown paper lunch bags and scoop a hundred cherries inside. They're probably going to cost twenty dollars, but I don't care.

I go through the store, having the time of my fucking life. You'd think Whole Foods was a vacation to the South of France for all the fun I'm having. I say hi to every person I see. I look into their eyes, notice their bodies, feel their energy. I've lived in a dead world for so long that I'm thrilled to be here. I want to kiss every baby, tell every woman she's beautiful, tell every man to be grateful for his wife and his job and his mortgage.

I want to preach.

People think they want to be free of all their responsibilities and dream of a life where they sit and do nothing. Well, I've sat and done nothing. It's the worst thing you can imagine. Now I dream of a life where I have people who need me and I'm so busy doing things for them I have no time to think of myself.

———

By the time Melissa gets home, I have dinner all ready. A nice Asian stir-fry with real ginger! Talk about luxurious. I didn't even mind cooking on that tiny electric stove. I hear the key in the lock and my heart actually jumps. That's an old sound with a new meaning. She opens the door with a really bright smile on her face.

"Hey there!" she says. "Smells good in here!"

The minute I see her face I know I'm in trouble. Big trouble.

She's light and happy. There's no hint of this being the first day of an illegal arrangement, no sign of wondering how to act. She just gives me a kiss on the lips like I'm her husband, then dumps her computer and bag on the side chair.

"Someone's had a busy day," she says.

Like this is her life now. *Shit.*

I can tell from her body language (relaxed) and the tone of her voice (breezy) that there is *absolutely no way* this woman is going to be able to keep this relationship in a compartment. No way. No how. Not only is she eventually going to think she's in love with me, she probably already does.

*What was I thinking?*

In the old days I would just cross out what's going through my mind right now and keep going. After all, Melissa allowed me to get out of the halfway house early, *and* without a job. Which means I'm going to be living on easy street. I can post up here, watch her TV, get regular blow jobs, for as long as I want.

But I can see right now that it won't be free of charge. There will be a heavy price to pay. Every day that passes Melissa will sink deeper into her fantasy that I'm going to be her man, that I already *am* her man, a fantasy she doesn't even know she's having. And if I try to explain it to her, she won't believe me, because women never do. I'm not saying every woman is like this, I'm saying the women who are willing to deal with *me*, the women who fall for *me*, the women who let *me* into their lives, are like this. It has to do with that door I knocked on, the one she opened for me, and if I walk through it right now, the lie will take hold of her and in a month, or two, or three, I'll never be able to leave. Not until my parole is over, or she says I can—whichever comes first.

Which means if I stay here, even for one night, I am putting myself back in prison.

*I've got to get out of here.*

But I only have one place to go.

# PART THREE

---

## Contingencies

# 9

# NICKI

I can tell something's off the moment I open the front door. I don't know what it is—is it a feeling, an intuition, or did I notice that the drawers in the dining room hutch are halfway open? I don't know, but it's something.

"Cody?"

No answer.

I move slowly through the living room. Nothing seems noticeably out of place. Pale late-afternoon sun filters through the west-facing windows.

I go into the bathroom. I sit down to pee, and something hits me.

*Where's Jake?*

I haven't heard from Jake since this morning, when he texted me a short *Morning. Meetings this a.m. but call u later.* I thought he was still mad about last night, and that's why he was terse. I texted him back *Heart U* and then I got busy with work, and now I am realizing he never texted me back. I pull my phone out of my purse to check it.

Nope. Nothing.

*That's weird.*

I tap out another text. *Where are you?*

I go into the bedroom and I can see that several of the drawers aren't quite closed. Also strange. I have a thing for making sure they're flush with the frame—I don't like accidentally running into them. Also, the drawers are off-white and it looks messy when they're even slightly open. I begin shutting the drawers but when I get to Jake's something makes me open it.

It's empty.

I look at my phone. Nothing yet. I text again. *Are you okay?* Then, *Jake?*

Jake has had his own drawer at my house since our fourth or fifth month of dating. Even though he keeps his own apartment, he spends so much time here he has clothes for every occasion—a couple of dress shirts, T-shirts, sweaters, jackets, jeans, socks, and underwear. The stuff migrated over here gradually, and there's never been any reason to take it home.

My phone rings.

"What's up?" he says. All casual, but also like he's in the middle of something and I'm interrupting him.

"What's happening?" I say, trying to match his casualness. But what I'm thinking is, *What's up? Really? That's what you're asking me right now? What's up is that I haven't heard from you. That's what.* I haven't seen Jake or heard his voice since he left last night while I was in the middle of my dad crisis, which I've now recovered from (sort of), but his weirdly offhand tone is bringing it all back. Something very strange is going on here. "How's your day?"

"Nothing," he says. "I mean, not much. Where are you?"

Oh, I see. He's not going to level with me. Because if he were going to, he'd be telling me why he came here when I was gone and emptied his drawer, instead of pretending he's busy and can't talk.

"Out and about," I say. Why should I give him any more information than I have to? "On my way to an appraisal."

"Cool," he says. "Listen, babe. I'm in the middle of something, can I call you in a bit?"

*I hate it when he says "a bit."*

"Jake, what's going on?" I can't help it, I just sounded like I'm accusing him of something. But I've got him on the phone and I want to keep him on the phone until I figure out what's going on. Because something's going on.

"Nothing, why?"

*Because I'm looking at an empty dresser drawer, that's why.*

I give him another chance. "Is something wrong, honey?" I soften my voice. Maybe he's scared of Big Mommy Girlfriend getting mad at him and needs to know it's okay to tell the truth. "Are you mad at me?"

"Nicki, I gotta go."

"Jake." *Level with me.* "Come on now."

"What?" *Ain't nobody here but us chickens.* "I'm parking, Nicki."

Okay, fine. I'll show my hand. "I'm at home," I say. "In the bedroom. For some reason I opened your drawer, and I see that your stuff is gone. What is going on?"

"Nicki, I gotta go," he says, rapid fire. Now he sounds guilty. Almost apologetic. "I'll call you later, I promise."

"Jake, wait, stop—"

I don't even have a complete sentence out of my mouth when my phone makes the little electronic sound that means the call has ended.

*He hung up on me.*

I look into the empty drawer. A feeling of confused frenzy takes over my body.

What in the fuck is going on with Jake?

———

Here is why I love Peaches. Because Peaches will bang on your door at three o'clock in the morning if you're a mess and you've called her. Just tell her your lame-ass boyfriend took all his shit and lied to you about it, then didn't answer any of your calls the rest of the day, then texted you two minutes ago to say he's *sorry, he just can't explain right now, but he's okay and he will as soon as the time is right,* and the next thing you know she will be sitting on your bed rubbing your feet in solidarity.

"The fuck?" She's scowling at the disappeared Jake in absentia, on my behalf. "He sucks."

I totally appreciate Peaches's ability to just side with me no matter what. She doesn't ask a bunch of questions like, *I mean, didn't he* warn *you that he was going to do something like this?* Or: *But you sort of knew this all along, didn't you?* In other words, she's not like me at all. All she says is: "You're supposed to be opening a restaurant with him!"

I couldn't cry when I was alone, but now that Peaches is here, the tears are pouring out of my face. It doesn't feel like they're about Jake, even. The thought that keeps happening over and over in my mind is *How could I be so stupid?*

"I really did think things were fine! I mean, I brought him a picnic lunch! Would I have done that if I thought he was going to bail on me later that day?" I'm aware of how pathetic this sounds, like what a chick on a reality show would say in the interview part. You know, where there's a Pottery Barn lamp in the background and it's a super close-up of her face? "He said he's going to explain. What does that even mean? Do you think he's going to come back?"

"Probably." Peaches waves the question away. "But I kind of fucking hope not. Who does something like this? I mean, I have, in the past, but I am lame! Now that I see what it looks like, I get exactly how lame." She thinks on that for a second, then goes back to her train of thought. "I know you love him, Nicki," she says, putting air quotes on the word *love,* "and I know you guys are going for this whole life together, but maybe he's just not up to it, you know? That's why I always leave. Because I can see that the person wants more from me than I'm ever possibly going to be able to give."

"Whoa," I say. It is not like Peaches to self-reflect. At all. "Did you just go deep?"

"Shut up," she says. She thinks some more. "You can figure out what to do later. Seriously. You are going to be fine. You really are." She says this like it's a movie title: *You Are Going to Be Fine.*

I search for a dry corner of my Kleenex to wipe my eyes. I'm smiling now, almost. "You mean FINE—the acronym for Fucked up, Insecure, Neurotic, and Emotional?" I read that on the Internet once and thought it was pretty accurate.

"Precisely."

We laugh for a half second, until I start crying again. "How could he do this?" My mind has lurched into gear again—I'm retracing my steps through the past twenty-four hours, looking for clues to what might have set him off. The biggest thing that happened was Ronnie showing up at my door. Maybe that freaked Jake out somehow. "Maybe it's my dad!"

"Definitely Daddy issues," Peaches says knowingly. "It's always that."

"No, I mean my dad showed up on my doorstep last night!"

I haven't told Peaches this yet, partly because I haven't had the time, and partly because I know she's going to have a big reaction and I'm just not ready to deal with it. Jake's disappearance has made me doubly unready.

"He *what*?"

Here we go. "He's out of prison," I say. "I'm sorry I didn't tell you yet. I literally haven't had time."

"That's bullshit, Nicki, and you know it." Sometimes Peaches and I are like twins who share brain cells that continue to transmit information even though they're in separate bodies now. "Who doesn't have time to tell their best friend that their dad is out of prison?"

The maddening thing is that instead of looking at herself, and the reasons *why* I don't want to tell her stuff sometimes, she gets mad at me. Under normal circumstances I would try to point out this discrepancy, but right now I just don't have the energy.

"It's not that big a deal. Calm down," I say. I'd rather keep this abandonment slumber party focused on Jake. "It really isn't. It was going to happen eventually and now it has. To be honest, it's sort of been in the back of my mind for a while now."

I pick up my phone out of habit, to avoid the look on Peaches's face and to check to see if Jake's texted me again yet.

"*What are you talking about, Nicki, it's not that big a deal?*" Peaches is yelling and her eyes are practically bugging out of her head. She swats at my phone. "Shut that thing off!"

"It's really not," I say, evenly. "I mean, maybe my dad had something to do with Jake leaving, but I don't really think so. I think it was just really bad timing. I don't know!" I start to cry again. "See, this is why I don't even want to tell you stuff. I knew you would overreact."

"*I'm hardly overreacting!*" She's shaking her head in tiny back-and-forths as if to say, *I can't even*. Finally she just says, "Fuck him."

"Who, Jake? Or my dad?"

"Both of them!" Peaches says. "Fuck them both."

We have a brief moment of uproarious laughter. High fives and all.

That's when we hear Cody yell, "*Can you guys be quiet!*" from the other side of the wall. Oh shit. I thought he was asleep.

"Sorry, mister!" Peaches yells back. Then she drops her voice to a whisper. "I'm sorry."

"I'm scared I'm never going to trust another man again," I say quietly.

"You never did trust men, lady. Don't you get that? That's how you got into this madness. You don't trust men, so then you pick men who aren't worth trusting," she says. For someone who would date Charlie Sheen, this is a pretty good insight.

"I lent him money, Peaches. I'm supposed to know better than that." I'd add I'm also supposed to be stronger than that. As well as smarter than that. "You told me I shouldn't. And I did it anyway."

"Men are jerks." Peaches says this like it's common knowledge. "Don't feel bad."

"Are they? Jerks, I mean." I really don't want this to be true. But right now, it definitely seems true. "All of them?"

"Not all of them. Just the ones we want to get with." Peaches explodes into laughter and holds up her right hand for another high five. She hugs me, and

I still feel terrible, but with her here, I feel a little better about feeling terrible.

"I'll wait up while you go to sleep," Peaches says. She's settling into the pillows, touching my head in the nicest possible way. Just like when we were kids. I was the responsible one, the good girl who would always go to sleep first. Peaches would stay up reading *Tiger Beat*, or later, getting sex tips from my mom's *Cosmopolitan* magazines.

"You just drift off and don't worry about a thing, because I'm here," she says, grabbing a magazine from my nightstand. "We'll deal with all this bullshit tomorrow."

I turn away from the light and comfort myself with the thought that tomorrow will be a new day.

———

I wake up the next morning, but it turns out to be 3 p.m. Peaches is gone. She had to go to work, but left a note saying to call her when I wake up. I thought it was going to be a new day, but I can already tell it's going to be the same day. Why wouldn't I be able to just get up the next morning and move on—Jake wasn't my whole life or anything, right?—but this feels cataclysmic. I can't get out of bed. My body feels like I haven't slept in ten years. My mind is covered in a dark blanket. I feel nauseous.

I guess it's the money.

It's one thing to believe someone loves you. It's another thing to believe they love you so much that you give them a bunch of cash. It makes me feel so foolish, so gullible, so so *stupid*. Like did he just want me for the money all along? Then I think, no, it couldn't be that. Because the one thing he wanted the money for—the restaurant—he left behind. So maybe it's not the money.

Maybe it's the restaurant.

Miguel has tried to call me three times already today. I know he's facing a thousand decisions—on countertops and espresso machines and chair styles and refrigerator equipment rentals, and now both Jake and I are just . . . missing in action. I'll call him eventually, but right now it's impossible. I can't lift up my head, much less my phone.

It's like I got hit by a bus and now I need to be in traction—only *traction* is where I just lie here in the dark and pretend like I'm in a coma while wanting to throw up. I remember a therapist once telling me what it felt like to be an infant—she said it's like you're on a Tempur-Pedic mattress and life conforms perfectly to your body because you're being held all the time. That's what I'm doing here. Trying to be an infant. Except without food. I guess I should be excited that if this keeps up, I'm definitely going to be wearing those twenty-six-waist-size jeans when this is all said and done.

From far away I hear a knock on the door.

"Mom?"

It's Cody. He's home from school and probably wants to know if I'm still alive. I've never lain in bed like this a day in his life. Even if I have the flu I get up and throw a burrito into the microwave. I'm that kind of overachiever.

"Yeah, honey?" Boy, do I sound bad.

"Are you coming out anytime soon?"

*Maybe. Maybe I'll come out soon.*

"I'll be right there." I force myself to sit up, slide out of bed, and slip my feet into my clogs. I pass the mirror on my way to the door. I look like hell.

I come into the kitchen and Cody's rummaging through the cupboards.

"Hi, Mom," he says. He looks worried about me.

"Hi, honey."

"Are you okay?"

"I'm fine."

"You look like you've been crying."

"I have. But I don't want to talk about it. Okay, honey?"

"Mom, can I just say what you would say to me?"

"No," I say. I really don't want to hear what I would say right now.

"You can't just pretend nothing's happening," he says anyway.

That *is* what I would say.

"I'm a mess, Cody," I say. Might as well tell him the truth. "Jake left last night and he hasn't come back and I don't think he's coming back anytime soon."

Cody stands perfectly still. He doesn't say anything for a breath or two. "I'm sorry, Mom."

That was the perfect response.

"I thought it was going to work this time. I really did. All I managed to do is just chalk up another failure. Another guy who has to come get his stuff and move out of the house." I'm trying not to sound angry or sorry for myself, even though I'm a little of both. I bury my face in my hand. "I can't believe I'm doing this to you again."

"Mom, it's fine." Cody does that thing where he shakes his head with a half smile on his face. It's like he's looking at me and the folly of the entire human condition. He's not judging, he's more like a Buddhist monk who already has knowledge that it's clearly going to take me years more to figure out. "I'm fine."

But is he? I've only had two main boyfriends during Cody's life. The first was Steve. Steve was short and quiet and didn't smile very much. He liked to eat licorice and used to bring bags of it home for Cody. Dude loved licorice. Steve was a good guy. We never lived together, so our breakup didn't have that much of an impact on Cody. Just the thing about the licorice. Cody missed the licorice.

Then there was Dash. Cody loved him. Dash was a sculptor, and lived in this crazy warehouse near the bridge in North Portland that had giant pieces of metal everywhere. They used to play backgammon together and go to the park to play frisbee. We were the cute, artsy family and everything was great until it wasn't.

Dash broke my heart. He broke Cody's heart, too. He cheated, of course.

What made it doubly worse is that I'd broken my rule for Dash. No live-in boyfriends. I swore I'd never be like my mother—with a rotation of guys coming in and out of my kid's life—but Dash was unlike anyone I'd ever met. He loved me and he loved Cody and I thought this time it would be okay. Because Dash was going to teach Cody how to be an artist, how to be a free thinker, how to do life on his own terms. Instead he hurt us in the worst possible way.

The day we moved out of the warehouse, I sat in the living room chair, all these boxes stacked up around me, and cried. I thought I was alone, but I didn't realize Cody had walked in and was watching me. I'm sure it was the first time he ever saw me cry. Up to that point, I'd successfully managed to present a pretty spotless version of "Mother," or so I thought.

After that, we moved into a one-bedroom apartment where there was this giant closet big enough for Cody's bunk bed. I asked him what color he wanted to paint the walls, and in a last moment of boyhood innocence, he chose a pinky-purple color—which I went along with in a moment of gender-free mothering. I hung a curtain across the doorway and the closet became his "room." Every night I would sit on the floor and read him books before bedtime. One night after I'd turned out the light, I heard him crying softly in bed. I asked what was the matter, and he replied, *I miss Dash,* and it was so crushing, so painful to admit to myself what I had done. *I did this. I let this person into his life and then he hurt us both.* But I had to admit it, because I knew that if I didn't let it land on me—I mean really hold myself accountable for the fact that *I chose* Dash and I was *the only person* who was responsible for that choice—I knew I would do it again.

And now I have.

"It's okay, Mom," Cody says. "Really." He sounds so sure, it's almost heartening. Is it possible he's really fine? Or is he just young, or compartmentalized, or both? "What about moving?" he says. "To the new house, I mean. Is that still gonna happen now?"

I slump over the kitchen counter. "Sweetheart, I think I have to go back to bed." I can't face it. Not right now. Maybe later.

"It's going to be okay, Mom." Cody takes a couple of steps toward me. He doesn't quite know what to do, but he reaches out and puts his right hand over the top of my shoulder and sort of half hugs me. Oh, my son! I am both moved and heartbroken that he is trying to alleviate my pain. Then he perks up. "I got an A-minus on the English test," he says.

"You did?"

"Yeah. I studied," he says.

"That's amazing, honey." I lift my body up to a full sit. It's a little like starting the car by popping the clutch, but I want to give this boy some positive reinforcement. "I'm so proud of you for making that effort."

"It's not that big a deal," he says, going back to his cereal, "about Jake, I mean." He takes a couple of bites and thinks. "You didn't like him as much as Dash, or anything."

He's right, I didn't. But I didn't know that Cody knew that.

Dash *was* a big deal—the only guy besides Gio I ever truly let in. But our relationship was so painful—his lies and drinking and flirting with pretty retail girls—that by the time he finally left, for me at least, it was a relief. The moment he was gone I realized I'd been living with a form of tinnitus: a pinging noise so constant, so pervasive, I couldn't rest. *Ever.* I lived in constant fear (without even knowing it) that Dash was going to just wander off, or be stolen by dingoes, or decide that whatever intriguing stranger he just met could do more for him than I could. Dash's cheating wasn't like one of those spiritual journeys where the person goes looking for some lost part of themselves they left behind somewhere along the way. Dash was a beautiful, tragic, empty soul who didn't come equipped with his own oxygen supply—so he had to borrow from women. Women at the coffee place, women in the parking garage, women working behind counters or sitting in parks. Each of them was a breath of—some were a gulp, I suppose—life-giving air. How ironic that he couldn't breathe without them, and I couldn't breathe without him.

And how amazing that Cody has this perspective on it all. It feels like this is maybe a moment of closure for us.

"Dash was really special," I say. I really don't harbor any grudges toward Dash. Now that I think about it, maybe he was just another swan man. "Bless him wherever he is."

"Do you know where he is?"

"I don't."

Cody drops his spoon in the bowl, seemingly done with this discussion. "Mom?"

"Yeah, honey?"

"Is it okay if I go play Magic?"

"Sure, honey."

"Thanks, Mom," he says.

He grabs his backpack and leaves. I watch him step into the fading afternoon light, feeling humbled. Life problems don't care that you have a kid, do they? Life problems barge into your house, tell you to move over, and sit down on the couch until they decide to leave. And there's nothing you can do about it.

I really, really have to go back to bed.

# 10

### RONNIE

No one answers the front door when I knock. But I see Nicki's car in the driveway, so when I try the door and it opens, I take a chance and let myself in.

"Nicki?" I take a few steps into the house and call out softly. There's still a spot on the white rug where she dropped the platter of meat the other night, but other than that, it sure is nice in here. My daughter obviously is doing a lot of things right to live in this place. "Are you here? Cody?"

The house is strangely silent. I can tell Cody's not here because I can see a bedroom door with a *C* on it, and it's open and there's no life coming out of it. I take a few more steps and call out again.

"Nicki?" There's another bedroom door, it's open a crack and I move toward it. "Baby?"

I push lightly on the door and I can see her lying there, asleep, looking just like she did when she was a baby. My God, she's beautiful! Her wide, slanted eyes are closed and there's this calm perfection on her face. When you look at someone sleeping, it's like you're seeing what she is for all time: what she was the moment she got born and what she'll be the moment she leaves. Nicki taught me that when she was a baby. After that, I realized it was true for all women.

Seeing her like this takes me back to the very beginning. Beth was so overwhelmed. I wanted the baby more than she did! I begged her not to drink and go out there and hustle. I wanted Nicki so bad and I didn't even know why. I think I knew she would save me somehow, or I wanted her to.

Then she was born and she was so perfect! As perfect as she is right now. I'd just stare at her going back and forth in that little swing and I could see everything that she could be. Her whole future—the pigtails, the jumping jacks, the kindergarten, the prom, the first car, the waitress job, the braces, the tears. The happiness. I have no idea if any of that happened, because I fucked it up. I caught my first case when she was five and after that it was a revolving door. She got bigger and so did the cases. They don't make it easy for a guy who's been in prison to escape the system. Because they don't care that you got a little girl who deserves a daddy. All they care about is proving that you are a criminal.

And I'm a criminal. So that's pretty easy to prove.

I know Nicki thinks she doesn't want me in her life. Part of me feels guilty—like I should go away and just let her live. But the other part of me is like, *deal with it*. You don't get to choose your parents, you take what you get and you make the best of it by learning to love them for who they are—not who you wish they could be. My only real choice is to stand here and claim my daughter and take whatever punches she wants to throw my way. Because I deserve them, and also because kids throw punches, it's what they do.

Parents have to deal with it, too.

I look around the room and notice how disheveled it is. There's a roll of toilet paper on the bedside table, some dishes stacked up, and the trash can is overflowing with Kleenex. Like she's sick or something.

Did I do this? Maybe it's because I came around.

"Nicki?" I set my hand down on the bed, just slightly. "Baby, it's your dad."

Her eyes open in a flash.

"Nicki?" I say it as softly as I can, half hoping she doesn't think I'm a stranger and pull a gun out from under her pillow. "Baby?"

She moves just a little bit so I say it again, "Nicki?" Nothing. "Nicki? It's your dad."

That does it. She sits bolt upright in bed and looks at me, terrified.

"What are you doing here?"

It really looks like she's still sleeping, so I keep my calm wake-up tone of voice. "Honey, it's your dad. I came back. Are you okay?"

She's awake now for real. She turns to me, just as calm as you please. "I don't want you here. You need to go away."

"I know you don't want me here. I really do," I say. I'm not trying to manipulate my daughter into taking me. I just want to level with her. Being completely honest is my only shot at having her see me as a person, her father, instead of a cartoon character in a comic strip about extreme family dysfunction. Because right now, I'm not human to her. Yet.

"If I could help it, I would not be here. Not like this. But I don't have anywhere else to go. I know this is not at all what you have in mind for your life, and I apologize deeply for the way this is happening, but if you could find it in your heart to help me, just until I can line something up, I wouldn't have to go back to prison, and baby"—I have to hold the tears back—"that would mean the world to me. But even more than that, I just want to spend a little bit of time with you and my grandson."

She twists her face into such disgust I almost don't even recognize her. "Are you fucking serious?"

I don't know what I was expecting her to say, but that's not it.

"Yeah, actually. I am."

"You are out"—she grabs a water bottle off the night table, opens it, and takes a swig all in one motion—"of your mind. I mean it. Are you serious?"

I see that she's mad, and she has a right to be. But that doesn't mean I don't have a right to know her. She's just going to have to get over it. I'll be patient. "Yes, baby. I'm serious."

"Oh my God. Don't *yes, baby* me." She tries to put the water bottle down on the night table but has to slide some dishes out of the way. "Please."

"Are you okay?" I ask. I mean the dishes and the tissues. "You're asleep in the middle of the day. Are you sick? Can I get you something?"

"Don't try to act all concerned," she says.

"Why not? I am all concerned, Nicki. I'm your dad."

"Sire, maybe."

Vicious, but at least she's engaged. "That's not true," I say.

"Oh, isn't it?"

No, it's not. "I took care of you from the time you were three until—"

She cuts me off. "Until you went to jail?" She doesn't wait for me to answer. "And then you got out and went to jail *again*." She says *again* like I stole food from a homeless person. "And then you went back again! It's like you only got out for vacations."

"Yes, that's true." I'm not going to let her bully me. I can own my choices. It took years of work to be able to look at what I made of my life without flinching. "That is what I did."

"You sound proud."

"I'm not," I say. "But I'm not ashamed, either. You want me to be ashamed?"

"It might be nice," she says. "A little shame might go a long way."

"I'm accountable, Nicki. You are right. That's what happened. Those are the actions I took. I harmed a lot of people. And I'm here to make amends," I say. There's a little more edge on it than I wanted, but hey, it's hard to be perfect when it feels like she's attacking me. "So what are you going to do? Reject me? Go ahead. Then you're no better than me." I can't help but add, "And something tells me you would rather be better than me."

Apparently, she would. Because she throws the covers off and gets out of bed.

"I'm hungry," she says.

———

"How about breakfast for dinner?" I stand at the stove, digging through a cupboard of pots and pans. "Do you have a cast-iron skillet?" I ask. Nicki's sitting at the breakfast bar, doing something on her phone.

"Look to your right, in the other cupboard." She slides her computer in front of her and opens it. "I'm not okay with this, I just want you to know that."

"Boy, you people just go from one screen to the next these days," I say. I'm going to ignore the jabs for now. Let her throw some punches, get the fight out of her system. It might take a while.

"Yep," she says, without looking up. "That's what us people do. These days."

I let the tone of voice slide and go over to the fridge. I pull out some eggs and a package of what looks to be bacon. It's brown and shriveled instead of fatty and pale pink. "Is this bacon cooked already?"

"Yep," she says without looking up. "That's how you buy it now. Pre-cooked. Just throw it in the microwave for thirty seconds. They had microwaves before you left, right?" *Now* she looks at me.

"Yes, they did," I say. "Eggs over well done?"

She looks surprised. "How do you know that?"

"I'm your father, girl," I say, making a *duh* face. "I *introduced* you to eggs."

Cody walks in at that moment, backpack over his shoulder. "Hi, Mom." He looks at me, and I detect that he's pleased to see me. Though he can't really show it. "Hi," he says.

"Hey there, Cody," I say. "I came back for a visit."

"Unannounced," Nicki says.

"Your mom has been very welcoming," I say. "Which I appreciate. Greatly. She didn't have to let me hang out. So, thank you, Nicki."

"Anytime, Ronnie," she says, mimicking my tone precisely. She finishes typing a word and speaks right to Cody. "Actually, my dad came here today because, as it turns out, he doesn't have anywhere to live. Probably he hasn't met the right woman yet. That'll be a couple more days, *at least.*"

"Now, now, daughter," I say.

"What?" she says, mocking innocence. "Surely, you're out there trying to round up a Serena?"

"Serena was a long time ago," I say. "I've changed."

Nicki's talking about my old girlfriend Serena. She's being rude about it, but there is definitely some truth in what she's saying. I have a long history of being manipulative. I would do anything to get what I want. I used a lot of people, people like Serena, and now other people, people like Nicki, don't trust me. That is what happens when you use people.

"Who's Serena?" Cody asks.

"Nobody," Nicki says.

When I got out of prison the second time, I took Nicki to the Portland Civic Center to see this boy band she was crazy about and brought along Serena. Man, that girl was hot. A stacked redhead, she looked just like one of the models on *The Price Is Right.* Anyway, Serena really loved to show herself off and wore a jumpsuit cut down to *there*—she didn't know how to dress to go somewhere with a teenage girl. Nicki was fascinated by her, but wouldn't say a word to her because being my girlfriend made her a suspect. Who in her right mind would date me? Even then Nicki had that chip on her shoulder.

When I got arrested a few months later, Serena put up her house for my bond *and* she paid for most of my defense. I didn't ask her to do it; she did it willingly. She'd probably *still* take me back, if I could find her and if she was single. So I understand why Nicki is so suspicious. She's seen what it looks like for the women in my life, and she has no intention of becoming one of them.

"Are you going to let him live here?" Cody brightens up, changing the subject. "That would be so cool."

Before Nicki can shoot the idea down, I reroute the conversation. "How do you like your eggs, Cody? I'm trying to make myself useful around here by putting together some dinner. When your mom was little, I used to cook her breakfast for dinner all the time."

"Uh, scrambled," he says. He seems intrigued by the idea of Nicki being little. "My mom was little? That's so weird."

"She sure was," I say. "Cute as a button, too."

"Since when do you eat eggs?" Nicki asks Cody.

"Since always," he says. He throws her a little scowl. "What was my mom like when she was little?"

"I was never little," Nicki says. "I was born eight years old and not long after that, I turned thirty-two. I've gotten straight A's and been very responsible my whole life." She laughs, half sad, half proud.

"That's not true," I say. "When Nicki was a baby, she used to stand up in her crib and jump up and down while holding on to the railing. We used to put on music and you would just dance for hours. You were very carefree."

"What happened?" Cody asks. He's doubtful that his serious and responsible mom was ever footloose and fancy-free.

"Oh, your mom is a dancer," I say. "You didn't know that? As a little kid, she really knew how to party."

"He believes the other story. The one about being thirty-two," Nicki says.

"Sorry, Mom," he says. "I just don't see you as the jumping around and dancing type."

"Wait a minute!" Nicki says, with just a hint of a smile. "I don't know if I like where this is going."

"Cody, look here," I say, pulling a couple of eggs out of the carton. "See how I do it? Crack it right *there*, on the widest part of the egg. Opens right up every time." I make a big show of breaking the eggs into a coffee mug. "I worked in the kitchen in the joint," I say. "So I got skills."

"What's the craziest thing that ever happened in prison?" Cody asks. "Did any guys ever shank another guy?"

"Oh my God," Nicki says. "Don't answer that."

"*Ha!*" I clap my hands and laugh. "Boy, you've been watching too much TV. I was in federal prison. Guys in there don't go around shanking each other. Unless maybe you're in Vacaville. They don't call that place Victimville for nothing. It's been years since I was anywhere like that, though. I've been in the medium-security joint with the smart criminals: the embezzlers, the interstate drug dealers, the bank robbers. State prison is where you got most of your riffraff. The murderers, the rapists—"

"Wait. You mean there aren't any—"

"Cody, go wash your hands," Nicki says.

"The boy's curious, Nicki," I say. She's worried I'm going to say something inappropriate, but I'm not. Prison is a little like war. You don't talk about the worst things you've seen to people you know can't handle it. At the same time, I wasn't destroyed by it, the same way millions of guys go to war and come back in one piece. There's a way of compartmentalizing what happens; maybe it's part of the male mind. Unless you were messed up in the head to begin with, you're probably okay. Not that the world is an easy place to handle, it isn't. But it's not because you went crazy in there, it's because The Man never gives an ex-con a break.

"Can I ask him about drug dealing?" He gives Nicki a pleading look. He really, really wants to know. "Is it like—"

Nicki cuts him off. "I don't think so," Nicki says. "Aren't you supposed to be in your room hunched over your computer talking to sixteen-year-olds in other parts of the world who are also hunched over their computers?"

"This is more fun," he says.

"Let the boy ask his questions. You should encourage him to learn about the world." I cast a thick-as-thieves glance at Cody, as I expertly tip the sauté pan over the plate, depositing a heap of fluffy scrambled eggs on it. "A guy's gotta get out in the world if he's gonna conquer it."

"Yeah," Cody says, probably thrilled to finally have an ally against his mom. "Did you ever shoot anybody?"

"Cody!"

"No, son," I say, nodding at Cody's plate as a signal to start eating. "Eat up." Which Cody, to his mom's surprise, does. "I'm a gentleman criminal. I rarely carried a gun."

"Oh my God," Nicki says. "I can't listen to this."

I've been heating up the cast-iron skillet on another burner, which I now pull to the front of the stove. "Got this bad boy all ready to go for your eggs, darling." I crack the eggs open and they sizzle as they hit the hot olive oil. For two whole seconds I breathe it in and my whole body says *Thank you, Lord,* just to experience a really primo olive oil. It's the simple shit in life, I'm telling you.

"What's a time that you did?" Cody says. "Shoot your gun, I mean."

"I said, stop," Nicki says.

"*Eeeee-yiiii!*" I yell as I pop two pieces of toast way into the air and catch them. "Now that's what I call toast. We don't have this kinda bread in the joint. All we got is that shitty"—he looks at Cody—"Sorry. That crap white bread. Got no flavor."

"My mom swears all the time," Cody says, eager to make me feel better. "Don't even worry about it."

I give the toast a swipe of butter. Then pick up the cast-iron skillet, slip a spatula under the eggs, drop them on the toast, and hand it to Nicki. "You didn't know your dad could make a perfect egg, did you?"

"I never imagined." She sounds a little snide, but I can see that she's warming up just a little, watching me and Cody together.

"Did anyone ever shoot at you?"

"No, son," I say. "Drug dealing isn't *Scarface.*"

"What's *Scarface?*" he asks.

*Only the best movie about a drug dealer ever made.*

"Don't tell me you haven't seen *Scarface*!"

"He doesn't need to see *Scarface*," Nicki says.

"All men need to see *Scarface*, Nicki," I say. "It's one of those movies, like *Apocalypse Now*."

"What's *Apocalypse Now*?"

"We'll watch it one night," I say.

"Oh my God," Nicki says. "You're glorifying violence to my teenager."

"It's men stuff, sweetheart." I can see that Nicki has a woman's distaste for male things: violence, power, risk. She doesn't understand that those things are buried as deep in the psyche of a man as shoes and princesses and babies are to a woman. Men evolved to be attracted to violence. It's how we survived. And just because feminism came along, and central heating, and grocery store meat departments, doesn't mean that part of ourselves just vanished. A guy has to get acquainted with these parts of himself. Not fear them. I remind myself to take Cody to a shooting range some time.

"I think it's cool," Cody says. "I want to see *Scarface*."

"Well, I don't," she says.

"These eggs are great," Cody says, chowing down. "I didn't realize how much I like eggs."

"Thank you, Cody," I say.

"Can I ask you another question?" Cody says.

"Sure, son. Go ahead." I shoot a look at Nicki to say *let the boy speak*.

"Did you ever do drugs?"

"Okay, that's it," Nicki says, taking Cody's plate. She glares at me. "Go be in your room. You can learn all about that stuff later. When you're thirty-five."

"Listen to your mom, Cody," I say. "Besides, she and I have some stuff to talk about."

Cody gets up obediently and heads into his room. But before he leaves he turns to Nicki. "Mom, I think you should let him stay."

We watch him disappear into the hallway. Nicki starts clearing plates, dumping them into the sink a little too hard and loud. "This was fun and all, but don't think you can just sail in here and, I don't know, think you're going to be part of—"

She doesn't finish the sentence, so I do. "Be part of your lives?" I say. "Why not, Nicki? Why can't I do that?"

"Because."

"Because why?"

"Because!" she says. "Because you're a bad person who spent half my life in prison and you don't deserve to be part of my life. That's why."

"There, you said it," I say. "Thank you."

I love this girl. I love how committed she is to her truth, and how real she's willing to get about her anger. It's a gift, really. She could be doing that thing some women do where they get on an IV drip of *never mind*. Where they pretend everything's fine because they're unwilling to show their hurt, their pain. But Nicki? Nicki is honest about her feelings with me and that's a good thing. I find it very encouraging, because if she feels safe enough to tell me the truth, she actually trusts me already. I can work with that.

"Don't 'thank you' me," she says. "It's patronizing."

"You want to know what I think?" I say.

"Not really," she says. Then she looks up at me, just slightly. "What."

"I think you're amazing." Then I look pointedly at her. "And I think you should listen to your son."

# 11

# NICKI

I said yes. I'm not 100 percent sure why. Guilt, mostly. Yes, I'm concerned about how this might affect Cody. No, I really don't want Ronnie here. Yes, I'm furious he would just show up on my doorstep and put me in this position. But it pretty much came down to this: I just couldn't throw my own father, a fifty-seven-year-old man without a cent or a piece of clothing or anything at all really, out on the street. They'll make him go back to prison, and I can't do that to him.

Ronnie's not a bad person. He just isn't. He's been in jail a lot. And he's desperate for the attention of women. And that desperation made him want money so much that he was willing to do really stupid things to get it. But at his core, he is basically good. Even my mom said so. One day we were standing in the kitchen after our every-other-week phone call from him. I must have been about thirteen. Beth had just hung up the blue wall-mounted phone and she looked at me and said, *Your daddy's not a bad man. He's actually sweet. Always was. He just goes about everything the wrong way.* The way she said it, I could tell that even though he was a world-class fuckup, she still loved him.

It was the only time she ever said anything like that.

I never forgot it, because it made me feel like maybe it wasn't so awful that he's my dad. Like maybe it was still okay for me to love him, too. Just by her saying that one thing, I grasped that regular people don't understand prison because they've never known anyone who went there. They've never been inside a prison visiting room and seen all the guys who, if they weren't wearing uniforms and there wasn't a guard in the room, would look like slightly rougher versions of the average person's uncle or cousin. In fact, the whole reason regular people are regular is because they've never had to deal with extreme life circumstances. If they had, they would know that going to prison is like doing drugs or going skydiving. It's only crazy the first time. After that it becomes normal because human beings can adapt to just about anything.

Anyway, there is just no way for me to justify forcing Ronnie back to prison. I have this thing I call the Grocery Store Exit Clipboard Test that I use sometimes to make decisions. It helps me figure out what kind of person I think I am, and whether the choice I'm making matches up with that person. For example: if someone stood outside a grocery store with a clipboard and asked me if I would force my almost-senior-citizen dad to go back to prison rather than let him stay with me for a week or two or even three or four, I would say, *Nooooo! I'd never do that!*

Of course, here I am in that situation and that's exactly what I want to do. But am I going to live up to the person I'd declare myself to be outside the grocery store? Or am I going to take the easy way out? I'm not so cold that I'm going to send an old man back to jail. Nor do I want to feel bad for the rest of my life if he drops dead tomorrow. So I said yes. Not so much because I wanted to say yes, but because I'm afraid to say no.

"You can put your stuff in there," I say, pointing toward the spare bedroom. I open the hall closet and pull out enough linens to make the bed. "Let me just grab some sheets."

The other thing is Cody. The way he looked at Ronnie—he just had this *light* in his eyes I'd never seen before. It was automatic love—my dad didn't have to do anything to earn it, and all the bullshit he's done can't take it away, either. Which, I don't know how that's possible. I'll probably never totally forgive Ronnie for all the ways he's fucked up. There's a part of me that wants to make Ronnie pay for every mistake he's ever made. Then here comes Cody saying, *Oh, don't worry about it, Grandpa. You don't owe me anything.* What, is he trying to make me look bad? If someone with a clipboard outside the grocery store asked me if I would deprive my son of the grandfather he never knew, I would have to say, *No. No, I wouldn't.*

"I want you to know I think you're making the right decision, Nickles," Ronnie says. He's trying to make me feel good about this by using my second-string nickname, but it's backfiring.

"Ronnie, with all due respect, and that's not a whole lot, everything you say to encourage me feels like manipulation," I say. "So I would stop that, if I were you."

"I get that," he says.

"What does that even mean, *I get that?*"

"It means 'fair enough.' I've hurt you a lot and you're not sure you're ready to forgive me yet."

"I'm fine with forgiving you," I say. "I just wish I could do it with you *over there*. Not in my face. But that's not what's happening, is it?"

"Peace is a practice, little girl."

"What?"

"You know what they say: what you resist, persists," he says. "I hear you trying to be in acceptance. I commend you for that."

I roll my eyes as hard as I possibly can. "I don't actually need your commendation." I don't know why I'm being such a teenager right now—I can see my behavior for exactly what it is, since I'm the proud owner of a sixteen-year-old myself—but Ronnie is, to put it politely, bugging the shit out of me right now. It's bad enough I'm letting him stay here—does he have to force all his New Age crap down my throat? It's all I can do to keep my mouth shut. "This is it."

I flick on the light in the spare bedroom. It looks like a storage bin. There's a rolling rack of clothes, an old futon couch, and a bunch of Cody's outgrown toys and clothes. The one thing the room really has going for it is a nice window that looks out onto the yard. The windows in this bungalow—giant, double-hung with original glass and hardware—are one of the main reasons I fell in love with this house in the first place.

"Why would you ever sell this place?" he asks. When I told him he could stay, I said it was going to be temporary because we're moving soon. Which I now realize I shouldn't have said because it made him think he could act like my father about it. "It's so nice."

"Please don't start asking a bunch of questions. I've lived without your advice this long," I say, "I don't need it now." I set the bedding down on the mattress. "I take it you know how to make a bed."

"Sure do," he says.

He starts singing out loud. *"A thousand kisses from you is never too muh–uh–uh–uuuuch . . ."*

"Ronnie." I say it all exhausted. "Please?"

"What? You don't like Luther? That was the jam back in the day! You used to love that one."

"Yeah, well, I don't now." I clear a path to the other side of the futon and pull it into the bed position. "You're driving me kind of nuts. Are you always this relentlessly upbeat?"

"That's called being happy, girl."

"It's a bit much," I say. "Can I ask you a question? How is it that you spent a million years in prison and you come out sounding like some sort of motivational speaker? All happy and carefree?"

"I told you," he says patiently, "I did a lot of work in prison. I read books, I studied, I learned meditation. I figured out where I went wrong and I healed myself."

That sounds a little too awesome. I'm not sure whether to believe him or not. On the one hand, there's what Cicero said: *res ipsa loquitur*. The thing speaks for itself. This man is not hardened, seemingly at all. He feels like an exceptionally bright Salvation Army bell ringer, or some homeless person who is at peace despite having nothing to his name but a cardboard box and a German shepherd wearing a bandanna. On the other hand, who comes out of prison after all this time with a smile on his face? Is that even possible? Isn't he supposed to be guarding his food with his forearm, and checking to see if anyone is coming up behind him? I don't get it.

"Prison was good for me." Ronnie grabs the other end of the fitted sheet and tucks it in. I notice his hands as he smooths the corner flat. I remember thinking how huge they were as a little girl. Now I can see they're just regular-size man's hands. "I never lived right, Nicki. Not one minute of my life. And this time I went away for long enough to figure that out. I'm grateful."

"Hmmmm," I say. I find it irritating how confident he sounds. It's not exactly arrogant, but maybe a little too sure. "Forgive me if that's kind of hard to believe."

"I understand," he says. "You'll see."

As I help him adjust the elastic over the top corner of the bed, I notice I haven't missed Jake or felt shitty for the past hour. Which almost makes me feel a twinge of panic. Like, is the bad feeling going to come back now? I wait for a second, but I still seem to feel okay.

"What's going on with your boyfriend?" Ronnie asks. "Is he going to be okay with me being here?"

*What, is he reading my mind?* Weird.

"Um, that's kind of complicated," I say. "He doesn't really live here, technically. He just stays here a lot. But anyway, we got in a big fight, so we're going to take a little break from each other."

"That's too bad."

"It's okay, actually."

"Is that why you were all messed up yesterday?"

I hate how observant he is. "I wasn't all messed up yesterday," I say. "I was tired."

"Okay, then," Ronnie says, making it glaringly obvious he thinks I was all messed up yesterday. He holds a pillow under his chin while he snaps open the pillowcase. "What kind of business is Jake in?"

It's an innocent question, but I feel a block of marble move into my chest. I don't want to tell my dad *one single thing more* about my life. Not one thing.

"I'm letting you stay here, but that doesn't mean you're going to get up in the details of my life," I say. "Not to be rude."

"You're right, baby. I'm sorry." He gives me an understanding glance, and to be honest, I hate that he's so nice. It would be much easier to be cranky if he wasn't. "It's none of my business. I'm just grateful to be here."

"Hey." Cody appears at the door. He sees Ronnie and looks all alive. "What's up!"

"Heyyyy!" Ronnie's excited to see Cody. He holds up his fist and Cody pounds it, all dudelike. "My boy! Come here and help me with this sheet."

Ronnie grabs the top sheet and hands the other end to Cody, who doesn't have a clue what to do with it, but takes it anyway.

"Just lay it down nice and flat, then tuck it under like this." He makes a perfect envelope corner on the mattress, no doubt learned in prison. "Then like this."

Cody takes his end and follows along, attempting to fold the corner of the sheet under the mattress. He struggles for a second, but ends up with something close to an envelope. When he's finished, he looks at Ronnie like a four-year-old would. As if to say, *I did it!*

"Nice, son," Ronnie says. "Now smooth it out a little. Like this."

I take a step back and watch them together. Maybe Ronnie being here is okay for tonight.

———

I plunge my feet into the warm water. This is the best I've felt in three days, almost normal. Peaches is in the chair next to me. I've purposely been avoiding her since all hell started breaking loose at home, because she's very judgey and she always finds a way to make everything about her. I don't feel like dealing with her, but she's my best friend and that means I can only respond by text and send her to voice mail for so long before she starts to get suspicious. The limit is about forty-four hours.

"I have to tell you something," I say, leaning back into the chair.

"Your dad is living with you." She says it like when a really great basketball player gets the ball, runs all the way to the other end of the court, and slams it into the net with such skill, flourish, and finality you just want to stand up and cheer. Even if you're on the other team.

"How do you know that?" I certainly didn't intend to give it away so quickly that she's right, but it slips out.

"A little bird told me." She stops. "Okay, Cody put it on his social networking," she says. "You know, those crazy little phones have all sorts of stuff going on inside of them. Like apps and whatnot. You're behind, bitch."

I used to check Cody's social networking, but I stopped doing it with any regularity because it felt like I was spying on him. Did I even really want to see what was on there? Not really. Once I became reasonably certain he wasn't going to become the teenage Unabomber I decided to trust him instead of trying to control him. Although I have to admit that maybe if I'd paid more attention I might not have been caught off guard over all those absences at school.

"Why didn't you say anything?" I don't like the idea that Peaches is hiding stuff from me, even if I'm hiding the same stuff from her first.

"I wanted to see how long it would take you to tell me," she says. "It was a test."

"That's sneaky," I say.

"Yeah, well, I'm sneaky," she says, balancing her cell phone on the arm of her chair. Peaches likes to live dangerously, even when there's absolutely no reason to. "Anyway, you passed. It only took you a couple of days, and I can understand that."

"Thank you, Peaches." I say it like *I appreciate this rare moment of being the bigger person; that doesn't happen very often, does it?*

"Yeah, you're welcome," she says back, not appreciating my tone. "Anyway, what's it like so far? Does your dad put his arm around his food so you guys don't try to steal it off his plate? I had a boyfriend once who told me that's how it goes down in prison."

I love that Peaches has the same stupid idea of prisoners as I do. Not that I'm going to tell her that. I'm too busy maintaining my air of superiority.

"No, Peaches. He acts perfectly normal while eating. It's only been a couple of days, so I don't really know yet," I say. "So far, the weirdest part is that it's not very weird. He seems almost unbelievably normal. Every once in a while I'll see him staring off into space. And sometimes he seems like he's in his own world. Like he's connecting the dots in ways that the rest of us probably aren't. But then again, he read a hundred books in prison and now he thinks he's some sort of cross between Joel Osteen and Dr. Phil, so who knows."

"Sounds fantastic. When am I coming over to meet him?"

"Yeah, um. Absolutely no rush." Peaches and Ronnie are like the two people from opposite sides of your life that you're not sure you want talking to each other at your birthday party. "I mean, you and he both annoy me individually, so together, I'm sure you're *really* going to annoy me, and I'm not in a big hurry for that to happen."

"You're just scared to have us comparing notes on you." Peaches sucks in a giant snort of air. "You might lose your precious feeling of control."

"Exactly," I say. "I spent my whole life dealing with Ronnie being out of control, and now that he's out of prison, everything's gonna go at my speed this time. So you can just take a number and have a seat." I finish it with a *got it?* face.

"So, next question," Peaches says. "Have you heard from Jake?"

"I actually haven't," I say. "But you know what's crazy? I'm sort of fine with it."

"I don't believe you."

"No, seriously. It's true. Okay, maybe not totally fine, but I'm not all broken down crying." No one is more surprised at this than me. But since my dad moved in, I've hardly even thought about Jake. It's like Ronnie's presence is so big he's taken up all the space Jake occupied and a whole lot more. Or maybe Jake's presence was just a lot smaller than I thought. He did work pretty much around the clock.

"He's going to come back, you know," Peaches says. "Not that I'm ex-cited for that. But you're the best thing that ever happened to him. I always felt like you'd have to peel him off of you to get him to go."

"Do you have to judge, Peaches?" I say. I secretly like that Peaches is so sure that Jake's going to come back—I think he will, too—but I don't like it when she implies that he's some sort of gold digger. "It's half the reason I don't like telling you things."

Hua taps my left calf, signaling me to change feet. I dutifully pull the right leg out of the water and put the left one back in. I relax into the feel-ing of the bubbles around my ankles. I have friends who think mani-pedis are a waste of money, but the way I see it, if someone said it'd cost twenty-seven dollars for a ninety-minute trip to heaven, wouldn't you say, *Deal!* Of course you would.

"I don't! Judge," she says.

"Are you kidding?" I say. "You're the most judgmental person I know." I didn't mean for it to come out that harsh. But it's sort of true, so I don't feel like taking it back. "Isn't she, Hua?"

"Not getting involved," Hua says. "Feet up." She grabs what is essen-tially a long skinny cheese grater and starts filing away at my calluses.

"I guess if you feel I'm judging because I *say* what I *see*," Peaches says, "then maybe, yes. I judge."

"You do more than that," I say, as Hua rips on the bottom of my feet with the grater. All the jostling around is undercutting my ability to make a point. "You just think the worst of every guy I go out with."

"It's not that I think the worst of Jake, Nicki. It's that I didn't trust him. I knew he was going to—"

"Going to do what?"

"Whatever he did." She picks up a bottle of nail polish and uses the cap to scratch her nose so she won't mess up her mani. "Something stupid. So, um, what *did* he do?" Before I even have a chance to answer she starts talking again. "I mean, besides steal your money."

"He didn't steal my money," I say. "You said it yourself, he's coming back."

"Nicki, you're crazy. You're pouring how much money into that restaurant? You never wanted a *restaurant* until he came along." She practically spits the words at me. "Get real."

"You're not helping me," I say. "Also, that's not true. I *did* want a restaurant. I wanted *something*. I've never said I wanted to appraise things forever." My whole body feels like it's on fire when Peaches confronts me on stuff like this. "You're making me feel even worse."

"I can't make you feel anything."

"Right. Did you read that in a magazine article or something? Was that in *Cosmo*? Right after '99 Best Ways to Blow His Mind in Bed'?"

Here we are again. I hate when things devolve like this, but somehow it always does.

Hua weighs in. "Say you're sorry."

We both glare at her.

"Who? Not me," Peaches says.

"You both," Hua says.

"Yeah, not me, either," I say.

Hua gives me a look that's the perfect proportion of kind and disappointed, which tells me her kids probably behave extremely well, because you wouldn't fuck around with that face. That look makes me want to say I'm sorry.

"Okay, I'm sorry. But Peaches, look what I did! I made a fool of myself," I say. "I thought it was okay because Jake gave me twenty thousand dollars. I did what you said! And he still screwed me over."

"He gave you the money in a paper bag, Nicki." She says *paper bag* like she's saying *dog poop*. "That should have been a hint."

I give Hua a pleading look. When I put down my dukes, Peaches is supposed to say she's sorry, not take my vulnerability and get a couple more punches in. "Do you see how she is?"

"Peaches. Maybe you soften some." Hua says it real quiet. She's either a better person than either of us, or she has a lot of sisters and has learned from years of practice.

"Hua, will you adopt us? We need you," I say.

Peaches almost looks tearful. Almost. "I just don't want anyone to hurt you. I'm protective of you, lady." She pauses, like she's considering whether she should say what she says next. "I love you."

When she says this, it's like there's a cotton candy maker in my heart. "Peaches! That is so sweet!"

Hua looks all proud. "You girls, good."

Peaches touches my hand. "I know I can be a bitch sometimes. But it's only because I want to protect you." She keeps going. "I didn't mean to be judgmental. But Jake isn't good enough for you. No one's good enough for you. Except maaaaaybe Prince William. Because Princess Diana was rad. And maybe Paul Newman, but he's dead, right? He *was* great, though—crazy good-looking and doing all kinds of charity *and* loved his regular-looking wife for a whole lifetime. That's what you deserve, Mama. That's the kind of guy I want to see you with."

"You're being weird now," I say. I don't know what's more uncomfortable: Peaches being mean or Peaches being nice.

"We're gonna get through this, chicky. We are. It's not even that big a deal."

She reaches out and grabs my hand, smearing my nail polish. We both fall into gales of laughter.

————

Eventually, I was going to have to face the restaurant. And now I am. Miguel stopped calling a couple of days ago—he's too polite to badger me—and I've spent the past two days deluding myself that somehow Jake was going to just miraculously show up and handle everything. That hasn't happened, obviously. When I walk in, all the workers stop what they're doing and stare. The lead man puts down his paintbrush and comes over to me.

"Hi, miss. I'll go get Miguel."

Ugh. My face is pounding. Is it possible for your heartbeat to be trying to escape via your face? Because that's what's happening to me. I look at the guys, who look away, and I try not to incinerate myself from shame. There's something about seeing the results of my stupidity—twenty thousand dollars I put into this thing!—that makes me want to die. If I ever imagined myself as a strong, independent woman, I now know the truth: I'm a strong, independent woman who is also a mess. A hot one.

Miguel comes out from the back of the restaurant. He's with a guy who I recognize as the heating and air-conditioning guy. "Hi, Nicki."

"I'm so sorry," I say. I feel like it's my fault Jake has disappeared, that I'm responsible for getting Miguel into this situation.

"It's okay." Miguel is such a sweetheart. He doesn't want me to feel bad.

"It's definitely not okay."

"I mean, I understand," he says. His eyes show he's being really nice. I can't believe my luck. If I had to stand totally defenseless in front of someone, I would want it to be someone like this. "Have you heard from Jake?"

I shake my head. I fight back tears. Why am I suddenly crying? I was fine an hour ago.

"It's okay," he says.

"It's most definitely *not* okay," I say again. I laugh while I cry.

"I called his job," Miguel says. He tilts his head down so he can see my face better. "Are you *sure* you're okay?"

I nod quickly, hoping this will stifle the tears. It occurs to me that for the past few months my life has been a little like when people only style the front of their hair. The parts you can see in the mirror are great. The bangs are perfect, the pieces are lying just right at the shoulders. But in the back, it's a rat's nest. I've always wondered. Do they not know it's looking like hell back there? Well, now I know. The answer is: *they really don't know*.

"They haven't heard from him," Miguel says. "I take it you haven't, either?"

I nod again, harder this time. Then I realize that's probably the wrong answer, so I shake my head. "Yes, I haven't," I say. Then I'm laughing at how stupid I sound. I can't help it. It's funny. Miguel laughs, too. The heating and air-conditioning guy must think I'm ready for a nice white straitjacket and a forty-eight-hour hold in a psych ward.

"It's going to be okay. We're on schedule down here. I want you to know, I'm still one hundred percent in this. I believe in this restaurant. This location. You."

"Are you serious? But I'm a disaster."

"Temporarily." He smiles. "That'll pass. But this is a good project, Nicki. You shouldn't give up on it."

For one second, I feel like the luckiest woman in the world. People say terrible situations have a way of bringing out the best in people. Now I know what they're talking about. "Are you for real?"

"Let me show you what we've been up to." Miguel proceeds to show me the new kitchen, the floors, the ceilings, the storage, the refrigerators. It's a real restaurant.

"I figure we'll be ready to open in early December," he says.

"That's a little over a month from now!" I didn't think we would be ready so soon. Then again, I've had no idea what's going on here. This was all Jake's project.

"Yep," he says. Clearly, Miguel is proud of himself. He should be. It's amazing. "I hope you don't mind. I just used my best judgment on things."

"Oh my God, of course!" I can't believe he's apologizing to me for the fact that he made decisions while I was busy lying in bed feeling sorry for myself.

"Miguel, I'm so sorry," I say. "I'll get your investment back. I promise."

"I'm not worried about that," he says. "I'm just going to keep doing the work until it's done. This place is going to be great."

Maybe he isn't worried, but I sure as hell am.

# 12

RONNIE

It's been three days since I moved into Nicki's house, which makes three days total I've been living in a place where no one tells me when to wake up, shower, eat, take a shit, eat, work, eat, hang out, or sleep. The halfway house wasn't really freedom. It was prison in a crappy 1980s apartment building. Not that I'm done with the Oregon Residential Reentry Facility completely. I still have to check in once a month, and technically, I'm supposed to get a job, but like Melissa said, no one's really paying attention. As long as I don't commit a crime (which really means don't *get caught* committing a crime), I should be fine.

Right now I'm making Cody and Nicki my job. I've been waking up early, doing a full breakfast for them, packing Cody a lunch, then cleaning it all up while Nicki gets ready for work. I'm like a stay-at-home grandpa and I love it.

Nicki wanders into the kitchen every morning around 7:15. I've already got the milk foamed and I'm warming up her mug for a cappuccino from the Nespresso machine. Talk about changes since I went into prison—as far as I'm concerned, real espresso you can make in the privacy of your own kitchen is right up there with the invention of the cell phone.

"What time are you guys gonna be home tonight?" I usually plan dinner in the morning, then go shopping while Nicki and Cody are out. "I wanted to make something nice for dinner."

"You don't have to," Nicki says. "I was going to get takeout."

"No, I want to," I say. "I love cooking for you guys. After all those years of feeding the masses, making dinner for you and Cody is a walk in the park."

Nicki looks me up and down, with a wince on her face. "Are those the same clothes you were wearing yesterday?"

I only have two outfits, so the answer is yes. A pair of khaki pants issued by the halfway house, some jeans, a golf-type shirt, a crewneck sweater, and an insulated winter jacket Melissa gave me that had been left behind by some other inmate.

"You know what? Come on, get in the car. You're coming with me today," she says. "We're going shopping."

"You don't have to do that. I'll take the bus to Goodwill and pick some things up. I've been meaning to do it, I've just been so busy around here, that I—"

"Ronnie. Come on," she says. "I'm in a good mood, you should take advantage of it."

This is how Nicki has been since I moved in. She swings from warm to angry—sometimes inside the same hour. I knew it might be like this. That girl has been hurt a lot in her life—and by me! She wants to get close, but she's also afraid. The moment she feels nice toward me, she gets scared and chases me away, usually with her attitude, which can range from irritated to sarcastic or aggravated. It's textbook anxious attachment. Beth wasn't a stable mother. And like I said, your attachment style becomes the way you deal with closeness (or don't) for the rest of your life. People don't realize that.

Anyway, I just have to ride it out. Keep reassuring her that I'm here, I'm not going anywhere. Which won't change Nicki at her core, but she will calm down. Maybe start to trust me a little more. I can start by taking her up on her offer.

"Well, okay then. I'll say yes."

"Good. I'll be ready in five minutes. I just have a couple of phone calls to make for work."

Fifteen minutes later we're walking through the Lloyd Center shopping mall, on our way to get me some new clothes. It's early, so the place is just about empty. I see that there's still a skating rink in here, though. Nice that some things don't change.

"Sweetheart, I really appreciate this," I say. "I have a hundred dollars left over from the halfway house. You sure you don't want to go somewhere cheaper?" I really don't want her to think I'm taking advantage of her in any way.

"Don't be silly, keep it," she says. "I have money. You might as well have some halfway decent clothes. It's fine."

"This is like old times for us, huh?" Nicki and I used to go shopping on our Saturdays together when she was little. It was one of the few activities we could both enjoy in a town where it rains five months out of the year. She'd get new clothes and I'd flirt with the salesgirls.

"I guess," she says, making it clear she's not about to take any trips down memory lane.

We pass Nordstrom. "That place hasn't changed, has it?" I say.

"It's Nordstrom, so that's the whole point," Nicki says. "Good taste never changes."

The rest of the mall feels like walking through Vegas. Everything's so slick and sensational. Bells and whistles everywhere. It is brighter, louder, and sexier than I remember it. Several stores have photographs the size of walls. Another one has computers and is lit like a hospital. In every store window, the mannequins are very skinny and they all have nipples. *The mannequins have nipples?* Pointy, jutting out, it's-freezing-in-here nipples. I guess that's what it takes to get people's attention these days.

We head toward the middle of the mall. There's a really cute young girl handing out flyers in front of a store. I take one from her because pretty girls are fun to look at and I like taking an opportunity to talk to them. I'm not sure why Nicki considers that such a crime. "Why, thank you! You sure are pretty," I say to the girl. "What is this?"

She tells me about a sale they're having. Twenty percent off everything in the store. Nicki is standing there, impatient, wanting me to leave. But I think a good deal is a good deal. "Let's check it out," I say. "Twenty percent off? I know a good deal when I hear one."

"The whole store smells like Axe body spray," Nicki says. I don't know what she's talking about. "Teenage boy aftershave. They all wear it and it's suffocating. They're all like extras in a party scene."

I agree that this place smells really strong, and the lighting is very low. It's downright dark in here. Once my eyes adjust, I can see that all the kids who work here are hotties.

"You're not kidding," I say. "That guy's body looks like a forty-hour-a-week job."

"Can we leave?" Nicki's looking like she might throw a temper tantrum. "This is where Cody would shop."

"I'll just take a look," I say. "Maybe I can find something in here."

I head straight for a rack of sweaters, passing stuff for women on my way. "Check these out," I say. I hold up two button-down shirts with collars. One polka dot. The other plaid. "These are you, baby. Tell me these aren't Nicki Daniels."

Nicki looks at the shirts, up at me, and back at the shirts again, and the expression on her face is just like—and I mean *just like*—when she was a little girl and we would go shopping together . . .

*I pull up in front of Beth's house, and Nicki's in the window, waiting for me. She jumps up and disappears from the window. By the time I'm out of the car, she has the front door to the duplex apartment open, letting all the cold, damp air into the house. "Close that door," Beth says. "It's getting wet in here." But Nicki doesn't care. She's so excited. Every Saturday I pick her up at noon and we drive around in my brand-new 1983 Mercedes. We listen to the radio, drive around, go get lunch, usually over in North Portland. I bring her around to Dixie's and the Hi-Lite and all my stomping grounds. She's so cute. Everyone loves her. She's like my mascot, the most adorable five-year-old girl in the world. So smart, and she talks like a grown-up. "Hello, Mr. Mal!" she says. "Good afternoon, Miss Phyllis!" She just charms the dickens out of everyone.*

*Then we go shopping. I always take her to Nordstrom and buy her the expensive stuff. Nothing but the best for my little girl! On this particular day, I'm going to get her something special for Easter. "Pick out whatever you want," I say, "it's yours." Nicki takes forty-five minutes to decide which dress she wants. She is not fooling! This is her opportunity to get what she wants, and she is not going to waste it. The choice comes down to a lime green number with a velvet ribbon and a pink chiffon princess-looking thing. She's in love with the chiffon from the pink one, and she's in love with the velvet ribbon from the green one, and she's trying to hustle the saleslady into taking the green velvet ribbon and putting it on the chiffon dress. That's my little girl. Takin' after her daddy. She must stand there for ten minutes, trying to figure out how to get what she wants. But she doesn't plead, or cry, or beg. She appeals to logic. And when the saleslady says no, she goes back to thinking. There is only one way to solve this:*

*I buy them both.*

*We leave that store and Nicki is probably the happiest five-year-old girl in the world. This might be the most powerful thing I have ever done in my life to make Nicki happy. I've never felt so proud of myself. That day, I lived up to being a good dad.*

*I take her back home and she can't stop talking about the dresses and how she got them* both. *Of course, Beth looks at them, disgusted. The two dresses together probably cost half her month's rent. She says something under her breath about my need to be worshipped. That I'd rather put stars in the eyes of a little girl than put a roof over her head. And you know what? She was right. I was so full of ego. I did what made* me *feel good. Still, it made Nicki damn happy, much happier than paying the rent, so I didn't regret it.*

*Besides, neither of us knew that two months later I would catch my first major case. I wouldn't see Nicki again outside of prison until 1989.*

I snap out of the memory. Nicki is standing at the next rack over, flipping through shirts. She wants to make this quick. "Are you a large or an extra-large? Large." She pulls out a blue plaid and a green-checked shirt. "I like the button-down better. Preppy."

She holds the shirt up to my chest. "What do you think?"

This is the most loving gesture Nicki has made toward me since I got out. I feel like she's the parent and I'm the child and she's taking care of me. She wants me to have a nice shirt that's preppy. If I think about this for more than a second I might break down. So instead, I tease.

"How do my eyes look?" I'm teasing, but serious.

"Like you could get a date if you wanted one," she says, teasing back. "But not in here." She chuckles at her own statutory rape joke. I chuckle, too.

For one second, I feel accepted by her. One second.

Nicki's phone rings, a nice-sounding chime. Reminds me I have to put a little more work into my cell phone ring game. Mine's still on the one it came with in the package. It sounds like a children's toy piano. Everybody else has something custom. At some point I have to ask about how you do that.

"I have to take this," Nicki says, looking down at it. "Figure out what you want and I'll be right back in to pay for it. Before I file a class action suit against this place for lung poisoning from this god-awful smell."

"This is Nicki," she says into the phone. "Yep. Go ahead."

She smiles as she walks into the mall and I smile back. She's right, the smell in here is god-awful.

———

The next day, I'm napping in my room when I hear the front door open. I've been sleeping like a mofo since I got out of the halfway house. Every night nine hours, plus a nap during the day—it's like I'm catching up on everything I missed after sleeping with one eye open since 1998. My daytime naps are packed with dreams, all the unconscious stuff I guess I'm trying to process, so I'm groggy as hell. It takes me a long time to wake up.

The first thing I notice is a man's footsteps. Heavier, but not real heavy. Must be Cody—but somehow it doesn't really sound like him. I slide my feet onto the floor, and that's when I hear the voice.

"No, man, I'm just running a quick errand. I'll be over there in fifteen minutes. Yeah, bye."

*It's the boyfriend.*

Nicki hasn't told me much of anything about what is going on with this guy, but I already know this: he doesn't love her enough. I know that because if he did, she would look different. She would feel different. Taken care of. Relaxed. Because that's how women come across when they're being loved by a good man. But that's not what's happening here, and she doesn't seem to see it.

I have a theory. This guy, he's a restaurant manager, right? They don't make that much money. He probably sees her as an opportunity to get a life he wants without having to earn it himself. She's got money—I don't know how much, but it's enough to drive that particular car, pay for this nice house, and buy me shit like it's nothing. She's also generous—I saw that yesterday. She bought me probably a thousand dollars' worth of really nice clothes. Talking cashmere sweaters. She did not have to do that. But she did. She probably did it for this guy, too.

If he loved her, he'd be here. He'd want to know about her dad. He'd want to protect her from me, frankly. He'd make me prove to *him* that I'm good enough for her. And he's not doing any of that. Instead, he's coming into the house in the middle of the day when he thinks no one is home. I decide to just listen a minute.

Nicki mentioned they're investing in a restaurant together. She said the boyfriend put up a bunch of money. But something's off there. From hearing her talk, and she only said a sentence or two, I got that they're more connected over the new restaurant than anything else. And what about the house she said she's buying? Is he in on that? The other thing is, she didn't smile big when she spoke about him. She didn't talk about babies and gardens and lifetimes and sunsets. All of which tells me there's not enough love here.

I blame myself. Because, using a woman? Being logical about what a woman can do for you? That's me. That's how I am. And a girl's going to bond to men who offer the same kind of painful feelings as Daddy did. You know, the sins of the father. Nicki doesn't even know what "enough love" feels like. She probably thinks this is all the love there is to have.

I peek out through a crack in the door. I don't see anything, but I can hear him going through every drawer in the dining room, opening them, rummaging around, then closing them with a slam. He must have found what he's looking for because the sound just stopped and he's going into the bathroom and peeing. Clearly, he doesn't think anyone is here. Which means Nicki hasn't told him about me. Which means Nicki probably hasn't spoken to him at all. Hmmm. I quickly calculate whether it is more to my daughter's advantage to have me confront this asshole or not.

I decide not to. When in doubt, don't. At least not yet. Let's see what he does. If I stop him in the middle of whatever he's doing, he can lie about it. If I witness it and he doesn't know anyone's watching, I've got him dead to rights. Better to see what he's up to.

Jake comes back into the hallway; he's fifteen feet away, still with no idea that I'm here and can see him through the crack in the door. What is he doing? He looks sweaty, like his heart rate is up and he's filled with adrenaline. He goes to what looks like the towel closet and yanks the door open. He pulls a thousand towels out, reaching way in the back, just dropping them onto the floor.

When he brings his arm back, he's got a small bag, which he reaches into and pulls out a bunch of cash. There's a roll of money—a thousand dollars? Maybe even more. I'm surprised Nicki would keep that much money in the house. But it's smart; you never know when you'll need cash.

I consider again stepping out into the hallway and letting this guy know I'm watching him, but another even bigger thing tells me to be perfectly still. He shouldn't know I'm here. When I see him stuff the money into his jacket pocket, I'm *sure* he shouldn't know I'm watching him. He thinks he's alone and I have to let him think he is. Once he's got the money in his jacket, he reaches over and picks up the towels he spilled onto the floor and carefully folds them. Perfectly neat. Then he puts them back into the closet and closes the door.

And that's when I know this guy's not just in a hurry to get somewhere. He's leaving. And he's leaving for a while.

# 13

## NICKI

It's been a week now and we're actually settling into a routine. My alarm goes off every morning at 7:15 a.m., the last possible minute I can sleep until and still have enough time to get everything done and get Cody to school on time. I roll out of bed, put on my favorite cashmere robe, and head for the shower. On the way I stop by Cody's room to give him his first wake-up call.

"Boo? Wake up, pumpkin." I open the door slightly, and he shifts in bed. It's the world's most-often-repeated parent cliché, but it's true: *he's getting so big.* He's beyond "big," he's *grown.* A man is lying in Cody's bed, and every time I open his door to wake him up it freaks me out. Will I ever get used to it? Probably right about the time he leaves home—if that ever happens.

"Morning, baby!" Ronnie's already up and in the kitchen making breakfast. He gets up at crazy o'clock and does yoga or meditation or whatever it is that he does. Then he goes into the kitchen, and by 7:40, he never fails to have a plate of something warm and/or interesting for Cody and a really nice cappuccino for me. He's even figured out my foamer.

"Here you go, baby," he says. "Three shots, just like you like it."

"Thanks," I say. I'm reluctant to get used to this, but I must say, it's damn nice to have a wife. No wonder dudes have been so unwilling to give up the benefits of traditional marriage. That is some good shit. "You know you don't have to do this every morning."

"Are you kidding?" he says. "There's nothing in the world I would rather be doing in this moment than making you a cappuccino. And look what I made for Cody this morning. Nutella crepes!"

I'm starting to calm down just a little bit about having him in the house. At first I had my guard up every second, but not only am I starting to get used to having him around, he's been a huge help. He does laundry, he cleans, and he cooks all the meals. For a single mom who is overwhelmed at work, what is not to like?

"Code?" I hear Cody's footsteps come into the kitchen. He's really been pulling it together lately. He's up every morning on his own, showered and with his teeth brushed—which never used to happen. Not without me bringing in some kind of crane to lift him out of bed. I don't really want to give Ronnie credit for that, but no doubt some of it belongs to him.

"Morning, Mom. Morning, Ronnie."

"Grandson," Ronnie says. "Look what I made for you!"

Ronnie's very proud of his crepes, and I'm not even feeling bitchy about it. "That looks more like dessert than breakfast," I say. That's pretty tame for me, considering all the arrows I've been slinging Ronnie's way since he got here. Which, yes, I'm beginning to feel bad about.

"You have a test this morning, right, son?" Ronnie asks.

*He does?* I think to myself.

Ronnie knows more about Cody's schedule than I do. I'm not sure what they talk about in the afternoons before I get home from work, but they seem to be bonding. I don't ask, because I know Cody—if you call too much attention to something or praise him too much, he'll want to stop doing it. I'm just glad he's engaged in life. "What subject is it again?"

"Social studies."

"Ohhh! Wonderful! Isn't that great." Ronnie sounds like a first-grade schoolteacher. "And what's on the test? Do you have a study sheet or something? I'll help you with it. You're gonna ace this thing!"

Cody jumps up and grabs his backpack from the living room. He's back in a flash, pulling out his social studies notebook and flipping through it until he finds his review sheet, which is right where it should be in the pocket. Whoa. Whose child is this?

"Look at you, so prepared," Ronnie says. He's doing positive reinforcement without seeming all momlike—in other words, like I would be. I'd be all teachy and annoying. "Let me at this thing."

"I'm speechless," I say.

"Don't be speechless, Nicki," he says. There's a hint of admonishment in his voice. "Your boy is doing great work here. Very diligent, son," he says to Cody. I guess Ronnie's showing me how it's done. *Fine, then.*

Ronnie takes the sheet and gives it a once-over. "Should I just start anywhere? Or at the beginning? Never mind. Start with the civil rights movement. That's my era. Who is Malcolm X?" He pronounces this like he's a game show host.

Cody knows this one. He can't wait to answer it. "He's that radical hitter who was all badass and got killed."

"I like that," Ronnie says. "Yes, he was a radical hitter. As opposed to Martin, who was all about peaceful, nonviolent protest."

"What's a hitter?" I say, turning first to Cody, then to my dad. "And how do *you* know what a hitter is?"

Ronnie and Cody make meaningful eye contact. "Should we tell her?" Cody asks. Almost at the exact same time, they simultaneously shake their heads. "Nahhhh!"

"Trust me," Ronnie says to me, "you don't want to know."

"Oh, it's some prison thing?" I suddenly realize I'm not used to Cody having an ally against me. This is what it would have been like if he had a sibling. I'm outnumbered.

"Because then you're right. I probably don't want to know."

"Sort of," Ronnie says. "It's more of a rap music term. A hitter is a friend. One of your homies. It's a substitute for another word that can't be played on the radio."

Cody giggles.

"Okay, next question." Ronnie goes back to the review sheet. "Who is Louis Farrakhan?"

"The Nation of Islam?" Cody knows this one, too.

"Exactly right," Ronnie says. He gets a back-in-the-day look on his face. "You know, I went to New York one time with a buddy who knew a couple of Nation of Islam guys and we hung out with them."

"You did?"

"Sure did." Ronnie clears Cody's plate and puts it into the sink. "Those were the days."

"You know I want him to clear his own plate," I say.

"Tomorrow, he will. Right, Codes?"

"Right, hitter." Cody smiles. It's hard not to admit that they're pretty cute together.

My dad goes on with his story. "Farrakhan, he's got a *lot* of followers in the penitentiary. Guys in there love him. I always felt like he appeals to them because he's radical and orderly at the same time. Prisoners crave order, you know. They don't have any ability to self-regulate on the inside, so it ends up that the state gives it to them on the outside. You hear me, boy?" He musters a look toward Cody that might pass for stern. Ronnie's not much of a meanie, though. "The moral of the story is: regulate yourself, or the government will do it for you."

I hate saying it, but Ronnie *is* interesting. He knows a little about everything and a lot about a lot. For a guy who has spent most of his adult life locked up, he sure did make the most out of the time he had. He's got more stories to tell than most guys half his age.

"Oh shit. I just remembered," Cody says, grabbing a permission slip out of his backpack and a pen. "We have a field trip tomorrow. It's lame. Can you sign this thing for me?"

I go to reach for the piece of paper, but Cody has already handed it to my dad. *Well, then.*

"Sure, son." My dad takes the pen and scribbles his signature. "There you go."

I'm watching all this like they're aliens who just landed from a distant galaxy.

"I'm going to go grab my purse," I say. "Cody, pack it up. You have to be at school in fifteen minutes." I clomp back toward my room, because I always have to wear my noisy-ass clogs. And as I go I'm wondering: am I even needed here anymore?

———

Later that night I'm looking at new real estate listings on my computer when there's a knock on my bedroom door. It's not late, but as we go deeper into fall it's getting dark early and it makes me want to get in bed. I didn't even watch any home-flipping shows. (Am I okay?) At first I think it's Cody at the door, but he doesn't knock like that. Sometimes I forget there's a third person in the house. Jake worked such long hours—The Echo did a lot of liquor business, so he rarely got home before 1 or 1:30 a.m.—going to bed alone is normal. "Come in," I say.

Ronnie enters wearing the pajamas I got him at Nordstrom. I'm getting used to him in some ways, much faster than I would have thought, but times like this are still weird for me. Who is this grown man walking around in a robe? My dad being here is underlining a realization for me: I don't have the same relationship to men that other, better-fathered women have. They've always seemed sort of like aliens to me.

Maybe that's the reason I've always favored artsy philosophy majors,

guys who are more poet than lumberjack. Serious male energy (okay, sexuality) is scary to me. Or maybe overwhelming is more the word. This is not something I'm in a hurry to admit—Peaches would have a field day with it, for starters—but now that my dad is standing in the doorway of my room, it's really obvious. Men are too much for me. Their physicality. Their hair. Their muscle mass. They're just so sizable.

"Is it okay if I sit on this chair?" Ronnie says. He seems a little tentative. Since that first day, he hasn't come into my personal space. Maybe he's like me in reverse: he hasn't been around women for all these years. So I guess we have something in common.

"Sure." I put down my laptop and give him my attention, since it seems like he has an announcement. "Is something going on?" Then, jokingly, "Are you moving out?" The moment I say this, I realize I might actually be *sad* if he said yes. Now *that's* interesting.

Ronnie doesn't smile at all.

Uh-oh. Now I'm worried.

"Nicki, I have something to tell you," he begins with his head down, unable to look me in the eye. "And it's hard to say."

My stomach flips, but I don't say anything. I just wait. I can't imagine what he's about to say, and I don't want to.

"I was here this afternoon, and your boyfriend—"

"Wait. Jake?"

"That's his name, right." He snaps his fingers, remembering. "Yes, Jake."

"What about him?"

"He was here."

"Here?" I lean forward. "Are you kidding?"

"I was in my room, napping. And I heard the front door open. He must have his key, because I know I locked it, and when I heard the door open, something told me to sit still." Ronnie is speaking carefully. Slowly. "Then he came in and started going through drawers. Looking for something."

"Which drawers?"

"The ones in the dining room hutch?"

That's where I keep the passports. I hold on to both of them because we always travel together. The last time we used them was in April. We went to Vancouver, British Columbia, for a couple's weekend. We rode bikes around Stanley Park and ate sushi and had sex in our room on the eleventh floor of the Hyatt Regency. We had such a good time even though everything was in bloom and I had full-blown allergies. After a night when I sneezed nonstop, Jake offered to go to the pharmacy at seven in the morning to get me the only allergy medication that works because he wanted me to feel better. We were so in love. Or so I thought.

I try to make sense of what I'm hearing. I know my dad's not lying, but it seems incredibly hard to believe that Jake would be so bold as to come back here. "How is that possible? He told me he was—"

Ronnie continues. "Then he went to the hall closet."

My gut sinks.

"And he took out a roll of money."

"That's the emergency stash," I say.

"I figured."

"It's thirteen hundred dollars."

"It looked like real money. Anyway, when he was done—and Nicki, this is a really hard thing to say—" He stops himself.

"Just say it."

"He folded all the towels perfectly and put them back in the hall closet," he says.

He stops. "What?" I ask. I'm not sure why that's so damning.

"That's when I knew," he says.

"Knew what?"

"He's probably leaving for good."

"That's not true," I say. My voice is high-pitched. My throat is closing.

And I'm just now realizing Peaches was right. *I'm delusional.* "He said he just needed some time to figure things out."

"Baby," my dad says gently. "He didn't want you to know he was here. That's why he folded the towels so perfect. But the universe wanted you to know, so it put me here . . ."

I've stopped listening. I don't want to hear about the universe. The universe is causing my life to implode. Fuck that. My whole body is shutting down. I swivel my head toward the window and float off into the blank space outside. I can hear everything around me and I know where I am, but I just can't move. I'm like a computer that's asleep.

"Baby?"

"I think you should go," I say. I can hear that I sound robotic.

"Baby. You're slipping into a trauma state," Ronnie says. "I'm not going anywhere. Here, take my hand."

"Go away." I can't take his hand at all. I can't even move. All I can do is just stare out the window. Even though there's nothing to see. "I hate you."

"Baby, I'm so sorry. I'm so sorry this happened," he says. "And I'm so sorry I hurt you in the past. Beth and I really hurt you. We didn't do our jobs as parents and I know that affects you still."

*We didn't do our jobs as parents and I know that affects you still.*

When I was small, I spent a lot of time looking at clocks. Right now I know why. Because the clock was the only safe place to look. When things are going down around you, just look at the clock. It's like an island in the middle of chaos. The second hand sweeps around the face. You can get lost in it going around and around, and you're not afraid of anything. You don't feel anything.

"Baby, I'm sorry," Ronnie says. It's like he's speaking from another room, in another dimension.

"It's okay," I say. I have a singsong voice, like when I was little. "It's okay."

I know that girl's voice. When adults would talk to her, when they'd try to ask her questions, she'd be like, "*I don't know; it's okay; I don't know; it's okay.*" Like a bluebird was saying it.

Well, she did know. *I'm in danger. No one's taking care of me. Where's my mommy?* And it wasn't okay.

I look down, where Ronnie has taken my hand and is holding it. And even though I can't say anything, and can't acknowledge it, it feels good.

I almost feel safe.

I guess Jake's gone for good.

# 14

# RONNIE

It's time to get me a license. Because I was away for so long, I've got to start from scratch. Learner's permit first. Then the behind-the-wheel test. It's not like I forgot how to drive, but I've definitely forgotten the rules—not that I ever played by them. Since Cody's sixteen, and he needs one, too, I figured we could do it together. I went online and found some sample questions for the permit test, and now we're sitting in the kitchen, where I'm making some black beans from scratch and quizzing us both at the same time.

"When is it legal to cross a double yellow line? A) When you're entering a business. B) When you signal first. C) On weekends and other nonpeak traffic times. D) Never."

"D! Never!" Cody raises his hand like an A student.

"Let's see," I say. I click on the answer. "That's right! The answer is D, never." I drop my shoulders in exaggerated defeat. "You are going to crush me, player."

Cody grabs the laptop and slides it his way. I toss in the chopped onion and green pepper, along with a pinch of salt. "Okay, now it's my turn to ask you one," he says. "What should you do if you see a railroad crossing sign?"

"Run."

*"Ha-ha-ha-ha!"*

I love making Cody laugh. His whole face just explodes into a million pieces of sunshine. You know how people love to make babies laugh? It's like that. I might have missed his babyhood. But what I'm learning is that making a sixteen-year-old laugh is seriously fun, too.

"You're an idiot," he says.

"I know," I say. "Ask me another one."

"Okay. What does a flashing red light mean?"

"Same as a stop sign."

"Right!" He goes again right away. "The number one cause of rear-end crashes is . . ."

"Checking out women as you drive."

"Ha-ha-ha!" He's tearing up from laughing so hard. "You're so funny."

"I just like making you laugh," I say. I put a cover on the beans and turn the heat down to simmer. They are going to be *good*. I wish Nicki could see her son like this. I think she would lighten up. About him, and about me. "Let me ask you some now," I say, grabbing the laptop back. It slides on the marble countertop and we both wince in unison. "Ouch!"

I click the pad thing with my left index finger and drag my right finger down to get to the next question—a trick I only learned to do after ten full minutes of instruction by Cody. He notices that I'm really getting the hang of it.

"Look at you! Killing that track pad!" He gives me a pound. We do a lot of fist-bumping around here. It turns out hip-hop is the language of both teenagers and prisoners.

"Thass right," I say. "I'm catching up. You watch. Next I'm going to get one of those Instabooks like you have. Or whatever you call them." I know I'm saying Facebook/Instagram wrong, I just like to exaggerate how stupid I am about everything online. It cracks Cody up, and like I said, nothing makes me happier than to see him smile.

Cody shakes his head. "Just give me the next question," he says.

"Before you leave your vehicle parked on a downhill slope parallel to the curb, what should you do to prevent your vehicle from rolling downhill?"

"Don't know," he says.

"You turn your wheels. But which way?"

"In?"

"Yes!" I give him a little round of applause. "If you turn the wheels in, the car will jump the curb instead of rolling into traffic."

"Makes sense," Cody says, shutting the laptop. "I think we got it, don't you?"

"I think *you* got it. Me, I'm not so sure about."

"Let's just go take the test," he says with a quick nod. He's a little too confident, the way teenage boys are.

"Boy, you have no idea how that test is going to be."

"It's gonna be easy," he says, dismissing me. "Trust me."

"I like your confidence," I say. "But you've never had to deal with the government before. They don't make it easy."

"What's it like to deal drugs?" Cody says, out of nowhere. "Do you get a lot of money?"

"I'm not sure I should answer that, son."

"Why not? Come on," he says. "My mom's not here."

"You want to get a lot of money?" I ask.

"Hellz, yeah," he says.

I don't want to encourage Cody's questions about drug dealing. I know he's curious, because he thinks it's all badass. He's probably going around telling all his friends his grandpa's a real drug dealer. When I was a kid, that would have been something to brag about. But I don't want to lie to the kid, either, or he won't trust me. So I say, "Yes. You make a lot of money. But everything you make you end up losing, and then some."

"Because you have to do time?"

"*Do time?*" I laugh and clap my hands at him using that phrase. The things civilians say about prison crack me up. "Where do you hear this stuff?"

Cody blushes. "I don't know."

"Let me tell you, Cody. Dealing drugs is like an addiction. You do it once, you think it's cool. You think it's easy money, you got it under control. It's a high, no doubt about it. You feel on top of the world when you got a couple dozen bricks stashed in your hiding spot. Then pretty soon, what was working for you starts to work against you."

There came a time in my life where I couldn't stop selling drugs even if I wanted to. During my second bid in the penitentiary, I even sold drugs inside. I had all these women coming to visit me in prison, and some of the California gangbangers couldn't help but notice a business opportunity there. They set me up with an operation where I'd have a woman (they called them *hyenas*) smuggle the drugs in a little balloon she held in her mouth, which she'd transfer to me when we kissed at the end of the visit. They would do this for me because, not to be vulgar or anything, but women go crazy for the dick. Anyway, I ended up in The Hole more than once, but I was eager to prove myself in the joint and it worked. I got a reputation as a guy who could, as they say, "go hard." When I got released that time, I went right back to it on the outside. It was all I knew. It wasn't until I got caught that *third* time, and I lost Nicki and Cody as a result, that I was finally able to see what it had done to me.

"There are more important things than making a lot of money, boy," I say. "There's being of service. You got to figure out how your experiences in life can help other people. You have to find a way to make a difference in people's lives. That's what makes a happy life."

Cody gets quiet, like he's thinking this over.

"Don't worry. I'm not going to be a drug dealer," Cody says. "I already have money."

Out of the mouths of babes. *Of course!* Cody has no reason to take that kind of risk. Why would he do that? He lives in a nice house. He goes to a good school. He has health insurance and new clothes and food whenever he wants it. He's socialized. He hasn't spent his life fighting The Man. He practically *is* The Man. Unlike me, Cody sees himself as someone who is entitled to every good thing there is to have in this world. He's had life handed to him on a silver platter. Once upon a time I resented guys like him—guys who come from good neighborhoods and have mothers who love them, who've never had to fight for anything. They don't have a care in the world. Now it's the opposite. I'm relieved and grateful my grandson is one of those guys. Proud, too.

My daughter has done a helluva job with her life.

———

"Hey, Ronnie," Cody asks. "What's our stop?" Cody calls me Ronnie most of the time now. For the first couple of days he called me Hey, and then it was Grandpa, but eventually I just told him to use my regular name, and since then, he has. I'm not trying to be his friend, but the fact is, we're getting pretty good at chilling together. He sees me as a fun babysitter—not the kind who will smoke a joint with you, but the kind who takes care of you without having to be an authority figure all the time. Kids know when you're being trustworthy with your power.

All those years as a prisoner—you become an expert in power. You learn how to use it. How to misuse it. You figure out real quick that most of the people who want power—cops, wardens, guards, even teachers and principals and mayors—want it for the wrong reason. Mostly because they feel weak, or they used to feel weak, and now they're going to even the score. I know this is true because I spent years at the mercy of some overgrown children who are gonna kick ass or die tryin'. I don't ever want to use my power like that. I'm glad Cody knows that.

Right now we're taking the bus down to the DMV to get our permits. We're sitting toward the back. Cody's next to the window, and I'm on the aisle. As usual, I'm being my outgoing self. Making friends, and appreciating folks. That's just my way.

"Afternoon, Slim." I nod at a nice-looking girl who takes the seat across the way. She nods back.

"Did you just call that girl 'Slim'?" Cody looks at me like he's never heard such a thing.

"I said 'Good afternoon.' Nothing wrong with that."

"Then you said, 'Slim,'" he says.

I check out the girl again. She's wearing a pair of those jeans that are skintight. "She's slim," I say.

Cody laughs out loud. "You are so funny."

"What? I say hello to everyone," I say. Just then a girl with a mouth like that movie star who's always on the cover of the magazines in Nicki's bathroom heads toward us. "Like her. Hey, Lips," I say. "She's got a nice pair of lips."

Cody laughs again. He's shocked. Obviously he's never ridden the bus before with a red-blooded man.

"Next one is our stop," I say. "Pull the cord, son."

"There's no cord," Cody says. "You probably mean the button." He pushes the button and we get up together, surfing down the aisle as the bus pulls up to the corner.

"You got pretty good balance," I say. "You ever play sports?"

"Not really. You?"

"Not really. The ladies were more my thing." I decide now is as good a time as any to find out more about how Cody's coming along as a man. "How are you doing with the ladies? You break a piece off yet?"

Cody's face turns bright pink. It's pretty clear that no adult has ever asked him about sex before. He shakes his head. "Naw."

"Well, you will." I'm trying to reassure him.

"I won't lie," he says, "it sucks. I don't know how to talk to girls. They're weird."

*Ha!* I clap my hands. "It feels like that at first."

"All they talk about is makeup, and, like, astrology."

"Well, son. High school is about everybody doing things that everybody else will approve of. Things change for the better the older you get. You just keep doing you. The more you do you, the more girls will do you." *Ha!* "I'm joking, but it's true." I pat him on the shoulder. I don't want to make too big a deal out of this—I'll embarrass him. I feel for the kid. When I was his age, girls and hustling were the *only* things I understood. I couldn't have written a paper like he can, and I was surely never going to go to college. But everybody's got their struggles, so I relate. "I'll give you some pointers. Just hang with me. Watch and listen."

The bus stops and we step onto the sidewalk. The Department of Motor Vehicles is across the street. I push the button at the crosswalk light and wait.

"How's your mom doing? She say anything about me I should know?" Might as well pump this kid for some information.

Cody shakes his head. "We don't really talk about stuff like that."

"What kind of stuff do you guys talk about?"

"Not that much."

Cody looks up at me, like he's ready to see disappointment. He seems surprised I'm not giving him any.

"A guy can't always talk to his mom," I say. "A guy needs other guys to talk to." The light changes and we step into the crosswalk. "Women don't really understand what it means to be a man. And we men don't understand what it means to be a woman. The sooner you figure that out"— I smile—"the better." I find this very true, so I laugh. "*Ha!*"

"You always laugh and then you clap your hands," he says.

"Yes, son. I do. I like to think a good laugh keeps you young. Even if you have to crack your own self up." I clap my hands. "*Ha!* See? I'm doing it right now!"

I hold the door to the DMV open for Cody. Inside, the line is a hundred miles long. "Don't worry," I say. "I made an appointment. Stay with me."

"You made an appointment?" Cody's surprised his old granddad has the know-how to make an appointment.

"Sure did. Right here, son." I walk up to the window marked Appointments. Behind the counter is a clerk who's hot in that messy way I've been known to like. The kind with very long fingernails with decorations on them. I lean right up on her.

"Excuse me, miss. We'd like to apply for a learner's permit, please?" I say it in my Official Business Voice, the one I use when it's important to sound respectable. It works, too. Because the clerk-girl looks up from her screen, and when she does, I switch to flirting. "I like your nails. You did those yourself?"

"No, I had them done," she says. She's tilting her head, so I know she's feeling me, as the young guys in the pen used to say.

"But you picked out the flowers and the colors?"

"That was all me," she says, tugging at her hair.

"Well, it looks real good on you," I say. I wink at Cody. He needs to see what real game looks like.

"Thank you," she says in that tiny-voice way girls talk when they're liking you. Then she hands me a clipboard. "Have your son fill this out and take it to that window over there." She points to the other side of the room.

"Oh no," I say, "we need two of those. I'm getting a permit, too." I don't even bother to correct her about Cody not being my son. "That's right. Gonna get a license. Haven't had one in years." Then I answer the question she hasn't even asked yet. "I've been away."

"Two for you, then!" She giggles. She grabs another form and throws it under a clipboard. "Fill these out. Take a seat and wait for your number to be called." Then she leans over the counter, flashing some major boobage. "Tell you what, let me see if I can't bump you up a few numbers. How's that sound?"

"That sounds wonderful," I say, stealing a glance down her shirt. "Why, thank you."

She winks and sits back in her seat. "You have a great day, now."

"Wait a minute," Cody says as we walk away. He's trying to figure out what just happened. "Aren't you supposed to *hide* the fact that you're a grown-up who doesn't have a license?"

"Son, here's the thing," I say patiently. "Women love it when you show your vulnerabilities. They want you to be strong, *and* they want you to go after them, but if you're also *real* with them—then they are putty in your hands." I smooth my right hand into my left to show *putty*. "You gotta bring all three things to the game. Vulnerability, strength, and realness. Very important."

"So you took a threat," Cody says in that nerdy *let-me-get-this-straight* way guys like him talk, as if he's doing a math problem out loud, "and figured out how to use it to gain on your opponent. In this case, the opponent is that girl."

"Exactly."

Damn, the wheels are *spinning* for Cody. He's translating this whole women thing into terms he can understand.

"In Magic: The Gathering, we call that 'card advantage,'" he says, slicing the air with his palms to keep track of his point, "where you handle two of your opponents' threats with only *one* of your cards. In this case, you're trying to 'kill' the hot chick, by making yourself seem superconfident *and* coming clean about what would normally be a liability."

"I don't really know what you just said, boy, but you sound like you got it. Now add some swagger to all that smarts, and you're gonna have to fight the girls off with a stick!"

Cody looks pleased with himself as we take a seat on the hard plastic chairs to fill out the forms. There's a guy next to me who smells like body odor. Cody looks at me and waves his hand in front of his nose. We smirk together silently.

"*Daniels, window three.*" Our name comes over the loudspeaker. We've only been sitting here about two minutes.

"Damn, what did you say to her? That's us," he says. I give Cody a shove toward window 3. It's a male clerk this time and I can tell Cody's disappointed. He wanted more lessons in talking to women.

"You're the boy's father?" the clerk asks.

"Yes, sir. I am," I say. I know I'm lying in front of Cody, but life is too short to explain to all these people that I'm the boy's grandfather, not father. "I'm taking the test, too."

"I see that," the clerk says. "Get your booklet, study it for twenty minutes, then go to that window and get your test." The guy directs us to the far corner of the room.

"We already studied," Cody says. "We are going to crush it."

The guy looks at him, bored. "Well, study some more. Because you're going to be here a minute."

*Ha!* I clap my hands. "Over here, son." I lead Cody outside to where a bunch of guys are smoking cigarettes to the left of the door. "Hey, you got an extra smoke?"

"I didn't know you smoke," Cody says.

"I don't," I say. "Just sometimes."

I get a light off the other guy and inhale. "You got one for my son, here?"

Cody's not sure he wants one, but the guy shakes his pack and out pops a brown filter. He pulls it out.

"Go like this," I whisper. I demonstrate a proper holding technique. Between thumb and forefinger.

Cody leans in for a light, like I did. He inhales like a pro.

"Look at you," I say. "Guess you've been practicing."

"From time to time," Cody says, smiling. I'm starting to get this boy. Underneath all that quietness is a kid who's thinking a lot, who's really paying attention to things. He's a little bit of a punk, but funny as hell and good-hearted, too.

"It's nice for men to have a smoke once in a while," I say. "Just don't get addicted to this shit." I give him a stern look. "You promise me that."

"I won't," he says. Him promising me doesn't mean he won't get addicted, but it does mean he'll feel guilty about it if he does, and if he feels guilty, eventually he'll quit.

We sit and smoke and nod at other guys as they walk in and out of the building. Two dudes are talking about the Mariners. I don't give a shit about baseball, but it feels sort of good to just be here among all men again. Prison is good for that one thing at least. When you're in a world of all men, you don't notice any difference between the way you feel inside and what's going on outside. When women are around, it's not like that—you have to be aware of what you're saying and doing at all times. I bet you this is what Cody likes so much about his Magic game, and the card store.

I stub out my cigarette in the ashtray. "We should go back in. We got a test to pass."

We hear our name over the loudspeaker. "*Daniels. Window fourteen.*"

As we walk across the crowded room I watch Cody walking ahead of me. He's got a long stride—my long stride—but you can see all the young-man insecurity right there on the surface. I can see he's going to shape up into a really fine young man, though. As we make our way through the room, people look at us. They don't know that a month ago he hardly even knew my name and I was sitting in a jail cell.

I'm so grateful I get to show him what the world is like and help him grow into a good person. I thought I'd never have the chance to matter to another person ever again. I hope I never take that shit for granted.

The clerk outside the testing room directs us to a bank of computers lining the walls of the room. "Good luck, bro," Cody says as he takes his place in front of the computer he's been assigned.

"You, too," I say, slipping into the spot next to his. I have no doubt that Cody's going to pass. No doubt I'm going to pass, either. "See you in a few."

I glance out into the main room and think, as soon as we're done here, I'm going to try to get that clerk's phone number.

# 15

## NICKI

There's only one thing I love as much as real estate listings: the *New York Times* wedding announcements. When you think of it, the two things aren't so different. With the announcements, you click from couple to couple, checking out the pictures. Except instead of bedrooms, bathrooms, and square footage, the copy is all about alma maters, high-profile jobs, and prominent parents. With each one, I imagine what it would be like to be those two people, to be living their lives. I scrutinize their engagement photos, noting the micro-gestures in their faces, predicting where the marriage is going to run into trouble. Sometimes it's obvious. The girl will have a slight sneer, or the guy will have a cheating look in his eyes. It really makes you wonder—why would people put a picture in the *New York Times* (of all places) that reveals everything about them for the whole world to see? I guess they don't know we can see it.

By résumé alone, though, every couple in there is some form of perfect: high achieving, from good schools and good families. They fascinate me not just because they seem to have it all together—no accidental pregnancies here, folks—but also because if you look deeply you see a lot of patterns. Like: how many women marry a guy who has the same career as their dad. Like: how many men in their late twenties are willing to commit to women they met in their early twenties. Like: how many really pretty women marry guys who aren't even all that good-looking, but feel lucky as shit to be with such a beautiful girl from such a great family.

I can't help but think those are the really smart girls—they're going to be valued for the rest of their lives. I marvel at such women. The ones with the bouncy hair and nice teeth who grow up in Greenwich or Chappaqua and whose mothers are on the board of the gardening society and whose dads have a private otolaryngology practice in Manhattan. Is it any wonder a girl like that is getting married? No, it is not. She believes she is worth committing to, and not surprisingly, so does everyone else. And if you try to tell me that half of these couples will be divorced in ten years, I will cite you a story published elsewhere in the *Times* that says the divorce rate among the college educated is something like 11 percent. Eleven percent! Messed-up relationships are just one more indignity of being born to the wrong kind of people. Like me.

Anyway, I can and do kill one hour of my life every seven days reading about these people. I have a special love for the outliers: older couples, interracial couples, the couples who've obviously made (at some level) an arrangement—because don't try to tell me that the only person that Korean or Indian or Nigerian girl ever fell in love with was also Korean or Indian or Nigerian. I'm fascinated that these girls were able or willing to put the family first, the culture first.

Fascinated.

As if my parents could ever be so important that I would only marry someone they approved of. That these women do must mean their parents gave them so much—time, energy, resources—that to lose their approval and support would somehow make their lives less.

My parents have given me nothing I couldn't risk losing. Not only have my parents not really given me anything, they actually sort of took from what I already, or might have, had.

I'm almost done reading this week's announcements when Ronnie comes into the living room wearing jeans (which rarely happens) and an old T-shirt, which probably means he's been out in the garden at some point today. "What's happening, darling daughter?" he says.

I'm getting less annoyed by all the ways he sweet-talks me. At first I saw it as completely manipulative and irritating. Now I just see it as somewhat manipulative, while also understanding that he's actually sincere about it. There's a paradox to a lot of what Ronnie does. In this case, it's like in a dream, where there are two things going on at once. You know how you're at someone else's house, but it's really your house? Still, I know when he begins like this he's probably about to ask for something.

"Not much," I say. "Going to pick up Cody in a half hour. How are the roses doing?"

Ronnie has been spending every Sunday—even the rainy ones—out in the yard working on the roses. Apparently he's a jailhouse botanist on top of his jailhouse therapy practice, because he told me I've been doing my vintage climbing roses all wrong and walked all the way to the garden store and back to get what I needed to make it right.

"I'm bringing 'em back to where they need to be," he says, clearly disappointed in my gardening skills. "They'll get there. But it's a long road ahead."

I want to laugh. It's hard to tell if he's serious. But since he's almost always funny and laughing, and very rarely ironic, I'm going to go with yes. He's dead serious.

"Speaking of which, I wanted to ask you something," he says. "It's a favor."

We haven't been speaking of anything, but this is more of Ronnie's behavior. If he wants to bring something up, he pretends like you just said something related to what he wants to bring up. Like I said, irritating.

"You want money?" I say.

"Well . . ."

"I was wondering how long it would take you to ask."

"I'm not going to lie. Yes, I need money." Ronnie takes a breath. "You know I wouldn't ask you unless I absolutely had to."

I've been waiting for this moment to come since he moved in. It's one of the main conditions of his release that he find employment. I know because I looked it up on the Internet. But he hasn't mentioned it once. "Shouldn't you be getting a job?"

"I've been looking."

"Really? Not hard enough, obviously." That was mean, and I'm sorry I said it. I try to soften it a little. "I mean, I thought you got some money from that woman at the halfway house?"

It's always safe to assume Ronnie has a woman doing for him what he won't or can't do for himself.

"That was a onetime deal," he says. "Listen, Nicki. I was thinking we could work something out."

"Oh, you mean I pay you for doing what you're already doing around the house?" I can read my dad like a book.

I actually expected this, and I'm surprised it's taken him this long to ask. So I don't know why I'm making it seem to him like I'm upset. Because I'm not—upset I mean. I sort of think it's a good idea.

"Yeah. That's what I was thinking." He pauses. "I don't need much. Just enough for my cell phone and bus money."

"How much is that?" Something makes me feel like if he wants to ask me for money, I'm willing to give it to him, but I don't want to make it too easy. Because if I do that, he might try to take advantage. "Just give me the ballpark."

"A hundred bucks a week?" he says, eager to sell his case. "You know it's reasonable."

He's right, it's reasonable. I am the first to admit that Ronnie is doing an exceptional job of making up for lost time in the being-useful department. He's basically jumped right into the job of house manager—he's handling everything from laundry, to beds, to breakfast, lunch, dinner, and yard work. It's making my life so much easier I'm starting to not only enjoy having him here, I'm wondering what I'm going to do when he leaves. So why does the thought of giving him a hundred dollars a week feel like I'm losing something somehow? Maybe if I give it to him, I'll find out. Ronnie would call it a "contrary action." In other words, doing the opposite of what I feel like doing. Apparently it's a "spiritual practice." *Argh*.

"Fine. A hundred dollars a week," I say. "You can have it."

Ronnie stares at me for a good long ten seconds.

"Wow, look at you!" he says finally, all surprised and delighted about my contrary action. "You made that look easy, baby."

"No, don't look at me," I say. I'm not really even joking. "Please? It just makes it harder to do the right thing."

"Okay, yes, you're right," he says. He's got a sympathetic look on his face that says he knows it's hard for me to take this baby step toward him. "Thanks, sweetheart. Now," he says, "pick one, right or left?"

He wiggles his elbows in my direction and I notice that all this time he's had both hands behind his back. I roll my eyes. "Is this some sort of game?"

"Come on now, pick one!" He's got this big smile on his face—like this is the most fun he's had in years. I guess it probably is. "Play along, girl. You need to loosen up."

I know I need to relax more and go with the flow—I'm so type A, which I hate to admit is really just controlling—but it always feels just slightly infuriating. Like, here's my dad, of all people, standing in front of me in stupid jeans and a stupid T-shirt having just pruned all the roses outside in the drizzling rain and he wants to play a stupid game and I'm supposed to just goddamn go along with it? I know the answer is yes—I mean, if I want to have a dad. Which actually, I'm not sure I do, but anyway—

I know, I know—contrary action.

"You can do it, baby. You can do it!" He's reading me again; he intuitively knows what my inner struggle is, and he's trying to cheerlead me along—talking to me like I'm a kid attempting to go off a diving board for the first time, or ride without training wheels. "Pick one. Right or left?" He's wiggling his elbows so I can't see what's behind his back. "Riiiiiight? Or leeeeeeefffffft?"

"Fine!" I give in. "Left."

He holds out something polka-dotted. I hold it up at a random angle. "What is this?" As it falls open, I see exactly what it is. It's from Abercrombie, the shirt he picked out for me.

"It's a Nicki Daniels shirt!" He's beaming at me. "I got it when you went to make your phone call."

"Are you serious?" I say. "But you don't have any money."

"I stole it," he says with a grin. "*Kidding*."

I hit him on the arm—just pretending, of course. It's actually really sweet and thoughtful.

"It's going to look really cute on you, baby," he says. "Really cute."

He's right, it is really cute and something I would totally wear. "Thank you, Ronnie."

"You're welcome, daughter," he says. "Now I gotta go clean up. I'm a mess." He turns and heads toward his room.

I hold the shirt up again and smile to myself. I can't believe he bought me that fucking shirt. I wonder if this is what it feels like to be one of those girls from Chappaqua.

———

I'm in traffic a couple of days later when I get the call. Stop-and-go traffic, my least favorite kind. This is why I hate the freeway at low speeds. Because if you're not watching every second, the next thing you know, it's like—*crash*! This is sort of what it feels like to see Jake's number pop up on the car's computer screen. He's showing up right when I least expect it—which is to say, after my dad told me what happened. Right when I had finally accepted Jake was gone and had stopped expecting him to call.

So of course he calls.

On the other hand, I've been waiting for this moment the whole time, rehearsing what I was going to say, and now that it's here I'm not even sure I want to pick up the phone. *He doesn't deserve you*, is the first thing that pops into my mind. Just thinking that makes me so mad that the only way to discharge my anger is to punch yes on the Bluetooth.

"It's about time," I say. I notice that I'm wearing the polka-dotted shirt my dad got me. "Where have you been?"

"I'm sorry, Nicki."

"Well at least you're not pretending you didn't fuck up." I'm seething. I wasn't seething before, but now I am. Before I was sad. Now I'm seething. "So that's something."

"I know I fucked up. But, Nicki—"

"Seriously? Are you about to start explaining something? Because that's what you just sounded like. Like you're going to try to explain where you've been for the past three weeks."

"I *can* explain—"

"No, you can't," I say. "I know you came back into the house and took the emergency money. My dad was there, and he told me."

"Please," he says. "Just give me a chance. I can explain."

Everything about his tone of voice and the way he's talking makes it sound like he's a normal person trying to converse with another normal person on a normal day. As if he's been coming home every night for the past three weeks, eating dinner with me, fixing things around the house, cracking jokes, and having sex with me three times a week. It's like he's daring me to mention that he walked out of my life nineteen days ago without saying a word and I haven't heard from him since. He's probably hoping he can psychologically manipulate me into just forgetting it ever happened. Is that what he wants me to do? Because if that's what he wants, *I really want to set something on fire right now.*

"Are you *kidding*? You have to be kidding. There is no possible explanation, Jake." The car in front of me stops on short notice, forcing me to slam on the brakes. *I hate stop-and-go traffic.* "I shouldn't have answered the phone."

"Nicki, wait—"

"You're just going to use that regular tone of voice, like this is just some sort of, misunder*standing*? Like you—"

"Nick, please—"

"Like you just *forgot to come home*?"

"I can't talk to you if you're going to—"

"As if now you're calling to say you *just remembered*?" I can hear myself making a terrible wheezing noise that I hardly recognize as my own. "Oh my God, are you *serious*? I'm in escrow on a house because of you. On a house I *don't even want*!"

"Can't you cancel the escrow?"

As if I am in a frame of mind to answer any logistical questions, but no, I can't. The seller of the new house is refusing to let me out of the deal. All he has to do is sign a thing called a Cancellation of Escrow and I'd get back my deposit. But he won't. There's no good reason—I guess he feels like he has a buyer (me) and he doesn't want to have to go find another one. So I basically have two choices: go forward with the purchase of the house, or forfeit the thirty thousand dollars of earnest money I put down. Oh, there's a third option. I could sue—which would cost me fifteen thousand dollars in legal fees. And if I lose the lawsuit, I still forfeit the thirty grand, or have to go forward with buying the house.

I am screwed every which way. And it's all Jake's fault. So I'm screaming at him.

"*Are you insane?*" At the top of my lungs. "*Seriously? Are you that idiotic?*"

"Nicki. Listen to me! Please?"

He's pleading with me. I can hear it right there, tucked into an inflection deep in his voice, he's pleading with me. It almost makes me calm down slightly—from an 11 on the Rage scale to a 9.5. I've never heard a tone of pleading in his voice before. He's usually either large and in charge, or not talking at all. This sounds more like truly apologetic. I mean, for him.

"Please," he repeats, this time softer. It's enough to make me take a breath. "Please?"

"Okay, what." I'm not relenting, I just want to hear him out.

"I need you to know that I'm working something out. And I hope when I work it out, you'll understand. That's what I hope."

Why does he—right this very second—sound like the person I've been wanting him to be for the last eighteen months? Like the person he made it seem that he was in the very beginning, that I knew he could be all along: a reasonable guy who would sometimes go, "*Yeah, you're right,*" instead of a narcissist who thinks every time I try to offer another point of view I'm trying to "teach" him something.

Just like my mother.

Why would he start sounding like that *now*? After there's almost no way I can go back to Peaches—or Cody, or Ronnie, or Miguel, or *anyone*—with a straight face and say he made it all up to me and it's okay now, we're going ahead with our house, our relationship, our life together?

"I'm never taking you back," I say, totally aware that I want this to be true more than I know this to be true. "I have to move into a house I don't even want because of you."

"I'm not asking you to take me back, Nicki."

Remembering the house is all it takes to get me back in touch with my fury. Jake surely understands that you can't just cancel an escrow, not once you've removed the contingencies. It makes me sick to think of how much my miscalculation-slash-delusion-slash-fantasy about Jake is going to cost me. "I'm hanging up."

"Nicki, *wait.*" He sounds reasonable again. The way you would imagine Denzel Washington would sound if he was trying to convince you not to hang up.

"No," I say flatly. I'm on the ropes now and I don't like it. How did that happen? How come I feel like the unreasonable one now, the one who won't listen, the one who needs to calm down? This is what I can't deal with about Jake. It doesn't matter what's happening, I'm always off balance. "I don't want to hear it."

"Okay, I won't. But I want you to know that there *is* an explanation. And I want to give it to you eventually." He adds for good measure, "I promise that I will. I swear, Nicki. I'm still in love with you."

He says this with just enough certainty to make me want to hear him out. I'm thrust back into confusion—can I trust him, can I not trust him? An image of Dave Armstrong pops into my mind. He was my boyfriend freshman year of college—I dumped him for Gio—but the thing about Dave was, he was trustworthy. Not just I-won't-cheat-on-you trustworthy. He was, like, globally trustworthy. He brought you soup when you were sick, listened to your tears, listened to your *friend's* tears, and never put bros before hos. In fact, Dave had no bros of that type. Dave would take you home for Thanksgiving, remember your birthday, and bring you Peeps on Easter. You could *trust* Dave. He was *there*.

Unfortunately, I didn't really want to have sex with him.

I consider this the cruelest trick nature (or is it nurture?) has ever played on me. That I've never wanted to have sex with a truly excellent guy. I'm not saying I've never *had* sex with a truly excellent guy. I have. But a truly excellent guy has never rocked my world. It's like when it comes to men, I have two channels: ho-hum and sociopath. At first I thought Jake was a slightly more interesting and fashionable version of ho-hum. But underneath the flannel shirt and the *aw-shucks* demeanor, he turned out to be a slightly tamer version of sociopath. Which I should have known, because from the moment I met him, I really wanted to have sex with him.

Maybe I'm like the female version of those guys who only want to date strippers. They *wish* they could like nice girls they could bring home to

Mom—and they do like those girls for friends—but when it comes to sex, only a girl named Pandora or Savannah will do.

I feel tragically stuck. How come other girls get to be dying to have sex with a guy who'll come home every night for dinner? Who are these women? These *New York Times* wedding announcements–type women. And can they give me a stem-cell transplant? Because I feel utterly, totally, and completely screwed. No pun intended.

"Nicki? Nicki? Are you there?" I can hear Jake asking if I'm here—it feels good for a second to make him wonder. I want to say to him *fuck you, buddy.*

But I know the deal: to engage with Jake will only open the door to him again. Arguing with Jake is like eating potato chips—the moment you eat that first one, there is no possible way to stop. You just want to feel that crunch between your teeth and that impossibly flavorful vegetable fat and salt coat your mouth *one more time.* Even though you know it's terrible for you. There's something sick about knowing a thing is bad for you and doing it anyway. When I argue with Jake, I just want to say one more thing, just one more thing, until three hours have passed and I feel sick and lonely and desperate. And I don't want to do that now.

So I quietly hang up the phone without saying a word.

Let him wonder.

I just wish I wasn't wondering, too.

# 16

## RONNIE

"You have to push the button, I think," Cody says. We're sitting in Nicki's very fancy car, getting ready for our first driving lesson. Trouble is, I haven't driven a car in almost twenty years. Good thing Cody's been paying attention. He points to a spot on the dashboard. "It's right there by the steering wheel."

I push the button, but nothing happens. "Nada."

"No, you have to do the brake first," he says, "then push the button. So you don't accidentally start the car."

"You mean like this?" I step on the brake then push the button in the dashboard and boom! The car comes to life. It's a really nice purr, too. My daughter got herself a nice ride. "Nice."

Nicki is out with her friend for the afternoon, and I have decided to take the liberty of teaching my grandson to drive.

"You're really going to let me drive my mom's car?"

"Of course I am," I say. "Why wouldn't I?"

"Because it's really expensive." I like that he's an honest kid, basically telling me his mom would never approve. "My mom wouldn't let me do this. She said she's going to get me a really ghetto car and let me practice on that."

"Well, that's not a bad idea she's got there." I wave it off with my hand. "But it's just a car, and you're starting driving lessons *now*. With me."

I roll out of the driveway and back to a stop. It's one of those rare sunny days in mid-November, before the rain comes for its annual six-month visit. Driving toward Southeast Thirty-Seventh reminds me of Melissa and the first night I came up this street. That was a lifetime ago. Now that I'm thinking of her, I almost miss that girl. I really should give her a call.

"Okay, get out," I say, opening my car door. "Your turn to drive."

"Here?" Cody has a shit-eating grin on his face. This is probably the best day of his life.

"Yeah, here." I'm already walking around the front of the car. I open Cody's door and stand there. "C'mon. Get out."

"Aren't we supposed to go to the mall parking lot or something?"

"I believe in sink or swim, young man," I say. "The old-fashioned way. You either got it, or you get it. In a hurry."

Cody scrambles out of his seat, runs around the car, and settles into the driver's seat. I push backward on my seat adjuster. At least I know where it is now.

"You know what to do," I say. "You've been watching people do this your whole life. You've been playing those video games. You've been riding your bike. You're just going to do what you already know how to do. But really, really carefully." I smile, and he starts the car.

This is going to be fun.

He pulls away from the curb but guns it a little too hard. "Sorry," he says, sheepish.

"No problem," I say. "That type of thing happens at first. You don't know your own power. Your car's power." I point toward the end of the block. "Just go down to that light and take a right. Start slow."

He pushes down on the gas.

"Uht, uht, uht," I say. "On a residential street like this one? You don't really need much in the way of accelerating. Mostly, you're gonna coast."

"Got it."

He pushes down on the gas again, makes it to the end of the block, and comes to a stop at the red light.

"Now you need to signal. Take that thing on your left there—"

He's already got it.

"Good work, boy."

"Can we listen to the radio?"

"Maybe once you're going." The light turns green and Cody takes a right, steering too hard and heading for the curb.

*"Stop!"*

He slams on the brakes, which lock up. We look at each other. He thinks he might be in trouble. "Shit."

"You'll get the hang of it," I say.

"Whoa. Did I almost crash?"

"Naw, not really," I say. "Just go forward."

We start moving again. Cody's got the car on a nice forward motion. When I'm sure he's got the hang of it, I give him the next set of directions. "So when you get onto Thirty-Seventh, just go straight for a long way. Don't think about any turns or lane changes or anything. Just get used to being behind the wheel, and being in the flow of traffic."

"I got it."

"You don't need to turn hard. A little bit will do it. Then you just let go of the wheel and it'll"—I mime steering with the heel of my hand—"go right back to where it's supposed to go. You'll see."

We come to a red light. Cody hits the brake kind of hard. "Gentle, son."

"The brakes happen so fast," he says.

"You'll get used to it. You're doing great."

The light turns green again. "It's green, boy."

Cody takes off nice and smooth. "Very nice!" I say. "You're getting this." He smiles, proud of himself. I flip on the radio. "You got any hip-hop?"

"I think it's number four," he says. "On the buttons."

I push number four and it's one of those fools talking about *money on the floor* or some shit like that. "This is a whole song about strip clubs?" I say. "In my day, there was romance. We had Teddy. And Luther." Cody doesn't say anything. "Don't you want to know who Teddy is? And Luther?"

"Not really."

I laugh out loud. *Ha!* Then I clap.

"Do you always have to clap when you laugh?" He's deadpan, face as straight as a board, which makes me laugh even harder.

"We've been over this," I say. "The answer is: yes, I do. When something's funny, I laugh." I clap, again. "And then I clap."

Cody stares straight ahead. Then he takes a right turn, even though I told him not to.

———

I'm not supposed to associate with my old associates. But I don't consider a brief visit "associating." I consider it being in the old neighborhood and dropping in to say hello. Cody and I had to drive the car somewhere, so I figured, why not here? It's almost like the car drove itself.

The Hi-Lite looks the same as ever. We walk in and there's Mal behind the bar, pretty much right where I left him. "Good to know some things around here haven't changed," I say. Mal's got more gray hair than he used to, but he's still the same curmudgeon.

"Well, look who's here. Ronnie Daniels! Hell musta froze over. I thought I'd *never* see this day."

"Me neither, man." We give a big half hug and a high five. "Me, neither. This is my grandson, Cody."

"Nice to meet you, Cody," he says. Then he looks me up and down, shaking his head. "Mm, mm, mmm. You just get out?"

"Little while now," I say. "Seventeen long ones, man."

"That's some *time*."

"It sure is."

"You see DJ in there? I heard he was up there at Sheridan."

"Yeah, man. We didn't see each other but once or twice. They don't like you having friends in there they didn't introduce you to."

"I know that's right." Mal's really checking me out. "Can I get you something, Cody? A Coke? How about you, Ronnie?"

Cody shrugs and nods. Mal gets out a highball glass and presses the nozzle on the gun until it's filled. He throws down a napkin and slides it across the bar toward Cody. Probably his first real bar drink. Even though there's no alcohol in it.

"Nothing for me, man. Maybe a soda water," I say. "I don't fux with alcohol. That shit ages you. And I like to look *good*." I wink at Cody. I know he'll like the proper use of the latest slang phrase *fux with*.

"Well you always did. And you still do."

"Thank you."

"And what about Beth? How's she? You see her still?"

People out on the street still associate me with Beth. At one point in the early eighties, we were the golden couple of North Portland. She looked like a movie star—long legs, great smile, long, curly hair—and carried herself like the beauty pageant contestant she once was. One time we flew down to LA for the weekend; people couldn't stop staring at her. One guy even asked for her autograph. Thing is, Beth was beautiful, but she was as down for the life as anybody I ever met, too. Maybe because she was from a small town in Eastern Oregon. Maybe because her dad couldn't hold a job. Maybe because her mom ate too much. Who knows? But Beth couldn't wait to turn a trick or do a line or run a game. She couldn't wait to hustle some dumb businessman out of a few thousand. She couldn't wait to get down with another girl. And all that made her perfect for me, because I couldn't wait to do that shit, either.

But after Beth gave birth to Nicki things changed. I knew they wouldn't be able to stay the way they were, because we were buck wild bats out of hell. But to be perfectly honest, I thought Beth would change into a good mother, and I would keep doing what I was doing. Instead, Beth took care of the baby, but her heart never really seemed in it. It seemed more like she was taking care of her baby because she was doing the right thing, not because she was done being buck wild. It always felt like she missed the life.

For a while, until I got my second conviction, she went back to it. We had this con where we would drive to a small town, and Beth would post up in a bar somewhere. We'd use her as the honeypot to attract a rich old rancher, always married. She'd take him to a nearby hotel room, sex his brains out, and once she hooked him, she would ask for a loan of fifteen thousand dollars for an emergency, or an investment, or her kid, or some other urgent situation. The detail would just depend on the mark's weak spot. He'd give it to her, and she'd go back to servicing him with the best sex of the guy's life, and when the appointed time came to return the money, we'd be *gone*. Presto! In and out of there in a week, and we'd walk away with a year's rent.

I didn't think Beth would ever settle down. But I heard through friends not long after I started my third bid in the joint that she met some kind of rich guy, a banker or something, got married, and went Junior League. I had a good laugh over that one. Because I know Beth and I know that the last thing in the whole world she would ever want to do is bed down with some wrinkly old fart in a suit. Nope. Beth is just committed to the long con. She always did have more patience than me.

Aw, Beth. When I think of her, I still get a flutter in my heart. She was my equal. Maybe the only woman I ever truly loved. Together, we were unstoppable. We were so famous in North Portland that Mal Martin is *still* talking about us—thirty-five years later.

"No, man. I haven't talked to her in years. She went straight anyway. Last I heard."

I tried to write Beth once or twice from the joint, but she sent those letters back Return to Sender. She didn't want a thing to do with me.

"Mm-hmm," Mal says. He's seen it all from behind this bar. "We gettin' old, all right."

"Too old," I say. There. I told him. "Too old" is code for, *I'm just here for a visit.* I'm not here to do any business—as if bringing a teenager down here didn't say that loud and clear already.

"Cody, what are you doin' hanging out with an old fart like Ronnie Daniels?" Mal says. "Isn't he boring you to death?"

"He's okay," Cody says, a little bashful, but playing along with the joke. "He lets me drive, so . . ."

Cody doesn't even take his eyes off the bar, swiveling back and forth on the bar stool. Nicki would probably shit if she knew I took him down here, but I say it's good for him. Boy is soft. He needs some exposure. Anyway, nothing's going on here—not really.

"You're a good-lookin' son of a gun," Mal says. "Nice work, Ronnie."

Mal is genuinely happy for me. He might be an old-school Portland go-between in the drug world—but he cares. This is what people don't get about people who commit crimes. We're just like regular people.

"And how's your daughter? She was a cute little thing," Mal chuckles. As my sidekick, Nicki had fans from one side of Northeast Alberta to the other.

"She got a real estate–type company she owns. I'm staying with her. Things are real nice. Getting to spend a lot of time with my grandson here," I say. "Like he said, teaching him to drive."

"Oh yeah?" Mal directs another question at Cody. "What kind of ride you sporting, young man?"

Cody dares to take his head out of his Coke and make eye contact with Mal. "My mom's BMW," he says.

"We're not going to tell her that, are we?" I say. *Ha!* "In fact, we better get going if we want to get that car home before she finds out we took it for a spin."

Cody whispers in my ear that he needs to use the bathroom and I point him in the direction of the men's room. He gets up off the bar stool, and the moment he's gone Mal leans across the bar and asks me point-blank if I'm wanting any action.

"So you sure you're not interested in a little something?" Mal says. I guess I can't blame Mal for asking. It's hard for people to believe it when the life of the party says he's leaving before midnight.

"Why, you got a hookup?" I'm asking this more out of habit, I guess. It's hard not to be just a little bit curious.

Mal wipes the bar in front of me. "You really wanna know?"

I know what he's asking. I take a swig of my water. "Not really. I just came here to say hello to my old friend Mal. See what's up. You know. Show my grandson my old stomping grounds."

Cody returns from the bathroom. "You ready, Freddie?" I say.

"Sometimes you get in the car for bread," Mal says, "and you end up getting a fifth of whiskey. If you know what I mean."

"I gotchu," I say. It's really time to go now. "Let's do this, Cody. You take care, Mal. And if you see anyone from the crew, give 'em my regards."

"Will do," he says. He knocks on the bar twice, the universal sign for acknowledging a tip—even though I didn't give him one. I down the rest of my soda water in one gulp.

I gotta get out of here.

I drive the car home, and while I'm cruising down the road, the thought enters my mind that one deal would give me the kind of money I'd need to help Nicki with her escrow situation. I could pay back the money she'd lose on the deposit without even thinking about it. And have something left over for myself. Not that me solving her problem would make up for all the lost years between us.

But you never know. It might help.

# 17

# NICKI

How is it that all I had to do was step across the threshold of a two-story colonial and instantly I'm able to breathe again? I don't recognize the agent (thank God), a good-looking guy, older than me, but sexy in a twinkly, gray-haired, blue-eyed, J. Crew sort of way. *Gray Crew, ha-ha,* I think.

"You're hot," Peaches says to him, like she just found a dollar bill on the floor.

We're supposed to be getting our nails done, even though it's only Tuesday. I needed an emergency session, because I still own a restaurant I have no idea what to do with, I'm still buying a house I don't really want, and my long-lost dad has become my wife. At least my son is going to school every day, and he's putting together two or three sentences *in a row*—which he's never really done before—so I can't say it's all bad.

"You been looking long?" The agent is twinkling straight at me. Normally I find it easy to ignore such overtures, but right this second, it actually feels nice. I could use a new fan, even if it's just for the next ten minutes. Of course Peaches jumps in. She can't help grabbing all the attention for herself, that's just her way.

"Oh, we're not together," she says to the agent. "If that's what you were thinking."

It's obvious he wasn't thinking that, but this is how Peaches flirts: she suggests something sexual out of whatever it is you just said—whether it was sexual or not. Then she touches your arm.

"We're just stopping by," I say. I give the agent an apologetic glance. Gray Crew twinkles some more. I'm hardly going to tell this guy I'm already in escrow on something and that, in fact, I've already removed the final contingency, despite having been left by my boyfriend, not to mention the shocking and unwelcome appearance of my incarcerated father at my doorstep. I can't tell him that. So I just say something benign. "We're neighbors. We saw the sign."

Peaches wants more eye contact and face time with Gray, so she mounts an explanation no one asked for or cares about. "This is what she does to relax," she says, meaning me. "Goes to open houses. We're supposed to be getting our nails done right now."

"He doesn't need to know that, Peaches."

That gets Gray's attention. "Your name is Peaches?" Yes, her name is Peaches. This is an exchange I've had four million times in the years I've been friends with Peaches. Someone overhears me saying her name and the next thing I know, she's taking her clothes off. Not quite that dramatic, but almost.

In this case, the guy's doing me a favor, though. Secure in the knowledge that Peaches has now found something to occupy her attention—such is the life of an emotional toddler—I wander toward the dining room, a boxy affair that has good light and the kind of six-over-one original windows any die-hard real estate lover can appreciate, whether or not a Monterey Colonial is your personal jam. Nothing, but nothing turns me on like original glass. Okay, chevron parquet floors turn me on like original glass, but those are usually in Paris, so forget it.

There is something about disappearing into someone else's kitchen, bedroom, bathroom, and guest bedroom that takes me further and further away from myself—or maybe it's just further from the painful parts. I can lose myself in someone else's family photos, someone else's wall coverings, someone else's choice of hand soap. By the way, who paints a bathroom the color of wet cement? It's hideous and it's making me look even more washed-out than I already am.

For the moment, at least, I don't want to have to think about my life, and now I don't have to.

"Let's go," Peaches says. Gray Crew has moved on to some other potential clients, a young couple who clearly have the kind of jobs where you don't have to wear a name tag. "I'm bored," she says. Right, because if she doesn't have some sort of plaything to occupy her attention, she's bored.

We say good-bye—I wave extra-cute on my way out, because that was flattering—and we head for the car.

"When are you gonna have me over to meet your dad?"

"Never."

"I was thinking you should have Thanksgiving dinner."

"Are you going to make the turkey?" I say, knowing that would never happen.

"I will if you want me to," she says. "But I don't think you want me to."

I start the car and pull away from the curb. "You still have time for nails?"

"Absolutely," Peaches says, going back to Thanksgiving dinner. "What about your dad? Make him cook it."

"Oh, he'd be the happiest man on the planet," I say. "But I don't know if I'm ready to be that nice to him."

"You're such a punisher," she says.

"No, I'm not. But if you had a dad who disappeared on you seventeen years ago, you might go slow, too," I say. "I think I'm being an extremely nice person even just to let him stay at my house."

"Yeah, you're right. If I had a dad, I might."

Peaches has a dad, but he's lived in California our whole lives. "I'm sorry, I wasn't thinking." I can be really self-centered sometimes. "I'm just trying to say that I don't have to fling open the doors to my heart just because Ronnie Daniels needs a place to stay or he'll go back to jail. Let him earn it."

"He could always earn it by cooking," she says. Then pops a bubble with her gum.

Maybe. Last Thanksgiving Cody, Jake, and I ate dinner at a friend of Jake's house. It was all restaurant people, so the wine list was amazing, but the gathering lacked any sense of family, or for that matter, soul. I knew it was time to leave when I got the feeling that people were doing coke in the bathroom. Some restaurant people—especially the ones who work at cool places like The Echo—are like that. It's just part of the culture.

"Perfect! It's done, then!" Peaches flips down the mirror and starts digging through my makeup stash, refreshing her lips and eyes. "I'll bring the tequila."

"Maybe, Peaches. I'm not committing to that. But I'll think about it." She's destroying my favorite brown eyeliner, dragging it across her lower lid like the former goth girl that she is. "Could you go easy on that thing? It was expensive."

"Damn! Calm down, sis." She plugs the cap back on the pencil and puts it away. "It's just an eye pencil."

"Yeah, but it's my favorite one," I say. It can be really hard for Peaches to care about something as much as you do. If you point something out to her that she's doing, she feels so bad she has to keep doing it. If that makes sense.

Peaches looks at me. "You're right. And you've been having a really hard time lately. I'm sorry."

Now I look at her. "Are you serious?" It's not like her to just drop something. She usually has to tug at it for a while. Fight about it. She's scrappy.

"Of course I'm serious."

"Because for a second there it sounded like you were making fun of me."

"I'm not making fun of you," she says, with a heavy emphasis on the *youuuuuu*. Everything Peaches says sounds like a pit bull is saying it. "I'm worried about you. Your life is falling apart."

"Thanks a lot," I say. It's true, though. My life *is* falling apart. "Jake called me."

"Of course he did," Peaches says. "Let me guess, there's some kind of explanation. Please don't tell me you're buying it, Nick."

"I'm *not!*" Oof. That was a little too much protest. "I mean, I'm not. Really. Trust me."

She eyes me. "You know what you should do?"

"What?"

"Start dating."

"Oh please." Dating is possibly the last thing I need to do right now. It would be down there with having another baby and starting a third business. "It's only been ten minutes since I was buying a house with someone."

"So? Where is that someone now? You know what they say: the fastest way to get over someone is to get under someone else."

"Who says that?"

"Sexy people." She's grinning while wiggling in her seat. "You know."

"I'm not a sexy person," I say. I personally think I'm sexy, but I know Peaches doesn't, so sometimes I like to play into her version of me. Because compared to her, I'm not.

"You could be, though. You're just afraid to go there."

Peaches thinks sex is the solution to everything. "There's more to life than sex," I say.

"Just think about it," she says, checking her lipstick. "It's a good idea."

It's definitely not.

"I think maybe you have a hard time letting people in, Nicki," she says. She really thinks she's having some kind of insight here. Which is annoying. "You don't want to get close."

"Those are called boundaries, Peaches," I say. "You wouldn't know anything about it."

"You call them boundaries, but we all know what they really are—you're a scaredy-cat. You're scared."

"I'm not scared." I say this like *skeered*. I'm making fun of her idea that just because I don't have sex with strangers I'm a scaredy-cat. "I let you in."

"That's different," she says. "Because I'm awesome." She does her little booty dance in her seat and laughs out loud. "No, but really. I'm all that's left. Everyone else you kick out." Then, like she knows what I'm about to say: "Cody doesn't count."

"Jake left all on his own," I say. "I didn't kick him out."

"I think if you look real close, Nicki, you made him leave." She's so damn certain of what she's saying right now. She's got this smug look of, *mm-hmmm*. Ugh. I want to wipe it right off her face.

"Whatever, Peaches. Just because you'll let anyone set up a tent in your life. Look around. I have two businesses, I'm a college grad, I'm a good mother, I own a home, and I did all that—*by myself*. I'm comfortable with my choices."

Every once in a while I have to say something like this to remind Peaches that our lives are not equal. Even when it's in a shambles, my life is a palatial estate compared to her one-room shack. I use this fact as proof of why I don't need to listen to her, why her instincts suck, and why my way of living is better than hers—because it results in a better life. *Obviously*. Sure, I know no one's life is *actually* better than anyone else's—we're all right where we're supposed to be, blah blah blah—but I'd way rather be where I am than where Peaches is.

"Wow, Nicki," Peaches says. "You're not a true bitch very often, but when you are, you *bring* it."

"Can we please just go get our nails done?" I want to put my feet in soapy water and have a chair be my boyfriend for an hour. Hold me and make me feel safe. "Please?"

"Yes, we can. But you have to tell me what Jake said. Every second of it."

"He—"

"Is this the *very* beginning?" She wants every single detail.

"Okay. First off, I was on my way home from work." I pull into a parking space outside Nail Station. "Be careful getting out, I don't want you to scratch my car door again."

"Fine," she says. She throws open her car door, even though I just told her to be careful. "Then what happened?"

"I answered it."

"*Shit,*" she says.

"And right away, he sounded sad. I can't explain it. He just sounded . . . the way I've always wanted him to sound."

My mind floats back to the first time Jake said he loved me.

*We're sitting on the sofa after dinner, drinking cabernet, talking about the Oregon coast. We both agree it's one of the most special places in the world. "I would love to take you there, Nicki."*

*Jake sets his glass down, takes my hands in his, inhales deeply. I have to stifle a nervous smile, because I know he's coming close to telling me he loves me, and as much as I long to hear him say those three little words, it also makes me feel exquisitely vulnerable to look into his eyes and let him really see into mine.*

*"You know, when I was younger," he says, "I used to wonder what it would feel like."*

*He stops. I'm not sure whether I should prompt him, or not. I decide I should. "What what would feel like?"*

*He looks almost misty. "Falling in love," he says. "I never knew."*

*I've never had a guy say something like this to me before. Usually, they just say it, "I love you," then I say it back, and from that moment on, you say it to each other all the time. Not really that big a deal. More like a relationship milestone that you just have to get out of the way, like cutting your toenails in front of each other. But this is different. Jake is saying he's never been in love before. At all. With anyone.*

*Except me.*

*Very quietly, I say: "It feels like this."*

*"I love you, Nicki."*

*He leans over and kisses me. Then he squeezes me and pulls me close, right on top of him. As I'm lying there, I can feel him starting to want me. His hands drop down to my ass, which he touches exactly the way I like. "I'm really turned on all of a sudden," he says, laughing.*

*We lie there and just look at each other. He gazes at me with his dark brown eyes like no one has ever gazed at me before. Like I'm everything.*

*There's nothing like the feeling when Jake focuses all his love on me like this. It's the same feeling as trying on a dress in a particularly good dressing room, where the lights are warm and bright and the mirror is slanted at an angle that makes you look especially skinny. In this particular light, in this particular mirror, you can see yourself not just wearing the dress, you see where you're going to wear it, and all the people you're going to be with, you see the glass of wine you're going to be holding, you see yourself drinking it. You're in Napa somewhere, or Malibu, or Italy, one of those places where people drink wine wearing dresses like this one.*

*And you want that life, you know it's meant for you, you want it so much the next thing you know you're opening your wallet and handing over your card and the girl behind the counter is asking, "Debit or credit?" And it takes you a second to realize, you're not really sure. All you know is: you want that dress. And you're willing to do what it takes to get it. No matter what it costs.*

*"I love you, too."*

Now that I think back on this, I realize that I did have a sense that Jake might not be able to live up to the big experience he was trying to have with me. I couldn't have named it at the time, but it was there, right at the very beginning.

"Get to the point," Peaches says, impatient. "What in God's name did he have to say?"

"Well, he said there's an explanation," I say, coming back into the moment. "So you were right."

"Okay, I'm worried again." She scowls. Her face is like an EKG, going up and down according to whether she thinks what I'm saying is leading me toward Jake, or away. She really doesn't want me to be with him. But like I said, she always feels like that about my boyfriends.

"No, wait," I say. "I hung up on him."

"Really?" The little needle on the EKG shoots up. Peaches is all excited. "That's my *girl*. You hung up on him? Did you tell him you were going to hang up on him, or did you just do it? Or did you do that thing where you pretend it's a cell phone problem and you're losing them, *You're cutting out!* and then, boom! They're gone as fuck."

I laugh. "I hung up on him without saying a word. I just got really sleepy all of a sudden, and didn't want to hear another word from him, so I just clicked the button and he was gone. Like that." I'm actually feeling pretty proud of myself. "And it wasn't that hard."

"And he didn't call back."

"No, he didn't."

"Amazing," she says. Then she goes somewhere surprising. "This is because your dad's here," she says. "He's changing you. I swear. You're not acting as stupid over men as you used to."

"You can stop now," I say, just as my phone rings. It's Miguel calling, probably with something about the restaurant. "I have to take this. Go ahead. I'll be right in."

"You know he's coming back," Peaches says. "You know that, right? You haven't seen the last of him."

"You mean Jake?"

"No, I mean Santa."

I wave Peaches away and answer the phone. I can't handle her theories about Jake, or my dad. I have to answer this call, because I still have a restaurant I need to deal with.

# 18

## RONNIE

Melissa sits across from me drinking tea at a little place not too far from the halfway house. This is the first time I've seen her since I moved into her apartment, then out of it, on the same day. At first I thought things might be tense, but she seems friendly, and my first check-in at the halfway house went off without a hitch. After I peed into a cup and filled out the paperwork, we started chatting, and next thing I know I'm sitting here staring at her mouth as she talks about her life—I don't know, to be honest, I'm not really paying attention.

I'll say this: she's looking good.

"What did you do with your hair," I say. "It's nice. I like it."

She blushes. "Really? Just some highlights. Nothing major," she says. I'm not sure if she knows it or not, but she's gazing at me, and it's making me want to have sex with her. "How are things with your daughter?"

"You know what? Surprisingly good. She was a little edgy for the first week or so, but I have to hand it to her, she's been really accepting."

"Of course she has," Melissa says. She's eating a berry scone, and instead of lifting the whole damn scone up to her mouth and biting some off, she's tearing little pieces off and placing them in her mouth. It's turning me on. "You're a good person, Ronnie."

"You don't realize. I didn't tell you this at the time, but before I showed up at her place, she hadn't spoken to me in years," I say. "I thought she might never speak to me again."

"Well, then she's a good person, too," Melissa says, popping another little morsel into her mouth. I see her tongue this time and I—

I lean over the table and kiss her. She kisses me back. And the moment I do it, I can't believe I did it.

Again.

———

I've got Melissa by the hand and I'm leading her down the narrow hall of her apartment. I open the first door I come to. It's the linen closet. "Shit."

"Next one," she says, giggling. She opens the next door and there's the bed. "Sit down," she says.

I sit on the bed and she stays standing, pulling her phone out of her purse. (Does anyone *ever* put those things away? Even when you're about to get laid?) She touches it a few times, different screens start popping up like it's a video game. I'm fascinated by the fact that all of life seems to be contained in these phones. A few more swipes and taps and she sticks it into a little clock radio thing by the bed. Music starts playing.

Sade.

"That's good," I say.

"I know, right?" Melissa smiles. "I love this song," she says.

She starts swaying to the music, totally in her body. A woman's body— every last woman, in every last body, is beautiful. If only they knew that.

"You're so pretty, Melissa."

"Me?" she says incredulously. "I am hardly pretty."

"You are. You just don't know it." I drop to my knees and face her, wrapping my arms around her legs, and bring her toward me until her knees are at my shoulders. I smooth my palms down her back, feeling the channel of her spine and the strong muscles on either side. She's being felt. Like if hands were eyes, she's being *seen*. "Look at you. You're amazing."

She almost makes a sound but stifles it. I run my hands over the lower part of her back, with the ten extra pounds that stand in the way of her loving herself . . . and I meditate on loving her there. Right there, where she can't love herself. As I move to that spot where the sounds begin to come out of her, she can't even hold it anymore—

"Oh my God," she says. "Ronnie."

I lower her to the bed and we look at each other a long, long beat, and then she lays herself back and I lie down on top of her and then we're just together with the intensity that only happens when there's no possible way the relationship will ever work.

———

That was a week ago. Now I keep sending Melissa to voice mail. I know she probably feels abandoned. But I just can't seem to pick up the phone. Sleeping with her again was a mistake that I don't want to repeat. And since I don't seem to have any control over it, the only way to make sure I don't repeat it is to just go cold turkey: don't speak to her at all. I have a month until I have to check in at the halfway house again, and by that time, I'll probably be fine. I hope I will.

There's something about living with Cody and Nicki that's getting me in touch with a more wholesome, more pure side of myself. I'd say it's a side of me I forgot—but I don't know that I ever had it. When you're locked up repeatedly for as long as I have been, and treated like a criminal for as long as I have been, you start to believe what the world is saying about you. You start acting the way they expect you to act. You lose your humanity.

There's a saying I read somewhere: *Use things, not people.* I never forgot it. Probably because I spent my life using people, not things. I don't want to use Melissa, or anyone else. That's new for me. Is it possible that making peanut butter and jelly sandwiches every day for a high school junior could take away my lifelong willingness to exploit people? And if so, now what am I going to do? Exploiting people is what I'm best at.

I'm only half joking.

Part of me is afraid that the Melissas of the world are just the gateway drug to going back to my old self. I've never been a 100 percent good person. I've been a person who's good "inside." Who could be truly good if I would only stop doing bullshit. Maybe I'm not doing bullshit today. But when you have a track record like mine, is it possible to just never do bullshit again? Could I dare to believe I could put all that behind me once and for all? I can't afford to slip back into my old state of mind, my old habits. My new life is too good, and for the first time ever, I'm willing to do whatever it takes to keep it. Even give up free sex. (Damn, that is *willing*.)

Melissa isn't making sainthood easy, either. Her messages have gone from friendly to worried to judgmental to martyr and I still haven't called her back. Yes, I feel guilty about just letting her hang there without an explanation. She probably thinks I'm rejecting her personally—women always have to go there. In her last message, she even tried to suggest that maybe she might make things difficult for me with my parole. She'd never really do that, but it's proof of how much pain she's in, and I feel terrible. The least I can do is write her an email telling her what's going on with me. She'll understand.

I'm sitting in my room, on the computer—those Gmail people deserve every billion they've got for making the Internet and email understandable to a lifetime convict like me—when Cody comes in, white as a sheet.

"I think I need to go to the hospital," he says.

He holds up his hand and there's a massive gash in his left thumb; I can practically see the bone. He's bleeding buckets of red blood all down his shirt and onto the floor.

"Ohmygod, boy!" I jump to my feet. "We have to call an ambulance! I need to get a towel! We should call your mom! Did you call your mom? *Shit*."

Cody's calm as anything. "I can't. My hand."

"We have to call the operator!" I grab my cell phone. "What's that number you call again?"

"You mean 911?"

"Right," I say, and start dialing.

"Who's the operator?" Cody's breathing isn't even heavy. Which means he's probably in shock.

They pick up in one ring: "*911, what's your emergency?*" I tell them our address and that Cody has nearly sliced his thumb off. While I talk, I'm frantically looking around for something to stop the blood from going everywhere.

"Here!" The only thing within reach is a pillowcase, so I pull it off and start wrapping, trying not to hurt Cody as I go around and around his hand. "How did this happen?"

"I was cutting a bagel," he says. "And I slipped."

I can hear myself shouting at the 911 operator. "He was cutting a bagel. And, uh, I don't—we don't—have a car. Hurry!" I hang up and run immediately to the bathroom. "Let me get something else for that blood. Hold on, son. They'll be here right away."

I grab four more towels from the hall closet and go back to Cody, who is calmly sitting on the edge of the bed, leaning over carefully so he doesn't spill blood on the bedspread. He's such a great kid. He fronts like he's a rebel, but he's really a very considerate boy.

"We got to call your mom," I say. I grab my phone, push every button at once, trying to get to my main page, then to my list of recent calls, then to scroll down to Nicki's name. I keep ending up on the wrong page, the wrong list, the wrong name. "Goddammit!"

Cody starts laughing.

"Don't you laugh at me!" I realize this must look pretty funny to him, and he's the one with his finger half cut off, so if he can laugh, then so can I.

"You look so—" He can't even finish the sentence because he's giggling so hard. "You're all—" He mimics me fumbling with my phone. "Sorry, dude."

I can hear the sirens screaming down the block. "They're almost here. Where's your shoes, and I'll get you a jacket. And is there an insurance card around here? You need your wallet for your ID."

"Go in my room," he says. "It's in there."

I charge into Cody's room and grab a jacket and the nearest pair of shoes. By this time, the ambulance has pulled up and I run out to the living room to open the door. "He's just about cut it off," I say. I feel crazy, but I sound okay. "I'm his granddad."

"Let's take a look at that," the paramedic says. He steps over to Cody and unwraps the towel. There's blood everywhere. Cody winces for the first time. I think the shock might be wearing off, or maybe it's just hitting him that he's got a damn awful wound.

"Okay, let's go," the paramedic says. He helps Cody stand and stays with him as they move through the house. "This way. We'll get you something for the pain."

I grab my phone as we walk out the door. I sure hope I can figure out how to dial Nicki's number.

———

We're in the back of the ambulance. Cody's lying down on a stretcher, and I'm sitting on a little stool across from one of the paramedics. The ambulance pulls down the street, lights flashing. I notice a couple of neighbors poking their heads out of their front doors as we go by.

"Dude, it's pretty chill in here," Cody says, looking around. He points at something hanging on the wall. "What is this thing?"

The paramedic, a young guy who looks like maybe he flunked out of firefighter school, gives Cody a tablet of some kind of painkiller. The boy happily downs it. "Should start working in a few minutes."

"Awesome," says Cody.

"Should we make some conversation?" I ask. For some reason, it seems like the thing to do is to try to take Cody's mind off what's happening. I land on asking him about Magic, since I don't know a single thing about the game, and it's literally the only subject Cody will speak about before being spoken to. "Tell me something about Magic, the—"

"Gathering?" he says.

"Yeah. I really want to know more about your game," I say. "For example, is it something I should be learning to play?"

Cody smiles. As if the thought of seeing me playing his game would be very absurd. "I think it's probably a little complicated for you."

"Oh, do you now?" I come back with some very exaggerated game face. "Because you know I could throw down on some chess in my day. In prison, we got nothing to do *but* play games. So you should know who you'd be dealing with."

The mention of prison gets a raised eyebrow from the paramedic. But not Cody, who loves it when I tell stories about prison. He can also see that it's probably true that I had as many hours to hone my game as he's had to hone his.

"There's so much to talk about, it's hard to know where to start," he says. "Basically, you put together a deck of sixty cards, from the ten thousand cards that have been invented for the game."

"Ten thousand? Are you kidding me?"

"The cards all have names, and they do things. Things that are too complicated to go into in an ambulance."

I smile. I love this boy's sense of humor.

"Another part is that there are five colors: white, black, blue, red, and green. Which we abbreviate to be WUBRG. Pronounced *woo*-berg." On cue, both the paramedic and myself say *woo*-berg under our breath. It's one of those words you really need to feel in your mouth.

Cody keeps going. "Each color has a different vibe. Like, white is the color of healing and light and peace and righteousness. You know, white creatures have First Strike and Lifelink."

"What's Lifelink?"

"Again, too complicated," Cody says with finality. He's very clear on the level of game he's willing to teach me. Level one, basically.

He continues. "Blue is intellect and knowledge; black is power and greed and death; red is passion and creativity; and green is nature and reality. Oh, and there's all this overlap with poker. So much that I sort of think one day I might decide to take all my MTG knowledge and parlay it into a sick poker career."

"Poker! Now that's my game," I say.

The paramedic cuts in. "We're here," he says. He looks at me. "After we pull in, you go to the intake and we'll bring him to a room."

The back doors open and there's a rush of energy as they take Cody and wheel him into the emergency room. I dial Nicki's number again and brace myself for her arrival.

# 19

## NICKI

It takes me half an hour to get to the hospital, that's how bad traffic is on 84 East. Lesson learned: don't ever have to go to the emergency room at rush hour. I know Cody's injury isn't life-threatening, but Ronnie made it sound really bad, and the whole way I'm having morbid fantasies of staph infections and MRSA and other calamities you hear about but never think could happen to you until you're on your way to the hospital. By the time I get there, Cody has already been given a spot behind a sliding curtain. I pull it back, half afraid of what I'm going to find.

"Hey, muffin," I say tentatively. With Cody, I have to keep my emotions in check. A hysterically worried mom is his worst nightmare.

"Hi, Mom." Cody seems pale and quiet, but fine.

"Aww, are you okay, punkin'?" I move toward the bed and run my hand across his head the way I used to when he was little, careful not to jostle him and hurt his thumb. "How're you doing? Does it hurt much?"

"I'm fine, Mom. You're totally overreacting," Cody says. "I'm fine. Seriously. Fine. I'm feeling pretty chill, actually."

"They gave him some kind of painkiller," Ronnie says.

"It's so chill," Cody says again. "If this is opiates, uh, I get why they spent so much time on them in drug education class."

I have to smile. I know Cody does drugs sometimes and drinks, but I don't make a big deal out of it. This is probably the only place in my life I'm not trying to control. Oh, I did at first. The weed smoking seemed to start the first day of high school—it was like someone said, *Here's your locker, here's your geometry book, and here's your bong.* I went crazy for the first few months. But the more I talked about it, the further away Cody went, until finally it became clear to me that if I kept searching his backpack, or scrutinizing him when he walked through the door on Friday nights, or gave him lectures about the dangers of drugs, I would lose him completely. And I couldn't bear to lose him.

Sometimes I feel guilty about this—you know, like a *real* parent shames you, punishes you, sends you to rehab if they find out you party. It's a fine line to walk, because I don't want him to think I approve (I definitely don't), but once your kid gets to that place where they've decided they want to drink and smoke weed you have two choices: accept it, or force them to lie. I'd rather accept it. Because I know there's no world where you take a kid who really wants to drink and smoke pot and turn him into a kid who doesn't. I mean, do you know one kid in high school who did that? Me neither. Everyone I know partied until they decided they didn't want to party anymore, and then they stopped—like me—or they wanted to stop but couldn't and went to rehab. Or they didn't want to stop and now they're a mess.

Ronnie is sitting on the bed next to Cody, and when I look closer, I see that he is the one holding Cody's arm upright, at the elbow. He sees me watching this and explains. "He got tired of holding it up, so I took over." Ronnie looks at me. "I'd stand," he says, "but then I'd have to—" He motions to Cody's elbow.

"No, don't. It's fine. Really."

Ronnie's got a concerned look on his face. "I'm more worried about you. Are you okay? This is a parent's worst nightmare, getting a call that your son's in the emergency room."

"Now that I'm here, I'm okay," I say. "I was having a lot of scary thoughts on the way over. But I can see now everything's going to be fine."

"It's fine, Mom."

I'm worried about my child, Cody, and my dad's worried about his child, me.

"Thank you for calling the ambulance and getting him here," I say. "Do they need me to fill out some papers?"

"It's done. Cody had an insurance card in his wallet, and I handled it when I got here."

"Wow, thank you." Again, I find myself feeling grateful to have my dad on the case.

At that moment, a doctor rips the curtain back and sails into the room. "Hello, I'm Dr. Povgoricz." She looks about twenty-seven.

"Hello, Doctor," Ronnie says. He must think she's hot, because he just patted his hair with his free hand. "Aren't you the looker?"

Dr. Povgoricz ignores this statement. As she should.

Instead, she launches into her diagnosis. "I've seen the X-ray and everything's fine," she says. Her voice is surprisingly husky and, together with her vaguely Eastern Bloc accent, immediately makes her seem ten years older—and yes, hot. "You didn't sever any of the most important things in there. Which is good news." She says it like *thingks* and *goot nyoozs*.

Ronnie is spellbound. "I love your accent," he says.

My dad can't even go to the emergency room without trying to pick someone up.

"Dad." The second I say the word, I realize this is the first time I've called him Dad since he came back into my life. I've always been okay with referring to Ronnie as my dad, or calling him Ronnie or Hey to his face. But not since he went to prison (the second time) have I called him Dad. It feels somehow excruciatingly vulnerable, and I am eager to shake off that feeling. "Leave the poor woman alone."

I can almost feel my face burning. Not that my dad's even noticing.

"Seriously," he says, beaming at the doctor. The way he's looking at her, apparently he's engaged in some fantasy halfway between love at first sight and Dr. Playboy Bunny. "Where are you from?"

"I am from Bulgaria," she says evenly. She goes back to her examination.

"Is that the one next to Romania? On, what is it, the Black Sea?"

Well, that got her attention, all right. Never in a million years did Dr. Povgoricz think this handsome older guy with the blue-blue eyes knew where Bulgaria was. "Very good, Mr. Daniels! Most Americans have no idea."

"Yeah, well I'm not most Americans." Ronnie's got a sly look on his face. He knows he just impressed the hell out of her. "Naw, man. It's just, I love geography."

I'll admit that part of me is a little bit proud that my criminal, Lothario dad is still one of the best-educated people I know. Not in a French-Existentialism-and-Critical-Theory way. But he's read more books on more subjects than half of my undergrad friends.

Dr. Povgoricz pulls the needle off of the tray and holds it up. "Now, Cody, you're going to need to sit very still." She holds it poised over the deep gash between his thumb and forefinger.

"Mom, can you take a picture for me? I have to Instagram this."

If there was ever proof he's going to be fine, I guess this would be it—he wants the world to know he's sitting in a hospital emergency room, getting stitches. I take the phone from him and wake it up. Even Dr. Povgoricz looks up at me and smiles.

"*Cheeeeese!*"

That is going to be a good one.

———

"I have seventy-two likes so far!" Cody posted a video of the hot doctor sewing up his cut, and apparently now it's blowing up on his social network. "That's one in every three people who follows me. I gotta do crazy shit more often."

We all walk out to the car. Ronnie's whistling and doing the occasional dance step, as he sometimes likes to do. When I'm stressed, which I am right now, I find this irritating. Does he not realize that in the history of the world, no one ever said to another person, "Oh, I love your whistling"? Whistling is like eating Doritos—it's only good for the person doing it.

"What do you all say we go get some ice cream?" Ronnie says.

I shoot him a look. "I think we're a little past ice cream."

"No one's ever past ice cream, Nicki," he says. He's almost mad, but not really, because Ronnie doesn't really get regular guy "mad." He does something more like peewee soccer coach mad. "Come on now. Give me those keys. I gotta practice my driving."

I surprise myself by handing over the keys. Ronnie slides in behind the wheel and Cody gets in the back. Ronnie hits a button on the dash and the radio starts blaring. Not what I'm in the mood for, but I go along with it.

"Oh! This is my *jam*!" Ronnie starts singing along.

*"Just hold on, we're going home."*

"Cody, when your mom was a little girl, I used to take her out in my car and we'd roll all over Portland, just hanging out." He claps loud, even though it means he takes his hands off the steering wheel for a second. "Your mom was so cute. Everywhere we'd go, people would be fussing over her. '*Look at your little girl! She's so cute!*' They couldn't get enough of you!"

"Oh my God."

"You're still cute, baby!" Ronnie actually pinches my cheek. "Do you remember that old car I used to have?"

"Was it blue? And it had a cool little thing on the end of the hood?"

"Oh shit! That's the one! Before the Mercedes." Ronnie claps again. He's getting all excited. "I had a big old Lincoln. It had a cool hood ornament. Man, that thing was posh." He hits the last word hard. "You loved that car, baby."

"I did?"

Sometimes it's crazy to think of myself as a little girl. I feel like I was born a grown-up. I'm so damn capable and I always have been. Except for my boyfriends—that's the one area of my life I've never been able to get right. Everywhere else, I'm like the efficiency police. On top of *everything*.

"Oh hell yeah. You used to say, '*Daddy? Can we go for a drive?*'" He busts out a little girl voice.

"I did not sound like that!" There is something really fascinating about hearing stories about myself. I guess regular people who have parents around are probably used to it. Which makes me wonder, do I tell Cody stories about himself? If I don't, I need to start.

"Did she really sound like that?" Cody says.

"Naw, man. I can't do her voice. But she was so cute. You had this little lisp." He sticks his tongue through his teeth and tries to say *My name is Nicki*.

"Mom, I want to see a picture of you when you were little."

"Forget it. There aren't any," I say. "I was neglected as a child." I wait a second. "And I'm only half joking."

"Of course there are!" Ronnie's shaking his head. "What are you talking about? We took a million pictures of you."

"I've never seen any of them," I say.

Ronnie stares at me for a beat. "Is that right? That's news to me."

It's true. That's the kind of mother Beth was. Even if she had the pictures, she would have been too lazy to get them out of whatever box in whatever place she'd stuck them. She'd rather just say they were lost. And even if she had found them at some point, I was long gone by then. I moved out of the house, more or less on a dare. *I dare you to go live somewhere else*, she said. *Go ahead, I dare you. You have nowhere to go.* She was right, but I didn't care. I snapped. I had Peaches come pick me up in her dented white VW Golf stick shift. For the next two months, I slept on the floor in her room.

I never talked to my mother again after that.

"I have one picture," I say. "Me standing with a big cotton candy. I think we're at the zoo or something." I turn around to look at Cody. "Are you good back there, honey? How's your hand doing?"

"I'm fine," he says. Then, after a long, customary silence, he says, "I'm thinking about how you only have one picture of yourself. And I have no pictures of me with my dad. We're a family of pictureless people."

Dude. It must be the opiates. I'm speechless for a second. I look over at Ronnie, who looks over at me. I make one of those *holy crap* faces and he makes one back like, *damn—smart boy.* And before either of us can say anything, Cody pipes up again.

"I mean, my hand's fine."

I can feel the tension rising in my throat, and in my face. Ronnie reaches out and touches me, but not like he's feeling sorry for me. It's just really light and like he knows something's up with me and he wants me to feel better. I pull my arm away.

"We definitely need a new song. Who's with me?" he says. Super upbeat. He punches buttons on the radio until he hears something that makes him stop. "Oh, now don't tell me you forgot this song! Oh shit!" He's popping his fingers and singing "Come On, Eileen" at the top of his lungs.

"You remember we used to sing this one together, baby?" he says to me.

"Jesus, that song is really inappropriate. I never really listened to it before," I say, grateful for the change of subject. I don't want to get all sad in front of Cody. I'm taken by surprise at how much emotion is just sitting there, right under the surface. You think you're in control of your life, you know what's going on. Then your kid says something that just breaks you open. "I should not have been singing that."

"Nickles! Come on, sing!" Ronnie keeps going, pointing out the words with his finger, bobbing his head up and down like invisible karaoke. When that doesn't get me to sing, he drops into a cuddly voice you would use to talk to a little kid. "You can do it. Come on, Nicki Beans."

"Yeah, come on, Nicki Beans!" Cody pipes up from the back. Then *he* starts singing, substituting, *Come on, Nicki Beans,* for *Come on, Eileen,* and next thing you know he and Ronnie are singing it over and over. "*Come on, Nicki Beans, too ra loo rye ay.*"

So finally, I quietly add the background vocal: "*These things they are real, and I know how you feel!*"

Then they sing the next line a little bit louder: "*Come on, Nicki Beans, too ra loo rye ay!*"

And I add my line: "*These things they are real, and I know how you feel!*"

"Hell yeah, little girl! You got it!" Ronnie's embarrassing himself, but he doesn't care at all. "Go, baby!"

Pretty soon we're going back and forth at top volume like we're in a movie. Even doing the parts that aren't even words, just *toora-loora* over and over.

Ronnie takes my hand like he did that very first day when I couldn't get out of bed, and this time it feels familiar and okay—better than okay, it feels good—and he holds it and he's smiling at me and I'm even smiling back at him. I've never in my whole life done something like this. Ever. I'm not worrying about anything or stressing out about what's going to happen next, or telling Cody to do his homework. I'm just being right here in the moment where I am.

I guess you could say I'm happy.

# PART FOUR

---

## Open Houses

# 20

# NICKI

I'm here to pull the plug. I've done the math, and in order to open the restaurant I need another fifteen thousand dollars—for the last of the interior work and the first three months of food and labor costs. I am down thirty thousand dollars already, not counting the twenty thousand Jake put in, and because I'm still committed to buying the new house, I simply don't have any more money to put into it. There's no other option. Now I just have to break the news to Miguel.

He's outside finishing up a call and when he comes back in, I'm going to tell him. Not going to be easy. This place is stunning! So simple, but so beautiful. All Miguel's choices—from the tile floors to the backsplash behind the counter to the perfectly understated lighting—are beautiful.

But without Jake, I'm in no position to run a restaurant. I'm a real estate appraiser. That's what I am. The idea that I could be part of a community, that I could make the world a better place by serving artisanal sausage and preserved Meyer lemon waffles? What was I thinking?

I wasn't.

I was dreaming, and that's not what I'm supposed to do. I'm practical, pragmatic Nicki. I can always be counted on to do the right thing, to be the stable one. I won't lie: fantasizing was fun. I guess I know why people do it now. Wanting this restaurant, dreaming big? I've loved it. It made me feel alive. But it's time to let go of the dream, because now look at me. As Peaches would say, I'm fucked. Actually, I'd say that, too.

Miguel walks into the room and tucks his cell phone into his back pocket. "Miss Nicki," he says. "How are you?"

"Oh, I'm all right," I say. "How are you?"

"Doing good, things down here are on schedule." He eyes me as if to say, *how are things going on your end?* "Did you get my messages?"

"About the chef? Yeah, I did." Miguel has been wanting to know who I'm hiring as the executive chef, so that person could consult on the final decisions in the kitchen. Naturally he wants to know this sooner rather than later, because he's good at his job.

Ugh. Here we go. This is where I need to say it: *there is no chef.* Then I need to say the rest of it: *because there is no restaurant.* Which Miguel isn't going to believe, because he's been working on the restaurant around the clock for the past six weeks. To him there's a restaurant and it's gorgeous.

I've thought over and over how I could solve this problem, but I can't come up with anything. Not even working will work. Work has always been my drug of choice. It's like Spanx for my emotions—it gives me something to bury myself in and, because of the money, makes me feel secure. There's almost no life problem I can't get through just by taking my list of things I have to do and places I have to go and dutifully marching from one task to the next, thinking about nothing in between except maybe the most efficient route to getting there.

I can pinpoint the start of my workaholism to the summer after I left home. I needed money to pay for my next semester of college. I think it was something like $2,850. An insurmountable sum! I already had a five-nights-a-week job working the five to ten p.m. shift at an answering service (a job too boring to discuss in any detail), but that wasn't going to get me the money soon enough. So when a friend asked if I wanted to work at the administrative office of a law firm five *mornings* a week, I said yes. Then I saw a job to work the breakfast shift at a hipster café on Saturdays and Sundays and I said yes to that. I worked seven days a week and it was brilliant. Not only was I able to anesthetize the pain of having a criminal dad and an absent mother, by the beginning of September, I had $6,240. In cash. All mine. I was a self-made six-thousandaire.

To me, that was serious money.

And I liked that. No, I loved it. I loved it the way people love vodka tonics, or cocaine, or pornography. I loved it so much that from that point onward, I always had a slush fund at least three times the size of anyone else that I knew. I once told Cody that the key to always having money is to never spend the last dollar you have. That, and working three jobs. He rolled his eyes at me, but it's true. Sometimes I think if I had had half as terrible a childhood, I'd have half as much money in the bank and be half as successful.

But getting three jobs isn't going to fix things at the restaurant. Maybe if Cody wasn't going to go to college soon (fingers crossed) or I didn't still have this house thing to deal with. The only real solution is to just let the whole mess go. Chalk it up, learn my lessons, and move on. I'm going to start looking for investors and as soon as I find one, I'm gone.

"Miguel?"

"Yes?"

He's looking at me expectantly. Why is my mouth not moving? Why are there no words coming out of my mouth? Why are there no thoughts in my mind? I'm drawing a blank.

"I'm going to have someone for you right after the holiday," I say.

Fuck it. Thanksgiving is at the end of next week. I'll decide after that.

———

Work might suck, but play is going great. For the first time in my life I've taken relationship advice from Peaches. I'm dating! I know that, technically, it's too soon—Jake's only been gone a little over a month—but I don't care. I'm feeling a way I've never felt before: like I'm fine just the way I am.

Normally, a breakup leads to a certain amount of loneliness and wondering if there's something really wrong with me. But not this time. I'm feeling the way I've always heard people say you should feel about dating—like I can take it or leave it.

So I'm taking it.

I'm on that dating site where it's a little app on your phone and you just swipe left if you don't like someone and swipe right if you do. It's only been a week, but I've been swiping my ass off. To the right, to the right. (Sorry, Beyoncé!) I've met more men in the past seven days than I have in the past seven years. I'm not kidding.

Not that I've ever been a hookup girl. I've had exactly two one-night stands in my life—and one of them turned into my baby daddy, so technically it wasn't even a one-night stand. Every other guy I've been with—and I could count them on two hands—I made wait a minimum of two to four weeks before I could even think of having sex with him. Not because I was playing some game of Hard to Get, but because I've found that I don't like people I don't know. At least not sexually.

Whenever I hear girlfriends talk about being sexually attracted to a stranger, I think, *What? Eww!* Because as far as I'm concerned, you just have to assume people you don't know are disgusting. That they smell weird, have dirty sheets, strange body habits—twitches, scratching, mouth sounds!—and you are definitely not going to like their feet. Sure, maybe they're awesome people, smell good, and have clean sheets and nice feet—but you have to assume they don't. Otherwise, you might end up back at their apartment discovering the dirty sheets—or worse yet, having them over to your place and discovering their gross smell. The only way to avoid such unpleasantness—for me at least—has been to wait two or three weeks, kiss them only after knowing them a reasonable amount of time, and only take your clothes off once you're familiar with them. Because once a person is familiar, they don't seem disgusting even when they are.

Which brings me to this park bench I'm sitting on. I'm waiting for someone named Alex and we're going to go for a walk. I'm four minutes early, which is totally not cool, but I'm over being cool. Alex is the third guy I've hung out with in seven days and this strange thing is happening—I'm not even nervous anymore. I'm excited. This is a big change from my old self. My old self hates people I don't know and expects the worst. My new self thinks dating is cool because I get new perspectives on life and I might even kiss someone at the end of it. And kissing is fun.

I've only seen a two-by-three-inch picture of Alex, but here are the good things about him:

*He's age appropriate.*

*He's got nice hair.*

*His teeth are the right amount of imperfect.*

*He's employed in an interesting capacity.*

Then again, here are the bad things about Alex:

*He's age appropriate.*

*He's a little too good-looking.*

*He's from California.*

*He works in tech.*

I've decided walking around this park is my favorite date because there is just the right amount of distance and closeness. For one thing, when you walk, you're side by side, and that's a lot better for a date than face-to-face. Side by side is kind of like the instant messaging of real-life conversations. It's immediate, but not so intense that you can't look away if you need to.

When Alex arrives, I'm texting Cody that there's some pasta with tur-key Bolognese in the refrigerator in case he gets hungry.

"Excuse me," he says. "Are you Nicole?"

Holy shit.

This is possibly the cutest guy I've ever seen.

Not the handsomest, not the tallest, not the builtest, not the best dressed. Just the most sparkling, twinkliest, funnest-looking guy I've ever seen. Even more than Gio. The minute I think this I remind myself to slow down, after all I've only just laid eyes on him.

"Do you mind if I have a seat?"

I like his tone of voice.

I nod, painfully aware that I haven't even said anything yet. "Hi, I'm Nicki." I hold my hand out and he sits next to me, not too close, and gives me a very charming (but not too charming) kiss on the cheek.

"You're lovely." He pulls his body back an inch or two to get a better look. "Your pictures don't do you justice."

I'm blushing. "Thank you," I say. Then I say: "Can you please stop being so charming? Or, I'll have to leave."

Alex laughs. I laugh, too.

Q: *When is the last time I laughed on a first date? And in the first five minutes?*

A: *Never.*

"Shall we walk?" He stands up and offers me his hand. It's a very Cinderella-type move, but somehow it doesn't seem insincere coming from him. "How's your day so far?"

I start to answer, just for small talk. But something's been happening to me as I go on these dates. I'm becoming more real. In the olden days, I would go on a date and act as close to "perfect" as I knew how to be. I'd sit across from the other person at coffee or whatever and make sure I said nothing offensive, didn't talk too loud, and wore something no one could object to (hello, Ann Taylor Loft!). But these dates have been different. I'm more like, *this is who I am.* I'm not being combative, but if a guy doesn't get my joke about him being too charming on the first date, then he's not going to be very happy with me two years from now. Because there's a lot more where that came from. So if it's not going to work, why put either one of us through it? I should just be my real self starting right now and not even bother to try to make him think that I eat continental style every meal, even when I'm having scrambled eggs and Cheerios for dinner.

Might as well show him the real me.

"Alex?"

"What?"

"Do you ever think this whole dating process is just . . . stupid? I mean, why not just cut to the chase?"

"You mean cut to the chase and go have sex somewhere?" He says this with a broad smile and I really like him for it.

I burst out laughing. "That's not the chase for me."

"What is the chase for you, Nicole?"

"Nicki."

"What is the chase for you, Nicki?"

"I don't know. Being real? Finding a friend? Someone who, eventually"— I glare at him playfully—"I'll want to have sex with?"

"Hmmm. I like that chase." He looks at me meaningfully. "But how would you cut to it?"

This is a good question. I've always imagined a world where people are real all the time—where they just stop faking everything and stop doing what they think they're supposed to be doing but is making them unhappy—but I guess I never quite thought about how you'd do it, say, on a first date. "I guess I didn't think it out that far."

At this point, I'm noticing something amazing happening. I haven't thought for one minute about whether or not Alex likes me—I don't know if that's because I'm assuming he likes me, or what—but what I *am* noticing, is how much I like being around Alex.

This feels like a revelation.

Like, you know it when you see it.

I think I'm seeing it.

"Never mind," I say. "I think I answered my own question." Alex gives me a slightly baffled look, but I stop him by jumping ahead one step and standing in front of him. I put a hand up near his chest in the "stop" position. "I have a very important question for you, Alex."

Alex gives me an elfin smirk. He seems to intuitively know how to play with me. "Yes, Nicki. I would like to answer it."

"When is the last time you played tag?"

He reaches out his arm and gives me a gentle tap. "Now—you're it!" Then he takes off across the park.

I run after him, giggling like crazy the whole way.

I think I'm really going to like Alex.

# 21

## RONNIE

If you're going to throw a dinner party, why not start with the most important dinner party of them all? Thanksgiving! I told Nicki and Cody I was making a turkey, and if they wanted to invite anyone, just have them here by 4 p.m. Nicki's bringing her best friend, a girl named Peaches, whom I met a couple of times back in the day when she and Nicki were kids, and Cody's got two of his homeboys coming over from down at the comic-book shop. At the last minute, Nicki even decided to invite the guy she's started dating, Alex, which seems really bold for her but totally in keeping with this more relaxed version of herself she's been trying out lately.

In the past, I'd be jumping up and down to take some credit for that, but these days, I'm really practicing keeping my mouth shut. Let her think it's her! Isn't that what a good parent does? Either way, I'm just glad she's feeling stronger. That little hum of sadness that's always been there for her, even as a little girl, seems just a little bit less. I don't even know if she's noticed it.

Today we went to Whole Foods together to pick up food for the dinner. I've been getting into some of those lifestyle magazines that they have at the checkout counter. You know, the ones with the great decorating ideas and the Healthy But Tasty recipes? I'm going to do a turkey, of course, but instead of the traditional sides I'm going for truffled macaroni and cheese and a carrot-and-roasted-fennel soup, with an Asian kale slaw for a salad. No one ever eats sweet potatoes anyway. I wouldn't let Nicki look in the basket because I want it all to be a surprise. She has no idea what I can *really* do in the kitchen.

Everyone shows up around four. Cody's Magic: The Gathering buddies are as geeky as you please—the skinny one is named Max and the one with the acne is named Justin. They are both wearing backpacks and have things to say about Free Jazz when they're not talking gibberish about duels, Planeswalkers, and the Multiverse. Nicki complains about how obsessed Cody is with this game. But I say it's the only thing he truly loves and I don't see why you'd want to take it away from him. Even though it's probably the number one thing preventing him from getting laid. There's time for that. Cody's showing me what it would be like if I'd grown up thinking about something other than sex. Let's just say my life would have been different.

"You guys want a beer?" I'm holding out an Anchor Steam to Justin, or it could possibly be Max. Suddenly I'm not so sure which one has the acne. Nicki's mouth falls open.

"They're a little young," she says.

"Sure, man," Max says, taking the beer. "Thanks."

"Can I have one?" Cody looks hopefully at Nicki, who shakes her head.

I hand him one anyway. "Let the boy have a beer, Nicki." I hate seeing her baby him. No wonder the kid still wants to play cards in a comic-book store; she hovers over him like he's seven. "He's seventeen years old. That's plenty old enough for a beer at a dinner party."

"He's not seventeen until next month," she says.

"The blink of an eye," I say. "Don't blow it."

Nicki gives me a dirty look but it doesn't bother me too much. No one knows better than me that men who live and die by a woman's approval are still little boys inside. Being okay with your decisions no matter who approves is the first thing a guy has to learn if he wants to be a man. I want Cody to see what that looks like.

"I'll be in the kitchen if you need me." I give Cody a glance to make sure he got the lesson correct. He did. He doesn't make a full smile or anything, but there's a knowingness in his eye. The two of us have spent enough time together to be able to communicate with just a nod and a look here and there.

When I come out ten minutes later with my portobello mushroom appetizer, Nicki is sitting next to one of the more amazing women I've ever laid eyes on. *Holy shit.* This must be Peaches. And she looks as street as her name—part motorcycle gang, part pinup girl. Damn, she grew up nice. I don't feel bad saying it, either, since she's got to be thirty-five or thirty-six. Old enough so that I'm not a creep or anything.

"Hey!" I say.

Peaches is in the middle of a story about how her car broke down this morning and she needs Nicki to give her a ride home when she turns and lays eyes on me.

"You must be Ronnie!" She jumps up and throws her arms around me and holds me a good three seconds, during which I can feel her body. All of it. The whole goddamn thing. "I'm Peaches."

*You sure are.* "Peaches! Nicki's friend! How do you do?" I notice I'm breaking out my good manners right now—my opening bid for flirting. Preflirting. I better pull it together. I have no business turning on the sparkle for this girl.

"I'm great," she says. "So excited to meet you. You know your daughter is only my very best friend in the whole world. Without me, she would be nothing. I want you to know that."

"Consider it known, then," I say.

Nicki tugs at Peaches's arm. "You can annoy him later. Come on, I need to finish talking to you."

Nicki sweeps Peaches into her bedroom. They're probably talking about Alex, who isn't here yet. I've never been a big fan of Nicki's choices in men. She generally goes for entitled princes of one stripe or another. Pretty boys or mama's boys, or daddy's boys, or just . . . boys. I can't respect these peo- ple. They've hardly worked a day in their lives, never broken a rule, never been in a fistfight. They're not men! How can they protect my daughter or give her what she needs? They can't. And that's why, sooner or later, they all go. Nicki doesn't know this is why they go, but it is. Someday maybe I'll tell her if she doesn't figure it out in the next couple of years or so.

The door opens and a tallish, brown-haired fellow comes in. Seems like he just left a library somewhere. Good-looking son of a bitch, but more of the same. Doesn't seem selfish the way the last guy was, at least to hear Nicki tell it, but hardly what I have in mind for my daughter.

"I'm Alex," he says. He's got one of those nasally voices college guys have. "You're Mr. Daniels?"

"I sure am." We shake hands. His hand is soft, with long skinny fingers and short nail beds. Back in my hustling days I used to like to buff and polish my fingernails to go along with my custom suits, and put it this way, Alex doesn't have a hustler's nail beds. Or attitude. Or game. "Nicki will be right out. Why don't you come help me in the kitchen, Alex?"

I head through the living room and dining room, Alex trailing behind me. I want to chat with him a little—take a crack at him before he gets on his best behavior for Nicki. "So, Alex, what do you do for a living?"

"I work for a start-up. We're, uh, mostly digital content but we got some VC for a messaging app that we really think could take off." Alex seems to think he's speaking English.

"Alex, I have no idea what the fuck you just said." I look him square in the eye.

He smiles nervously. "Seriously?"

"Yes, I am. Serious." This kid has no idea what just hit him. I take it this isn't how college people do Thanksgiving. "But I'm also not." I bust out a grin.

"Oh, irony! That's so good." He chuckles. "Heh."

I hand him a bag of heirloom tomatoes and a knife. "Here, cut these into quarters for me? And be careful. Knives are dangerous. No offense about the thing you said earlier."

"Nicki said something about her kid slicing his thumb off," Alex says. "No offense taken."

"It wasn't quite that bad, but yes. There was a trip to the emergency room." I'm whisking rice wine vinegar and sesame oil together in a bowl. I dip my fingertip in and give it a taste. Not enough sesame oil. "He's healing up good, though."

"Scary. Glad he's okay."

"Where you from, Alex?"

"I'm from the Bay Area. Grew up in Palo Alto." Rich people. This is not the least bit surprising. Sometimes I can't tell if Nicki lives her life in denial or if she really does identify with these rich kids. She didn't grow up with money, yet she's always surrounding herself with pampered people. Poor folks scare her. What happens when she shares her life story with one of these jackasses? They must just stare at her. People need to be with people who understand their hurts, their pains. And these guys are never going to be able to do that for her.

"Alex, did Nicki tell you I've been in federal prison for the past seventeen years?"

For a moment I think Alex is going to slice *his* thumb off. "Uh, no. She didn't."

"Well, I was," I say. "I just got out a couple of months ago."

"I'm sorry," he says. "That's terrible."

I forgive this kid for acting like I have cancer. He's never met someone who's been in prison before.

"Alex, let me ask you a question. What's it like to grow up in Palo Alto? Did you just never have a care in the world until . . ." I stop and think. "Wait, maybe you *still* don't have a care in the world."

To his credit, Alex is not just jumping to his own defense. He's sitting stock still. "I'm thinking about what you're saying," he says.

"I see that," I say. "Thank you. I really appreciate that, Alex."

"And you're right. I don't really have 'cares,' not in the sense you're talking about. All of my basic needs are met, and they always have been. The only thing I have to worry about is—"

"Self-actualization," I say.

I'm referring to Maslow's Hierarchy of Needs. It's a psychology thing I'm sure Alex knows about. Most college people do. The theory is that human beings have basic needs: food, shelter, etc., and once those are taken care of, they move up to the next level of things to worry about, like security or friendship. And eventually, there's nothing left to worry about but the meaning of life. That's where Alex has been his whole life.

"Exactly," he says, a little shocked. "You know Maslow?"

"I studied a lot in the joint. Psychology, child development, attachment, a little evolutionary biology," I say. I pour my sesame oil dressing over my kale slaw, then sprinkle in some sesame seeds. *Hell yeah, this is going to be good.* "Lotta time on my hands in there. I sort of think of myself as an *un*-licensed therapist. *Ha!*" I clap and laugh real loud.

"That's hilarious," Alex says, laughing with me. "I love that you know Maslow."

I'm not hating this Alex cat. I grab the hand blender. "You ever work one of these before?" Alex takes the blender, just as Nicki and Peaches walk into the room. They're surprised to see Alex. Well, Nicki is.

"Alex!" She goes over to him, and before she can pull him into a hug, he takes her by both hands and gives her a polite kiss on her right cheek.

Peaches looks at me and raises an eyebrow as if to say, *Are you kidding me?*

And I think, I'm going to like sitting next to this Peaches girl.

———

"Dinner's ready!" I'm shouting at Cody's bedroom door. "Time to come to the table."

The three boys mosey in. I wait at the door until the kids are moving, then usher them into the dining room. I notice Nicki is holding the hand of the new boyfriend, but she drops it when Cody walks into the room.

"You guys sit there," I say, pointing toward the corner of the table. "Cody, you're on the end. You fellas, one on each side." I want the kids at one end so us adults can make conversation.

"The table sure does look nice," Alex says. He makes a moon face at Nicki.

"Thank you," Nicki says. Then she introduces him. "Cody, this is Alex."

That's it, just his name. No explanation. None necessary, I guess.

"What's up?" Cody gives one of those head dips men use to acknowledge each other. "Um, that's Max, and that's Justin."

"Hey, guys," Alex says. "Nice to meet you."

"Cuuuuute!" Peaches says. "Codes, you think you're going to like your new dad?"

"Peaches!" Nicki's pissed. "Stop."

"I joke, I joke," she says. "Jesus, people. You have no humor?"

That Peaches sure is a scoundrel. "Peaches, you're next to me. Nicki, you're to my right. And Alex, you're next to Nicki." We all take our seats.

Shit. This is beautiful. A Thanksgiving table and I got my daughter and my grandson here? And I'm free? Dear Lord, I'm grateful.

"Let's say grace."

"Grace?" Nicki says. "We're not religious."

"We're going to be thankful for our food, daughter." I take her hand. "Everybody take the hand of the person next to you." Nicki really wants to protest, but I keep talking. "Just go along with me."

She takes Alex's hand, but refuses to bow her head.

"Universal Creator," I say, "thank you for this food. These friends. This family. We thank you for the blessings we continue to receive. Our health, our open hearts. We thank you for the opportunity to spend time together, and get to know each other better, and we ask that you heal the scars from the past."

"Amen, already," Nicki says, jumping in.

"Amen." I squeeze her hand before I let it go and smile at her. "I love you, darling. Thank you especially for letting me be here. Our first Thanksgiving together. This is really special."

"So sweet!" Peaches says. She's beaming at me. Which I like, naturally.

Nicki doesn't say anything back. Again, that's fine. I don't expect a response. The way I see it, I'm chipping away at her defensiveness. I've got the rest of my life for her to come around. It's two steps forward, and one step back.

"So, guys," I say to the kids' side of the table, forking a big piece of white meat. "Why don't you tell us more about your game? The whole thing. Starting with what's so great about it."

"That's boring," Cody says.

Max starts talking even though he just shoved a huge spoonful of macaroni and cheese into his mouth. "What's so great about Magic? Only everything."

"I was into magic when I was little," Alex says. "But I couldn't ever make a coin disappear, and I finally gave up."

The boys all snicker. Cody says, "This is why I hate talking about Magic."

"Just tell him what it is," Nicki says. "Don't talk about what it's not."

"It's too confusing," Cody says.

"Oh, I think I can handle it," Alex says. "Why don't you try me?"

"It's not, like, David Blaine magic," Max says.

Cody cuts him off. "Basically it's strategy, fantasy, and competition all in the same game. And it's constantly evolving." The way he talks, it's obvious Cody really knows the whole deal. "So it never gets old. Also, it was invented in 1993 by a guy who was getting a PhD at the University of Pennsylvania. In combinatorial mathematics."

"Richard Greenfield," Max says.

"Bro, they don't need to know his name," Cody says.

"Yes, we do," Peaches says. "Was Richard Greenfield hot?"

"Peaches, stop," Nicki says. "You're being inappropriate."

"Peaches is always inappropriate. That's what we like about her," Cody says.

"I didn't know you liked me!" Peaches says, clearly in fun. "Awwww!"

"I don't," Cody says. He's got that blank face he wears sometimes, and right now, I can see that he doesn't really mean it. It's a way of being funny and in control at the same time. This kid has some really interesting levels to him. "I was joking."

The whole table breaks into whistles and catcalls. Maybe Cody's got some game in him after all.

"That's enough," Nicki says. "Next subject."

"You know who I want to hear from?" Peaches looks right at me. "*You*, Ronnie. I want to hear from you."

She leans into me and I can feel her body graze my arm, and I know right then and there that I am in trouble.

———

I grab the car keys without even asking Nicki. Peaches needs a ride home and asked me to take her. Nicki's walking around the block with Alex, pretty drunk the last time I saw her, and she's been letting me drive the car a little more lately, so I figure she won't mind. We're only a couple of minutes away from the house when Peaches puts it out there.

"Do you want to get some tea?" Peaches says.

She only said those seven little words, but she said them while sliding her long blue nails through the right side of her hair. I know that look on her face and I know what the deal is when a woman tries to spend more time with you at ten o'clock, after a great meal and too many drinks. It only means one thing.

She wants to get down.

"No, I don't think so," I say.

I'm lying, obviously. I want to go wherever this woman is suggesting we go. I want to go there no matter what, because I'm not a normal person. When you have what I have, you don't really choose whether you go get tea or not. You just *do it*. Even when you know it's a bad idea. But maybe if I say no enough times, this feeling will pass.

"Come on! How good would some tea be?" She giggles. "Tea-be. It rhymes!"

"I said I don't think so, Peaches." I'm trying to keep it light.

"It would be good, you know it would." She's dropped her voice an octave, she's almost whispering, and she's looking at me that one way. "Don't you like tea?"

She's saying it that one way. The way I can't say no to.

*Oh fuck.*

So I don't.

"You know what?" I say. "I do like tea."

"I thought you would," Peaches says. The air in the car is electrified. "Take a right at the next light."

Oh shit. It's on.

# 22

# NICKI

I don't usually drink this much. Normally, I try to keep it sane, one glass of wine, *maaaybe* two. But after we cleared the dishes from the table, the discussion turned into a tutorial on Magic: The Gathering, which is when Peaches got bored and decided to break out the blender and the tequila. Three margaritas later, Alex and I went for a walk around the block and ended up at the park down the street. Now I'm sitting on a bench and Alex is walking around picking up leaves off the ground. There's a single park lamp shining on us, and the ground is wet, as it usually is in Portland anytime between November and May.

"Remember our first date?" he says to me. "You were sitting on a bench just like that, and as I walked toward you, I saw you sitting there and thought to myself, *I sure hope that's her*. And it was."

"Awwww," I say. "You're sweet."

"No, you're sweet. Here." Alex hands me a bouquet of wet leaves that he just pulled together. He bobbles just slightly, thanks to the tequila. "For the lady."

"Are you for real? These are *so* beautiful! Seriously," I say, also tipsy as shit. I don't even care that the leaves are all soggy and brown. "No one's ever given me wet leaves before!"

We giggle and Alex sits down next to me and kisses me, really long and warm.

The past couple of weeks with Alex are making me realize I've spent my whole life choosing guys who could be warm or close but not both. Either they could be affectionate and loving but have to disappear for a couple of days at a time until they couldn't take it anymore and they disappeared forever—or they were aloof and distant but stuck around until one day when *I* couldn't take it anymore and I broke up with them. That's pretty much my entire relationship history in a nutshell.

Part of me wants to second-guess this whole thing. Like: this is too good to be true, I just got out of a relationship with Jake, I'm supposed to cry and feel bad for a long time before someone awesome comes along. How in the world could this good thing be happening to me? But then I just stop questioning it because here it is, it's happening, and how do you argue with what *is*? What *is* is the only real thing.

Which I know sounds totally like something Ronnie would say.

Alex puts his hands around my waist and then we're all into making out and he is possibly the best kisser ever.

"I like kissing you," I say.

"I like kissing you," he says.

We go back to kissing and I open my eyes and look at him and think that being here, right now, making out with Alex outside in the night air in the park down the street from my house on Thanksgiving might be the most romantic thing I've ever done since Gio and I walked across the Hawthorne Bridge.

*This is the only real thing.*

Except then a few minutes pass, and I remember that I'm a grown woman with a houseful of people and a kid and a whole bunch of dirty dishes in the sink and I have to get back home. Twenty-five minutes is the limit for walking around the block and impromptu make-out sessions in the park. I pull my shirt down and steady myself.

"I better go. I gotta check on everyone," I say. The night air and the

make-out session has sobered me up just a little, to where I'm now pleas-
antly warm inside and feeling wonderful.

Alex touches my cheek and gazes at me for a long moment. "You're
so beautiful, Nicki." He traces the curve of my cheekbone and kisses me
again, really lightly. "I really, really like you."

This is probably the most sincere thing any man has ever said to me.
Sure, I've had guys say nice things, but not in this tone of voice, with this
much eye contact, and so un*guarded*. It's making me squirm. I've spent a
lifetime dreaming someone would say something like that to me—and
now that someone has, I feel itchy. Not that I like admitting that. I don't
even know what to say.

So I just go, "Thank you."

He smiles at me like I'm adorable. "It's not really a compliment, Nick,"
he says. "It's the way I feel. I like you and I want you to know."

*Holy shit.* Is this what it's like when someone is just, like, *there*? Present?
Available? If so, it's going to take some major getting used to. I'm feeling
so shy I can only look at my fingernails. They're really chipped, by the way.

"I don't even know what to say," I say.

"You don't have to say anything. I just wanted you to know." He kisses
my cheek, then lifts up my chin with one finger and looks me in the eye.
"I really like you."

I start to get up, and Alex offers me his hand to help me off the bench.
Home is only five minutes away, but that's not far enough. I don't want this
moment to end. We walk in a nice silence, and I feel this sense of calm wash
over me. Nothing's missing right this second—nothing at all. As we walk
the one hundred yards to my house I look into people's windows—I have
the same fascination with people's homes at night that I have during the
day. At night, you can see right into their lives—just a snapshot—a corner
of wallpaper, a split-second of doing dishes, a glimpse of someone walking
from the living room to the kitchen for another glass of bourbon.

"I love houses," I say. "They're my favorite thing in the whole world."

Alex squeezes my hand like he understands this. "What do you love about them?"

"I love how they have rooms, and windows, and roofs, and . . ." I start laughing. "I'm joking. Kind of." Then I think about it. What exactly *is* it that I love about houses? And all at once the answer is behind my eyes, at first a little burning feeling, then a welling of tears. "It's that all I ever wanted was a home, you know? A really beautiful place to live and be safe and belong." I'm trying to keep the sound of the tears out of my voice, but he can probably hear them anyway. "That's all I ever wanted."

I look over at him and smile. He looks at me and smiles back. "And now you have one," he says.

He's right. I do have one.

I haven't told him I'm moving—it's way too messy a story for three weeks in—but I feel safe with him, and I know when I finally do explain it, he'll understand. He was so great at dinner—Peaches didn't hate him and he completely won over my dad. It turns out they know a lot of the same stuff because Alex was a psychology minor.

"You know I've never had my dad meet someone I'm dating before? You were the first. Ever!" I say. "And you really had his attention at dinner. Not that you were trying to impress."

"He's nice, Nicki," Alex says. "I like him."

"Yeah, everybody likes him," I say. It's true. Everybody likes Ronnie. "He's a storybook charmer, all right." Alex looks at me like, *huh*? So I explain. "In real estate, they always call a certain kind of really cute house a 'storybook charmer.' It means the kind of house that's going to make you get all emotional and go against your better judgment. Just like Ronnie."

Alex seems to get this. Then, out of nowhere he says, "You know what I want to do?" He's all excited. "I want to give your dad a job. He said he needs a job for his probation or parole or whatever it is, right? I'll get him something down at my work."

"You would not!" I can't believe Alex is serious. His tech start-up is the toast of the so-called Silicon Rainstorm—Portland's cutesy name for the small congregation of tech firms based here. "But your company is one of Portland's top-ten hottest tech firms!" I'm always giving Alex a hard time about a magazine article that came out listing his company as one of the most desirable to work for.

"Yeah, and everyone who works there went to politically correct schools like Reed and Stanford," Alex says. "They believe in the whole idea of reha-bilitation, and I'd say your dad is clearly rehabilitated. Why not challenge them to walk their talk?"

I kiss Alex. "You're awesome," I say. "But this sounds like one of those great ideas people get when they've had too much tequila." Although I'm secretly thrilled Alex would even talk about making such a grand gesture on behalf of my dad (and me), I feel like I need to give him an out so he doesn't feel so bad when he realizes what he said and wants to change his mind tomorrow.

"I'm serious, Nicki," he says. "I haven't had *that* much tequila. I don't know, it just seems like your dad is actually a really good guy who just got caught in the system and now he's worked his ass off to live right. He deserves a chance."

"You're such a liberal," I say playfully. But seeing my dad through Alex's eyes is making me soften a little. "I like that about you."

"I also want to do it for you," he says. He kisses me. "I'm serious."

I can't believe he would do something like that for me. In fact, having a guy be this nice to me is giving me anxiety. Good thing we're almost home. I can already hear Cody's music coming from his bedroom window.

"Cody!"

I shouldn't yell, but it's too late, I sort of did. You can hear some shuf-fling from inside the room. I poke my head in the window.

"What's going on in there?"

"Mom, are you drunk?"

"I wouldn't say drunk." I feel momentarily grateful that unlike me, Cody's growing up with a mom where being drunk is newsworthy and it's okay to say it out loud. "Sorry. What's happening?"

"I'm fine, Mom."

"Are your friends fine? Do they need a ride home?"

"Their ride already came," Cody says. "And Ronnie took Peaches home."

"Oh really? Shoot, I told her I would give her a ride."

Cody looks at my condition. "Yeah, um, no."

"Okay, honey," I say. Maybe now that I'm talking to a sixteen-year-old, I'm drunker than I realize. "I have to pee. I'll see you in there," I say, meaning inside the house.

I head into the house toward the bathroom. For a minute I think about putting in my diaphragm, but immediately reject the idea as lame. That's not my particular brand of Bad Mom. I'm more the lady who works a little too much and wants her kid to do well in school a little too much and gets a little too much takeout. I'm not the lady who's trying to get laid a little too much. Thank God.

I flush the toilet and head back outside. Alex is lying down on the grass now, looking up at the sky. "The stars are really beautiful tonight," he says.

I like guys who like stars.

I don't care what Peaches says. Alex is a good guy and I think this relationship has possibilities.

———

The minute we leave the doctor's office, Cody asks if he can drive. "Mom, please?" He's just had his thumb injury checked and lucky for him, he only partly lacerated his tendon, so after two weeks of wearing a hand splint that made him look like he was half dressed in a mummy costume, he's now been given a clean bill of health. Which means he's able, if not exactly ready, to get back behind the wheel. "Please? I'm so far behind. I really, really need to practice."

I make an *I don't know* face and mumble something about how Cody just got his splint off.

"Let the boy drive, Nicki," Ronnie says. "He wants to get his license, and he needs all the practice he can get."

It's getting to the point that when my dad tells me something about Cody, I just shut up and listen. It's like the two of them have some sort of mental telepathy that I'm not in on, and never could be in on, unless of course I had a penis. I had no idea I was so out of touch with my kid, and I said as much to Ronnie one day. He told me it's not that I was out of touch, it's just that a woman can never teach a boy how to be a man. Only another man can do that. At first I was dubious, but over the past few weeks I've been "schooled" (as Ronnie would say), and now when Ronnie uses his *it's a dude thing* tone of voice I just step aside and let the testosterone happen.

"So I guess this leaves me in the backseat?" I open up the car door and get in.

"Yeah, Mom," Cody says, giggling. "Welcome to my world. I had to sit back there until I was eleven. You'll get used to it."

"*Ha!*" Ronnie laughs. He motors the passenger seat back a few inches, forcing me to tuck my legs in, and gives Cody a fist bump. "Son, you're killing it."

Cody pushes the start button in the dash and it's immediately obvious he's done it before because the car is roaring to life. At the same time, he adjusts the rearview mirror and kicks back in his seat, shoots a glance at the shifter, and with his right hand confidently throws it in reverse like it's no big deal. Then he checks his first mirror, then the other one and with his uninjured hand, sweeps the steering wheel half a rotation to the right, and pulls out of the parking spot in one clean move.

"Damn, boy." Ronnie throws a look my way. "You got skills."

I'm not sure whether to be terrified or impressed. "How do you know how to do all that?"

"Because," he says, as he swipes the blinker down and pulls into traffic. "Ronnie."

"Because before he cut his thumb, I was teaching the boy to drive. That's how." Ronnie smiles impishly. "And I'm a great teacher, right?"

"Right," Cody says. He has a look of self-satisfaction on his face that belongs to a guy in his midtwenties. He holds out a fist for another bump.

"You took him out without asking me?" I say to Ronnie. "In what car?"

"In this one!" Ronnie claps. "Which car did you think?"

"Whenever you walk to your yoga class, or get your nails done with Peaches, Ronnie takes me out," Cody says. "Or he did, until I cut my finger. But I'm good, Mom. Just watch. You'll see, I'm awesome."

"He's right, baby," Ronnie says to me. "He's really good. Look at him!"

I'm astounded as Cody pulls into traffic. It's hard to get too mad, though. How did I not realize until this very moment that Cody's childhood's going to be over in about ten minutes and I'm extremely not ready for it? On the other hand, thanks to Ronnie, he appears to be readier than I imagined. If Cody can do life the way he drives this car, maybe I don't have to worry about him so much after all. He's damn good.

"Cody, you're lucky I think you're so cute," I say. "Because otherwise you would be in major trouble."

"I hope you think I'm so cute," Ronnie says back.

"Actually, Ronnie," I say. "You *are* in major trouble! Taking out my car without permission." I make it clear from my voice that I'm kidding.

"The boy needed to learn to drive," he says. "I hadda do what I hadda do to help him. Anything for my boy, here."

"You're forgiven. Now for the important questions," I say. "What's on the radio?"

Maybe there's something we can all sing along to.

# 23

# RONNIE

I finally found a job. Actually, I didn't "find" it—it found me. A couple of days after the Thanksgiving dinner party, I got a call from an unknown number (I almost didn't even pick it up) and it turned out to be the office manager from that company Alex works for. They said Alex recommended me for a PA position and would I like to come down and interview for the job? I'm like, what job? I was down there in a half hour! Not that I even knew what a PA does.

I started on Monday. Now it's Thursday, and I know what a PA does—everything. PA is short for "production assistant," a term from movie sets where you basically do all the things no one else wants to do. I answer the phones, make coffee, deal with the mail, and grocery shop for all the snacks in the break room. But my biggest responsibility is handling lunch. Every day I choose a restaurant from a list of places nearby, then pass out the menu to everyone in the office so they can pick something. I start with the CEO, who is something like twenty-nine and dresses like a lumberjack, and work my way down the hierarchy. There are twenty-three people total, and they all get a free lunch. I have half a mind to offer to cook for everyone because I could save this company an awful lot of money if I did. But maybe I'll try to stick around for a while before I suggest that.

Most of the day I sit in my "office area," which is really just a desk off the break room, and watch the world go by. There are also some good-looking girls working here, I won't lie. They flit around all day—from their desks to the bathroom, back to their desks, to the break room, and back to their desks again. Some of them have on little skirts and boots and giggle all the time. Others are the kind who just wear sweaters and jeans and don't like to show their bodies too much. I wouldn't have given them a second look when I was younger. In my advanced age, I can appreciate their beauty, too. They are all way too young for me (or "obvs," as the girls would say), but that doesn't mean I don't enjoy looking at them.

The best part about my desk is that it's right in the middle of everything, so people stop by and chat with me. I want to know where they're from, what kind of music they listen to, how long they've worked here, what their job is, and whether or not they're in a relationship. I think I've learned more about the world in the past four days than I did in the previous seventeen years combined.

"What's for lunch today, Ronnie?" I look up from the menu book where I'm trying to decide between the Italian place and the soup-and-salad place. It's Addie, one of the sweatshirt girls who works in coding. "Better not be the soup-and-salad place."

"Addie! Well, miss, I'm sorry to say, I think it is going to be exactly that," I say. There are two factions in the office—the miniskirt girls who don't eat any bread, rice, pasta, basically any white food, and the sweatshirt girls who do. It's practically a civil war. "We had carbs yesterday, I'm afraid."

"Sucks," Addie says. "The marketing girls need to realize that becoming Taylor Swift isn't a life goal."

"*Ha!*" I laugh, and clap my hands. Addie's funny and very real. "You're a good girl, Addie. You got a boyfriend?"

"Ronnie, I'm not into guys," she says. "Is that not clear?" She motions at her flannel shirt.

"Okay, you got a girlfriend?"

She smiles. "No, but I'm working on it." She leans over the little pony wall that separates my desk from the walkway and lowers her voice. "Do you know that girl Liz in IT?"

I lean in. "As a matter of fact, I do! She's cute!"

"Isn't she?"

"Should I put in a word for you?"

"You actually talk to her?" Addie sounds excited. "Is she in a relationship?"

"That, I don't know," I say. "But I can certainly find out." I open the three-ring binder and take out the soup-and-salad menu. "I'm about to take the lunch order. When I get to Liz, I'll drop a hint real sly. Get the lowdown."

"Yes!" Addie gives me a big smile before heading back to her desk. "You rock, Ronnie."

I have to admit, these kids are good people. So nice, they're forcing me to change my mind about people who go to expensive colleges and have doctors for dads. I woulda thought they were stuck-up or rude. Turns out to be far from the case. They are some of the most thoughtful and sincere people I've met in my life.

My first day here, the office manager introduced me as Ronnie Daniels, a guy who just spent a whole bunch of years in prison, who is doing this job as a condition of his parole. I told them when they hired me that I didn't want to hide my past. It's part of who I am, and I think being honest about it might even mean I can help some people. At the very least, they'll be a little less prejudiced against convicts if, once upon a time when they were in their first job, they met a guy named Ronnie who actually spent some time in prison. Since then, a couple of kids have dared to ask me what prison was like—so I dared to tell them. I told them it wasn't that much different from what they're doing right now. I told them everything changed for me the day I realized I could spend most of my time in there waiting for the moment I was going to get out. Or I could just be where I was and be free right now. My choice.

Sometimes I want to sit all of these kids down and give them a big speech on everything I've learned about life. I want to tell them being young is a lot better on TV than it is in real life, so they shouldn't compare their insides to other people's outsides. Being young is about trying to find yourself, figuring out who you are, and just as important, who you aren't. Everyone they know is wondering how their lives are going to turn out. Will they get the great job? Will they get a boyfriend/girlfriend who is nice and fits with their life plan *and*—this is the big *and*—they want to have sex with really bad? Why does that seem so hard to find?

The truth about being young is that it's just a phase. Everything is just a phase. It all passes. You go from being a kid, to being a kid in college, to being a kid with a job, to being married, to having kids, then a house and a dog. And then pretty soon your kids grow up and you get older and all the stuff you spent your life putting together starts to go away—you downsize the house, retire from the job, trade full-time kids for part-time grandkids. None of it lasts. You just have to enjoy it while it's here.

Not that they would believe me.

In twenty minutes, I'm done taking all the lunch orders and I'm about to fax them in, when Carmen, the receptionist, approaches me. She's still got the little phone system earpiece sticking out of her ear.

"Ronnie, there are some men here to see you." She seems a little tense.

"Are they delivery guys?" I have paper and office supplies coming. But they never arrive *that* quick. "I only ordered it a half hour ago."

Carmen shakes her head. "I don't think so. These guys are wearing suits. And there's two of them."

My heart skips twenty beats. *I'm in trouble.* My whole body knows this feeling. It's like my subconscious does a million little calculations and spits out a warning: *I'm in trouble.*

"Who are they?"

"I don't know," she says, impatient this time. She glances over her shoulder. "They want you to come out and talk."

I have to pee. My stomach is rumbling and I feel like I might just have diarrhea on the spot. Not good. "Can you tell them I'm gone?"

"Too late." Carmen looks sick, like she knows she's gotten me in trouble. "I already told them you're here."

Carmen turns to look again, and once she moves her body I can see that they are at the far end of the room, heading in my direction. If I could burst into a dash I would. But I'm frozen. I can't move even though I know what's about to happen.

They are coming and I can't stop them.

The biggest thing I'm feeling is mortified. Nicki's boyfriend got me this job and now I'm going to embarrass him and humiliate her and him both. Why is it that I can never stop hurting my child? Is there some part of me that can't stop screwing up? What is my problem?

"Ronald Daniels?" the guy on the right says.

"Yes."

"Multnomah County Sheriff's Department," he says evenly. "You're under arrest."

———

I've been in here three days now. Back into the world of buzzers and slamming doors. Of voices over loudspeakers. Of keys and uniforms. Of strip searches and screamers. Of a world painted cream and light blue—colors scientifically proven to induce "calm." (Yeah, right.) Of stainless steel toilets, and trays passed through tiny windows in doors, and shades that can only be drawn from the outside.

Back behind bars.

I've called the house three times so far. First no one picked up. Then Nicki picked up and hung up. Then, no one picked up. I'm trying to figure out what's happening. Is anybody coming? Am I going back to Sheridan? I'm tormented by the not knowing.

One thing I'm sure of: Melissa put me here. She had me picked up on a parole violation. (I don't even know what exactly yet, but it's not hard to find a violation—all parolees are breaking at least one of the rules most of the time.) It's my fault. You can't just get a woman all strung out on you and think she's going to let you walk away—I know that. Even worse, I never officially broke it off with Melissa. I was hoping I could let her down easy by slowly letting the whole relationship fade out. You know, let it die of neglect. I got so caught up in my new life with Nicki and Cody I thought she'd just forget about me. Just let it go real easy. I'd moved on, why couldn't she? It's not like in reality we were really going to have a future together. But Melissa Devolis doesn't give a goddamn about reality. She's lost in a time warp of Daddy issues, and isn't about to let me leave without fulfilling her fantasy of getting the bad boy to turn good *for her*. After I didn't love her the way she wanted to be loved, she decided to punish me by taking the only thing I have: my freedom.

"What the fuck." My cellmate is awake. And he's talking. "*What the fuck.*"

I'm in a cell with three other beds. The beds are filled with a rotating collection of drunk drivers, assaulters, car thieves, drug addicts. People being human in ways that make other people want to lock them up. People who still have people in their lives who will bail them out.

Right now there are just two of us. Me and my friend here, who's been lying dead on the floor on a dried river of old pee since he arrived four hours ago. Now that he's sitting up, I can see that he has a busted lip and his left eye is puffed almost shut.

"Looks like you lost," I say.

"I'm lost?" He's still trying to figure out where he is. He must have been really drunk.

"Looks like you lost," I say, louder. "The fight."

He's in his midtwenties. Working guy. Probably went out for some darts and a few beers and his big mouth got him here. He touches his face and winces. Pain is the only thing about this experience so far that isn't confusing to him.

"Can't remember it, huh?"

"Fuck, man," he says. "No."

"You're in jail."

"I see that." He stands up and goes over to the bars. "Hey! Hey! Somebody! *Hey!*"

Nobody comes.

He looks at me, because I seem like I know what's going on around here. "They'll be back around eventually," I say. "Maybe just have a seat." I pat the cot next to me, not in a threatening way. Not a lot of dudes in County are willing to share a seat with you, but this guy doesn't know that. Probably his first time and he can't tell the difference between a good guy and a bad guy. He shakes his head and sits back down on the dry pee river and buries his head in his hands. He might even be crying.

"Sorry, man," I say. "You and me both." He doesn't even look up at me.

I know how he feels. Time stops when you sit in a jail cell like this. Days turn into nights turn into days. You fall into a sort of animal state of poised alertness, where you imagine—expect?—something will happen at any moment. A fantasy place where you hope against hope that someone, anyone, will magically appear to get you out of here. My mind goes to the most far-fetched possibilities. If Nicki won't come, maybe Melissa? Peaches? Alex? Cody?

*This must be how Nicki felt as a child, waiting for me—Someone! Anyone!— to come home.*

Here's what will happen to me: at some point a court-appointed lawyer will show up to go over my options. It won't happen very quickly. Since I didn't murder anyone or commit some other high-priority crime, I could sit here weeks. If I can't find someone to bail me out, or sort out the parole violation with Melissa, I'll probably be forced to go back to Sheridan to do the rest of my time.

But there's not a goddamn thing I can do about that right now.

So I sit.

Meditating on what's happening.

Which is not much.

Mostly, I think about things. Life. There's this spiritual idea in the Bible—actually, all religions come to it sooner or later—that your life, and the people, places, and things in it—is a reflection of whatever you believe. Whatever you hold to be the deepest, truest thing about life—that's what will manifest in your life. It took me a long time to understand this. I thought the Bible was telling me that everything that happens to me *is my fault*. That if my life is shit, it's because I wasn't a good Christian. I "created" my life, right? So God must hate me, probably because I did things wrong, like sell drugs and masturbate. But once I went a few trips around the sun in prison, I started to get it. I didn't end up in jail because of bad circumstances, bad timing, or bad breaks. No one was against me. I ended up in jail because I made the choices you make when you believe what I believed.

And I believed I was bad.

I'm not even sure exactly how. I was just bad somehow. Some invisible way that I could never quite put my finger on, but women were always trying to point out.

Maybe you can't go home again. Maybe seventeen years is too long to be away and have anyone remember you, love you, want you. Maybe they never wanted you in the first place. Maybe the people who invented three-strikes laws were right: once you're a criminal long enough, you'll always be a criminal.

It doesn't matter that I didn't commit a crime this time. My crime is being a criminal now.

The fact that I'm sitting here means at some level I still believe I am alone and always will be. The question now is: am I willing to change that belief?

# 24

## NICKI

The glow of Thanksgiving didn't last very long. On Sunday, Peaches canceled our mani-pedi date. She said she was hungover, which is hardly a reason to cancel. She's always hungover. That doesn't ever stop her from getting a mani-pedi. In fact, getting her nails done is usually the *cure* for a hangover. Then, later that night I called her, but she didn't pick up. Also weird. When she didn't return my calls or my texts on Monday, Tuesday, or Wednesday I started thinking she was lying in a ditch somewhere, having finally succumbed to her bad driving or choices in men or both. So today I finally went to her work and cornered her. I guess I sort of knew something was wrong. Though I never in a million years would have guessed what.

"Are you okay?" We're standing in the little waitress station off the main dining room of the restaurant where she works. She's making a side salad, sprinkling croutons and ladling Italian dressing on it.

"I'm fine," she says. "Why do you ask?"

"Because you canceled on Sunday and you haven't responded to me for days?"

"So?" Peaches can be difficult, but usually it's *I'm-in-your-face-about-your-new-boyfriend* difficult, not *I'm-saying-nothing's-wrong-when-it-obviously-is* difficult. "Do I have to answer to you for everything? I swear, you want me on some kind of leash."

"Peaches." I have no idea where this tone of voice is coming from. "It's been a week."

"Nicki," she says, "it's not that long."

Now she's mocking me. I feel a little lump in my throat. I don't know why this is making me want to cry, but it is. "Are you serious? You're going to mock me right now?"

"I'm fine," she says. She practically slams a bottle of ketchup onto her tray. "I'm not sure why you wouldn't believe me."

"Probably because you're not acting fine."

"Will you hand me that mustard?" I'm annoyed that she's asking this, but I do it anyway. She grabs it from me. "Why do you have to sweat me all the time?"

"Peaches, what's going on? Are you mad at me?"

"Why, should I be?"

She drops a fork and picks it up and puts it on the tray anyway.

"Obviously something's wrong. Tell me what it is."

"I'm working, Nicki." She scoops up the tray. "I'll call you later." She pushes the flap doors open and walks out into the restaurant, leaving me standing there.

I follow her out onto the floor. "Peaches!" I'm whispering loudly. "Stop!"

She ignores me as she goes to her table and puts down the side salads, the drinks, and the ketchup and mustard. The customers look at me like I'm crazy. "She's training me," I say. "It's my first day."

Peaches pretends like I'm not even there and heads back for the kitchen. I struggle to keep up. The moment we are out of the main room, Peaches hisses at me. "Leave me alone!"

"No, Peaches. I won't. What's going on?" Somehow I'm getting the idea that whatever's happening, I need to know what it is immediately. Peaches has never acted like this in the history of our relationship. Ever.

"Okay, fine. There's something going on, but"—she looks at me dead serious—"I can't tell you."

I drop my shoulders, relieved that I'm not insane. I was really starting to worry there. "You can tell me anything! You know that you can."

"Not this." She turns her back to me. "Now, please stop asking. I have to work."

All I can think is that she's pregnant or someone died. But both of those she could tell me.

"Are you pregnant?" I say.

"Please, Nicki."

"You tell me everything!"

"I know." She looks terrible. "That's why if you keep pressing me, I'll probably tell you."

"So, tell me."

"This is different."

"Peaches, I'm worried about you. Whatever it is, it's a bad idea to keep it bottled up. This is how people get cancer." I don't know why I just said that. It's clearly not scientific, but a part of me still thinks it's true. Anyway, it was just one last gasp trying to get her to tell me whatever it is that she won't tell me.

She pulls her hair out of her eyes and lifts her head. She wants to tell me, I see that. Peaches has a lot of faults, but keeping secrets isn't one of them. What you see is what you get. "Are you sure?"

"Of course, I'm sure. You can tell me absolutely anything."

"And you won't get mad?"

"I won't get mad."

"I didn't mean to do it."

"Do what?" I prompt her the way I used to have to prompt Cody when he had to admit he was the one who broke the lamp or the cup or whatever. "You didn't mean to do what?"

She starts to cry. Big tears, of a variety I have never, in all these years, seen her cry.

"What?"

"Nicki, I slept with your dad."

I didn't see that coming. Not at all.

———

The day is going from bad to worse, if that's possible. I was supposed to go to the restaurant after stopping by Peaches's work, but I'm sick to my stomach and I had to come home and get in bed. I can only think about one utterly bad life decision at a time. And right now it's Ronnie's. Or maybe it's mine, for letting Ronnie into my life again.

Of course he fucked my friend.

I should have known when I let him move in here that something like this would happen. This is who he is: a person who is so self-centered, so narcissistic, so unable to think about anyone but himself that he'll just mow down whoever gets in his way. He doesn't care about me, Cody, or even Peaches. He just cares about knowing he can have power over some dumb woman who needs to know she can have power over him.

They both disgust me.

He's at work right now, so I have the next three hours to figure out how I'm going to tell him I know what he did. Thinking back on the last week—I had no idea anything was amiss. That's how messed up he is, that he can do something so wrong and then just act like everything's fine! He can go out with me and Cody and get pizza after the doctor's office and make breakfast and lunch and do laundry—all as though he didn't just betray me in the grossest possible way.

Obviously I'm going to kick him out. But I'm not going to call him to tell him that. I'll just wait until he gets home from work. It needs to happen face-to-face.

Speaking of which, how am I going to tell Alex? This is such a mess. What am I supposed to do, ask Alex to fire Ronnie? I can just see me going to my new boyfriend of a month and saying *you know that awesome thing you did for me because you're amazing? Well, now I need you to undo it because I have god-awful family baggage and I'm virtually radioactive as a result. Don't even think of wanting to be in a relationship with me because this is what you're going to get more of.*

I'm untouchable.

I was so stupid to think maybe the war was over. To think that maybe I was going to get to be a normal person with a kid, a dad, a boyfriend, a job, a business, a house. And now it's all gone, of course. Because that's me: Nicki Daniels, the girl with the smelly plastic shoes.

I pick up the remote control and am about to click on the DVR—quick, get me some *House Hunters International*—when the landline rings. Normally, I wouldn't even answer that phone, but I haven't heard from Cody all afternoon, and sometimes he'll call me there if my phone dies, which it did, so I pick it up.

"Hello?"

There's a beat, and a familiar pause that I recognize from some faraway place in my mind, like a face that is hard to place. *I've heard this before, where do I know this from? I've heard this before, where do I know this from?* I'm running through the options in my mind when the voice begins:

*"This call is from the Multnomah County Jail. You will not be charged for this call. This call is from . . . 'Ronnie.' To accept this call, press five. To decline this call press—"*

Fuck him. I decline.

An hour later, Alex comes over and tells me the whole story, or what he knows of it. Ronnie was at work when two guys showed up and put him under arrest, apparently on a parole violation. Even though Ronnie's embarrassed him at his job, Alex has brought flowers, and is offering to bail Ronnie out of jail. That's how awesome he is, even when I don't really deserve it.

"I'm so sorry, Nicki," he says.

"I should be saying I'm sorry to you," I say. "I'm so embarrassed."

Alex tells me it's not my fault, and chances are it's probably not Ronnie's fault, either. He's so sweet and trusting. I shake my head and snort cynical laughter.

"You don't know my dad, Alex. He's probably guilty as shit."

Alex looks stunned, his expression a mixture of disbelief that my dad is guilty, and fear that I sound so unforgiving.

"Wait a minute, now," Alex says. He's trying to slow me down; you know, maybe there's some kind of mistake. "You don't know that."

"Really? Really, Alex?" I sound scary now. "I kind of *do* know that. Every time you give him a chance, he fucks it up. *That's what he does.* And now he's doing it again."

"Nicki, calm down."

He doesn't mean for this to come out patronizing, but that's how I take it, because I'm furious. Furious that my dad would do something like this, *again.* That he would not only drag me through it, *again.* But that he would drag Cody through it, too. Not to mention Alex.

"I will not calm down, Alex," I say. I'm angry now. "You have no idea."

Alex backs down. "You're right, I don't."

"I'm *pissed.* You did something nice for him and what does he go and do? He totally takes advantage!" My chest is heaving and I feel sick that Alex is seeing me like this, but I can't control it. I feel so unworthy of such a good person. "This is who I am, Alex. I'm a messy, fucked-up chick from a terrible background and this is how it is. This is why I date losers who bail on me out of the blue—because I'm not worth being with a nice guy. I'm just going to bring you down and make you look bad at work, and be a burden to you."

"Nicki!" He sounds genuinely shocked. "That's not true!"

"It's okay, you can go now. I'm giving you an out," I say. I can hear that I sound insane, but I also believe what I'm saying. This is the truth about me. I might have it all together on the outside, but if you get too close, you're going to discover who I really am. And who I really am is a girl from the wrong side of town, passing as a normal person who grew up in an upscale suburb. "You don't have to get involved with me. You can get out now, while there's still time."

Alex drops his head. "Nicki, no," he says. He looks seriously hurt, as if I'm rejecting him. "You're not going to get rid of me that easy."

"Go, Alex."

He just sits there.

"Alex, *go!* Please."

I can't stand to see myself in his eyes. It makes me feel so small and so ashamed.

"Okay, I'll go," he says, getting up. He grabs his car keys off the coffee table. He doesn't seem angry, just confused and hurt. "But you're not going to get rid of me that easy."

I watch as he walks toward the door, giving me one last meaningful glance before he closes it behind him. I hear his footsteps go down the wooden stairs, and I'm relieved.

I'm also nauseous.

———

I spend the whole next day in a whirlwind. Nothing like a crisis to make me triple my productivity. I do four appraisals, tear through a massive pile of paperwork, do two loads of laundry, and grocery shop, all before Cody gets home from school. All this activity does the job of pushing the drama with my dad to the background, where I almost can't see it or feel it. I say almost, because it's still there, draining my energy like a data-sucking application you leave open on your phone. And you wonder why you're at 14 percent battery and it's only 3 p.m.

I'm still livid at Ronnie. I was just starting to trust him and now, *bam!* He's back in jail. This is the worst-case scenario.

I'm mad at myself, too, for making Alex leave last night. I woke up this morning going, *What did I just do?* Now I haven't heard from him all day and I'm blaming myself. I was stupid to take my frustration and anger with my dad out on him. Alex is a good guy. He's better than good, he's amazing. And now he thinks I'm not speaking to him.

Also, I never thought I'd say this, but I miss Peaches. She is the only person I could really talk to about what is happening right now. No one else would understand. I feel betrayed by my dad. It feels something like getting fired from a job, finding out a boyfriend is cheating, crashing your car, and getting an F on a test—all rolled into one.

At least I'm not missing Jake. So that's something.

I can't bring myself to tell Cody what's going on, either. This is exactly why I never wanted him to know my dad. Because this is what my dad does. He gets you to love him, then he leaves you. Right when you least expect it. I want to kill my dad for doing this again. First to me, and now to my son.

Except for how much I got done today, this really, really sucks.

———

At dinnertime, the phone rings again. This time Cody picks it up before I have a chance to stop him. Instantly, I know it's Ronnie again—I can tell from the blank look on Cody's face that he is listening to the lady with the automated voice:

*This call is from the Multnomah County Jail. You will not be charged for this call.*

"Hang it up," I say from across the room. "Cody." This is not how I want him to find out that Ronnie's in jail again. But I can already see that it's too late.

Cody looks up at me, but doesn't move.

*This call is from—*

I grew up with that recording. I know every second of that recording. That recording framed every major moment of my life with my father: my first starring role in a school play, my first period, my first kiss. And now my son has to hear it.

*An inmate at—*

"Hang it up!" I say again, louder this time. Too loud.

But Cody doesn't hang it up. He presses five. *God, no, please.* Then he starts talking.

"Ronnie?" Cody sounds worried, fearful, shocked. My worst nightmare. "Are you okay?"

My stomach feels like I just ate a giant spoonful of sour cream, which I'm allergic to. I want to barf. Right now. I want to get up and rip the phone right out of Cody's hand, but something in his body language, the look on his face, is stopping me.

"What happened?" I can only hear Cody's side of the conversation. "It's okay, dude. We're going to get you out."

*No, we're not.*

"Don't tell him that," I say. Cody's so trusting. He believes every word Ronnie is saying right now. "I don't know if that's true."

Cody looks up at me. "Talk to him, Mom."

"I don't want to talk to him."

"She doesn't want to talk to you," he says into the phone. He listens another moment, then turns back to me. "He says he understands. But there's been a mistake, and if you'll just let him, he can explain. He got picked up on a parole violation. For not having a job."

"That's bullshit, he has a job," I say. There are times I wish I still smoked. Like now. Now would be the perfect time to light up a menthol 100 and instantly feel in control of my life.

"That's exactly it," Cody says, pleading ever so slightly. He's giving Ronnie the benefit of the doubt, but as far as I'm concerned, Ronnie used up the last of his benefits in the 1990s. "It's a mistake. Something to do with the caseworker down at the—" He speaks into the phone again. "What was that again?" Cody relays the rest of the sentence: "The caseworker down at the halfway house. You need to go talk to her. He never reported his job to her, and that's why they arrested him. He would do it himself, but he needs twenty-five hundred dollars' bail to get out."

"That doesn't make sense. They arrested him *at* his job."

"I don't know, Mom!" Cody's frustrated with me. "Can't you just help figure it out? Ronnie's sitting in jail!"

I need that cigarette because right now my son is playing hostage negotiator between me and my dad.

What has my life come to? It's come to where it started from, that's what.

"The line's dead," Cody says. He clicks off the phone. "He hung up."

"No. They cut you off after ten minutes," I say. "The calls are timed. That's how it is. I'm sorry, baby," I say. "I know it's a disappointment."

"You don't sound sorry," Cody says. It almost sounds like a threat. But he's right, I don't sound sorry. Probably because I'm not. Not really. "You're going to get him out, right?"

"I don't know, honey," I say. "My dad is responsible for his own life. If he got himself in there, maybe he needs to get himself out."

Cody's horrified. "Are you serious?"

*Yeah, I'm serious.* "People are responsible for their own lives."

Cody scans my face, looking for some sign that I don't mean what I'm saying. Some sign that I'm going to give Ronnie a break and bail him out. But there isn't any, because I have a callus in the spot where I'm supposed to give Ronnie a break.

"But that's not fair," he says. "It's a mistake."

"It's always a mistake, Cody," I say. I'm tired all of a sudden. So tired. "It's been a mistake with him since 1986."

Cody glares at me—it's the ugliest face he's ever made at me. The most intense fear and disgust. I feel like he just plunged a dagger into my lung. "I hate you right now," he says quietly. He gets up and leaves the room.

Part of me is like, *fuck you, Ronnie.* The other part of me is like, *fuck.*

I feel so alone.

I'm only doing this because Cody hates me right now. I haven't decided yet whether I'm going to ask/beg Melissa Devolis to let Ronnie out. But I figure I should at least hear what she has to say. I arrive at the halfway house first thing in the morning. Melissa pokes her head into the waiting room and says she'll be right with me. She seems nice enough. Sort of plain, but then again if she had more spectacular looks, she'd probably go for a bigger career than midlevel federal employee. Something in public relations, or marketing. Something where you need style to pull it off. What this job lacks in glamour, it makes up for with power. Melissa can get my dad out of jail all by herself. And all by herself she can get him sent back to Sheridan until 2017.

"Hi, I'm Melissa," she says as she buzzes me through the door. "Thanks for waiting. Right this way."

She gives me a light handshake and I notice her tiny hands, which look too young for her face. There's a ring on her right ring finger, something semiprecious, probably a garnet. I wonder where she got it. Did she buy that for herself? Was she trying to do some self-help kind of thing about loving herself? I can tell she's got major self-esteem issues, in a *You Spot It, You Got It* way. You know, how you can only see something in another person when you have it in yourself? Melissa hasn't had a great relationship in, like, ever.

*I feel you, sister.*

I think about Alex, and whether I should call him and apologize. Or maybe I should just text? I haven't heard from him, but I feel intuitively— at least I think it's intuitive, maybe it's more of a hopeful delusion—that he hasn't forgotten about me, he's just giving me space to work all this stuff out. The longer I'm away from him, the more I'm thinking he's the best guy I've ever dated. If one positive thing comes out of all this, it will be that I finally know that I can want to have sex really bad with a guy who is really good. Even if Alex doesn't ever want to see me again, that's major.

I follow behind Melissa as she leads me down a hallway to a cubicle where there's a PC on the desk and a large tower on the floor. It's definitely 2006 up here in the Oregon Residential Reentry Facility, or whatever this place is called. She points toward a chair and I take a seat. I'm trembling a little bit, surprisingly nervous. She sits in her chair, which squeaks, and asks what she can do for me. I start by simply asking what happened.

"Your dad got arrested because he failed to get a job and then failed to report according to the terms of his parole," she says. She sounds super-official. "That's what happened."

"But he had a job." I'm not trying to argue, but Alex gave him a job, so if that's why he's back in jail, that's not fair.

"Yes, and he failed to report that," she says.

"But he *has* a job," I say again. She's doing that thing where she forces me to argue with her. "Isn't that the point of the rule?"

"The point of the rules, actually," Melissa says, "is to follow them."

"Does it not strike you as ironic that Ronnie's getting arrested for not having a job at the job he's failing to report?" It is very difficult not to raise my voice at all. "So is the parole violation not having a job, or failing to report the job?"

Blank face.

Oof. I've only been sitting here two minutes, but it's superobvious Melissa had some kind of relationship with my dad. If I had to guess, I'd say he stopped communicating with her when he moved in with me (I never even heard him mention her name), and as a result, Melissa felt jilted. And when Ronnie didn't follow the terms of his parole to the letter of the law, she decided to get revenge by having him arrested.

"Are you going to send him back to prison?" The moment I say this, I know I don't want it to happen. No matter how mad my dad makes me, he doesn't deserve to go back there. It's clear to me that he may be guilty of being Ronnie—because he, as he might put it, has a hard time with boundaries—but that doesn't mean he needs to be locked up. "He hasn't done anything to deserve that."

"That's up to the judge," Melissa says.

"But you can make a call, surely," I say.

Melissa stares at me dead in the eye. The answer is clearly *Yes, I could*, but *no, I will not*. I am instantly furious. Ronnie is a criminal, yes, but suddenly my heart opens to the fact that the reason he's been gone for so long is that there is an unjust system where the punishment far exceeds the crime. He's never had enough power to force the legal system to be fair to him. Well, I have that much power.

*I need to get my dad out of there.*

But in order to do it, I have to figure out how to leverage Melissa's relationship with him—how to force her to let him go. I can't decide if saying this directly would be the right tactic, or if hinting at it would be better.

"Melissa, I know you had a relationship with my dad." Why not just go for broke? Subtlety is not going to take the day here. "He told me."

I'm a halfway decent liar when I need to be—which is, like, every five years. When you grow up with someone like my mother, you learn to lie if you have to.

"Excuse me?" Melissa clearly had a better mother than I did, because she's looking down at her shoes. If that's not a "tell," I don't know what is. This is going to be easier than I thought.

"Look, Melissa. I get it," I say. "I totally get it."

"Get what?" She's either not-so-brilliantly playing innocent, or she's really naive.

"*It*. I get *it*." I sigh so big it might seem like I'm being condescending. But actually I'm being real—this whole situation makes me sigh. "Ronnie's my dad. I've been dealing with him my whole life. He's the most awesome person in the world *and* he's a total nightmare. That's just how he is. In fact, I've often thought to myself, *Thank God I'm not one of his girlfriends.*"

Melissa's blank face is now starting to show some movement. A little bit around her eyebrows, a little bit around her mouth. It looks like a glacier getting ready to break apart.

"Maybe I shouldn't have said that," I say. "I'm sorry."

I don't want to hurt Melissa's feelings, but it's true: I have often thought I'm glad I'm not one of Ronnie's girlfriends. Because then you'd have to deal with Ronnie's worst side—his grandiosity, his entitlement, the way he's often willing to exploit you and lie to your face while doing it. Ronnie wouldn't (doesn't!) do that to me. Daughters are their whole own category of woman. For a man like Ronnie, they're the last, best, and sometimes *only* chance of getting true love from a woman.

"Look, you probably got involved with him for the same reason everyone does: he's charming and handsome. And he makes it seem like he just might be able to give you what you need in that moment, right?" She's listening to me, I can tell, so I keep talking. I'm trying to get it all in before she can change her mind. "And then, he doesn't come through. One day, he just disappears and you wonder, where did he go? It seemed like he loved you, or at least liked you a lot, right?" I nod a little bit. "I get it."

Melissa doesn't protest, so I'm assuming I'm onto something here.

"And you're pissed about it," I say. "But, Melissa. Can I just say something? For all of his faults, he's taught me some of the most useful life stuff I know. And one of the things he taught me is that you've got to assume people are giving everything they've got. If you're not getting something from someone, it's not that they don't want to give it to *you*. It's that they don't have it to give."

I reach out and put my hand on her arm, because I'm about to close this deal. "Ronnie can never be more than what he was to you, except to one person. Me."

Melissa looks away from me. Like maybe she might want to cry and she doesn't want me to see her. She doesn't realize we have the same pain—

of being let down by men. Just like every woman who loves Ronnie. Even Peaches.

*Oh shit. Even Peaches.*

"Actually he can only be more to two people. Me, and my son," I say. Now I feel like maybe I might cry, too. "Can I just tell you that Ronnie's been the most amazing person since he got out. I think he really is that rare case. He rehabilitated himself! When he showed up on my doorstep, I was in a really dark place and he just . . . swooped in and handled shit. He cooks and he cleans and he takes my son, Cody, to school. My son has never had a dad, and Ronnie has been a friend to him and helped him study for his permit and taught him to drive, and made him feel like a young man instead of a little boy. I couldn't do that for my son, I couldn't. But Ronnie could, and he did.

"He's healed, Melissa. Somehow, in there, he healed. And now he's healing me. And I bet if you look deep enough, he healed something in you, too."

Even as I say it, I know it's true: we are all connected. Melissa spins halfway away from me, her office chair squeaking as she turns.

"We need him, Melissa." I really mean this and not just for Cody, for me, too. "We need him in our lives."

# 25

## RONNIE

I've never been so nervous. I'm lined up with all the other guys getting ready to leave. We've already been through the checkout procedure—this place is like the Holiday Inn from hell—and we've changed back into our regular clothes. We've gotten back our watches and key chains and cigarette lighters. We're about to board the elevator, ride down to the basement, go through the last two doors, and take the final staircase up. Then they'll open the door and I'll be free. Again.

You would think the last five days have been a nightmare, but actually, they haven't. I got time to reflect, and I needed that. Yeah, county jail is a lot worse than federal prison. But that just reminded me what I needed to remember: what got me behind bars was me. The bars might be outside me, but the prison cell is inside me—and it just manifests on the outside. Like the Eastern philosophers say: *As above, so below. As within, so without.*

See, these past two months since I left Sheridan have been a Shrinky Dinks version of my whole life. Basically, I got born, I had gifts (freedom, good looks, smarts), and I squandered them by placing too much attention on the outer world (sex, money) and not enough attention on the inner one (love, peace, humility). I've spent a lifetime imprisoned by my selfishness—getting what I thought I wanted, then trying to keep it. All those years in Sheridan taught me how to let go of that. I learned to live without getting what I wanted. Without sex, and money, and the five other deadly sins.

And then I got out of prison and promptly forgot. I let my guard down. Got lazy. Started slipping into my old states of mind. My old behaviors. Next thing I know I'm sitting in a jail cell again. It doesn't even matter that it wasn't my fault. Coming this close to losing everything again has been a wake-up call. The way I was going, I was probably going to end up right back at Sheridan. But this gave me a chance to go within. To search my heart. To think about what I want to be for my girl and her son. And what I want to be is a blessing to them. I want to matter to them. I want to serve them. I want to make their lives a better place.

When that door opens, I don't know exactly what's going to happen. All I know is that Melissa signed the papers for my release. I'm assuming there will be someone from the halfway house waiting to take me back there. And that's fine. I'll do a thousand days in that place if it'll give me another chance to make it up to Nicki and Cody. I know how lucky I am to get out of here this fast. I could be on my way to the penitentiary right now, but I'm not. So whatever happens on the other side of those doors, I'm prepared for it. All I want is another chance to get my family back.

The second to the last door buzzes. There's a long hallway as we move toward the final door, the one that leads to the outside world. Another inmate shoots me a quick glance; his heart is pounding through his eyes. He's scared—we all are. No matter how many times you've done this walk—and most of us have done it a lot of times—you never really know what's on the other side of that door. Actually, you do know. The world's out there. And if you're a criminal, the world is a cruel place. That's why you keep going back to jail.

"You got someone waiting for you?" the guy asks me.

"I don't know, man. You?"

"Naw," he says. "But that's okay."

The door opens and we pass through it. "Hey, good luck, okay?" I put a hand on the guy's shoulder and take the few remaining steps toward daylight.

As I move from the shadow of the doorway, I look around, expecting to see a guy holding a sign that says Oregon Residential Reentry, or something like that. Instead, there she is: Nicki.

She's smiling.

I don't know what I did to deserve the love of this girl. She could have told me to rot in hell, but here she is, holding two shiny metallic balloons that say Welcome Home! And there's Cody standing next to her. There's a light rain and it looks like they've been standing there awhile. Cody pounds his fist into mine.

We hug.

"Welcome home, Ronnie," he says.

For the first time, I feel like I have a place in the world that is safer than my cell. What I have now is a home. I have a real home.

# PART FIVE

———

## Home Equity

## 26

# NICKI

I walk in the door after work and Peaches is there. She's lying on the couch, her feet up, flipping through one of my fashion magazines. Like she lives here. I didn't expect anyone to be home, so I should be startled, but in the back of my mind, I knew she would just show up at some point. After all, that's what I did when I needed to talk to her. It just took her longer. Because she's Peaches. She's more stubborn than I am.

"What are you doing here?" I put down my purse and take off my coat. It's harder to get out of the coat than usual because I just had to wear this cable-knit fisherman's sweater that's too bulky.

"Sorry about the surprise." She hardly even looks up from the magazine. "You're not answering my calls."

"I know," I say. "Because I don't really want to talk to you."

"Are you still mad at me?" Peaches shuts the magazine and chucks it back onto the coffee table. Then she wings her feet off the arm of the sofa and onto the floor. She's staring at the little ceramic vase where I keep a dried dandelion. "You are. You're still mad at me."

I head for the bathroom, due to the fact that I have to pee like crazy. I'm actually not still mad at Peaches—I just don't trust her yet. I figured it out while talking to Melissa that we're all the same—we're fucked up over men and that's why we make bad choices. But that doesn't mean I was ready to let her off the hook like that. I've been feeling like I wanted to take my time coming back into my relationship with Peaches. Because even if I'm not holding a grudge against her, there is something between us that needs to change for me to be comfortable to be here. Some power imbalance. I want to be equals with her, instead of riding a seesaw where one of us is always down, and the other is always up. Even if we trade off who's down and who's up.

"Where are you going?"

"The bathroom," I say without turning around.

Peaches jumps up from the sofa and follows me to the bathroom. We've always gone to the bathroom together. Whoever wasn't in "active duty" would sit on the edge of the bathtub while the other one picked up shampoos and cleaning products and pretended to be a *Price Is Right* model—gesturing at them with gusto. Sometimes I would even announce the product's benefits, just like Johnny Olson, Bob Barker's sidekick.

"We need to talk, Nicki," Peaches says. "I've been sitting here almost two hours."

"We don't need to talk." I shut the door to the bathroom, right in Peaches's face. "There's nothing to talk about."

She keeps talking through the door.

"First of all, I'm sorry."

"I know. You said that," I say. She's left me numerous voice mails and text messages. "About a thousand times with a million emojis."

"It was a terrible thing to do," she says, not quite hollering, but loud enough that I'm sure to hear her perfectly through the door. "I'm weak and there's no excuse."

I let the silence happen as I finish tinkling. Part of being in a long-term friendship like this is letting the other person know how bad you're really hurt. Not just faking a truce for the sake of peace. You owe it to the relationship to be honest about where you really are. If you're still mad, *be mad.* That's our motto. So even though I'm technically not still mad, I'm not ready to let Peaches know that. She needs to understand that there are consequences for breaking the trust.

I flush and open the door without washing my hands.

"Please, please, Nicki," she says. "Don't make me beg."

"Why not?" I say. "It might be good for you."

She laughs, which is okay, because it was sort of a joke. A joke that's true. "Peaches, I hear you," I say. "But I should probably go figure out what to feed my child when he gets home from school." She's dismissed.

"That's not it, Nicki." She lightly pushes me toward the living room and sits me down on the sofa. "I have something for you." She reaches into her handbag and pulls out one of those white plastic drawstring bags from the Apple Store. "Here."

I take the bag. It's a little bit heavy. "You got me a new keyboard?"

"Look inside."

I open the bag and inside is cash. A whole bunch. Not as much as Jake gave me, but a lot. "What is this? You're Jake now?"

"My life savings. I've been keeping it underneath my mattress for the past five or six years. That's everything. Probably around ten thousand dollars."

A lot of thoughts are running through my mind right now. First of all: What? Why is Peaches handing me this money? Second of all: Where did she get it? I can't believe Peaches saved ten thousand dollars. She doesn't seem capable of delaying that much gratification. "Did you steal this?"

She shakes her head.

"Did a Harley guy give it to you? Because you know that means it's stolen, right? Or drug money."

"No, I swear." Peaches looks more vulnerable than I've ever seen her. Is that an *I could just cry* face? If so, we're in some entirely uncharted territory. "It's everything I have in the world, Nick. And I want you to have it. I mean, not *have* it—have it. I want you to use it to open the restaurant. I want to be an investor!"

Underneath her twisted, fearful expression you can see another one of pure glee. She's really thought about this. And she's serious. I know when Peaches is serious. Her mouth turns down at the corners and she smiles at the same time. If that's possible. "And I am going to manage the place!" She puts up her hand before I can start to protest. "No! Listen. I'm ready! I've been working in restaurants since God was born. And I know I can do it."

Let me try to comprehend this. On the one hand, this is bananas, given that I'm furious with her, and her judgment sucks, and she's hardly someone you would ever want to go into business with. On the other hand, now that it's in front of me, I can see that this is the perfect solution. Absolutely, totally perfect. I can't believe we didn't think of this before. I didn't even know I wanted a restaurant, and suddenly now it's the rightest thing in the world?

Yes, it is. I can see that.

"You don't have to do this," I say tentatively. Peaches starts jumping up and down a little bit because she now knows I'm going to say yes.

"I want to do it! You think I want to spend the rest of my life serving drunk people bar food and side salads? Nicki! Please."

I should probably just say yes and throw my arms around her, but lately it has become clear that life decisions like this one are like long division—you might know the answer, but you have to show your work. I need to go through every single one of the remainders.

"I'm going to drive you crazy," I say. "I'm such a perfectionist."

"So? That's not new. We already know how to drive each other crazy and come back from it."

"You're going to have to wake up earlier in the morning." Peaches is the laziest person I know. She hardly ever wakes up before 11:30 a.m. Like I've said to her a million times, all the money gets made before noon. "Because I'm not going to be some kind of mom person and push you to do something you don't want to do."

"Not a problem! It's about time I started getting up earlier," she says. "I'm ready."

"I don't know, Peaches."

"Yes, you do know. You need me. Don't try to tell me you don't, because I went down there and spoke to Miguel."

"You what?"

"He's *really* cute, by the way." She's not even kidding. "How did you not even tell me that?"

"You can't sleep with people we work with. Not even the people you think it's okay to sleep with."

"I know, I know."

"You probably will anyway."

"Probably. But not Miguel. I swear. Unless you say it's okay."

My mind-chatter is like four songs playing at once. In business with Peaches? Even though it makes no sense, it makes as much sense as anything in my life has ever made.

"Oh my God. We're serious, aren't we?"

"So serious." She takes both of my hands in hers. "But you can only take this money—this deal—on one condition."

"What's that?"

"You forgive your dad completely."

Here come the tears—they're mine, of course. I think I'm so tough sometimes. Until I'm not.

"It wasn't his fault, Nicki. It really wasn't." She drops her head onto my shoulder and my arms automatically go around her. Peaches is my dearest friend. The only person who truly knows me besides Cody. I need her and it doesn't matter how bad she screwed up. She sobs into me. "I'm so fucked up."

"You're not that fucked up," I say through my tears. In my opinion, if you know you're fucked up, you're not actually that fucked up. The real problems in life come from people who think they're fine. "Really, you're not."

"You're wrong," she says, wiping her tears with the crumpled-up paper towel she was using as a napkin. "I'm a disaster. But I'm going to be a helluva business partner. I promise."

I believe her.

———

We haven't had a Christmas tree in five years. It's not that I hate Christmas, it's just that I think Christmas is really, really overrated. I decided Santa was bullshit when I was four years old and robbers broke into our house on December 23 and stole all the presents. And to be honest, I don't miss any of it: Santa, trees, lights. Even if I had aunts and uncles and cousins to sit around and drink eggnog with, I don't think that's what I would want to do. Aren't most people just pretending to like their family anyway? I'd rather get on a plane and go somewhere exotic and wonderful. Cody never protested, either. The furthest thing from a sentimentalist, he was just as happy as me to spend December 25 in Tokyo, Paris, or Rome. Game Boys are everywhere, after all, and that's all he needed.

Unfortunately, Ronnie is not having our humbuggy ways. Which is why we're now at the Boys & Girls Club Christmas tree lot on the corner of Southeast Belmont trying to decide between the Douglas fir and the balsam.

"I want the balsam," I say. "This is what a Christmas tree is supposed to look like."

"But this is the Pacific Northwest, girl," Ronnie says. "You gotta go with the Doug fir. That's our people up here. Douglas firs are who we are."

Now that he mentions it, I remember learning in fifth grade that the Douglas fir is the Oregon state tree. The problem is, I don't really like Doug firs all that much. Their needles are too dense and point upward, making the lights hard to string. And since I don't want to get a tree to begin with,

I feel like I should be able to get the unwanted tree that I want. If that makes sense.

"I don't like the way the branches are on those," I say. "It makes it hard to put the ornaments on. They don't dangle right. These"—I put forward a sturdy balsam—"are American classics. They are the Dallas Cowboys Cheerleaders of the Christmas tree world."

Cody's a few feet away, pulling out trees he likes. "How about this one!" He's got an eight-footer in his hand. It's massive.

"That's huge!" I don't mean this in a good way.

"Blue spruce! Now that's a beaut," Ronnie says. He walks around the tree, checking it out from all angles. "Nice shape on that one, too."

Of course he has to talk about it like it's a woman.

"Mom, please!" Cody has the pleading eyes of a fourth-grader. Usually he would just do some kind of shrug and leave the choosing to me. Clearly, not all of Ronnie's influence has been good. "This one's so chill."

"That's way too tall! Will it even fit into our living room?" I don't know why I'm resisting. It's clear this is going to be the tree, but there's some unknown part of me that just wants to pump the brakes. I guess there's some feeling about the whole Christmas thing that I don't really want to deal with. Not that it matters, because Ronnie has taken over the whole project. He's decorated the house with lights and put up a wreath and now we're getting a tree. The whole shebang. "And what about the stand? I'm not even sure where ours is, much less if that thing's going to fit in it."

"We'll take it," Ronnie says to the lot assistant. "How much? Give us the good price. The one you're going to give us after I pretend to walk away and go to another tree lot."

The guy tells Ronnie it's going to be a hundred dollars.

"What!" Ronnie's shocked. "Even after I pretend to go down the street to buy a tree somewhere else? What has happened to the world," he says, "when a Christmas tree costs more than a nice dinner for two?"

"That's how much trees cost," I say. "Now you know why I'm not in such a hurry to get one."

"We're getting it, Mom," Cody says. "Deal with it."

Ronnie fishes a wad of cash out of his pocket and counts out five twenties. Then he takes a sixth one, and gives it to the lot assistant. "That last one's for you. Merry Christmas." The guy takes the money with a flash of gratitude.

We tie the tree to the top of the car and slowly drive the half mile home. It's misty out, and even though it's only the first week in December, some people already have their houses decorated. I guess they're the diehards, the people who love Christmas so much they're first in line to put the lights up and the Rudolph display on their front lawns. Normally, I would wonder what possessed grown adults to take a whole Saturday out of their lives to pull boxes of shit out of their garage, put up a ladder, climb onto the roof, and hammer stuff that's only going to be up there for three or four weeks, max. But listening to my dad and Cody sing soft-rock Christmas carols on the way home, maybe I'm starting to figure it out.

Maybe Christmas feels good when you belong somewhere.

# 27

## RONNIE

Mal comes into the back office and shuts the door. I know I shouldn't be here, but I don't have a choice. I need something, and Mal is the man. He is the guy in North Portland who knows the guys in North Portland who can deal with shit. Pretty much anything you need, any problem you have—Mal can solve it, or he knows someone who can.

"What can I do for you?" Mal says. "Don't tell me you're trying to go back into business. I thought you were clear on that."

I'm here to get Nicki out of that bullshit real estate deal.

"Naw, man," I say. "It's for a favor. Nothing major, but it's important."

It's understood that whatever I need, Mal can take care of—probably up to and including murder. Though I doubt anyone's ever asked him for a murder. Mostly, Mal handles drugs and loans. There's also gambling, forgeries, fencing stolen merchandise, large-scale pharmaceutical orders, locating missing persons, and other assorted activities. That makes it sound like he's a gangster, but he's not. He's really just a guy who used to be wild as a young man, then he settled down into owning this bar, and slowly people came to him to fix various problems they couldn't fix the legit way, and now it's sort of his ministry. A criminal ministry. But if you understand that crime is just people accessing power that they can't get another way—whether that power is to control people, money, property, or themselves (through an experience like a "high")—then you start to understand what criminal activity really is. Just another one of humankind's crazy attempts to get some needs met. If you want to know how desperate someone is, look at what they're willing to do to get a need met.

It's straight-up Maslow.

Right now, I'm desperate. I want to fix Nicki's problem for her. Am I doing it to try to make up for all the crap I've put her through? Probably. But I desperately want to do it. I know a fix is just a phone call away. Mal will go to someone who will pay someone else to turn down Nicki's loan, or intimidate the seller into canceling the deal, or bribe the seller's agent into losing some paperwork, or get the house inspector to forge a document that'll give Nicki an out. Mal will find a way to get my daughter out of having to buy this house—and she will never have to know what happened or who did it. Neither will I.

"You sure you're ready for this?" Mal looks at me steady.

What he means is that in order for him to do this for me, I'm going to have to do something for him. I don't know when and I don't know where—and I don't even know what. I just know that one day he is going to call in this favor, and then I will have to pay up. No matter what that means. That's how it works.

"Absolutely." I don't want him to think I'm nervous, because I'm not. I'm a man who can do a cost-benefit analysis and take responsibility for the risks involved. The risk on this is relatively low. I'd say there's a 35 to 40 percent chance that I'm going to have to do something illegal for Mal if it comes to that. But I want so badly to make a difference in Nicki's life that I'm willing to take that chance, because this will fix things for her now. I won't have to pay up until later, if ever. "Let's do it."

I'm just going to have to trust Mal that he's not going to force me back into a life of crime just because I want to take care of one little thing for my daughter, and I'm doing it the only way I know how. Mal understands what I'm doing and why, and he doesn't want me to go back to prison any more than I do. I trust him. Because Mal knows that if I had the other kind of power, I would use it. But I don't. I never have, and I never will. Not in this lifetime.

A man does what he has to do to take care of his own.

———

I get home and Cody is there, sitting at the breakfast bar, on the computer. He slides the computer away from me as I walk into the room.

"Checking out some porn, young man?" I'm only half joking. Cody's almost seventeen years old, so there's no need to pretend he's not like every other American male. I'm sure he's looked at the stuff at least a few times, and more likely on a regular basis.

Cody blushes bright red. "No," he says. "Like I would look at porn in the kitchen."

True. "At least you're not denying it," I say. "Where's your mom?"

"Yoga."

"Okay, is that it?" I say. "Just yoga?" Sometimes I get frustrated that Cody never uses two words when he can use one. Even though I know better, it's hard not to feel he's holding out on a brother. You gotta work for every interaction. It's a fine balance between asking more questions to get him to talk, but not so many he retreats into his room. I usually like to keep it real general. "What're you up to?"

"I'm checking out cards for the new deck I'm putting together." Now I remember that Cody and his buddies are going up to Seattle this weekend for a big Magic tournament. They'll stay in a hotel room on Friday night, then play the game all day Saturday and Sunday. I had to talk Nicki into letting him do it. She thought he was too young to go.

"It's gonna be so hype. We're totally all going to make day two." Cody picks up his deck and starts shuffling through it. "Last time, Justin came in sixth out of one hundred and forty-seven people. Everyone else in our group day two'd."

I don't know much about the particulars, but I think day twoing means you won a lot of matches on day one.

"I'm at least gonna top eight and win money," he says. If there's a gambler gene, this family has it. But at least Cody's got it channeled in a direction that won't get him in trouble. "I really wish I could get this card, Force of Will? You need four of them for a Legacy deck, but they're so amazing. They make your deck, like, unstoppable. The only problem is that they're seventy bucks each."

"Whew! That's steep!"

I always have a hard time following when Cody starts talking about Magic. He throws around these card names and terms and rules of the game so fast it makes my head spin. I step behind him to get a glance at his computer screen, thinking maybe that'll help me understand what he's talking about, but what I see instead is a Google search:

*Gio Recari.*

I glance from the screen to Cody. He didn't want me to see that.

"Son, you're searching for Gio?" I pause a moment. "Is that who I think it is?"

He snaps the computer shut. There's a moment of silence—I'm not sure what to say. I know what I saw. Cody doesn't want to talk about it. But I know from my studies that the worst thing an attachment figure can do when they see a child in pain is to ignore it.

"Codes . . ." I sit down on one of the stools next to him and put my hand on his shoulder. "Hey."

He starts talking fast, like he's trying to talk his way out of doing something wrong. "I was researching cards and I just got the idea that I wonder where my dad is. No big deal. It wasn't even really anything, the thought just popped into my head. So I put his name in and—"

"That's perfectly understandable," I say. "You're probably just curious."

Cody studies my face. Between the look in his eyes and how fast he's talking, I can see that a bunch of feelings are coming to the surface for him.

Not surprising, since his mom is dealing with so much dad business—of course his own issues would start percolating. He shrugs it off. "I don't even know why."

"I think it makes perfect sense. I mean, here I am, back in your mom's life, and even though it's been cool, it's bound to stir up a lot of dad stuff," I say. Then, as casually as I possibly can, I say, "Do you have any memories of him? Gio, I mean?"

"No," Cody says a little too fast. He looks braced against the possibility that if he opens up the box that contains Gio, he might never be able to shut it again. He thinks a second. "I mean, my mom says I met him once. When I was a baby. She said he took me to a park. Sometimes I drive by a park and I wonder whether that's the park."

Cody exhales. What a therapist would call a "release" breath.

My heart is flooding for this little boy who has never known his dad. My dad was a bastard who got drunk every night, but there were some good times in there, and at least I knew who he was. On the other hand, he had no ability to regulate his emotions, and he raged. He beat me and my brothers and sisters, and who knows what he put my mom through. Cody grew up feeling more safe and secure than I ever did, because Nicki's a good mom who has money. But in prison, you realize 99 percent of the people there suffered serious trauma in childhood, and the deeper I get into learning how that affects people, the more I've come to the conclusion that having no father is better than having an abusive one.

Then there's the fact that until two months ago, both he *and* Nicki were fatherless. Now things have changed: she has a dad, and he doesn't. No wonder he's searching for Gio.

"Maybe your mom's dad coming back," I say, "made you wonder about your own dad?"

"Maybe." Cody stuffs some papers into his backpack and scoots back his stool. "I'm going to my room."

"Wait. Son," I say. I pull the computer over and open it. "Maybe I could help you check it out. It's okay to be curious. We could check it out to-gether."

Cody looks at me. There's this expression he gets where he looks just like Nicki. Same combination of thinking and feeling. I take his silence as a go-ahead, and open the computer. "Have you ever searched for anyone online before?"

"You mean, like stalked girls?"

"Probably like that, yeah," I say with a laugh. "I got pretty good at this in the halfway house." Melissa taught me how to search the Web that first day there. I spent at least one full week Googling every person I'd ever met. I learned a lot about finding people, then I learned a lot about how well I'm aging. Man, back in the day, you just lost track of people. You never knew how unattractive they'd become. Now there's very few people from your past left to fantasize about. "What's his date of birth?"

"I don't know."

"The year?"

Kind of strange to realize Cody knows almost nothing about his own father. Maybe we should call Nicki? But then something tells me he wouldn't want her knowing about this. "Let's start with 1974," I say. "Do you know what state?"

"Oregon?"

"For some reason, I remember Nicki telling me Gio was from New York. Let's try that." I type in *Gio Recari,* then click into the little drop-down box and track down to the N's. "It's not a very common name. Let's see what happens." I hit return and wait.

Cody stands right next to me, so he can get a better look at the screen. The page loads. We got something. I start reading off the screen. "Gio Recari, thirty-eight? Used to live in Portland, then Seattle, then it looks like . . . Los Angeles?"

That's gotta be him.

Cody pulls the laptop in front of him and clicks on a link. "Look." He turns the laptop toward me. It's a Facebook page with a picture of a guy who looks like Cody in that one way people look like their less dominant parent—as if one parent's face is seeping through the other. Or is it hovering over the other? "That's him. Is that him?"

We stare at him a minute.

"Click on some more pictures," I say. "Where is he, is he married, does he have other kids? What's his deal?"

"Wait a minute," Cody says.

That's when I see all the comments. The whole right side of the page is lined with comments, and they all say the same thing.

*RIP man.*

*We'll miss you, Gio.*

*Heaven has a new angel.*

*RIP. 1976–2014.*

*Gio! Your smile will not be forgotten.*

I put my arm around Cody. Mother of Christ. Gio is dead.

"Is that him?" he asks. Even though we both know it's him, I understand why he asked. He only just met this man and he's already having to say good-bye to him. "Are you sure that's him?"

"I'm sorry, Cody."

I squeeze him tight as he just stares at the screen. He doesn't cry or anything. He's just scrolling down the page, trying to process everything he's seeing. *Is this my dad? Those are my eyes. That's my dad. It says rest in peace. Is that my dad?*

Finally, he says, "It looks like he died. In a car crash."

"Cody, I'm so sorry."

What do I say to this boy, my grandson, who just lost the father he just found? There's no way for him to absorb the impact of what's happening. It'll probably take the rest of his life to figure out how he feels about this. I shut the computer.

"Can we not tell my mom?"

"We don't have to tell your mom," I say. Even though I think Nicki would really want to know, there is time for Cody to process it before Nicki needs to hear it. "Not for a long time, if you don't want to. You just tell me when. It's up to you."

"Thank you," he says. This boy has such a sweetness to him. Way down underneath the nonchalance is a deeply feeling person who is trying to become a man. Not an easy task for anyone, much less a kid who has never had a dad.

"Come on, let's go for a drive," I say. I grab Nicki's extra key from the kitchen drawer. "You're behind the wheel."

Driving isn't going to bring Cody's dad back. But it might give him some space to make sense out of it.

———

Later that night, Nicki and I are sitting in front of the Christmas tree. The tree is truly spectacular. I made Nicki and Cody go with me to Target and buy a whole cartful of ornaments, not just the mirrored balls, but the expensive ones, too. At the store, we had a big debate over whether to get all-one-color lights or multicolored lights. Cody wanted all blue, Nicki wanted all white. I voted multicolor and I won. Or I should say: they let me have my way, since this was my first Christmas out of prison. It's the most beautiful tree I've ever seen in my life.

I made a fire in the fireplace, and in the background, I have my favorite Motown Christmas record on the iPod, which I have finally figured out how to use—even the downloading and syncing part. I'm feeling so full of spirit. Not holiday spirit, just spirit. God. Yahweh. Divine intelligence. The most high. All of it.

"Thank you, Nicki," I say. I hand her a cup of mint tea, which I used to drink with the Muslim guys in the penitentiary. It's one of the few rituals from in there that I've continued on the outside. "Thank you for letting me back into your life. You didn't have to take me back in."

Nicki generally winces when I get grateful on her. I'm not trying to embarrass her. But those days in County reminded me that you got to tell people how you really feel about them. Life is too short not to. I expect to see her brush it off, but she doesn't.

"You're right. I didn't want you here," she says evenly. "At all."

"I know," I say. "I know you didn't." I read somewhere in a relationship book that when two people each want different things—say, one wants Hawaii for a vacation and the other wants Mexico—the solution is generosity. One person says yes to their second choice and the other person gracefully receives that as a gift. This is what Nicki has done for me. I needed her, and even though she didn't need me back, she gracefully accepted her second choice. Me. She put what she wanted behind what I needed. When I think about it, that's what the parent is supposed to do. Have the maturity and grace to willingly put the other person first. I was never able to do that for her, and yet, she's doing it for me. This is the most humbling thing I've ever experienced in my life. Even more humbling than seventeen years in jail.

"There's no way I'll ever be able to repay you," I say.

"I didn't do it for you," she says. "I did it for me. Because I wanted to be a person who wouldn't make an old man go back to prison. And in order to be her, I had to let you stay. Even though I didn't want to."

This is my Nicki. When she was a little girl, she was so practical, so logical, I worried about her. I remember one time she was looking at one of those *Tiger Beat* magazines, with the posters of teen idols. I asked her if she was going to put the poster of John Stamos up on the wall. With a serious face she answered no. "I'm never going to meet John Stamos," she said. "First of all, he would have to come to Oregon. And second of all, he would have to be in the same place I was. Which probably isn't going to happen." She was so earthbound. Any other little girl would indulge herself in a fantasy of John Stamos. Not Nicki. She wouldn't dare to want anything she couldn't have.

"And you know what?" Nicki's thinking while she talks, staring into the blinking lights on the tree, almost in a trance. One of her curls falls across her face and she looks just like the little girl I took shopping every Saturday, who loved to ride in the front seat of my El Dorado.

"What?"

"In the end, I didn't do it for you. And I didn't even do it for me," she says. "I did it for Cody." She snaps out of her thought, taking a sip of her tea. Her voice drops a bit as she addresses me directly. "I've been looking at houses for my whole life, really. I thought that's what I needed to give Cody and me a good life. Give him structure, you know? But it turns out—" She hesitates, like she doesn't want to say this. "It turns out that what he really needed was you."

In the background Stevie Wonder sings "One Little Christmas Tree."

Finally, after a long time just listening to Stevie, she says to me, "Thank you for all the cards you sent." She means those Hallmark cards, the ones I made sure to postmark in time for birthdays, Christmas, Easter, and even Halloween. "I know I never said so, but I appreciated them." She takes another sip of her tea and brushes a curl out of her eye. "And I'm sorry I never came to visit."

My first thought is that Nicki doesn't need to apologize to me. And my second is: *maybe I'm a good dad after all.*

# 28

# NICKI

Hiring Peaches has turned out to be a great thing. Okay, interesting. Okay, good. She's running the place like a real restaurant, doing everything Jake would have done: putting together a staff, setting up accounts with food and beverage vendors, making choices in glassware, plates, forks, knives—everything. She says we are on track to open December 1. I can't imagine how that's going to happen, because we still have to hire the most important person: the chef.

We're unpacking boxes of dishware from Ikea when Peaches springs her latest brainstorm on me.

"You're going to find this outrageous, but I want you to say yes."

"No," I say. I don't care what "great" idea Peaches has, the answer is no. Her best ideas are usually her worst. "Your last idea was roller skates. So, just, no."

"You can't say no," Peaches says. She's mobilizing her troops on the battle line, I can see it in her eyes. And in her shoulders. "This one's different. It's so good, so on-point, the minute I say it you will immediately know that it is precisely the right idea for our restaurant. And you will say yes."

"Is this some of that manifestation stuff you're so into where you say it like it's already happened? Or are you trying to hypnotize me?"

"Both," she says. "Just hear me out."

I am not going to be able to dismiss Peaches. There have been a lot of those times over the past three weeks with her. There are going to be a lot *more* of those times with Peaches moving forward. It's what I knew I was getting into with her, so I might as well just surrender. Not that this makes me regret taking her on as a partner—it doesn't. Letting Peaches get involved took this restaurant from being a project of Jake's ego—a cool guy who wanted to open a business so he could surround himself with stylish hostesses and hot parents-about-town—to being a labor of love. Now it's about two little girls who grew up in a really bad way coming together to save *ourselves*, about creating a great life *together* that we now get to share with other families.

"Fine. What's the idea?"

"Well, you know how we've been having, um, challenges when it comes to staffing," she says. This puts me on my guard, because the more time Peaches spends trying to set up an idea, the more I know she'll go to hell and back to convince me to do it.

"No, I don't really know that."

"Well, we have."

"You mean about the chef? It's not that big a deal, we'll find one. They're a dime a dozen, right?" I say. I'm wondering where this is going. "Just spit it out, Peaches."

"We should hire your dad," she says. "To cook."

My eyes go so wide I can feel the air on them. I'm trying to find an objection to this idea, but it's been .071 seconds and I still got nothing.

"I'm not saying no yet," I say.

"Good! Usually you reject things way too fast," she says. "So, before you say no, let me tell you why this is the rightest idea you are ever going to hear me come up with—"

I don't actually want to say no. I actually think it's a great idea.

"Yes," I say.

But Peaches doesn't even hear me. She just keeps talking. "See, he's a *great* cook, for starters. And he doesn't just cook anything, he cooks *home food*. Stuff people like to eat at home, like awesome macaroni and cheese with truffles, but that takes too long. Who's got time for that after battling traffic on the Banfield Freeway? Not me, boy. Or stuff that's too messy and hard, like fried chicken. Stuff like that."

"I said yes."

"I know, but you said it too fast," she says. "I have a bunch more arguments I want to give you." She gets that one expression on her face. "Because I've thought about this a lot."

"It's okay, Peaches. I think it's a great idea."

Peaches stares at me, slack-jawed. She slowly shakes her head from one side to another. "Excuse me, but are you Nicki Daniels?"

I smile. "Okay, okay."

"No, seriously. Because the Nicki Daniels I know would put up way more of a fight over this. So I'm wondering if some kind of Roswell-type thing happened to you. Did you get abducted by aliens who took you to their planet, implanted a chip that would make you agreeable, then dropped you back off all in what seemed in human time like thirty seconds?"

"I understand why you think that," I say, humoring her. "But I'm fine with my dad. He needs a job. The one Alex gave him is great, but this would be better. He's a kick-ass cook. And he has a great personality."

"And he's hot."

"Please don't say that," I say. "You're not allowed to say that."

"I wasn't going to, but you know how I like to keep it real," she says. Then she gets a very grave look on her face. "I won't touch him. I promise."

"I know, Peaches."

"I'm still sorry for what happened."

"I know you are," I say. It's true. I know she is. Everything's cool. Ronnie apologized, and somehow it really did all just evaporate. There are bigger things to worry about in life than when people make the same dumb mistake they always make. I feel like both of them learned a big life lesson, and my life lesson is to just never bring it up again. So far, I'm doing great.

"Shit. I'm so excited. We have a restaurant, girl!" Peaches jumps up and gives me a ginormous hug. We're jumping up and down shouting, *"We have a restaurant! We have a restaurant!"* like it's a playground song, when Miguel comes in.

He looks at us like we're crazy.

But of course, Peaches pulls him in. "C'mon, Miguel! Say it with us!"

*We have a restaurant!*

*We have a restaurant!*

We all jump up and down together.

As Cody would say, it's going to be so hype.

————

Later that day something amazing happens. My real estate agent calls me and tells me the seller on the Southeast Burnett house has decided to sign the cancellation of escrow. I'm out of the deal! I ask why, and she says she doesn't know the details. Only that the seller's agent called her and said they wanted to end it. They're going to give me back my deposit money and I'll be free and clear. Maybe they have another buyer? I have no idea— but I don't need to know.

There are no words for the level of relief I feel.

I promise myself that I will never again override what my gut says in order to do what my mind says. Putting an offer on that house was not a decision that came from deep down. It came from my head, churning out solutions to my so-called problems: my kid, my relationship, my future. I didn't know what to do and I didn't want to wait around for any sort of answer, so I just pulled the trigger and hoped for the best.

Now that the whole ordeal is over, I can see that my gut *was* trying to tell me something was wrong. I had a sense about that house the moment we pulled up to it—even the orange door bothered me! But because I couldn't understand it with my mind, I allowed myself to be bowled over by how perfect it was on the surface. How it seemed to be the answer to the question I had only just asked. It's like a smoke alarm was going off and I was walking through the house saying, *Will someone please turn that alarm off? I'm trying to buy a house here!*

Maybe I'm starting to understand what Ronnie means when he says the universe has three answers: 1) yes, 2) not now, and 3) I have something better in store for you. If I just relax and let go, everything that is mine will stay, and everything that is not mine will go. I've never trusted something bigger than me—God, or whatever—because my experience in life is that things only work out if you force them to. But maybe that was only my experience because I've never even *tried* another way.

All I know is, I don't think I need to look at houses anymore. Because the one I have already has everything I could ever want.

———

Opening day is only twelve hours away. So tonight we're doing a whole evening of dinner service to try to get the kinks out before our first day of business tomorrow. Not really a "soft opening"—more of a practice run. Miguel, Peaches, and I each recruited five people to invite whomever they wanted and told them to show up anytime between 6 and 9 p.m. We figured that would approximate what a regular dinner rush would look like. It's now 8:23 p.m. and the place is packed.

Everyone came at once.

Ronnie's cooking, Cody's the busboy, Miguel is playing host, and Peaches and I are waiting tables—something I haven't done since high school. I'll say this, I have a new respect for Peaches. I've been in a blind fury—screaming orders at Ronnie, throwing dishes onto tables like a blackjack dealer, and getting into a dysfunctional relationship with the fountain soda machine. We are going to be switching to canned and bottled sodas starting immediately and also, I quit—the waitressing, not the restaurant.

Other than that, things have gone smashingly. We are finally wrapping up—I just dropped the last check on the last table—no thanks to the temperamental credit card machine—and all in all, it was pretty damn good. We made a profit on the menu items—organic free-range fried chicken, local heirloom mashed potatoes, and three different kinds of sautéed greens, plus an arugula salad with shaved fennel—and everyone said they'd definitely be back. Of course they said that, they're all people we know. But still.

Now the five of us are sitting around an empty table, going over the night.

"One of my customers said she loved the truffled macaroni and cheese, but she'd like it better without the truffle oil," Peaches says.

"Let me guess who that was. Mrs. Finley," I say.

"Who's Mrs. Finley?" Ronnie says.

"Our next-door neighbor."

"She's so weird," Cody says. "I hear her, like, singing opera all the time."

Ronnie's gnawing on a chicken wing, his favorite part of the chicken. "Mrs. Finley doesn't know what she's talking about," Ronnie says, pulling a bone out of his mouth. "The truffle oil is the best part."

"One night in and you're already a diva? By next week you're going to be throwing saucepans," I say. "Or doing that chef thing where there's no substitutions."

I have to admit he looks kind of adorable in his checked pants and white chef's jacket. He said he got them because he wanted to go old school. His enthusiasm is infectious. He kept the kitchen staff rolling in laughter all night, sang most of Billboard's Hot 100 from 1991, *and* got all the food out on time. As I'm watching him talk, I'm trying to figure out what this feeling is, and then I realize: I'm proud of him.

"*Ha!* I can't wait to throw a saucepan," Ronnie says, clapping and laughing. "Everybody better watch out. I'ma go all Gordon Ramsay on your asses."

"Hey, Cody," Peaches says. "Who was that girl at table four you were talking to? Hmmm? Who was she?"

"No one." Cody turns bright pink. He shakes his head back and forth ever so slightly, the way he does when he can't believe the person talking to him is saying whatever they're saying.

"There was a girl who came to see you tonight?" Ronnie asks. Of course Ronnie wants to know all about it. If it turns out that Cody's found some success with women, he's going to want full credit for it, I'm sure. "Who was she?"

"Just a girl from school," Cody says.

"That's nice that friends from school came," I say, trying to make it seem a little less dramatic. "Did you invite them or did they just happen to come?"

"*Mom*," Cody says. This is my cue to STFU. But I take it to mean he invited her.

Peaches just keeps going. "She was sitting at my table with her mom, it looked like," she says. "She was supercute. She had long hair, and a hat on. Sort of a young Elizabeth Taylor, but not goth. And I swear to God I saw her mouth the words *text me*."

Cody gives Peaches a dark look. "Peaches, you're so annoying."

"I know I am. But that's what you love about me!" Peaches laughs and throws her arms around Cody for an enthusiastic side hug.

I give everyone glances as if to say, *stop, you're embarrassing him*.

"Sounds like Cody's got himself a lady friend." Ronnie claps his hands as a way to change the subject. "I'll toast to that. And a kick-ass first night of business!"

Miguel has returned with a bottle of champagne, which he gives to Cody to pop open. We all have a glass (everyone except Ronnie, that is, who has mint tea, because he doesn't drink), even Cody. We're just finishing the toast when I see Peaches's face fall. She looks over my shoulder, then looks at me, then looks back over my shoulder, then back at me.

"What?" I shift my body in a hard right from the hip, trying to see what she's seeing. "Oh shit."

It's Jake. And from the look on his face, he's drunk.

"The place looks amazing," he says. Right at me. "Hi, Nicki."

Everyone freezes. I take a very deep breath. My heart is beating fast, yes, and my stomach just flipped, but strangely, I wouldn't say that I'm scared. Surprisingly, I'm more ready. I guess I've been waiting for this moment.

"How did it go? Looks like it was everything I thought it could be," he says. He has this wounded look in his eyes. Jake is an asshole, yes, and he's lacking character, yes—but I do think he sincerely wanted to create a great restaurant. It pains him that we've gone and done it without him. He looks at everyone. "Miguel, how's it going? Great job you did here. Place is rockin'."

Ronnie sits up, poised, getting ready to leave the table.

"It's okay," I say. "I got it." I unfold my legs and slip my feet back into my gold clogs. Why I decided to wear these shoes, I have no idea. My feet are killing me, but I did get a million compliments. Jake waves me toward the back of the kitchen, near the walk-in refrigerator.

"Jake, stop." I stand where I am. I want to stay in full view of my people. My family. They're my power now. "We don't really need to have some big conversation."

"Please, Nicki. I'd like to talk," he says. "Privately."

"I'm sure you would." Of course he wants to separate me from them. I'm much more vulnerable to him alone. Having Ronnie and Peaches here—they're like UN monitors, those people the United Nations sends to oversee elections in unstable countries. Having a third party in the midst of chaos forces people to act right—or more right than they would if no one was watching. Maybe this is why I've chosen the kind of men that I have—I've never had a group of people who loved me backing me up, keeping the guys in check. Or me in check. I address Jake: "You can say whatever you have to say right here. In front of everyone."

"Nicki." His eyes are pleading with me. "I'm sorry. That's the main thing, really. I'm just really sorry."

His face does look very twisted with guilt. He holds up a check. "I brought you some money. I know it's not that much, but it's a start on what I owe you. And it's a check this time." He lets out a very thin chuckle—like he knows there's nothing funny about this, but he couldn't help trying to make a joke. "I know when we talked before, um, the last time we talked, I said there was an explanation and I'd give it when I could, and now I'm here to give it."

"I don't need your money," I say. "And I don't want your explanation."

No one's moving an inch. I really want to turn around and see what is happening here reflected on everyone's face—each of them would reveal something different about this situation to me. But then I realize that I already know what I would see. My dad is guilty because he knows that if he hadn't gone to jail for my whole life I probably wouldn't be dealing with losers like Jake; Peaches wants to 1) kick Jake's face in, and 2) tell me off for getting involved with such a pretentious asshole in the first place; Miguel is ashamed for me and for himself that he put so much work into this and then Jake turned out to be so unreliable—but he's grateful it's looking like it's going to work out okay; and last but not least, Cody is holding his breath and feeling worried that his mom is going to go down the tubes over a guy *again*.

Well, I'm not.

I also realize that I don't need to be looking for the truth on other people's faces. I need to be looking for the truth *within*. There's no such thing as a "sign." There's only that small voice inside me, guiding me quietly, if I'm willing to listen. And what I'm hearing right now is that not a single bone in my body wants to take that check. Nor does any part of me want to go to Jake, hug him, or make him feel better. I'm not scared of him, or fearful for him, or wondering where he's been. I don't want to talk it out or understand what happened. I'm not even angry. I just see how lost he is. He wasn't lying to me exactly when he promised me the world. It's more that he really wanted the world—the house, the family, the business, me—and he was dreaming out loud that I would be in it with him. He wanted it all and he wasn't ready for it.

Was I that lost?

Maybe. I wanted the world, too. But you can't make yourself whole from getting the world. It can only happen from the inside. My dad is teaching me that.

If you had asked me when I woke up this morning what I would do if Jake walked into the restaurant tonight, genuinely sorry and bearing money, I'll be honest—I probably would have wanted him back. I might not have admitted it out loud, but deep down, I might have thought I wanted it. But now, at this moment, I see one thing more clearly than I've ever seen anything in my life.

*He's not worthy of me.*

# 29

## RONNIE

They call Cody's name first. He's really nervous. We're at the DMV, where we both have appointments, fifteen minutes apart. Last night, I took him out and together we did a whole course on city streets: right turn, left turn, backing up in a straight line. He's got it, I know he does. Now if only he knew that. I give him a fist pound and a half hug, like rappers give. "Break a leg, man."

Cody has to pull the car around to a driveway where the guy who is going to administer the test gets in. Nicki and I stand under the overhang, trying not to get wet so we can watch. The test administrator is an Asian man who looks like he's in his sixties, retired, probably doing this to keep busy. He checks a lot of things off on a clipboard, walks around the outside of the car as Cody shows that he knows how to work the turn signals and the wind-shield wipers. Then he gets in and they're off. I have a good feeling about this.

"He's going to pass," I say to Nicki as we walk back inside the DMV to get out of the rain. "He's got it."

"I hope so."

"You gotta know so, baby," I say. "Hoping will get you up to the door, but *knowing*, way deep down in your heart, that's what opens it."

"Fine, I know so," she says. "I'm not even going to roll my eyes at your sermon."

I know I drive Nicki a little bit crazy with the comments, observations, and spiritual lessons I'm always dropping all over the place. But I was gone for a lot of years, and I have a lot of catching up to do if I'm going to pass along what I've learned in this life. I'm about thirty-eight years behind.

"How about you, do you think you'll pass?" she says. "You nervous?"

"Oh, I got this," I say. "No worries there."

"You sure?"

"I'm sure."

"All right, then," she says. "It's okay to be nervous, you know."

"You don't believe me?"

"Sure I believe you," she says. "I'm just checking to see how you feel."

We pass the time sitting on our hard plastic chairs. Nicki jumps on her phone and starts texting. She's always doing business. I excuse myself to the men's room. I make small talk with a nice-looking lady at the drinking fountain. When I return to my chair, it's time to go back outside and wait for Cody.

He's parked in one of the spots near the door, sitting in the car. I can see the test guy going over some stuff on his clipboard. They're in there a full four or five minutes. It gets to the point where it's not looking good.

"What's going on?" Nicki says. "This seems like a long time."

"Now, now," I say. "Don't look where you don't want to go."

"What does that mean?"

"It means don't imagine things you don't want to happen. Stay neutral."

Nicki closes her eyes like she's trying hard to keep her mouth shut. A few seconds later, the car doors open and Cody and the tester get out at the same time. The tester doesn't even smile. He just rips a form off the top of his clipboard and hands it to Cody.

Cody looks down at the piece of paper. He has a sad look on his face.

Nicki squeezes my arm. I can tell she's controlling her facial expression so Cody doesn't feel bad. She's trying a little too hard. "Well, how'd it go?"

Cody's face is so straight. I pat his back. "It's okay, bud." I pull him toward me for a hug. "You okay?"

"Yeah," he says. He's hanging his head.

"Awww, pumpkin . . ." Nicki's frowning.

I feel terrible for Cody. Failure sucks, but there's always something to learn from it, too. "It's okay, you can come back in two weeks and take it again."

That's when Cody yanks his head up. "*Ha!*" He shouts and claps his hands together. Just like I do. "This is so dope, I have both of you totally going." He smiles *huge* and throws his hands up in the air, fists pumping. "*Woooooo-hooooooo!* I passed, bitches!"

"Cody, that word." Nicki flinches slightly as she throws her arms around him. But she's relieved. "Congratulations, honey! That's wonderful!"

"Are you serious, son?" I pile onto the group hug. "*Hot dog!* I knew it the first time I saw you. I said to myself, that boy's a good driver, I bet you."

I'm so proud of this kid!

"I got a ninety-six!" Cody says. "The guy said I did great on the turns and he's never seen a teenager parallel park like I did!"

"I am so damn happy for you," I say. "We did it!"

"Stop taking credit for it," Nicki says. She's joshing me, but only sort of. "You are not the reason he passed."

Cody jumps to my defense. "No, Mom. He is. If it was up to you, I wouldn't even have my permit yet!"

"Are you saying I'm a bad mom? I would have gotten you down there eventually!"

"No, Mom. I'm saying I'm lazy as shit," Cody says with a laugh. It's true. Cody wasn't motivated enough to deal with the DMV. "Ronnie deserves all the credit."

"Thank you, son," I say. "You don't know, but that means the world to me."

I can't even show him how much it means. It would scare him. He's on to thinking about more important things anyway. Like where he's going to drive first.

"Can I drive to Magic tonight?" Cody says. "Please? Please please please please?"

At least he's predictable. Nicki makes an *ugh* sound. The place where he plays Magic is all the way out on Sandy Boulevard. At least twenty minutes from here—and despite the fact that the kid just got his license, I can tell Nicki is about to say she doesn't want him driving that far. This is one of those times I have to jump in before she can burst Cody's bubble.

"Of course you can!"

Nicki glares at me. "Why, that sounds perfect!" I say. "Doesn't it, Nicki?"

"Not really," she says. She opens her mouth to say something else; I'm guessing it's about the car, but I cut her off—

"The question is," I say, "what car are you going to drive?"

We both look at Nicki. "Please, Mom?" Cody's pleading. "Pleeeeeease?"

"Wait a second. I have an idea," I say. "Come over this way."

I head across the testing area toward the main parking lot. I'm walking fast, not because of the raindrops, but because I want Nicki and Cody to follow me. Fortunately, they do.

"What are you doing?" Nicki skips a step to catch up.

"Right over here," I say. "Just a couple more steps."

We round the corner, stepping past a small bank of bushes. There, right behind the bushes, is parked a 2005 silver Toyota Corolla. With a big bow on it.

"Right where I left it," I say. And I dangle a pair of car keys in Cody's face. "These are for you, son. Congratulations."

"This is for me?" Cody is shocked. "You bought me a car?"

"This car is for him?" Nicki asks. She's shocked, too. "You did this?"

"Yeah, I did."

This might be the proudest moment of my life.

"*Oh shit, yeah!*" Cody grabs the keys out of my hand, opens the car door, and gets in. He grabs the steering wheel like he's still a little boy pretending to drive, bobbing up and down in the seat. Cody rolls down the crank-style window. I purposely got a very basic car, without any bells and whistles—because you can't drive very recklessly with only four cylinders. "This is dope!"

"Go ahead, start it," I say. "It has automatic steering, transmission, air-conditioning, and only eighty-six thousand miles on it. This car is going to go for a long, long time."

Nicki still hasn't recovered from her surprise. She's wide-eyed, just walking around the outside of the car, checking it out. "Can I ask where you got the money?"

She says it in a low voice, like she's accusing me of something.

"I've been saving, girl." I'm not going to try to talk her out of her suspicion. I know I got the car on the up-and-up. First of all, it didn't cost that much money. And second, I planned this a little while ago and got Alex to give me a little advance on my paycheck for a down payment. Now that the restaurant's open and doing well, making the $127-a-month payments is not going to be hard. "And, I have a job."

"This is awesome," Cody says. "I'm going to Magic right now. Can I go right now? Just take it by the comic-book shop and show everyone?"

"Ronnie still has to take his test, " Nicki says. Sometimes that girl doesn't know when to quit with the control. I think too much excitement scares her.

"We'll figure it out. It's okay, the boy can go ahead." I do have a couple of ground rules for the car, though, that I need to get out before he starts driving. "No driving buzzed or drunk or high," I say. Cody nods. "And no friends in the car for a while, a long time, until I say so." Studies show kids get in accidents ten times more often when there are other kids in the car. "And, last of all, we're going to be sharing this thing sometimes, so you have to go along with that. You got that?"

"Totally! I totally got it." Cody starts the engine. It turns over like a dream and purrs like a kitten. A four-cylinder kitten. Cody puts the car in reverse and starts backing out of his spot.

"You got it, kid!"

"Roll up your window, you're going to get all wet!" Nicki says.

She's standing very still, her hand balled up in a little fist at her mouth. This is probably a really scary moment for her, watching her son get his independence. It hits me that this is where childhood really ends. With the car keys. No one tells you that. You think it's high school graduation. Or going off to college. But I can see it happening right now in front of my eyes. These car keys are going to change everything.

"It's okay, baby. Look at him," I say, as he drives off. He goes the twenty feet to the exit of the parking lot and puts his turn signal on. Good work. "He's as happy as a boy could be."

Nicki's shaking her head at me. She looks like she might be tearing up. I put my arm around her shoulder, but not too hard. I know she can be skittish, especially when she's feeling vulnerable.

"*Ronnie Daniels*." The sound of my name comes over the loudspeaker.

"Sounds like it's my turn," I say. I give Nicki a kiss. "Wish me luck, little girl."

"Break a leg," she says. She smiles as I walk toward the tester. The same guy Cody had.

———

The following Tuesday I drop Cody off at school so I can use the car. I have a mission today. Something I've known I needed to do ever since the day we found out Gio was dead.

I can't stop thinking about Beth.

I can't stop thinking about how Nicki said she's only got one picture of herself as a baby. I can't stop thinking about how she has a mom out there somewhere—right in the same town—and doesn't speak to her or want to know where she is. I can't stop thinking about childhood trauma and attachment issues and repetition compulsion and corrective experiences and how everything I've read about in my psychology books comes down to who raised you.

I can't stop thinking maybe there's some way to bring them back together.

Beth is talking with a client when I walk in the door. She's an interior decorator now, a successful one, and has an office downtown on Southwest Taylor. I just typed her name into Google and boom, there she was. Not only was she not hard to find, it turns out she's actually kind of famous. Portland famous, but still. Like with Nicki, this has to be a surprise visit. There's no way Beth would take my call and make an appointment with me. It was either show up unannounced or forget it. And I didn't want to forget it. I might be fifty-seven years old, and I might have missed half my daughter's life (and all of my grandson's life), but I'm finally out now, and if I can do something—anything—for Nicki or Cody, I'm going to do it.

Of all the things I did wrong in Nicki's eyes, nothing was more devastating than leaving her with Beth. Nicki blames me for that. Even though Nicki doesn't want to be close to Beth, I know Beth's silence feels like a rejection. So if I can broker some sort of gang truce between the two of them, I'd feel really good about that. Beth always loved me. I'm thinking maybe I can soften her up some. Make her see things with her daughter a different way.

Beth spots me the moment I step into the office. The amazing thing about Beth is that her game is so on-point not a muscle on her face moves an inch when she lays eyes on me. She doesn't do a double take. Doesn't even *flinch*. She simply turns right back to the woman she's talking to and continues showing fabric swatches. And she hasn't seen me in thirty years.

I'll say this, too: she looks good. She always did, so I'm not surprised. Five feet, eight inches, and still got her shape. She must be, what, sixty-one? And pulling off a tight (but not too tight) red suit, three-inch heels, and long curly hair. She's stunning. Just like Nicki.

"Hello, there," I say. She pretends to see me for the first time, looking at me without a shred of recognition. It gives me chills. I'd almost wonder if she knows who I am, except I'm certain she knows who I am. She's just refusing to acknowledge it. Maybe I spoke too soon about the love she had for me.

I turn to the client. "I beg your pardon," I say. "But I'm here on something of a very urgent matter. I need to talk to Elizabeth privately." I turn to face her. "Beth, right? Is it okay if I call you Beth?" Two can play this game.

"Excuse us for just a moment," Beth says to her client. The expression on Beth's face is placid but furious. "This will just be a moment."

Beth leads me to a side office area, curtained off from the showroom.

"What kind of stunt is this?" Her eyes are on fire. Her arms are crossed. It feels like she would hit me if she could.

"Aren't you going to say hello?" I say with a smile. "It's been a long time." I observe the feeling of wanting to flirt, but this definitely isn't the time, and besides, I don't do that anymore. I also notice that when I just stand there, I feel very tiny. Like a boy.

"No, I'm not going to say hello. I'm going to say, 'What do you want?'" She has her hand on her hip. This is how she stands when she's not having any of what you're giving. "I'm not interested in you, or how you are."

"Okay, fine. I'd like to talk about our daughter," I say.

Beth drops her arm to her side. "She wouldn't want you talking to me about her."

"You're right about that. I came here without her knowing," I say. It's like there's something in Beth that steals my thoughts right out of my mind and my mouth. I have no idea what to say, and I feel like even if I did, I wouldn't have the right to say it. She still affects me this way after all these years.

"Just as well you leave it that way." She glances out to the main room, I guess to make sure her client is still there. "I have to go."

"Why would you say that, Beth? She's your daughter. Aren't you even curious? Don't you want to know how she is?"

"She doesn't want a relationship with me. And even though it makes me sound like a bad mother, I'm okay with it," she says. "I'm just being honest."

I wince. What would ever lead me to choose this woman? She is missing something so key, so crucial to being human. She's missing the ability to put another person before herself. She's missing the ability to open her heart—at all. I want to cry for the twenty-two-year-old man in me who went to this woman to get love. I want to cry for my daughter. My heart aches for her.

"You have a grandson," I say.

"Save the sentimental face, Ronnie. I'm not mother material. *Or* grandmother material. That's been obvious since the very beginning. I did my duty for Nicki. I raised her. She seems to be having a fine life without me. And I'm living a fine life without her."

My stomach is sick with shame. Because back then, it wasn't about love. It was about sex. I didn't really care about anything else. Or anyone. I created this.

*I did this. This was my doing.*

My selfishness, my bad choices—they cost me, yes, but they cost Nicki even more. All those years, I tried to convince myself that Beth would treat Nicki better than she treated me. I don't think I could have survived my first prison sentence if I didn't think that. But standing here, it's clear I was in denial. Beth is a broken person.

For years, I have punished myself for my choices—you could even say (at a spiritual level at least) I put myself in prison and I threw away the key. Beth was a bad mother. In many ways I was a bad father. The great unfairness of life is that ultimately our failings were Nicki's problem to deal with. Just like I had to deal with my parents' shortcomings, and Cody will have to deal with Nicki's.

Parenting is the world's best worst thing. Your baby is born and you think she's perfect—she's going to be everything she could ever possibly be. Even more crazy: you think you're going to be perfect. Slowly, it dawns on you that your child isn't perfect—which you can accept. But then you realize that you're not perfect—which is unacceptable. Then you have the most awful realization of all: your child's biggest challenges come as a result of *you*. You cause them, but you can't cure them. Your child has to do that for herself. The only thing you can do to help her is to trust that she will figure it out. Trust that she will choose to heal herself of the things *you did to her*. Everyone has to make meaning out of their own mistakes, disappointments, failures, triumphs. All of it.

Nicki's doing that.

But I still want Beth to pay. I'm sorry, I do. I want Beth to feel guilty. I want her to feel remorse. I just want her to fucking *feel*. I want her to own what she's done to our child.

"She told me she's only got one picture of herself as a baby," I say.

Beth looks at me like I'm a beggar on the street. She pulls back the curtain and peers into the main room. Her client is still there, sifting through upholstery options.

"I think we should leave well enough alone," she says finally. "I've made my peace with it. Now you have to make yours."

She's right.

Without another word, she disappears onto the other side of the curtain. Behaving as if nothing just happened. Because I guess for her, nothing did.

# 30

# NICKI

The restaurant is taking over my life. In a good way. We've settled into a routine where I arrive after getting Cody out the door to school, usually around 8 a.m.—although now that I don't have to drive him, I could actually be here even earlier. The minute I show up, I hit the ground running, and today is no exception. There are four or five tables in progress, and the moment I walk in, Peaches starts barking orders.

"Thank God you're here!" She's using her nice voice, so I take it things are going pretty smooth. Our server, Felicity, is clearing dishes from table 12, and it looks like she just dropped the check at table 5, which Peaches is about to pick up. "Can you bust out two cappuccinos to go? And the banana nut muffin. I'll run this tab."

"Sure," I say. I give a little yell toward the kitchen—which is basically open at the back part of the main room—where Ronnie is flipping his specialty: the goat cheese omelet. "Morning, Dad."

"Morning, baby!" Ronnie sounds chipper, too. Boy, does he love his job! You've never seen a more enthused chef. He waves and winks and sings and claps his hands *all day long*. Chef Ronnie is so energized by engaging with the customers and the kitchen staff it makes the guy we've known at home for the past two months look like he was on Thorazine. "It's a real good one today!"

Ronnie busts into the hook of "Here Comes the Sun," probably because today is the first day we're seeing full sun in more than two weeks—always cause for celebration in the middle of Portland winter.

I step over to the cappuccino machine and grab two white paper cups. As one of her first management decisions, Peaches declared we should open at 6:30 a.m. so we could do a coffee business for people who don't want to go to Starbucks. She came up with the idea of Curbside Coffee, where people text their orders on the way over, then we make the cappuccino or whatever, and she runs it out to the curb. It's a flat five bucks and she has one of those little doohickeys on her phone to take credit card payments. *Genius.* Then she added a muffin option, which makes the total almost ten dollars a person. We are doing almost sixty of those a day on weekdays, and it's growing. A lot of them come back on the weekends for the full brunch.

I pour in the foam, secure the white lids (that was a whole ordeal: white vs. black plastic lids, I won), and put them in a tray along with the two banana nut muffins. Peaches glides by and sweeps them off the counter. "Thanks, lady. Love you, mean it."

Ronnie's kitchen is going strong, too. He does breakfast and lunch from 7:30 to 2 p.m. Then we close until 5:30, when we do dinner until 9 p.m. on weeknights and 10 p.m. on weekends. Sundays we're closed. Ronnie insisted on having a Lord's day. He said he didn't care which lord the employees chose, he just wanted them to have one day to tend to the spirit.

Oh, Ronnie.

I don't mind, though, because it's crucial to have a day off. The restaurant is more a stream of income, and a way to be part of our community, than it is a means of financially supporting ourselves. We're making enough to pay Peaches and Ronnie and the staff and turn a small profit—but we don't need the restaurant to pay my mortgage or Cody's college. I have my job for that. I plan to keep my appraisal business going. I really do love it, and as money goes, it's easy.

I'm about to head back to the office to take care of some ordering when the door opens and Alex walks in. It seems like forever since I told him to go away, and I've done everything in my power to stop myself from texting or calling. I just couldn't take the risk that he would reject me. I figured if he wanted me, he would come back for me. But now, even though he's walking toward me, and he's smiling, I don't dare believe that that is why he's here.

"Hi," I say. This seems like a weak opener, but I don't know what else to start with. I can't very well launch into *I'm sorry, I didn't mean it, I don't know what I was thinking.* For one thing, we have customers. And for another, it seems presumptuous. Maybe he's just here to say hi. "How are you?"

He seems a little nervous. He's pressing his forefinger into the cuticle of his thumb, which I now remember he used to do as a nervous habit. *I missed him.*

"I'm here for the goat cheese omelet. I've heard great things about it," he says. I'm not sure if he's kidding. "But if you think I'm cute, and you wouldn't mind being in a relationship with me, I don't know, maybe we could go back to the office and make out?"

"That sounds awesome," I say. "I mean, if you don't mind that I was raised by wolves and that sometimes it means I get really scared and tell people to go away when I totally don't mean it."

"Oh no, not at all," he says. "Wolves are very misunderstood. Not very many people truly get them. But I do." He takes my hand. He leans in and kisses me. "In fact, I love wolves."

I take his hand and pull him back toward the office. As we pass the kitchen, Ronnie gives us a *good morning, people* nod.

"Hey, Ronnie," Alex says. "What's good?"

"Business is good. The weather is good. And God is good. All the time." Ronnie then gives a big *ha*! And claps his hands.

I remember when Ronnie used to say stuff like that and I would roll my eyes. But I must have been converted, because as I shut the door to the office, I think it's true. Not only do I know what Ronnie means by God—he means *everything that is*—but I also know he's right.

God *is* good, all the time.

———

Later that day, I hurry into the school. Cody has asked me to be here at 2:30 p.m., sharp, in the auditorium, and I'm not sure why. All he said was, "Don't worry, it's not bad."

There are lots of people milling around outside the auditorium. I search the crowd looking for Cody's face, but I don't see him. I better find a seat before whatever this is starts. The place is packed. The whole school is obviously in here, and lots of parents, too. I wave at one of the other moms, a woman I've known since Cody was in preschool. I've never really understood the whole school mom thing. I'm actually more like a school dad. I sail in for assemblies and performances and never volunteer to bring the cookies. It's all I can do to get out of work long enough, and in time, to be here. Forget about being on the volunteering committee for the book sale or whatever.

Out of the corner of my eye, I see someone waving at me. The lights are down slightly, so at first I don't recognize him—mostly because I had no idea he'd be here. It's Ronnie. He's pointing at the chair next to him, which he must have been saving, because it's a good one, down in front, in the middle.

"What do you think is going on?" I ask as I fold down the old wooden seat and slide onto it. They are just as hard and uncomfortable as I remember. "It looks like the whole school is here. Something's definitely up."

Before Ronnie can answer, Principal Borman comes out and stands behind the podium. He looks a lot smaller from this vantage point than he did in his office that day. He taps the microphone, which lets out a sharp squeal. The whole crowd covers its ears. Then he starts talking.

"Ladies and gentlemen, students. As you know, we're here to elect offi-cers for Freshman, Sophomore, Junior, and Senior Board." He goes on to explain what Class Board is, how it's different from student council, how it only handles very specific business pertaining to each class, and other details in a monotone that I'm having a hard time paying attention to. "To help you in your decision making, you're now going to hear a short speech from the three candidates for each class."

The curtain parts and there are twelve kids sitting in chairs.

One of them is Cody.

I shoot Ronnie a surprised look. He taps the arm on my chair a couple of times in excitement.

We have to wait thirty interminable minutes—during which I hear more than I could ever care to know about the freshman lunch area and the Sophomore Winter Fest—before it's Cody's turn. Finally, Principal Borman announces him.

"And now, for one of the more . . . unorthodox . . . members of the class of 2016, Cody Daniels."

Cody gets up and lopes to the podium. From here I can really see how much he's grown in the past couple of months—he's standing a little taller, with a half smile on his face, not smug, but definitely more confident. He takes his place behind the podium and looks out at the crowd.

When Cody was little and he had to perform, I would always avoid star-ing at him too hard. I intuitively knew it would make him self-conscious, and I wanted to free him of the intensity of the mother gaze—the expec-tations, the judgment. I didn't want him to have to be up there performing Shakespeare or whatever, worried about whether I was assessing him or not. But right now, I can see that that part of him is gone—like a baby tooth that's fallen out and been replaced by something you can take into adulthood with you. Something that's going to last for fifty years.

Cody catches my eye and I give him a teeny wave. Ronnie nods to him. We're both so proud of him and he hasn't even opened his mouth yet.

"Juniors of Garfield High School, I'm here to ask that you elect me to the Class Board. Now, I'm sure some of you are wondering why you would want to elect me to the board. After all, most of you don't even really know me. Or if you do, you know me as the guy who got suspended for skipping class twenty-six times last term. Again, Principal Borman, I'm totally sorry for that."

The whole auditorium erupts into laughter. Cody smiles; this is the effect he wanted.

"Normally, a guy like me wouldn't dream of running for a position of importance in the school. Because in the world of Garfield High School, just like the world at large, once you make a mistake, once you get known as the Guy Who Skips Class, that's it—that's who you are, from that moment forward.

"But recent events in my life have convinced me that making mistakes, I mean totally fucking up—whoops—"

Again, *howls* of laughter, and a facial admonishment from Principal Borman—

"Sorry. That was a slip of the tongue. Anyway, recent events have taught me that the places where you've made your biggest mistakes are also the places where you have the most to give. Like me, for example. Truancy isn't what I'm about. But I didn't know that *until I skipped all those classes* and dealt with the consequences. Since my suspension, I've had a perfect attendance record. And what I've learned lately is that rather than just giving up on school, what I really needed to do was become part of it. I needed to be of service. This is why I'm running for Junior Class Board. To me, high school government shouldn't just be for the perfect kids who are slam-dunking their way through life. I want to advocate for regular old juniors—I'm talking about the C-plus guy, and the B-minus girl—people who usually get nothing. The kids with the honors classes and the 4.2 GPA's have enough power already! They don't need any more!"

That gets a *big laugh.*

"Elect someone to Garfield High School Junior Board who will advocate for you. Who knows you're not mediocre, you're just 'preexcellent.' I didn't know who I could be until I got inspired by someone who taught me that there's more to life than getting money and playing Magic: The Gathering. Someone who showed me that no matter what you've done in your life—or haven't—it's never too late to turn it around."

A cheer goes up from the juniors section. Cody's thrilled, his face is bursting with pride and self-esteem.

I turn to my dad and he has tears streaming down his face. I kiss him on the cheek, then stand up and give Cody a standing ovation of one.

———

When I get home, there's a small package on my doorstep. It's from UPS and there's no return address on it. I lean over and pick it up on my way into the house—I don't have time to look at it. Every afternoon, I do a mad dash into the house for my twenty-minute turnaround—I come home from my last appraisal, and in no particular order, grab a shower, change clothes, make a couple of calls, then jet back down to the restaurant for the evening shift.

This part of the day is the only peace I get. It's the time when I get to sit on the sofa for five minutes and realize how good my life is and how grateful I am to live here. I'd call it "meditation," but that would mean Ronnie's having way too big an effect on me. So I just call it my QT (quiet time) and leave it at that. I never thought five minutes on the couch could mean so much.

I've never been so fine with being alone.

Alone used to mean all by myself in the world with a kid to take care of and no one to back me up except a best friend who can hardly manage her own life. Now my life is so full of people and love and work that being alone just means sitting on the sofa taking a breather. So that's a relief.

I rip open the UPS package. It's sort of dense, about the size of an old-fashioned paperback book and about as heavy as an iPhone. I'm wondering what this is—I didn't order anything from anywhere that I remember, though I have been known to go shopping online in a procrastination blackout. Inside there's a smallish manila envelope with one of those metal clasps. I bend it up and lift the flap.

It's a stack of photographs. They're all me.

Baby me. Toddler me. Preschool me. Elementary school me.

I flip through them: it's like taking a memory drug—it all comes flooding back. Me at Cannon Beach, me on the first day of kindergarten, me at Christmas, me on ice skates, me with a Burger King crown on my head. The most disconcerting thing about it is that the second I see each picture I immediately remember almost everything about it. I remember that shirt, I remember wearing my hair like that, I remember that dog. *How did I forget a whole* dog? Is it possible that you could have this many memories—I'm holding years' worth in my hand—and just . . . blank it all out?

Obviously, it is.

But how?

I know how. Because contained in every picture is not just what or who you're looking at—me with the balloon, or the dog, or the Burger King crown—but also in there, right there, but unseen, is whoever took the picture. The person seeing the person in the picture.

Beth.

She's right here; I'm holding her in my hand. And I want to forget about her. Forever.

But if the past few months have taught me anything, it's that forgetting is impossible. There is no past. Everything that's ever happened is still in there, ready to show up—to be called up—at any moment. And even if you manage to convince yourself that you forgot, the moment you see it again, you'll know.

# Acknowledgments

To write a novel is to navigate a paradox—it comes from you, but it's not about you; it's yours, but not yours. Utmost thanks to my editor, Karen Kosztolnyik, for helping me find my way. Your insight, kindness, enthusiasm, patience, and faith made this book possible. I have so much appreciation for you and everyone at Gallery Books.

Deep gratitude, love, and respect to my agent, Andy McNicol at WME. I adore you and our partnership! Thanks also to the rest of my WME team: Tom Wellington, Nancy Josephson, Simon Faber, Ivo Fischer, Chris Jacquemin—it is a wonderful gift to feel so supported by you all.

Gratitude always to my dad, who is unfailingly loving, supportive, sunny, and understanding—even when I go too long before returning his calls.

Special thanks to Charlie, for being a fearless, thorough, and above all seriously loving partner. And kisses on the top of the head to Lee and Luna. I'm grateful to be part of your lives.

Finally, deepest thanks and gratitude to my son, Joseph, who inspires me every day with his intelligence, wit, honesty, character, and insanely good comic timing. You have been the North Star on my life's journey to understand what it means to have a family. I love you, Muffin.